Greenwich Council
Library & Information Service

IN HOUSE
QUALITY
SYSTEMS

Mobile and Home Service at Plumstead Library
Plumstead High Street, SE18 1JL
020 8319 5875

B

Please return by the last date shown

New label MAR 2013

Lewis

- / MAR 2013

- - MAY 2013

DEC 2013

- 4 FEB 2014

Halton

Serca

- - OCT 2015

- - MAY 2013

- / JUL 2013

- - MAR 2014

- - MAY 2014

- - JUL 2014

- - OCT 2014

- - APR 2016

- - FEB 2017

Thank You!

AUG 2015

Gregory

- - JUN 2017

Elliot

- - OCT 2017

- - JUN 2018

Central C

To renew, please contact any Greenwich library

Issue: 02   Issue Date: 06.06.00   Ref: RM.RBL.LIS

YESTERDAY'S SHADOW

Ella Gough is leading a comfortable – if unexciting – life at Burleigh House looking after her invalid husband and seven-year-old daughter Penny. Though determined to be a good wife and mother, part of her longs for something more – and then Daniel Hampton walks back into her life. At seventeen, Ella had loved him desperately, but he betrayed her. Now married and in debt, he needs work and applies for the post of assistant gardener at Burleigh House. Ella is drawn to her first love but she has her husband and daughter to consider. Then fate takes a hand...

YESTERDAY'S SHADOW

YESTERDAY'S SHADOW

by

Pamela Oldfield

Magna Large Print Books
Long Preston, North Yorkshire,
BD23 4ND, England.

British Library Cataloguing in Publication Data.

Oldfield, Pamela
    Yesterday's shadow.

    A catalogue record of this book is
    available from the British Library

    ISBN   0-7505-1635-6

First published in Great Britain in 1999
by Judy Piatkus (Publishers) Ltd.

Published in Large Print 2001 by arrangement with
Piatkus Books Ltd.

Magna Large Print is an imprint of Library Magna Books Ltd.

Printed and bound in Great Britain by
T.J. (International) Ltd., Cornwall, PL28 8RW

Chapter One

Mr Saville sneezed. Startled out of her dark reverie, Ella thankfully brought her thoughts back to the present.

She said, 'Bless you!' and looked at him sharply. There was a lot of flu about.

The old man fussed with his handkerchief, and her fingers drummed impatiently on the burnished table top as they waited while he blew his nose. Why did he always have to trumpet like an elephant, Ella wondered, exasperated. When he had finished, she assumed an expression of interest as he continued to read the list of tombola prizes.

'...a bottle of whisky, a boxed set of wine glasses – from your good self–' he gave her a little bow '–a hand-embroidered tablecloth, one of my watercolours, an owl in a glass case...'

Mr Saville's querulous voice sputtered on and Ella glanced around at the rest of the small committee seated around the large dining table. Mrs Grey's bulbous eyes were on her knitting. The secretary, Miss Spinney, was smothering a yawn with a delicately veined hand and there appeared to be very few jottings in her notebook.

Unable to endure it any longer, Ella said, 'Thank you, Mr Saville.'

He turned towards her, eyes blinking. 'Oh, but I haven't quite finished–'

Ella said firmly, 'I think we've heard enough to know that you've been most successful as usual. Asking for prizes is such a thankless task, but you always do it so well.' Her smile disarmed him as she had known it would, for she had used her charm quite shamelessly since she was a child. Combined with her good looks, it had rarely failed her. 'And you've donated another of your own watercolours, Mr Saville – that's so generous.'

The small protest died on his lips and with an answering smile he sat down. Ella slid her fingers through her softly waved hair. They were all very sweet and well meaning, but she didn't think she could put up with them for much longer today without screaming. She caught sight of the carriage clock on the mantelpiece and frowned. It had stopped at five to eleven.

'Excuse me.' She left her seat at the table, crossed the room, adjusted the hands and rewound the clock.

'It's a rather nice little view of Sidmouth,' Mr Saville told her as she returned. 'I was down there last year, or was it the summer before that? Where are we now?'

Mrs Grey said, 'Nineteen thirty-three.'

'Nineteen thirty-three? Is it really?' He shook his head in amazement. 'So that makes it... Yes, it *was* last year. July thirty-two. I remember–'

'How splendid!' Ella decided she would make her excuses as soon as she could and escape to the library.

She turned to the secretary who was rolling her pencil between her fingers. 'You have noted Mr Saville's tombola prizes, haven't you?'

'Yes. Yes, I have.' Miss Spinney began to write rapidly.

Ella turned to Mrs Grey. 'And you say the cake stall has been organised?'

'Oh yes, Mrs Gough. All the regulars will contribute and I shall be making four dozen of my lemon-curd tartlets. Homemade lemon-curd, that is.'

Mr Saville, ever gallant, said, 'A perennial favourite, Mrs Grey. Quite delicious.'

She smiled at him and then at Ella. 'Another Autumn Fair! Where has the last year gone to?'

Ella shrugged slim shoulders. 'Time just flies. Well, if there's nothing else we'll close the meeting. Annie will be bringing our refreshments.'

Outside the large sash windows an early October wind blew flurries of brown leaves from the chestnut trees, hurling a few

9

against the window and scattering the rest across the lawn. Inside the large room a fire burned in the grate, but most of its heat went up the chimney or rose to the high ceiling, forcing the members of the committee to rely for comfort on warm jackets, cardigans and warm socks and stockings. Heavy lined curtains kept out draughts from the deep windows, but nothing could alter the fact that it was a north-facing room and never cosy during the cold months.

Ella glanced at the mantelpiece. Three o'clock. Thank heavens for that. A reasonable time to stop.

Mrs Grey held up a navy-blue sock for their inspection. 'Nearly done,' she said, folding the needles together in the middle of a row. 'I turned the heel last night and that's always so encouraging.'

Ella's mouth twitched. The unfortunate grandson would have grown considerably before the socks were finished. She said, 'Well done, Mrs Grey.'

Rising to her feet, Ella wondered briefly why she bothered with all this committee work when she hadn't the slightest interest in the repairs to the church roof. As long as the rain didn't fall directly on to her own head, she wasn't too bothered by the leaks.

She said, 'Well, that's it for today, ladies and gentlemen. I think we can adjourn to the sitting room.'

Miss Spinney closed her notebook and pushed back her chair. 'I wonder what the new doctor will be like. They say it's only his second practice. He's been in Dorset for eighteen months working with his father. It'll take some getting used to – a new doctor. The last one was such a dear. Never too busy. It seems almost unfair that he should fall ill himself. You don't expect doctors to get ill.'

Mr Saville was struggling to his feet and Ella watched him with sudden compassion. His wife's death a few months earlier had turned him overnight into a broken old man with no one in the world, except a godson who worked abroad. I know what it's like to lose someone, she thought with a flash of bitterness. Losing someone you love brings the whole world crashing around you. At seventeen, rejection had left her bitter and wary; the loss of the man she loved had left emotional scars that were slow to heal. Even now, with the love and support of a devoted husband, Ella had neither the ability to forget nor the will to forgive.

With a determined effort she pushed the dark memories to the back of her mind. Stop it, Ella. Count your blessings, she told herself. Because she was blessed and she knew it. Financially they were secure – more than comfortably off, thanks to her

11

husband's skill with his stocks and shares.

She was also blessed with a healthy child. Penelope, known as Penny, was a sweet, bright seven-year-old – the apple of her father's eye, as Roland never tired of telling anyone who would listen.

They had a large comfortable home – the house in which Ella had spent a blissful childhood. Only later did it acquire unhappy associations for her, but her husband knew nothing of these. When her father died and Ella inherited the house, Roland had insisted that it made sense to move into it instead of putting it on the market. They were living in Croydon at the time and Burleigh House on the outskirts of Tenterden was surrounded by rolling countryside. Initially reluctant, Ella had finally been persuaded when Roland pointed out that by keeping the house they need not sack the staff. The gardener and the housekeeper had remained.

Ella glanced at Mr Saville who was dabbing his face with his handkerchief. For a moment he seemed to sway, and she forced herself to take hold of him. Inside the sleeve of his jacket, his arm felt alarmingly thin. Did he eat properly, she wondered.

'Tea in the sitting room, ladies and gentleman,' she said again.

Miss Spinney said, 'Oh, how nice!' injecting, as usual, a note of feigned

12

surprise. Ella smiled at her, groaning inwardly. The committee of Friends of the Church had been meeting at Burleigh House weekly for as long as she could remember, and Earl Grey tea and almond biscuits were invariably offered as refreshment.

Miss Spinney went on, 'I'm longing for a cup of tea. My throat gets so dry.'

'Wet our whistles!' Mr Saville offered and began to cough.

Ella didn't answer. He was rather flushed, she thought, and a little more shaky than usual. Leading him along the passage, she felt his arm tremble and was dismayed by his frailty. Please God I shall never be reduced to this. The prospect sent a shudder through her slim frame.

'Are you feeling all right, Mr Saville?' she asked as they negotiated the doorway into the sitting room. It was warmer here, a smaller room with fewer windows to let out the heat. Softly coloured chintz covered the armchairs and the deep pile rug added a little luxury. There was a recently lit fire in the open hearth and the smell of wax polish and smoke mingled in the air.

Mr Saville coughed, then shook his head. 'Just a head cold, I expect.'

'Not feverish, are you?'

She certainly hoped not. Ella herself was never ill, claiming that she was 'too busy to

13

succumb' and found illness alarming. When, six years ago, her husband had contracted polio, the prospect of nursing him had appalled her. They had therefore employed a private nurse. Professionally Nurse Baisley had proved herself beyond reproach and Ella was grateful to be relieved of the intimate nursing tasks which she would have hated. In the opinion of the rest of the staff, however, the nurse was 'entirely too big for her boots'. Naïvely, Ella had expected her husband to recover totally from the polio and was disappointed when his doctors were unable to restore him to full health. The nurse had remained with the family ever since.

With mixed feelings, Ella watched Mr Saville lower himself into the wing-backed chair which had gradually come to be regarded as 'his'. The phrase 'soldiering on' was a favourite of his, and it dawned on her as she watched him that that was what he was doing. Soldiering on until it was his turn to die and he could follow his wife into their joint grave. Since her death, he had said several times that he had nothing left to live for. She ought to sympathise, but illogically she felt only impatience.

In a brisk tone, she said, 'I hear they need volunteers at the hospital. Someone to take round the library trolley, perhaps, or to write letters for the patients. Have you

14

thought of offering your services?' Perhaps thinking about others would take his mind off his own troubles and act as a foil to his loneliness.

He shook his head. 'They wouldn't have me. I've tried several times. I lied about my age, but they said I wasn't fit enough.'

The housekeeper handed him a cup of tea.

He said, 'Thank you, Annie,' and set it down on the occasional table beside him while he helped himself to two lumps of sugar with fingers that could hardly hold the tongs. Then he took up the cup, clutching it with both hands, and sipped the hot liquid gingerly.

'I'm sorry.' Ella had misjudged him. She awarded herself a black mark. 'Never mind. You've been a very valuable member of this committee.'

He glanced up. 'I do hope so.'

'How's that godson of yours?' she asked, helping herself to a biscuit. 'Is he still abroad?'

He brightened. 'Young Charlie, you mean? Oh, he's doing very well. He was in New York last time he wrote, but he's coming home soon. I'm hoping he's had enough of foreign parts and is willing to settle down. Put down a few roots, so to speak.'

'Will he stay with you? You've plenty of room and he would be company for you.'

'I did once hope so, but he may need to

work in London. I have a small flat in Baker Street which he can use. I used to stay overnight when I went to my club, but it hasn't been used for a long time.'

Ella smiled. 'You must sing the praises of Kent, Mr Saville. Tell him the country air will do wonders for his health.'

'I must certainly try. He's wonderful company. My wife adored him... She used to say, "Why doesn't he find himself a wife and settle down?" but he never did. He always seemed to have plenty of lady-friends, but he's nearly forty and still a bachelor.'

'Some men do marry late. Your godson is probably Gemini, like Roland. He didn't marry me until he was over forty.'

'Really?' He looked bemused. 'Well, he made a very good choice when he *did* marry.'

She was delighted. 'Thank you, Mr Saville. That's a very nice compliment.'

Miss Spinney giggled. 'You watch him, Mrs Gough. He's a bit of a devil with the ladies!'

Ella laughed with them, but the little joke disturbed her. Looking at his rheumy eyes and trembling mouth, she wondered if he had ever been a bit of a devil. Perhaps he had, but if so there was no sign of it now.

She remembered her excuse. 'Well, if you'll all forgive me,' she said, 'I promised to let my husband know how the meeting went. He's always so interested in the Autumn Fair.'

Leaving them to the ministrations of Annie, the housekeeper, she hurried up the broad staircase and along the passage towards the library. She tapped on the door and went in without waiting for an invitation.

'Ella!' From his wheelchair beside the desk, Roland smiled a welcome.

At fifty-two Roland Gough was not unattractive. He had never been tall or slim, but had put on very little extra weight over the years. He was undeniably vain about his dark hair which showed no sign of turning grey. Pale grey eyes lent a shrewdness to his face, but he smiled readily.

'I've left them to it,' she told him and leaned down to put an arm across his shoulders. 'And before you ask me, it went well. Did you remember to write to your brother?'

He smiled. 'When do your meetings *not* go well?'

'They're all too terrified to cross me!'

'You mean they all adore you! And yes, I wrote to him. Told him how proud we are of him. It's not every day one's brother is elected to parliament.' He gave her a long look. 'I *also* adore you, you know, Ella. I don't want you to forget that.'

17

'And I adore *you!*' she replied lightly, knowing it to be a white lie. She loved Roland in her own way, but she had never adored him. As for her husband, she knew that he adored her, although real passion had always been absent from their lovemaking and his illness had put an end to dutiful nights.

Ella pulled a chair up to the desk and leaned on it. 'Did you miss me?'

He laughed. 'You were only gone an hour!'

She had always liked his smile. 'The longest hour of your life, I expect!'

'One of them, certainly.' He stared down at the pages spread out in front of him. Ella watched him guiltily. Why doesn't he touch my heart, she asked herself. Why hasn't my admiration grown into love over the years? When they married, she had admired and respected him; had been a willing student as he taught her about art and music; had listened as he read to her from Trollope and Thackeray. They had enjoyed the Noël Coward plays and the Covent Garden opera in winter and in summer had toured the countryside in his beloved Bugatti.

She stifled a sigh. And then I developed a mind of my own, she thought. Very thoughtless of me. Short-sighted, too. Her independence had brought about a subtle shift in the relationship and the tutor had lost his student. Nobody was to blame, but nothing had happened between them to compensate for her maturity. Ella's pregnancy had provided a spark, but the child had failed to draw them closer together. The love that Ella had hoped to feel for him had never been more than a deep affection.

Roland shook his head. 'It won't come together,' he told her. 'And they want it by the middle of next week.'

'What is it?'

'What is it?' He raised his eyebrows. 'The article, of course, dear! What else would give me this much concern?'

To hide her confusion, Ella crossed to the window and stared down at the windswept lawn. How could she have forgotten? He had been working on his article for weeks now. It was intended for *The National Geographic* and dealt with a little-known area in Kenya where he had spent some years as a child. The acceptance of the article would open doors for him and might lead to further commissions. They had no need of the money, but the prestige mattered enormously to him.

'Of course,' she said. 'Your article. Forgive me, darling, I was worrying about Mr Saville. Poor old thing looks very unwell.'

Roland frowned. 'I'm going to have to redraft the damned thing – for the *third* time. I'm beginning to wish I'd never agreed to write it.'

'He looks quite feverish.'

Roland murmured something non-committal and Ella watched the gardener raking the leaves and stuffing them into a sack. Pointless in this wind, she thought, but he was very set in his ways. Winter or summer, he wore the same clothes – a greasy cap, a worn suit with a collar and tie and a large green apron with a roomy front pocket.

As she watched him her thoughts shifted to the auditions which the Dramatic Society was due to hold the following week. She supposed she'd put in for the lead as usual, and was surprised to realise that she felt less than enthusiastic at the prospect of the twice-weekly rehearsals. Am I losing my zest for life, she wondered. Tired of the limelight? The trouble was that there were too many hours in the day. They had to be filled somehow, but with a nurse, a nanny, a housekeeper and a gardener there was little left for her to do.

Below her, unaware that he was being watched, Evans paused, put a hand to his back and slowly straightened up. He certainly was too old to manage such a big garden and she appreciated that he must retire. Her eyes strayed across the wide sweep of lawn and well-tended rose-beds. Further out there were flowering shrubs around the old summer-house, and beyond the far border of rhododendrons mature oak, chestnut and the occasional elm cast their shade in summer and scattered their leaves in winter.

To the right of the swing there was a tennis court, and Ella frowned. It would have to be resurfaced soon or they wouldn't be able to play the club's tournament on it next summer. Her frown deepened. Five years earlier, in a moment of desperation, she had started the club, but the membership had grown at an astonishing rate and they now had a waiting list of eager players.

As she watched Evans resume his raking, a man cycled up the drive and she considered him without much interest. He dismounted, lowered the bicycle to the ground and walked across the grass. Ella stared, her eyes narrowed. Something about the way he walked reminded her of someone she preferred to forget. The gardener turned at his approach and the younger man raised a hand in greeting. They began to talk and Ella turned to her husband.

'Did you advertise for another gardener, Roland?'

He glanced up. 'Yes, I did. Evans suggested that I should. I told you at the time.'

'That was weeks ago.'

He rolled his eyes. 'I know it was, but I've

21

been busy with this article. We just haven't found the right man.'

'I was only going to say–'

'There's no great urgency, anyway.'

'–that there's a youngish man talking to Evans. Brown hair. Tallish. Is he coming for an interview?'

Roland looked harassed. 'An interview? I certainly hope not. I've already seen two who were no use at all. Unless it's the third chap who couldn't attend when we first invited him. Hammond, I think it was. Maybe he's just turned up to take a look around and see what it would entail.' He wheeled himself to the window and looked down. 'It's a damned nuisance if he has.'

Ella said, 'I'll speak to him for you, if you'd like me to.'

'I would, darling, actually.' He slid a casual arm round her waist. 'Offer him two-thirds of what we give Evans and specify a seven-thirty start and no turning up late. Finish on Evans' say-so – and no bad language. No drinking. He can have his midday meal in the kitchen with the others. I'm sure Annie can rustle up an extra helping of whatever it is.'

'How many days do we want him? Part-time? A full week?'

'Mondays to Fridays. Talk to Evans. Find out how much help he needs. If the chap's any good and he stays the course, he can step into Evans' shoes when he goes. Make that clear. Bit of a carrot to go with the stick.'

He wheeled himself back to his desk while Ella continued to watch the two men below, her brow furrowed in concentration. There was something about the stranger ... something about the set of his head. A certain arrogance? With a shrug, she dismissed the idea as fanciful.

She had just decided to go down and investigate when she was startled by a loud scream from somewhere downstairs.

Roland looked up. 'What in God's name is going on?' he demanded.

'It sounds as though someone's been murdered!' she said. 'I'll go down and see.'

The tranquillity of Burleigh House was rarely disturbed and Ella hurried down the stairs with mounting curiosity. Half-way down she was greeted by the housekeeper who ran towards her, her face chalk-white.

'It's Mr Saville!' she cried. 'He's collapsed. He's bleeding something terrible!'

'*Bleeding*, Annie?' Ella stopped abruptly, clutching the banisters. She had a terrible vision of a full-scale haemorrhage.

But Annie was already rushing back the way she had come, and Ella followed close behind, her heart thumping. In the sitting room she gently pushed Mrs Grey aside and stared down at the prone figure on the floor.

23

Mr Saville lay sprawled on the dark carpet, his clothes stained with a large amount of frothy pink blood which was still bubbling from his nose.

'A *nosebleed!*' said Ella, relieved that it was not as bad as she had imagined.

Mrs Grey was whimpering with fright. Miss Spinney had retreated to the sofa with a hand pressed to her forehead. She said, 'It's a bit more than a *nosebleed*, Mrs Gough!'

Annie, keeping her distance from the still figure on the floor, clutched her apron defensively. 'Oh Lord! He's not dead, Mrs Gough, is he? Don't say he's gone and died!'

Miss Spinney said, 'He might have fainted. I had an aunt who fainted quite regularly. Even in church. Down she'd go for no good reason.'

Mrs Grey shook her head. 'He's never fainted before. Not to my knowledge, anyway. That was more of a ... a collapse, I'd say. Or a *seizure*.'

Ella thought that if they didn't stop *she* would be the next one to go down.

Miss Spinney now pressed a hand to her heart and breathed deeply.

Hiding her distaste, Ella knelt beside the old man. 'Mr Saville? Can you hear me?'

There was no reply. She picked up his wrist and felt for a pulse.

Annie looked anxiously at Ella. 'One

minute he was reaching for another biscuit, the next he just slid from the chair and all this blood...'

Ella said, 'He did look a little flushed earlier.' She leaned closer, listening for breathing. 'Mr Saville? It's me, Ella Gough. Can you hear me? Can you open your eyes?'

There was still no sign that Mr Saville was regaining consciousness.

Annie leaned forward. 'His chest's moving. It *is*. I'm sure I saw it move.'

Ella turned to her. 'Go and ring for the doctor, Annie. The number's in the book under "D". Tell him what's happened *calmly* and ask him to call round immediately.'

Mrs Grey wiped her eyes. 'Poor soul!' she quavered. 'First his wife dies and now this – whatever it is. And he's so frail. A puff of wind would blow him over.'

Ella sat back on her heels, wondering what to do next. Was it wise to move him?

The two women watched her anxiously, but before she could decide what to do next the housekeeper returned with a bowl of water and a towel.

'Should I bathe his face, ma'am?' she offered. 'Cold water might bring him round.'

Ella seized the offer. 'Please do. He's still breathing. What did the doctor say?'

She watched unhappily as the house-keeper settled herself beside the un-

25

conscious man and began to wipe away some of the blood.

Mrs Grey was murmuring something and Ella caught the words 'sal volatile'. 'Of course!' she cried. 'Sal volatile! That should restore him. I've a bottle in my bedroom. How stupid of me! You must fetch it, Annie, please – but before you go, what did the doctor say?'

'I spoke to his wife. She can't reach him at the moment, but she'll send him round as soon as he's finished his house calls.'

Ella stiffened. 'When he's *finished?* Did you explain that this was an emergency?'

'I did, but what can she do if she doesn't know–'

'I should have spoken to her myself.' She frowned. 'It's simply not good enough. He's not in Dorset now.'

'I'm ever so sorry but she–'

'It's not your fault, Annie.' She shrugged. 'Let's hope that poor Mr Saville is still alive when he finally gets here! If not, I shall have something to say to him.' She stared around her, unwilling to remain. 'I have to speak to the gardener's new assistant,' she told them. 'I shall be in the garden. Please let me know as soon as the doctor arrives.'

Before anyone could protest, Ella hurried from the room, her heels tapping briskly across the parquet floor. She paused at the downstairs cloakroom to throw a raincoat over her shoulders as she tried to remember her husband's instructions.

Outside, the wind was cooler than she had expected. She walked round on to the flagged terrace, took one look at the damp grass and decided the two men must come to her. Deep in conversation with their backs to her, they had not noticed her approach.

'Mr Evans!'

Her tone was peremptory and, startled, they both swung round to face her. Ella looked curiously at the younger man – and then, with a small gasp, took an involuntary step backwards. *No!* It was impossible.

Under her breath she whispered, 'Please, God! It can't be!' Surely Roland had said his name was 'Hammond'.

As they walked towards her she saw with a shock of dismay that it *was* Daniel. Somehow an unkind twist of fate had brought Daniel Hampton back into her life and Ella didn't know how to feel about that. As he drew nearer, she found herself staring at him with undisguised fascination. The smooth fair hair had darkened a little in the intervening years, the face was thinner and the expression harder, but the eyes were as fine and as green as ever. Even as she sought a way to extricate herself from the situation, she saw with growing panic that recognition now flickered in *his* eyes. She thought, 'Oh,

God! Let him hold his tongue!' and struggled to regain her composure.

Evans said, 'This is Dan Hampton, ma'am. Come about the job.'

She said, 'Good day, Mr Hampton,' but her voice trembled.

She could see that Daniel was as shocked as she was. He stared at her for a moment wide-eyed, opened his mouth to speak but then bit back the words.

Mr Evans said, 'This is the master's wife, Mrs Gough.'

Daniel's eyes didn't leave her face. He said, 'Good day, Mrs Gough.'

Was it her imagination or had he laid a little emphasis on the word Gough?

He went on, 'Mr Evans was just telling me about my duties – that is, if I were to be given the job.'

He seemed remarkably cool in the circumstances, she thought nervously, and there was something about the way he said 'my duties'. Also she detected a subtle hint of mockery in his expression. Would Mr Evans notice anything? She prayed inwardly that her own confusion was not obvious, but she could feel the heat in her face as she fought down a rising panic. Was this deliberate, and if so why had Daniel returned after all these years? He surely didn't want a job as a gardener. And if not, then *what* did he want? Even as these thoughts were running through her mind she was aware of his voice – low and husky. A voice she had never been able to forget.

She said, 'You could learn a lot from Mr Evans,' and thought frantically. He *would* have known the house, but presumably he had never known her married name. So by answering an advertisement from a Roland Gough, Daniel would never have expected to find her back at Burleigh House. In which case his presence here could not be deliberate. Reassured, she took a deep breath and told herself to relax. She was a grown woman and she could deal with this.

Mr Evans was looking at her, waiting for an answer to a question she hadn't heard. To gain a little time she glanced up towards her husband's study, her right hand raised as though to protect her face from the swirling leaves. Then she glanced back at the gardener who was regarding her expectantly.

She said, 'I'm sorry – what did you say?'

'I was saying as Mr Hampton has some experience of greenhouse work.'

'Indeed?' Her voice no longer shook. 'That would be an advantage, naturally,'

To Daniel she said, 'We have quite a variety of fruit under glass.'

Evans said, 'Mr Gough will want to interview him I expect, ma'am.'

He spoke with an eagerness that told Ella

he was impressed by the new applicant. Oh God!

'My husband is busy and has asked me to take his place.' Ella was recovering quickly. She would have to keep up the pretence, she told herself. Ask the questions. Treat Daniel as a complete stranger. 'How much experience do you have, Mr Hampton?' Of *gardening,* she added silently. Now that the shock was wearing off it was being replaced by anger. As the memories flooded back she was once more a young and vulnerable woman, betrayed and humiliated by him.

'I've never loved you that way,' he had told her. 'I never pretended I did. It was all in your mind.'

'No!' Seventeen-year-old Ella had screamed at him. 'You *said* it! You *did!* You can't love *her! I* don't believe it.'

But it was the truth. Ella, young and inexperienced, had misread all the signs. Daniel Hampton, only a few years older, had been in love with Lydia.

Forcing herself back to the present, Ella realised that Daniel was speaking and tried to concentrate.

'...with my last family in Blackheath,' he said, keeping his eyes fixed steadily on her face. 'Colonel and Mrs Hacker.'

Ella saw a small vein pulse in his temple. Perhaps he was *not* as calm as he pretended. Perhaps underneath the façade he, too, was angry. The Daniel Hampton she had known all those years ago had been more volatile, but presumably the disgrace and all that followed had changed him. Perhaps exile and the intervening years had been unkind to him. A *gardener,* for heaven's sake!

Evans drew a letter from his pocket. 'Mr Hampton's reference, ma'am. Seems quite in order.'

Ella took it from him, furious to see that her hand shook. She had to read it twice before she could concentrate sufficiently to understand it: *'Daniel Hampton has worked for us for two and a half years and has always been punctual...'*

Ella drew in a sharp breath. So Daniel had been back in England for the past two and a half years, maybe even longer, but had made no attempt to find her...

He is a hard worker and a quick learner. His outdoor work included flowers as well as vegetables and latterly he spent some time in the greenhouse. We found him honest and reliable. His employment is terminated only because we are moving to Scotland.

Edward Hacker (Col. ret.)

She stared at the letter, unable to meet Daniel's gaze while she tried to decide what to do. At last she looked at Evans.

'It's a very fair reference, I agree. I ... I'll

leave you to show Mr Hampton round, and I'll speak to my husband as soon as he's free.' She glanced up, forcing herself to look into the green eyes. 'Leave an address, Mr Hampton, and we'll be in touch. May I keep the reference for the time being?'

He said, 'Of course, Mrs Gough.'

'Then if you'll excuse me... We have a minor emergency at the house.'

She turned and walked back the way she had come, her head erect, her heart thumping erratically. They did not speak but she knew they were watching her.

'You might be a wonderful gardener, Mr Hampton, but you won't get the job!' she whispered. 'Never in a million years.' She drew in a slow, deep breath that was almost a sigh. The idea of him working for them was out of the question. Daniel Hampton was dangerous to know and she would never allow him to get close to her again.

Doctor Clarke arrived half an hour after Mr Saville's collapse, by which time Miss Spinney and Mrs Grey had departed.

Ella faced the doctor. 'Mr Saville could have *died*,' she told him, her eyes flashing. 'Where on earth have you been? And why didn't you treat this visit as urgent?' He was young and good-looking, but Ella was in no mood to appreciate good looks. She went on, 'You will discover, Doctor Clarke, that

32

Kent is very far removed from Dorset. People in Tenterden–'

He broke in. 'Don't you think this conversation should wait, Mrs Gough? Since as you say it's a matter of urgency, I would like to examine the patient.'

His insolence stung her, but even as she searched for a crushing rejoinder she knew he was right and changed her mind.

'I'll take you to him,' she said. 'He is still in the room where he fell – I was afraid to move him far – but we have tried to make him comfortable.' As she led the way she spoke over her shoulder. 'We applied sal volatile – old-fashioned, I know, but it brought him round. He's conscious anyway.'

In the sitting room, the sick man lay on the sofa. Nearby Annie sat on a small stool, watching him anxiously.

The doctor strode briskly across the room. 'Mr Saville, I'm Robert Clarke, the new doctor.' He shook the old man's limp hand and smiled encouragement. 'Now, what seems to be the trouble? Can you tell me what happened – in your own words? Are you up to that?'

Annie rose to allow the doctor to take her place. She glanced at Ella, who indicated that she should leave them. As the housekeeper returned to her duties, Ella asked, 'Is it necessary for me to stay?'

But the doctor's fingers were round the

thin wrist. He shook his head slightly, concentrating on his watch.

Ella bit her lip, incensed by his attitude towards her. Studied indifference, she thought, but then immediately told herself she was being unfair. In any case, her own frosty greeting was hardly likely to inspire friendly feelings. She had only herself to blame. Aunt Florrie's words came back to her: 'Think first, then speak.' Ella sighed. Now she watched the doctor, his hair falling untidily across his forehead as he stared into the old man's eyes. It immediately conjured up Daniel's hair as he had looked down into Lydia's face. That summer the sun had bleached it from golden brown to a deep straw, and a strand had brushed the face of the woman beneath him...

To break the spell, Ella turned abruptly towards the fireplace and tossed a few more coals into the blaze. Oh, Daniel! For a moment or two the longing for him was intense. Damn the man!

'And now say "Ah!"'... Hm.'

Ella turned back to see the doctor take a stethoscope from his bag. Unbuttoning Mr Saville's shirt, he helped him to sit up and then listened carefully to his heart and lungs.

Mr Saville rallied a little. 'I was feeling a little under the weather...' he began in a shaky voice. 'Then I felt a bit hot... Next thing I was lying on the floor and someone was holding sal volatile under my nose... I'm so sorry ... such a nuisance...'

The doctor smiled at him. 'Not your fault, is it? Nobody chooses to be taken ill. I'll just check your temperature. I think it may be a touch of flu. There is some about and it can knock you for six.' He shook down a thermometer and slipped it into Mr Saville's mouth.

Then he stood up and turned towards Ella. 'I came as soon as your message reached me. I can assure you, Mrs Gough, that my patients in Dorset expected just as efficient a service from their doctors as people in Kent.'

'I apologise for that remark,' Ella said quickly. 'I was worried about Mr Saville.'

'I understand, of course.' He turned back towards his patient. 'Do you live far from here, Mr Saville? And is there someone at home to look after you?'

Seeing the old man's face crumple, Ella lowered her voice. 'His wife died recently. I think there's a daily woman, but apart from her he has no one except a godson in New York. I might be able to reach him.'

'Notify the godson, you mean? But will he come back – all the way from America?'

'I've no idea, but he is due to return to England *sometime*. At least I can warn him that Mr Saville is ill.'

The doctor nodded and turned to his patient. 'In the meantime, you'll have to be admitted to the hospital. The almoner can sort out–'

Mr Saville snatched the thermometer from his mouth, panic-stricken. 'The *hospital?* Oh no, no. Don't send me into hospital. My mother died in a hospital. I swore never to enter one voluntarily.' He turned to Ella. 'Don't let them send me to hospital, Mrs Gough. I can manage on my own.'

Firmly the doctor returned the thermometer to the old man's mouth.

Ella knew exactly what Mr Saville was going through. She asked, 'Couldn't the district nurse visit him?'

Dr Clarke lowered his voice. 'He needs full-time care for at least a day or two. At his age he shouldn't be left alone at all. I suspect that the hospital is the best solution.'

'I might be able to spare my husband's nurse for an hour or so each day.'

'I'm afraid it wouldn't be enough, Mrs Gough.' He removed the thermometer, studied it and then nodded.

Mr Saville looked from Ella to the doctor, his anxiety growing. 'I won't go into hospital. It'll kill me, I know it will.' His faded blue eyes were wide with terror. 'My mother had an operation ... something went

36

wrong. Oh yes! The anaesthetic! That was it.'

Ella said, 'But you only have an anaesthetic if you have an operation. You just need nursing care–'

Her words fell on deaf ears as Mr Saville's eyes filled with tears. 'I can't... I *won't*... Oh, *please*...'

Ella glanced at the doctor. 'Perhaps he has a neighbour who would sit with him?'

Doctor Clarke shook his head. 'I'm afraid it wouldn't do,' he insisted and turned back to his patient. 'You'll be perfectly safe. Things have moved on since your mother's day. Everyone hates the idea of hospitals, but once you're in there you'll realise–'

'Oh – oh, Mrs Gough, *please!*' begged Mr Saville.

The doctor's mouth tightened. 'The staff are all professionals, Mr Saville. Your mother may have been an unlucky exception, or there might have been complications. I don't know the facts. There is no reason to suppose that you would come to any harm. Quite the contrary, in fact.'

Ella looked at the old man and made a sudden decision. 'Mr Saville will stay here for a day or two.' She faced the doctor. 'Then we'll see.' She cut short his protests. 'We've several spare bedrooms and my husband's nurse lives in. Mr Saville will be in good hands.'

She would have to convince Roland, but he could scarcely say 'No' once the sick man was installed. They would pay Nurse Baisley generously for the extra work.

'Well, I really don't know...' Taken aback, Doctor Clarke stared at her.

Mr Saville was stammering a very unconvincing protest, insisting that he couldn't possibly make such a nuisance of himself.

Ella lowered her voice. 'As long as you will supervise his progress,' she told the doctor. 'If it turns out to be a bad attack I appreciate that he may need hospital care.' She turned to the old man with a smile. 'You're in no position to argue, Mr Saville. It's a choice between us and the hospital.'

'Oh dear! Well, if you put it like that...' He smiled weakly. 'You really are very kind.'

The doctor threw up his hands in a helpless gesture. 'Well, it's remarkably generous of you. Are you sure that your husband...'

'My husband will be perfectly happy about the arrangement, doctor. He is in a wheelchair most of the time and leaves the management of the house to me. I'll have a word with Nurse Baisley and...' She stopped.

How on earth would they get the patient up the stairs to his room? He was in no state to walk; they would need someone to carry him. At once she thought of Daniel and an image rose clear and sharp in her mind. A much younger Daniel sitting on the sand at Camber wearing a pair of swimming trunks and her father's old panama. He was squinting into the sun, laughing at something her mother had said. Her father was with them and also Edmund Hampton, her father's closest friend. Ella saw Daniel's arms, still speckled with water from his dip in the sea, his skin sprinkled with gold hairs. All the seventeen-year-old Ella had wanted was for those arms to close around her.

They were all there, a happy group, frozen in her mind like a holiday snap. Her mother in a hand-knitted bathing suit, sitting with her hands clasped round her knees; Father in his deckchair next to Uncle Edmund who had the inevitable binoculars pressed to his eyes...

Daniel had leaned round her mother to tickle Ella's leg. 'Coming in again before we eat?'

'Yes!' She jumped to her feet. Just the two of them, she prayed.

He asked, 'Anyone else game?'

Her father said, 'You youngsters go. I'm nicely relaxed.'

Uncle Edmund, his eyes on the horizon, muttered, 'That looks like a tanker. Pretty low in the water, too...'

Ella crossed her fingers. It *would* be just the two of them.

Daniel smiled at her mother. 'Lydia?'

She shook her head. 'You two go. I've swallowed enough seawater for one day!'

'Then I won't,' he said.

She gave him a half smile.

Ella pulled a face. 'Oh, come on, Daniel! It was *your* idea!'

He shrugged. 'You'll just have to persuade your mother, then.'

Ella hesitated. 'Mummy? Will you?'

'No, dear! I've had enough.' She trickled a handful of sand over her feet.

Ella tried again. 'Daniel? *Please?*'

But he rolled over on to his back so that his right shoulder was touching her mother's foot, and Ella was immediately consumed with jealousy.

He said lazily, 'I've changed my mind, Ella. You go.'

Ella felt betrayed. First he tried to include her mother, then he refused to go in at all. What was the matter with him? This was their chance to be together away from the others.

Blindly, she stumbled towards the water and waded in. She headed straight out to sea. A moderate swimmer, she swam with fierce concentration. She would punish him; she would punish them all. She would swim too far and she would drown. He would be sorry then. He would live with the knowledge that he had killed her. Ahead of her there was nothing but sea and she didn't dare look back. They would find her body washed in with the tide... Her breath was laboured now, but she could hear faint sounds from the beach. They were shouting to her...

'Ella! Come back, you idiot!'

She turned at last and saw Daniel thrashing through the water towards her – but so far away. She felt a lurch of fear as she saw the beach behind him – an indistinct blur. At the same moment she realised that her energy was spent and she began to panic. She went under, then fought her way slowly back to the surface with leaden legs. Gasping and spluttering, she screamed for Daniel. It seemed an age before he reached her and then she punched and slapped him, fighting him off with what remained of her failing strength...

'Mrs *Gough!*'

With an effort she dragged herself back to the present. 'Yes?'

She caught the words, '...just ring me and I'll come as early as I can tomorrow.'

'Yes,' she repeated, wondering what she had missed.

As though sensing her confusion the doctor said, 'And remember – plenty of liquids, a custard, maybe, or a fruit jelly.

Keep it light.'

'I'll see to it.'

In a daze she saw him to the front door and watched him go. She was breathing heavily, waiting for the anguished memories to fade, but instead her treacherous thoughts returned with a greater clarity than before.

As Daniel carried her back to the shore he had been grinning. *Grinning!* Nobody had seen the darkness in her soul. Daniel had made light of her escapade and she had never forgiven him. Ella's mouth trembled...

Recalling Annie to keep an eye on her patient, she went into the garden in search of Daniel. She couldn't deny that she wanted to see him again, but with another part of her mind she knew that it was not a good idea. Best to get it over quickly, then.

At first there was no sign of the two men and she felt a wave of something akin to relief. She was too late; he had already left. Now she need not make a fool of herself. Almost immediately, however, she heard voices and realised that Daniel and Evans were in the greenhouse. Reaching the door she took a deep breath, rapped sharply on the glass and went inside. It was warm and humid with the green smell of growing plants trapped within glass. A healthy vine curled its way overhead, still bearing a few clusters of late grapes. A long table was given over to small seedlings neatly potted out into a regiment of small flowerpots. On the other side she saw empty pots, canes, seed packets, a watering-can, balls of twine and a pair of secateurs. Sacks of potting compost and fertiliser jostled for space on the floor. Both men glanced up.

Ella ignored Daniel. 'Mr Evans, I'd like to ask Mr Hampton a favour,' she said. 'One of my visitors is unwell, and I need someone to carry him upstairs to the bedroom.'

When at last she turned towards Daniel she noticed for the first time how tired he looked. The light filtering through the green leaves of the overhead vine cast an unhealthy shadow across his face. Was he thinner, she wondered, surprised by a flash of compassion. Daniel Hampton had no right to be asking for a job as an assistant gardener. He should be in chambers in Lincoln's Inn Fields, following in his father's footsteps.

Evans said, 'All right by me, if Mr Hampton doesn't mind.'

Daniel said, 'Of course not. Excuse me, Mr Evans. I'll be right back.'

For a moment or two he walked silently beside Ella and their feet sounded companionably on the gravelled path. Somehow she resisted the urge to slip her hand into his.

He said, 'Ella–'

She couldn't bear it. 'Mrs Gough!' she said sharply.

'Mrs Gough. I'm sorry, I forgot.' But he wasn't sorry, nor had he forgotten. She allowed herself a sideways glance and could see it in his expression. He intended to ruffle her feathers; he wanted to remind her. She said, 'My visitor ... he's elderly and quite frail and I don't think–'

He lowered his voice although no one else was near. 'This job, Ella. I need it.'

Ella dared not look at him. Her mind was a black whirling mass because already his presence and his words had broken through her flimsy reserve and the memories were flooding back. Briefly she closed her eyes and at once recalled the feel of his shoulder warm against her head, the pressure of his arms thrust under her legs and the rhythm of their bodies as he strode with her through the waves and out on to the beach. There he had lowered her on to her towel and watched as her mother wrapped her in another. Burdened by a deepening despair, Ella sat exhausted, aware of the curious looks of the other holidaymakers. The family, aware of the interest, had made light of it.

She stole another glance at Daniel's set profile. Once Daniel Hampton had carried *her* in his arms, she thought. Now it would be someone else's turn.

He said, 'Ella, *please!*'

'Don't!' she begged and her voice cracked treacherously.

'Don't what?'

'Don't upset me ... please, Daniel. It – was all so long ago. It doesn't – *shouldn't* – matter any more.'

He stopped, staring at her. 'Don't *upset* you? My God, that's rich. After what you did to us. To me.'

'I was very young, Daniel!'

'You got off scot-free.' His voice was rising.

'If you believe that...'

He swallowed hard, then made a visible effort to control himself. 'I need this job, Ella.'

'It's impossible,' she said. 'You must know that.'

'I don't want to beg–'

'Then don't!' She quickened her steps.

'Ella!' He grabbed her arm and swung her round to face him.

Ella snatched her arm away. 'Don't you *dare* touch me!' she told him breathlessly.

He said, 'Listen. Please. I have debts ... serious problems, Ella. You can help me. Big house. Rich husband. Servants. All I'm asking is the chance to–'

'It wouldn't work, Daniel.'

'We could try it. I'd keep out of your way.'

'No!' Ella almost ran the rest of the way

and hurried in through the front door. Raising her voice she said, 'Mr Saville is in the sitting room. This way, Mr Hampton.'

Without a word to anyone Daniel followed her, stony-faced. He lifted the old man from the sofa and carried him up the stairs and into the spare room which Annie had prepared. A small fire was already blazing in the hearth and there was a stone hot-water bottle in the bed.

'Thank you, Mr Hampton,' said Ella, glad of the housekeeper's presence. 'We won't keep you any longer.'

He went without a word. Ella dared not look at him, but let out a sigh of relief when she heard the door close behind him.

Almost at once Nurse Baisley knocked and entered the room, carrying a pair of Roland's pyjamas. The large figure beneath the uniform was stiff with disapproval and her mouth was a thin line. Ella knew that the woman disliked her, but had never bothered to ask why.

In a cold voice the nurse said, 'I should have been consulted about this.'

'I'm sorry. There wasn't time.'

'Bringing influenza into the house with Mr Gough in a weakened state of health...'

'Mr Gough is in perfect health apart from his disability.'

'Anyone who has had polio has been weakened by it, Mrs Gough.'

Ella was in no mood for penitence. 'Well, it's done now,' she said, 'and no doubt the extra money we pay you will compensate you.'

'The money is not an issue,' Nurse Baisley told her. 'It's my patient's welfare that concerns me.' She tossed the pyjamas on to the bed. 'If you had asked for my opinion, I would have advised you that it was most unwise.'

'I didn't ask for it because I didn't need it.'

The nurse was right but Ella couldn't bring herself to say so. The wretched woman would be so smug; she would *gloat*. But Ella knew she *should* have considered whether or not the infection would be dangerous. However, the solution was a simple one. Roland and Penny must be kept away from Mr Saville. Nurse Baisley was making a fuss about nothing.

'The influenza was already *in* the house,' Ella reminded her. 'Mr Saville had been here for nearly two hours before he collapsed. Rather a case of horse and stable door, wouldn't you say?'

She smiled at Mr Saville who was eyeing them nervously. 'Nurse Baisley will look after you,' she told him, 'and I'll be up later to see how you are.'

Without another look at the nurse, Ella followed Annie out of the room.

Outside the door, Ella drew a long breath.

47

'Thank you,' she said. 'You'd better get back to the kitchen now.'

Annie hesitated. 'He'll be all right, won't he?'

'Oh yes. He's in good hands.'

As Ella watched the housekeeper make her way downstairs she muttered, 'Mr Saville will survive – but will *I*?'

Walking slowly along the passage towards the library, she found her courage gradually returning. She must *not* allow the past to haunt her in this way. Pausing at the landing window, she stared out. Suddenly she brightened. She would telephone Aunt Florrie. Maybe she would visit her. For the first time in years Ella felt the need for reassurance. In a very short time Daniel had stripped away the protective layers with which she had surrounded herself for so long.

'But you have only yourself to blame,' she muttered. She needn't have gone back to him today to ask for help. 'You're a fool, Ella Gough!'

Suppose he made trouble for her. Could he? Would he?

Ella closed her eyes as panic flared.

Half an hour later, Evans watched Dan Hampton cycle away down the curving driveway, passing a small girl on his way out. Evans smiled. Young Penny. A good name for

48

her, he was fond of saying. Bright as a penny, she was, and no mistake! Now he frowned and scratched his head, still puzzling over Dan Hampton. The mistress had had no right to call on him like that, before he was even an employee. Not that it wasn't a good cause – he wasn't saying that – and they *did* have to get the old chap up the stairs. He shook his head. Not that Hampton had objected either. He'd gone off all obedient like, but it wasn't *right*. Still, it was between the two of them ... but it was odd.

Penny, seeing him in the middle of the lawn, left the driveway and ran towards him, fair hair flying, her hat askew. Behind her came the nanny, calling to her to stop.

'Penelope-e!' she shouted. 'Slow down. You'll fall!'

'Mr Evans! Mr Evans!' Penny gasped, coming to an abrupt halt in front of him. 'I saw a man on a bicycle and he rang his bell and he called me "young tiddler"! One day I'm going to have a proper bicycle. I'm too old for a tricycle. Who is he, Mr Evans? The man with the bell?'

Mrs Granger, a little overweight, toiled across the grass behind her. Evans watched her with approval. He liked women with a bit of flesh on them. He'd often wondered why Enid Granger had never remarried. If he'd been a younger man he might have been tempted to ask her himself.

'Penelope Gough!' she cried. 'How many times do I have to tell you? You will do as you're *told!*' she grumbled. '*When* you're told. Not five minutes later. I told you to wait for me, not race ahead like a hoyden. And who he is is no concern of yours.'

'But I *liked* him,' the child protested, artlessly twisting one of her curls around her finger.

Evans, smiling, was already bending down to straighten Penny's hat. 'Don't want your ma to see you in this state,' he warned. 'She wants her daughter to be a little lady, not a gipsy!'

Mrs Granger put a hand to her side. 'Gipsy? Little monkey would be closer! I've got quite a stitch, chasing after her.' But her expression belied the words. All the staff knew that Mrs Granger adored her young charge.

The child repeated her question and Evans said, 'He's the new gardener – or I hope he will be.'

'What's his name?'

'Hampton.' Turning to the nanny, he said, 'Seems a very steady sort of chap. Head screwed on the right way, although...' He shook his head.

Mrs Granger spotted the hesitation, 'Although?'

He frowned. 'I don't rightly know. Seems to know it all – even the Latin names and suchlike what I could never get my tongue round. But there was something odd about him. Something I couldn't quite place, if you know what I mean.'

Penny threw a handful of leaves into the air. 'What *is* a young tiddler?'

He laughed down at her. 'A young tiddler? That's a little fish, that is. But I saw you running away from poor Mrs Granger. I reckon he meant you're a bit of a handful. Are you?'

'Of course I'm not! Am I?' She appealed to her nanny.

'Of course you are!' she replied. To Evans she said, 'No, I don't know. How do you mean "odd"?'

The gardener shrugged thin shoulders. 'A bit la-di-da. A bit too – well, not *humble*, like you'd expect. Still, he knew his stuff, garden wise. And he didn't haggle over the money or the hours. I shall put in a good word for this one with Mr Gough. I as good as told the man the job's his.'

Mrs Granger smiled. 'You like your assistants humble, do you?'

'I like a bit of respect!' Glancing down he spotted a stray dandelion leaf, bent to ease it from the soil and tucked it into his apron pocket. 'Blasted things. Not that he wasn't respectful. It was just ... somehow he ... oh, blow it! I don't rightly know what I do mean.'

Mrs Granger rolled her eyes. 'Well, he can't be worse than the last lad. I used to see him from the nursery – lurking behind the wall, smoking those terrible cigarettes of his when he thought no one was looking.'

The gardener nodded. 'And his language! Many's the cuff I give him, but it didn't do no good. He had his six weeks' probation, but I was glad to see the back of him and that's the truth.'

Penny began to drag the rake over the grass. 'I heard him say a rude word once, but when I told Mummy she grumbled at *me!*'

Mrs Granger said, *'Don't* tell us what it was, thank you, Penelope.'

The gardener grinned at the child. 'What big *ears* you've got, Grandma!' he teased. 'Don't miss much, do you, Penny?'

Mrs Granger shook her head. 'Don't encourage her, Mr Evans. You know how she loves to show off.' She held out her hand. 'Come along, Penelope. It's nearly tea-time.'

Penny dodged the outstretched hand. 'Just let me show Mr Evans my handstand. Just one!'

'Handstand? Certainly not.' Mrs Granger made a grab for her but missed. 'Tea-time now or no story at bed-time. I mean it!'

'A cartwheel, then?'

'Good heavens no! Who's been putting

these ideas into your head?'

'Meg Cutts can do handstands *and* cartwheels!'

The nanny caught Penny's hand and held on firmly. 'Forget about Meg Cutts and say "Goodbye" to Mr Evans.'

'Goodbye, Mr Evans.'

He lifted a gnarled hand in farewell and watched, smiling, as they crossed the lawn. When they had turned the corner and were out of sight he allowed his gaze to wander along the paths and flowerbeds. A few weeds were appearing and the grass needed mowing again already. He would soon be seventy, although he kept his age a secret, but it was too much for him single-handed. He needed someone with a young back and strong arms so that he could ease himself into a nice retirement. He needed Dan Hampton, he told himself.

'And the sooner the better!'

Chapter Two

At the other end of the town, in a ground-floor flat, Lizzie Hampton was about to start the ironing. It was a job she disliked even more than cooking, and as she set the iron against the stove to heat she glanced around the dingy room and gave a heartfelt sigh. She hated the threadbare mats, loathed the cupboard doors that needed repainting and glared resentfully at the worn gingham curtains. The entire flat was ripe for improvement but it was rented and, since summer eviction was already a possibility, they had no incentive to spend money on it. Even if they had any to spare, which they didn't.

Lizzie took a striped pyjama top from the pile beside her and spread it out on the table. Beneath the top there was a badly scorched sheet folded double, and beneath that a thin blanket. Lizzie pushed a stray lock of auburn hair from her damp forehead. With her freckles and her golden-brown eyes she had once been pretty and there had been plenty of men chasing her.

'Those were the days!' she muttered with a faint smile.

Sighing over past glories and lost opportunities, she took the flat-iron from the top of the stove and spat on it. The resulting sizzle told her that it was too hot and she held it aloft, waiting for it to cool.

'Get back here, Dan!' she muttered.

After a moment or two she began, urging the heavy iron with such careless force that it created almost as many creases as it removed.

She needed her husband to share the news of the latest problem – one that might well overshadow all their other difficulties. A glance at the dresser revealed a bundle of bills which never seemed to grow any smaller, tucked behind the large meat platter which they could never afford to use. It was one of the few remaining pieces from the set Dan's uncle had given them when they married in the small church on the outskirts of Cape Town. Breakages had accounted for some of the missing pieces – some could be attributed to the usual accidents, but a few had been hurled at Daniel by his wife during their more violent rows. Lizzie would be the first to admit it for she was secretly rather proud of her fiery temper, inherited through her father's side of the family.

Stanley Chapman, a stoker, had been a trouble-maker from the day he was born, and later his activities on various cargo ships had earned him the label of agitator. When he finally overstepped the mark and was sacked the ship was in Cape Town, and that's where he had settled, married and raised his two children. Lizzie's brother Frank took after his father and was quickly fired to anger and always ready with his fists – especially when he'd been drinking. He'd gone back to England but had never prospered. He'd been barred from so many pubs that he'd been forced to buy one of his own. At least, that was the way he liked to tell it.

Lizzie shook her head. She folded the pyjama jacket, placed it on a chair and reached for the bottom half of the pyjamas. These she ironed with marginally more consideration, afraid that the worn fabric might finally fall apart. When they'd run out of luck in Cape Town, she and Dan had returned to England to share the running of Frank's pub but it had been doomed from the start. A large 'once-only' loan from Dan's father had saved it from immediate disaster, but it had simply delayed the inevitable. Frank had run up huge debts which he had hidden from Dan, had borrowed from unscrupulous moneylenders and had finally ended up in prison for dealing in stolen goods.

'Bloody *fool!*'

A faint 'meow' reached her ears and she

glanced up at the kitchen window where a half-grown black cat sat on the outside sill. It was a miserable-looking creature with a mangled left ear.

She said, 'No, you can't come in. Go home.'

Whenever she allowed it inside the kitchen it made a beeline for the cellar and mewed at the door, reminding her of the mice that surely inhabited the dismal room. Lizzie, more than a little claustrophobic, thought about the cellar as little as possible and never ventured down into the cramped, gloomy depths which the landlord had once described as 'a valuable storage area'. She sent Dan down each morning to bring up a bucket of coke for the stove and kept the door firmly latched.

'And stop that yowling!'

As the cat continued to mew, she crossed the room and opened the window with a sharp movement that dislodged it. She grinned to herself as the animal disappeared with a wail of protest. Standing the iron back on the stove, she reached for the basin. Dipping her fingers into the water, she sprinkled her best blouse and skirt and rolled them tightly to spread the dampness. A glance at the clock showed five minutes to five. The grandfather clock had been in Dan's family for years and he thought the world of it. He said it was worth a few bob, she thought, with sudden interest. If they were really desperate ... but she would miss its cheerful ticking if it ever joined a number of other articles recently relegated to the pawnshop.

'Which might be sooner rather than later!' she told the cat which had already resumed its place on the windowsill.

Unless, that is, her husband had finally found himself another job. 'For heaven's sake get lucky, Dan!' she muttered. 'We deserve it.'

At the thought of him her cold heart softened a little. After she met Dan there had never been anyone else for her, and she had thanked God more than once for allowing his first wife to die. Curiosity had driven her to ask him about Lydia, but although his obvious reluctance had finally deterred her she had gleaned enough from his attitude to know that he had been deeply in love. The knowledge fuelled her insecurities, but she had to admit that Daniel had tried to make his second marriage work. He had given up his studies to find a job that would support them and had never reproached her for what might have been. Neither had he ever blamed *her* for her brother's stupidity, and she would always be grateful for that.

'Ten minutes more,' she promised herself, with a glance into the laundry basket. 'Then what's not done can wait until tomorrow.'

She understood, too, why Dan had refused to ask his father for more money. Edmund Hampton had helped them once, but he was disappointed that his son had given up his career and he had made it clear that he didn't want to see him or his second wife when they arrived back from South Africa. Lizzie knew that whatever had come between father and son all those years ago was still there. For some reason Edmund Hampton had disapproved of Lydia, and there had been a tremendous row. Whenever Lizzie asked for more information Daniel said, 'Water under the bridge!' in a voice that discouraged further probing.

'Blooming marvellous!' she said, beginning on the blouse with small careful movements. She had married into a wealthy family only to discover that Dan and his father didn't get along. 'Just my luck!' she muttered.

Her mouth drooped. If only she had kept the child! She had fallen for it soon after the wedding but, immediately panic-stricken, had consulted a more worldly girlfriend who had reluctantly taken her to a back-street abortionist. The ensuing nightmare had left Lizzie with a lot of pain and she had been forced to consult a real doctor. Fortunately, taking pity on her, he had turned a blind eye to her crime but had warned her that she might never conceive again. Dan, comparatively ignorant of the inner workings of women's bodies, had known nothing about it which was just as well. He had been longing for a child ever since she'd known him.

Too late, with the benefit of hindsight Lizzie had realised that a grandchild might have made all the difference where Dan's father was concerned. The magazines she read frequently had stories about unhappy families who were joyfully reunited after the birth of a baby.

Lizzie sighed. There was no one to blame but herself, but it still might not be too late. How would Dan's father react, she wondered, if he wrote to say Lizzie was expecting? If feeling queasy was anything to go by, then perhaps she was expecting twins!

'Twins? God, I hope not!' she said, rolling her eyebrows expressively as she stood the airer in front of the stove and began to drape the clothes over it.

Her best skirt, blue linen with front pleats, came out of the washing basket next and for a while concentration kept more sombre thoughts at bay. She might not be the world's best cook but she *could* sew. Even Dan was surprised when she'd first turned one of his collars and he had shown no particular interest when, a week ago, she had let out her waistband.

'Getting fat in my old age!' she'd joked, crossing her fingers. If she *were* expecting a baby, the timing was terrible.

She arranged the skirt on a hanger and carried it into the bedroom where she hung it from the top edge of the wardrobe to air. Ten minutes later the blouse, two shirts, socks, pants and vests went over the airer and the kettle was almost boiling. As soon as he came in she would make a pot of tea and, if his luck had changed, she would tell him the news. If he was still out of work, it could wait until she had seen the doctor.

She folded the ironing blankets, stowed them away in the bottom of the dresser and stood the iron upright on the floor to cool.

'Dan ... *Dan*...!' She swallowed hard. The gardening job with the Hackers had been a godsend. They had paid off the rent arrears and Dan had been able to buy himself a decent pair of boots and a sturdy jacket. They were much happier together and Lizzie had dared to hope that maybe Dan still loved her. The Hackers' move to Scotland had put an end to all that.

The rattle of her husband's key in the lock sent her flying to the mirror to fluff out her hair and dab on some lipstick. Then she fixed a smile and saw with relief that she could still look attractive.

Dan came through the passage and into the kitchen and stood with his back to the door. There was an odd look on his face which Lizzie found disconcerting.

Her heart pounded. 'What?' she demanded.

He pushed himself upright. 'I don't know... They'll let me know.'

'That's good! Isn't it, Dan? I mean, they didn't say "No".'

'Maybe.' His expression was guarded. 'The gardener seemed to like me. He showed me round. It's a big garden – bigger than the Hackers' – but nothing I couldn't deal with. He was a nice old boy. When he goes I could probably step into his shoes. Money's not bad.'

'There you are then!' She stepped forward and put her arms round him. 'That's good, Dan. If they *hadn't* wanted you they'd have said. Wouldn't they?'

He closed his arms around her and she leaned her head against his chest. He stroked her hair and she closed her eyes.

'We mustn't count on it, Lizzie. I didn't see Mr Gough, I saw his wife instead. She was ... I don't think she was quite so keen.'

She craned her head to look at him. 'Not keen? But why, Dan? Just because she didn't take to you? You wouldn't be working for her, anyway. You'd be working for *Mr* Gough, and you have that wonderful reference. Hell's bells, Dan, they *must* give it to you.'

Gently he pushed her away and sat down at the table, rubbing his eyes. Not tiredness, she knew, but fear. So much was hanging on the Goughs' decision.

He went on, 'We mustn't hope for too much. She may already have someone else in mind. I don't know. She, she may have her reasons.'

Lizzie was silent as she spooned tea into the pot and poured on hot water.

He said, 'Anyway, how are you feeling? Still a bit under the weather?'

She shook her head. 'Not too bad,' she lied.

'That's the ticket.'

He sounded as though his mind was on other things, she thought, but at least he had asked about her. Surely that showed that he cared? Her mother had suffered with poor health most of her life and her father had *never* asked how she was feeling – but then he'd been a selfish pig most of *his* life.

When the tea was poured out they sat with their elbows on the table, staring wordlessly into the steaming cups.

Lizzie said, 'Does she know how much this job means to us? Did you tell her?'

'I tried. She was rather unsympathetic.'

'Miserable devil!' Lizzie drew a long breath.

He covered his face with his hands. From behind his fingers he said, 'It was just the most awful bad luck.'

'Bad luck? How d'you mean?'

He lowered his hands and said quickly, 'That it was her, I mean, and not the husband.'

A little too quickly, thought Lizzie, her senses suddenly aroused.

He rushed on. 'It's easier to talk man to man. But we'll just have to wait and see. The gardener must surely have a large say in who works under him.' Forcing a smile, he reached across and patted her hand.

Lizzie hesitated, watching his eyes, longing to help him. 'Why don't I go to her, Dan? I could explain why it's so important–'

'No!' He stared at her, startled. 'You stay away from her.'

'Dan!' She held up a hand in mock defence. 'No need to shout at me. I only meant woman to woman I could maybe talk her round.'

'I said "No", Lizzie. I don't want you involved.' He swallowed. 'I'm sorry if I shouted, but I know her – I mean I've *seen* her and you haven't. She'd make mincemeat out of you and I won't have you humiliated. Promise you'll leave it to me?'

She looked at him, puzzled by his vehemence, hurt by the rejection. 'OK! So I can't help you. What do I care?'

'Promise, Lizzie?' He waited, but she said nothing. 'Look, you mean well but I know you. You get carried away. You'd go too far and make things worse.'

'I wouldn't.' He didn't trust her, she thought resentfully.

'You *would*, Lizzie! You always do. Remember that woman on the ship coming home? You ended up *hitting* her.'

'She was *rude* to me! She said I was drunk.'

'You *were* drunk.'

'You should have stuck up for me!'

'You were in the wrong. You spilled her drink and refused to apologise, and then you were rude to her husband when he intervened.'

Lizzie knew that everything he said was true. 'I didn't mean to hit her. She just made me so mad. Stuck-up pig!'

'You went too far, Lizzie.' He put down his cup. 'I want you to promise.'

'Oh, for Pete's sake! I *promise!* Cross my heart and hope to *die!*' She fitted actions to the words, mocking him. 'I promise to stay away from your precious Mrs Gough.'

'She isn't mine.'

It was not the words but the way he said them that set alarm bells ringing in Lizzie's brain. 'What happened?' she demanded. 'Did she make eyes at you?' Her anger had disappeared, to be replaced with appre-hension. Her voice shook. 'Did you make eyes at *her?* Is that it?' When he failed to

66

deny it her suspicions deepened into panic. 'She did, didn't she!' Her eyes narrowed. 'What's she like, this Mrs Gough? Pretty, is she? Maybe that's why the last man left!' She was breathless with fright, but she only knew how to attack.

He shook his head slowly. 'Lizzie, please. If you could hear how ridiculous you sound.'

'So if I'm wrong, tell me it isn't true. Go on, Dan! Tell me.' She felt ill with shock. Another woman in Dan's life would be more than she could bear.

He gave a slight shrug. 'It's not like that at all. What's she like? Good-looking, I suppose, but much older than you. She looked at me as though she didn't want me there. She seemed set against me right from the start and...'

He was telling the truth. Wasn't he? Lizzie wanted to believe it. She was *sure* she could see it in his eyes. Yes, he was telling the truth. Her heart rate slowed and the fear began to seep away.

She said, 'Maybe she was having fun with the last gardener. *Maybe* that's why they got rid of him.'

He shrugged but said nothing.

Poor Dan. He looked so unhappy. Damn Mrs Gough!

'Perhaps she'll come up trumps,' she suggested, without much conviction.

Dan shrugged. 'God only knows! But there's nothing either of us can do about it – except wait.'

Later that day, Ella went back into the study where Roland was searching one of his books for a reference he required.

'Damn index is virtually useless.' He looked at her expectantly. 'Well? How was Hampton? Is he going to fill the bill?'

Ella sat down near him. 'I'm afraid I'm not totally convinced,' she told him. 'He comes with a good reference and Evans seems to think well of him, but...'

'Then let's take him on. Save putting another advertisement in the paper – and he can make a start. We've wasted enough time already. Poor old Evans is really past the heavy work. I was watching him...'

'I was going on to say that there's something about him I don't like.' She fought back a feeling of disloyalty. 'Something I don't quite trust.'

'Dishonest, you mean?' Roland raised his eyebrows. 'But you said the reference was a good one. Let me have a look at it.'

Ella said, 'Oh, there's no need for you to bother with it, dear. You asked me to interview him on your behalf, and I did, and I'm telling you that-'

'Ella! I'd like to see the chap's reference. You do have it, I take it?'

Reluctantly she drew it from her pocket and handed it to him. He unfolded the letter and scanned the page.

'As you say, a good reference. So what exactly is your concern, Ella?'

Frantically she searched her mind. 'It was his general attitude more than anything,' she said. 'A surprising arrogance about the way he spoke and a ... a rather familiar way of regarding me. As though I were a woman and not a prospective employer.' God forgive me, she thought. I'm crucifying him, but it has to be done. 'I really do think we should let him go, Roland, and look elsewhere. It's worth a little effort to find the right man, don't you think?'

She could see that her husband was more than a little annoyed with her. He wanted to continue with his article and she was delaying him.

'Does his attitude towards women matter that much?' he asked. 'It's how well he can dig and plant that's important, surely? How often will you come into contact with the man? Half a dozen times a year if that. As long as he treats Evans with proper respect, I can't see why–'

Ella jumped to her feet. 'So you are ignoring my recommendation, Roland. Does that mean you no longer trust my judgement? Because if so you–'

'Ella!' His annoyance was growing. 'You

know very well that I trust your judgement over practically everything. The choice of a nanny, for instance. I simply think you have taken an unreasonable dislike to the poor chap. I'll bear in mind what you say and I'll talk to Evans. Now, if you don't mind, I've got work to do.'

He turned back to his book and Ella felt herself to be ignominiously dismissed. Like one of the servants, she thought furiously.

She turned to go but hesitated at the door. She wanted to tell him that if he crossed her on this he would probably live to regret it, but even to her it sounded melodramatic and at the last moment her courage failed.

Instead she said very firmly, 'I wouldn't ask if I didn't think it important, Roland,' and closed the door before he could answer. For a moment she waited in case he should call her back into the room; but when no such summons came, she walked away. She had done her best to warn him. On balance, she thought it was enough. If she went too far he might become suspicious. She crossed her fingers. *Please, Roland.* If he supported Evans and gave Daniel the job, she could not be held responsible for the consequences.

Engrossed once more in the final paragraph of his article, Roland almost missed the tap on his door.

He looked up. 'Oh, for God's sake! Come in!' The door opened and Evans came into the room. 'Oh, it's you. I thought – never mind. What is it, man? I'm trying to work.'

'It's about the new man, sir,' Evans began. 'I thought you'd like – that is, that maybe you was expecting a bit of a report on him since you wasn't able to see him yourself.' He stood with feet together, his back straight as though on parade, his battered cap clutched in both hands.

Roland sighed. 'I'm going to advertise again. My wife didn't like him for some reason. She seemed set against him.'

The man looked genuinely surprised. 'Don't *like* him?'

'So she said. Didn't like his attitude.'

'Well, sir, that's new to me, that is,' Evans said indignantly. 'Mrs Gough said nothing to me. Said as how the reference was a good one, though. He called her Mrs Gough and she was polite to him. I didn't notice nothing. Nice chap, I thought. Knows his stuff and isn't afraid of hard work. I showed him all round, like, and he said as he could take over *all* the heavy work. *Offered* to. I was most impressed.'

Roland said, 'Dammit!' and threw up his hands in a gesture of resignation. 'So you saw nothing amiss, Evans? Nothing to take exception to at all?'

'Nothing, sir. Except ... well, it was

71

nothing really, sir, unless Mrs Gough took against his manner of speaking. I was saying to Mrs Granger earlier that he spoke very well. For a gardener, that is. A bit la-di-da, but I soon got used to it. He was proper respectful. I liked him, Mr Gough.'

Roland hesitated. 'It's really up to you, Evans. You have to get along with him. Do you think he's the man for the job or would you like us to re-advertise the position?'

'I'd like to have him, sir. Oh, yes. We'd have to go a long way to find a better man. I don't see no problems, begging Mrs Gough's pardon.'

Roland came to a decision. 'Then you shall have him, Evans. Let my wife know when you see her that I've made up my mind. He shall have a fair chance. Tell him he'll get the usual six weeks' probation.'

A smile split the old man's face as he touched his forehead in a half salute.

'Thank you very much, sir. I know you won't regret it.'

Tucked away behind the High Street, the church hall was bright with morning sunlight which streamed through the high, coloured windows on to the small dancers beneath. It was Saturday and nine little girls from five to eight years old were tapping their way to possible stardom, but probably doing no more than gaining a little poise and confidence. They wore the uniform of Janet Bell's Dancing Academy – pleated red skirt with shoulder straps and a white silk blouse with puff sleeves and a Peter Pan collar. Red tap shoes tied with wide satin ribbons completed the outfit. Five mothers, a nanny, an aunt and a big sister sat in a row and watched as Miss Bell put her young students through their paces.

'And tap and step and tap . . .' she cried breathlessly. 'And step and turn and step, double step, ball, change!'

Her rounded figure quivered with effort as she stepped through the routine with them – her arms flung out dramatically, her head tossing provocatively. Her own very short skirt twirled skittishly and the flounced satin blouse quivered. In spite of the fact that the small oil stove gave out very little heat, Miss Bell sweated to an unladylike degree.

At the piano her mother pounded the keys with relish, pausing only to beam with great pride at her daughter and the children.

Out of breath, Miss Bell stopped, one hand to her heart. 'And step and step a-a-and *stop!* Arm outstretched, Brenda, if you please. No, straighter than that. Right out, pointing over the heads of the audience. Look at Lucy's arm... Ah, that's better.' She drew a deep breath as they all relaxed, sensing the end of the lesson. 'Well, that's all for today. See you next week and remember

... what do you have to do, children?'

'Practise, practise, practise!' they chanted as one.

'Good! Practise between now and then. Ask your mummies to help you.'

She smiled at the spectators who, taking their cue, clapped with enthusiasm to mark the end of the session. As the children drifted back to their escorts, the older girls waiting outside for the last class of the afternoon could be seen through the frosted glass of the door.

'And ladies!' cried Miss Bell. The children stopped in their tracks at the sound of her voice. 'Please don't forget that the concert is less than six weeks away. Next week we'll have a look at the costumes. Check for fit. If any child is taken ill – Heaven forbid, but these things *do* happen – let me know at once so that I can arrange a replacement. Tickets are going nicely, but if any of you can sell any more so much the better.' She smiled down at the children. 'Right then. Off you pop!'

At the mention of the tickets, Enid Granger sighed guiltily as Penny ran towards her, her feet still tapping.

Miss Bell called, '*Thank* you, Penelope!'

Unperturbed, Penny grinned, sat down and began to tug at the bows of her shoes.

Enid said, 'Let me undo them. You always pull them into knots.'

She should have spoken to Penny's mother about the tickets, she reflected, but Mrs Gough had been in a funny mood for the past few days. Everyone had noticed it. Ever since the new chap had arrived to help Evans – or so Annie had told her. And Annie had got it straight from Mr Evans, who said the mistress had wanted to re-advertise the post. Probably had a falling-out with her husband over it. That usually put her in a bad mood, Enid reflected with a wry smile. Not that it happened very often, but when it did they all suffered. Enid decided to put off her news until her employer was in a better mood. She knew that Mrs Gough would object to her leaving but elderly parents needed care. Enid's mother was managing on her own but only just. The arthritis could only get worse and she was going to need her daughter's help. Mrs Gough might decide to take on another nanny, although Penelope was really past the age when she needed one. Finding a suitable replacement would take time...

She became aware that Penny was glowering at the sensible brown shoe which was now being buttoned around her small foot.

'Why *can't* I have shoes like Lucy Barnes?' Penny grumbled. 'It isn't a bit fair.'

'Life isn't fair, Penelope. I've told you that before.'

'But why *can't* I?'

Enid lowered her voice to a whisper. 'Because they're not very nice. Ankle-straps are rather vulgar and black patent leather is not very practical.'

'Is Lucy Barnes vulgar then?'

'Hush! Keep your voice down!'

'But is she?'

'No – at least...' Enid glanced up to see Mrs Barnes moving towards them. Lucy pranced behind her, the maligned black shoes much in evidence. 'Oh, Mrs Barnes...' Enid began, flustered. Had the wretched woman *heard* her?

Lucy's mother smiled as she handed her a small deckle-edged card. 'For Penelope. My daughter will be seven,' she said by way of explanation. 'Seven! Where do the years go to?'

'Where indeed?' Enid, waving the card, gave Penny a look which spoke volumes. 'An invitation to Lucy's party. Isn't that lovely, Penelope? We'll ask your mother, but I'm sure she'll say "Yes".'

Penny took the little card, her eyes sparkling with excitement. 'Oh, *thank* you! I'd love to come.' She glanced up at her nanny. 'I could wear my pink dress with the silk ribbons.'

Mrs Barnes laughed. 'I'm sure you'll look very pretty, Penelope.' To Mrs Granger she said, 'It will be a small group. We've invited

76

seven girls – one for each year.'

Penny said, 'Is Meg Cutts coming? I like her.'

Mrs Barnes' expression changed and she lowered her voice. 'Meg Cutts? No, Penny. She isn't quite the sort of girl we want our daughter to play with.' Lowering it even further, she whispered to Enid, 'Her family is very unsuitable and her language is dreadful. I'm surprised at Miss Bell allowing her to join a class like this but there you are. What can one do?'

'Exactly.' Enid tugged Penny into her leggings and buttoned them securely. Next the coat with its neat fur collar, lastly the matching hat. She ignored Penny's wriggling.

At that moment a thin-faced child paused beside them, looking eagerly at the invitation which Penny was holding. Her coat was shabby and she wore galoshes. 'A party?' she said, looking hopefully at the adults.

Lucy said kindly, 'You're not coming, Meg. Only my best friends.'

Mrs Barnes reddened. 'Lucy!' She smiled at Meg. 'I'm sorry, Meg. We – we just don't have the room for a big party. We can't invite everybody.'

The child's face fell.

Penny said, 'Never mind, Meg. When I'm eight you can come to mi–'

She stopped in mid-word as Enid tugged her round to face her. 'No time to stop and chat, Penelope,' she said. 'We have to go. Say "Goodbye". Your mother will be expecting us back.'

'No, she won't. She–'

'Penelope Gough! That's enough!' Enid, mortified, threw a helpless look in Mrs Barnes' direction. To Penny she hissed, 'Now what have I told you? *Do* as you're told–'

'*When* you're told. I know.' A scowl spoiled the pretty face as Penny pushed her tap shoes into her slipper bag with an exaggerated sigh.

Mrs Barnes said, 'Goodbye, Penelope,' but Enid was already hustling her young charge towards the door. Outside she said, 'That awful child. Meg Whatsit. She was as good as *asking* to be invited. The cheek of it!'

They walked in silence while Enid tried to reassure herself that she had handled an awkward situation as well as possible.

'I *like* Meg!' Penny said again.

'You like everyone, Penelope. No discrimination, that's your problem.'

'What does discimination mean?'

'Dis*crim*ination. Never mind.'

Penny hung back, ignoring Enid's efforts to hurry her along. 'Meg makes me laugh. Her mother's lucky; she doesn't have to pay because they're so poor and an old lady pays for the dancing lessons.'

Intrigued, Enid slowed her pace. 'An old lady? Who told you that?'

'Lucy told me, and Lucy's mother told her.'

'Really? How very odd.'

'I like her.' They reached the kerb and Penny looked both ways. 'Nothing coming,' she said dutifully. They crossed the road and turned left. Penny giggled. 'Meg makes me laugh. She says "bum" and "dicky dirt" and "titty" and–'

Enid rounded on her, shaking her by the arm. 'Now you just *stop* that, Penelope Gough! You only do it to upset me, and if your mother ever heard you talking like that she'd ... she'd be horrified! "Titty", indeed ... and what's "dicky dirt" supposed to mean?'

'It means shirt.'

'Shirt? *Shirt?* Don't be ridiculous!'

'It *does!* Meg told me.'

'Meg! Meg! I'm tired of hearing about her.'

They walked on in silence for a while and then, inevitably, Enid's irritation faded. Dicky dirt, indeed! How could it mean 'shirt', she wondered. Unless the real meaning was rather rude. *Dicky* dirt? Better not explore that any further. She rolled her eyes. She could never be cross with the child for long, and as they turned the corner she

79

was hiding a smile.

'Semolina for tea,' she said, 'and if you're very good you can have jam on it!'

Lizzie was peeling the last potato when Win put her head round the door. A peroxide blonde with the roots showing, as neighbours go Win was less trouble than some, but her husband was a noisy creature and bad-tempered when he was drunk. Lizzie glanced at the clock which said five thirty-five. Add on ten minutes because it was always slow, so it was getting on for six. Win had better not stay too long in case Dan got off earlier than usual. He disliked Win; called her 'that loudmouthed lump from next door'.

'Come in, Win.' Lizzie cut the potato into quarters and added it to those already in the pan. 'Where's the baby?'

'Asleep, thank God. He had me up twice in the night. I feel like a washed-out rag.'

The black cat followed Win in and headed for the cellar. It mewed loudly, staring at the crack below the door.

'Chuck it out,' said Lizzie.

Win picked it up and shut it outside.

'It's always trying to get into that blessed cellar,' Lizzie told her. 'Mice, I suppose.'

'Or rats!'

Lizzie gave a little scream and said, 'Don't!'

Win asked, 'Where's that kid of mine? Up with Mrs Levine again?'

Lizzie nodded. 'I said just for a few minutes. Showing off her dancing. Tap, tap, tap! Not that the old girl's sight's very good, poor old soul, but she likes a bit of company. I hear Meg chattering away.'

Win settled herself on the chair and helped herself to a Woodbine from a packet in the pocket of her apron. 'Want one?'

Lizzie pulled a face. 'Gone right off them, but thanks anyway.'

'So how you feeling? Still a bit umpty first thing?'

'Not quite so bad this morning.'

'So d'you think you are?'

'Don't know really.' Lizzie had still not plucked up the courage to see the doctor, but she was beginning to enjoy talking about the possibility. 'Be a blinking miracle if I am after what the other doctor told me. Perforated something-or-other.'

'Ulcer?' Win drew on her cigarette with deep satisfaction.

'A bigger word than that.'

'You don't seem like the motherly type, Liz. Have you told him yet?'

'No, I haven't – so you keep your trap shut when he's around. I don't want him getting his hopes up.'

Win grinned, blowing out a careful smoke ring and squinting through it. 'What's it worth, then, not to tell him?'

Lizzie felt a flash of anger. She leaned closer and poked Win in the arm with her knife.

'Ow!' Win rubbed her arm. 'Watch what you're doing with that ruddy knife!'

'No, *you* watch it, Win Cutts! If anyone's going to tell him it'll be me.'

Win scowled. 'I might. I might not,' she said recklessly.

Lizzie leaned forward and grabbed hold of her. 'You say a word out of place and I'll make you very sorry!' she hissed, pleased to see the sudden alarm in Win's eyes as she drew back.

'Make me sorry? Don't talk so daft!'

She scared easily, thought Lizzie, retreating. 'I mean it, Win. You keep your big nose out of it!'

She could imagine the row there'd be if Dan learned about the baby from Win – or worse still, Len. Neighbours! Lizzie sighed. If only they could get some *decent* money. Get out of this place. Tenterden was all right – a nice little market town, really, but she was sick of living in a flat. Kids playing up and down outside, the old dear pottering about upstairs and everyone knowing everyone else's business. If only Dan could get a job on a farm in the country with a cottage to go with it! That's the only way they'd get a place of their own.

It was all right for people like the Goughs. Her mouth twisted bitterly. It was all right for God's chosen few. She sighed, thinking of South Africa. They'd had very little money there, but at least they'd had room to swing a cat and she had enjoyed the wide-open spaces. They'd been happy there ... for a while, anyway.

Win had recovered and she tapped cigarette ash on to the floor. 'Still, now your old man's got a job...'

'Oi!' Lizzie pushed a saucer towards her. 'You're not at home now, you know!'

Win said, 'Sorree-e!' and made an exaggerated show of tapping nothing into the saucer. 'How's Dan liking it at the new place?'

Lizzie gave a short laugh. 'How would I know? I don't ask and he doesn't say. He gets *wages*. That's all I care about.' She began stabbing a fork into some sausages. 'Pity the Hackers left. The old colonel was a bit pompous. Always had to be called Colonel; that sort of thing.' She arranged the sausages in the frying-pan. Footsteps clattered on the stairs and Meg came in. She looked at Lizzie, who grinned.

'I suppose so,' she said.

'Suppose what?' asked Win.

By way of answer, Meg went to the cupboard and brought out a lollipop. She said, 'Red today.' Giving her mother a sly look, she began to unwrap it.

Win said, 'So *that's* why she never finishes her dinner!' She shook her head at Meg. 'Don't let your Dad know.' To Lizzie she said, 'You shouldn't spoil her.'

Lizzie shrugged. 'Her eyes was all red when she came round. Wouldn't tell her Auntie Liz what was wrong.'

Win shrugged. 'I gave her a tap, that's what. She was driving me mad. Grumbling on about this blooming party. The other kids got invites and she didn't. Real upset, she is, but what am I supposed to do about it?'

Meg climbed on to her mother's lap and Win hugged her.

Lizzie tutted. 'Aren't you a bit big for that?' she asked. 'Mummy's lap?'

Win said, 'She likes a cuddle. Why shouldn't she?'

Meg saw that she had their attention. 'They're all going,' she wailed. 'Brenda Letts and Mary Burch and Maud Stuckey and Penny Gough and Susan–'

Lizzie's head snapped up. 'Penny Gough? *Penny Gough?* Does *she* go to your dancing class?'

Meg nodded. 'And Susan Wells.' She began to sniff, screwing up her face.

'Well, I'm damned!' Lizzie looked at Win, amazed. 'Penny Gough!'

'So?'

'The Goughs' kid. Where Dan works. It's Penelope, but they call her Penny. Dan thinks she's the bee's knees!' She laughed. 'On and on about the kid. It's all he *does* talk about.'

'I *want* to go!' Meg was making the most of her audience. 'I want to go to the party.' She rubbed her eyes with small fists.

'Well, don't look at me,' her mother told her. 'You're not Cinderella and I'm no fairy godmother.'

'But I *want* to-o-o.' Meg began to force out a few tears.

For Pete's sake! Lizzie groaned inwardly. It was enough to put you off motherhood for life!

She said, 'You should count your blessings, Miss Grizzleguts. Forget the blinking party. Just think yourself lucky that you can go to the dancing classes at all. If it wasn't for her upstairs you couldn't even do that. It's very ungrateful to keep on moaning.'

Win threw her a poisonous look. 'I'll thank you not to call my kid ungrateful. She's disappointed, that's all. It's only natural.'

Lizzie regarded Meg with growing impatience. Anyone would think the girl was a blasted angel. Why were women such fools about their kids, she wondered? A good smack would do wonders for Meg Cutts.

She rolled her eyes disparagingly. 'She doesn't have to go on about it, though, surely? Like a blinking gramophone. Big girl like that grizzling for nothing.'

Lizzie knew she was pushing things, but suddenly she didn't care. If Win got the hump she'd stay away for a few days, and that would be no great loss. She'd be back as soon as she wanted to borrow some sugar or a drop of milk.

Win's face darkened. 'The trouble with you, Liz, is you're hard. Hard as old boots. I hope to God you *don't* have a kid because God help it with you for a mother!' She pushed Meg from her lap and stood up.

Lizzie got to her feet also. 'And you're a saint, I suppose? Well, for your information, Win Cutts, I've heard you yelling at your kids. Calling 'em everything under the sun. So don't try and come the old acid with me!'

Sensing trouble, Meg backed away to the door and slipped outside into the back yard.

Win's eyes narrowed. 'And I've heard you and your precious Dan going hammer and tongs. And it's you that starts it with your nag, nag, nag. If I was him, I'd have walked out long ago, and that's the truth.'

'Nag? I *don't* nag. I don't!' Lizzie could feel her anger mounting and suddenly she welcomed it. She stared with disgust at Win's plump face with its wobbly jowl and curranty eyes.

'You bloody do!' Win shouted. 'If you

must know, my Len calls you a bad-tempered bitch – among other things. You know what? I *pity* your old man. So does my Len and he–'

'Oh, he does, does he?' Lizzie almost spat. 'Well, it doesn't stop his hand creeping up my skirt when he thinks no one's looking! Oh yes!'

Win's colour faded and Lizzie knew she had found a weak spot as Win began to stammer. 'You – you lying tart! You ... Why, he ... my Len wouldn't touch you with a barge-pole!' She gave a defiant toss of her head as she spoke, but her words lacked conviction and Lizzie sensed a kill.

'Wouldn't he, then?' Lizzie's eyes glittered with malice. 'Well, you ask him what happened Christmas Eve when you were all round here. *You* won't remember because you were tipsy! Not that he'll admit it. He'd lie himself blue in the face first.'

She certainly hoped he would, otherwise he might reveal that Lizzie had led him on by pretending to fasten her stocking. Dan wouldn't be too pleased, but she'd deny it. It would be her word against Len, but Dan was a gentleman. He'd stick by her.

Staring into Win's eyes, she became aware that the woman looked almost frightened and suddenly she couldn't resist a little bullying. She gave Win a hefty push in the direction of the door and it felt very good.

'Get out of my kitchen, you stupid cow, and don't come back.'

Win was backing away. Probably afraid to turn her back on me, thought Lizzie with satisfaction. She struggled with her mounting rage, waiting until Win had turned and was half-way out of the door. Snatching a heavy mixing bowl from the dresser, she yelled, 'Sod off!' and hurled it with all her might at Win's retreating back. It struck her squarely between the shoulders, making her gasp with pain. As it smashed on the floor, Win half turned to face her attacker. Somehow she lost her balance and stumbled backwards down the step where she landed ignominiously, sprawled over the paving. Meg gave a scream and fled back through the hole in the fence to the safety of her own backyard.

Lizzie slammed the door on the ungainly spectacle and watched from the window as Win scrambled back to her feet, brushed herself down and followed her daughter's retreat.

Lizzie leaned against the sink, gulping for breath. She had gone too far this time and the knowledge worried her. It would get back to Dan. No doubt Win would send Len round. Oh Jesus! She ran the tap and, tilting her head to the stream of cold water, drank greedily. The cold water calmed her a little and she went to the cupboard and fetched a dustpan and brush. Dealing with the broken bowl gave her something to do, but when she had tidied it away she was still trembling.

'Think, Lizzie!' she told herself. 'Get it right!'

She must decide on a more suitable version of events – one that made her the victim instead of the aggressor. She sat down in the chair recently vacated by Win Cutts and thought frantically.

'Win started it,' she whispered. Yes, that was what she would say. That Win went for her. Pulled her hair. Called her names... Or better still, called *Dan* names. That would make it difficult for him. She drew a long, slow breath as her panic subsided. Suddenly she screwed up her eyes and raked the fingernails of her right hand down the left side of her face.

It hurt more than she expected and she snatched up a cloth and pressed it to her skin. After a moment she crossed to the cupboard, opened it and peered into the small mirror that hung there. The lines were faint but they would develop.

'Jesus!' she muttered and went in search of some soothing ointment.

Next, she found the second-largest mixing bowl and put it on the dresser. He'd never notice.

Ten minutes later the potatoes were

coming to the boil, the sausages were on a low heat, the table was laid, the crumbs from breakfast banished to the bin. Lizzie sat drinking a welcome cup of tea. She felt quite pleased with herself. She had her story ready and the 'proof' of Win's assault was developing nicely. Finally she allowed herself a thin smile.

While Lizzie was quarrelling with her neighbour, Ella was playing tennis with her daughter at Burleigh House and longing for Mrs Granger to fetch the child for her tea. Although the sun was shining there was little real warmth in it and Penny's erratic strokes sent Ella backwards and forwards. Her only chances to relax were when the ball went right out of the court and Penny was despatched to search for it among the rhododendrons, a job which kept her occupied for a few minutes and gave Ella time to catch her breath.

'Found it!' Penny squealed with triumph.

'Oh, good!' To the right of the court a squirrel ran soundlessly up the chestnut tree, its brown body sleek, its tail fluffed out. She pointed. 'Look, Penny! A squirrel!'

Penny paused, staring up into the branches, and Ella watched her with awe. She thought, not for the first time, how perfect the child was with her silvery-blonde hair and large blue doll-like eyes. When

Penny was born Ella had developed a fever which caused the midwife to keep mother and baby apart. By the time Ella had recovered the baby had developed a worrying cough, wouldn't take a bottle and was losing weight.

Penny cried, 'I'm going to serve!' She threw up the ball, swung her racquet and missed.

Ella said, 'You should throw it a bit higher, sweetie. Try again.'

Penny retrieved the ball and gave it a hard scrutiny. 'The ball's gone wrong!' she offered. 'It *keeps* going wrong.'

'No, Penny. The ball's all right. You just have to throw it up higher.'

Because of the initial separation, Ella regretted that she had never experienced the heart-stopping love which she had expected to feel for her first child. Once the maternity nurse had left, Enid Granger had been engaged as a nanny and had soon settled in. The arrangement worked well; but seeing the growing rapport between nanny and child over the ensuing years, Ella could not help feeling a sense of loss which was compounded by her need to spend more and more time with Roland after his illness.

Ella told herself that she had much to be thankful for, and that she had learned to deal with the loss just as she had come to accept her passionless marriage. Life was too short for regrets.

The ball came over the net now and Ella patted it back carefully. Penny rushed forward and it bounced past her and disappeared.

Ella pointed with her racquet. 'I think it went into that bush, Penny.'

One mistake still haunted her, however, and that was Daniel Hampton. Whenever she woke in the treacherous small hours of the morning, she thought about him. He had been impossible to forget and now he was close by, working in the gardens, a constant reminder of her youthful folly.

'Mummy! You're not ready!'

Ella looked up to see Penny waiting on the other side of the net, her small racquet poised inexpertly. 'Sorry, sweetie!'

At that moment she heard Daniel's voice as he spoke to Evans somewhere nearby. Ella froze and the ball flew past her and stuck in the netting which bordered the court.

'You weren't looking, Mummy. Shall I do it again?'

Ella nodded distractedly, disentangled the ball and threw it back.

She had found the past few days extremely difficult, afraid to walk in the garden in case she met him. She felt like a prisoner in her own home, reluctant to look out of the windows in case she caught sight of him wielding a hoe or wheeling the barrow. To compound her distress it seemed that everyone else found something positive to say about him and she was constantly hearing his name. No doubt he thought he had won, she thought bitterly. Well, he was wrong. He was here on probation and she was trying to find a way to get rid of him.

'Mumme-e-e!'

She swung the racquet wildly but missed again.

'I'm sorry,' she told her daughter. 'I have a really bad headache and it's nearly your tea-time. We must go in.'

Ignoring Penny's rueful expression, she crossed the court and held out her hand.

Penny gave an exaggerated sigh and took her mother's hand. 'Did I win or did you?' she asked.

'I think it was a tie.'

'You always say that. Mr Hampton said it can't be a tie in tennis. Someone has to be the winner.'

Ella stopped abruptly. 'Mr Hampton? Haven't I told you not to talk to... I mean, not to bother him? He has work to do.'

'He wasn't working, Mummy.' She looked up earnestly into Ella's face. 'He was having his lunch by the cabbage patch.'

'Don't tell fibs, Penny.' Ella walked on. 'Mr Hampton takes his meals with the rest of the staff in the kitchen.'

'Sometimes he doesn't. If it's a nice day he doesn't. He brings a sandwich and he sits outside all on his lonesome. He likes to be alone. He told me.'

Ella swallowed. She must be very careful what she said in case the child repeated her words. 'Then if he wants to be alone you shouldn't bother him, Penny. I want you to stay away from him. Do you hear me?'

Penny looked up. 'Oh, but he doesn't mind me. He told me so. He said he likes my company. He tells me about his house and his dog that died and his wife and his–'

Ella stopped again. 'His *wife?*'

'Yes.'

Ella stared at her, a sick feeling in her stomach. 'Mr Hampton has a *wife?* Are you sure?'

Penny nodded. 'What's the matter, Mummy?'

'Nothing,' Ella stammered. 'Nothing at all.'

She walked back to the house in silence, her heart hammering. Why had it never occurred to her that Daniel Hampton might have married again?

Chapter Three

As soon as Daniel stepped inside the kitchen he knew there was something wrong. The room was unnaturally tidy and that meant Lizzie was feeling guilty. Probably frittered their money on something they could ill afford. She was a fairly hopeless housekeeper, but over the years he had grown tired of trying to teach her new ways. Give Lizzie some money and she would spend it and ask for more. He had found her lack of housekeeping skills endearing at first and had teased her gently, expecting her to learn. Eventually her lack of domesticity had begun to grate until, dogged by financial problems, it had become a source of friction.

'Lizzie,' he murmured, giving her a peck on the cheek and moving to pass her.

She said, 'Well, say something, then!'

He looked up. 'Say something about what?'

She pointed to her face. 'This!' she cried. 'These scratches! You blind or something?'

His spirits sank a little. 'Not another row. Not Win again?' He took hold of her face and turned her scratches to the light. 'Not too bad. I don't think you'll be scarred for life!'

He moved to the sink, ran the cold water and soaped his hands, keeping his face averted from her while he struggled to stay calm. His wife seemed to thrive on conflict – he had learned that long ago. He had learned it in time to abandon her but somewhere, deep within him, he wanted to love her. A small spark of optimism convinced him that there *was* a Lizzie who was still lovable. A year after Lydia's death, still dizzy with loss, he had met Lizzie at a dance. His first glimpse of her had never faded. Vivacious Lizzie Chapman, with her sweetly freckled face, her golden eyes and fiery temper, had reminded him of a delightful wild animal. And in those early days she had made him laugh; had driven away the misery and given him hope that one day he might be happy again. She had helped him to believe that he could make a new life for himself which would be almost as good as the old one.

Now Lizzie said, 'Yes, it was Win, the stupid bitch – but a fat lot you care.'

'Of course I care, Lizzie.' He reached for the towel and wiped his face and hands, urging himself to remain calm. 'I care, but I can't keep my eye on you twenty-four hours a day. If you choose to fight with the neighbours...'

Her expression darkened. *'Choose?* Well, you've got a damn nerve, Dan. I didn't choose for her to run you down, did I? What was I supposed to do? Agree with her?'

He hung up the towel, his stomach beginning to churn. 'About what exactly? If you can't stay friends with her, then perhaps you should refrain from your constant reconciliations. Every time you quarrel you say–'

Lizzie had thrown her head back. 'Refrain from reconciliations? God! Just listen to yourself, Dan! Anyone would think you'd swallowed a dictionary!'

It was one of her favourite jibes and it never failed to irritate him. When they first met she had loved the way he spoke; had been impressed with his upbringing and education. Now she objected to the words he used, ridiculing him whenever she could. It was just another flaw in their failing marriage.

'You can be so spiteful!' he told her wearily. He pulled the folded newspaper from his jacket pocket and opened it up, but before he could read a word Lizzie snatched it from his hands and tore it in half.

'I'm talking to you!' she screamed, crumpling it into a ball and hurling it on to the floor. 'You're my husband, and if you were half a man you'd go round there and tell Win where to get off!'

He glared into her furious face. 'I won't do that, Lizzie, and you know why. Because I'll tell her she's not welcome and to stay away, and in a few days you'll be friends again and somehow *I'll* be the ogre. I told you last time, Lizzie, you sort out your own battles from now on.'

For a long moment they glared at each other.

She said, 'Don't you want to know what she said about you? What she called you? Why I went for her?'

'I'm not interested. Forget it, will you? I've been working hard all day and I'd like something to eat – if it's not too much trouble.'

She shot an angry glance at the clock. 'And you're late again! How am I supposed to get a meal ready if I never know–'

'I never know so I can't tell you, can I?' In spite of his resolution, his voice was rising. 'I can't walk off half-way through a job. I should have thought you'd be delighted that I've *got* a job instead of moaning all the time. They're decent people, we can pay a few bills and get back on our feet. What does it take to please you, Lizzie?'

They're decent people, he told himself again. Reasonable, fair-minded people. With the exception of Ella who had tried to ensure that he didn't get the job; tried and failed. But now that Evans and Mr Gough had gone against her wishes she was making sure that he, Dan, understood the position – that he was there on sufferance. But he had six weeks' grace and he would make sure that she could find no fault with him. OK – she could make a point of avoiding him and of saying as little as possible when their paths did accidentally cross. He could bear that. In a way he understood it.

Lizzie said, 'That's right! Stick up for them. Because they're your sort, aren't they? People like your father who turn up their noses at people like me.'

'Leave my father out of it, Lizzie. He was very good to us; he lent us money. If your bloody brother hadn't been such a crook–'

'He's not a crook!'

'So why is he in jail? And why am I working my heart out...?'

She faced him furiously, her face chalk-white, her hands on her hips.

'Why shouldn't you work?' she demanded. 'Too good for it, are you? Too stuck-up to get your hands dirty, is that it?' She went on, 'Born with a silver spoon and a daddy who's a lawyer! Trips to France and outings to the theatre. Well, Dan Hampton, now you know what it's like for the rest of us – *and* you can't blame me for where we are. My brother did his best–'

Daniel brought his fist down on the table. 'He did his best to cheat us, Lizzie, and he's where he ought to be and I for one am *glad!*' He gasped for breath. 'We had a chance to make a fresh start with the pub and he wrecked it.'

'Your father could have loaned us some more.'

'I wouldn't ask him.'

Daniel would never again make contact with his father. His pride stood between them and Daniel didn't want it any other way. Against his better judgement he had gone cap in hand, asking for a stake in Frank Chapman's pub in Bath: a partnership. His father had agreed and Daniel had promised to repay every penny with interest over a five-year period. But he had failed to do so because eighteen months later Frank Chapman had absconded with most of the money. The police had been called in and the ensuing investigation had led to fresh charges of handling stolen goods. When, months later, they caught up with him in Deauville the money was long gone and Daniel's and Lizzie's new start had gone with it. From that moment their relationship had deteriorated with a terrible inevitability.

As though reading his thoughts, Lizzie's face suddenly crumpled and her anger was replaced by despair.

Before she could speak he said, 'Not sausages again!'

She nodded. 'I'm sorry, Dan ... about everything, I mean.'

That was his cue to take her in his arms and say she was forgiven, but today the words stuck in his throat. He had stood for a few moments watching Ella and Penny play tennis. If only he had been able to fall in love with *her*, how different the world would be now. He'd be a lawyer and a child very like Penny would be *his* daughter. He looked at Lizzie and at that moment she seemed to represent everything that was wrong with his life. He had no prospects, no family – and no one to love.

She looked at him fearfully, frightened by his silence. 'Dan? I really am sorry.'

He missed his cue. '*You're* sorry! That makes two of us. I'm more sorry than you'll ever know.'

She looked stricken, opened her mouth, changed her mind and said nothing. Without a word she snatched her coat from behind the door and ran from the house.

Daniel listened to the slam of the front door and whispered, 'Oh God, Lizzie!'

Then he sighed so heavily that his chest ached. 'I think it's over.'

Next morning, to the accompaniment of heavy rain, Ella, Roland and Penny were enjoying eating breakfast together in the dining room. Since his illness, Roland had taken to having a tray sent up to his bed-room or to the library, because this removed the necessity for him to make the painful and undignified journey down the stairs. However, Penny had complained that she hardly ever saw her father and Ella had suggested that on Sunday mornings he made the effort to join them.

Penny was eating scrambled eggs on toast, while Ella had egg and bacon and Roland enjoyed the same with the addition of sausage and fried bread. There was jam and marmalade on the sideboard and toast would be brought as soon as they were ready for it.

Roland glanced surreptitiously at his wife. He was still puzzling over her hostility towards the new gardener. From his talks with Evans, Roland understood that the man was doing very well and that Evans wanted to keep him on when his pro-bationary period ended. Penny had taken a fancy to the man and the rest of the staff found him amiable enough. Only Ella remained decidedly cool.

Penny said, 'Please, Daddy, may I have some new shoes for Lucy's party? Some shiny black–'

Ella laughed. 'Penny Gough! You sly baggage!' She turned to Roland. 'She's been nagging me for days about these awful shoes. Black patent leather with ankle-straps. I've told her "No" and so has Mrs Granger but ... will she give in gracefully?'

Penny scowled. 'They're not awful. All the girls are wearing them.'

Ella held up a warning finger. 'Don't tell fibs, Penny. *Some* girls are wearing them, but they're simply not suitable.' To her husband she mouthed the words, 'Very common!'

His mouth twitched as he pushed his plate to one side and helped himself to a second cup of tea. He smiled at his daughter. 'What about satin ballet slippers?' he asked. 'Pink satin to match that pretty dress?'

'Oh yes!' cried Ella. 'The sort of slippers fairy princesses always wear.'

Penny considered for a moment, regarding them both with suspicion. 'Black patent are best, Daddy,' she insisted. 'They're much nicer than satin.'

Roland exchanged an amused look with his wife.

Ella said, 'Pink satin or none at all.'

To distract his daughter from what promised to be an unseemly tussle of wills, Roland said hastily, 'Would you ring for the toast, please, Penny?'

She slid from her chair, immediately delighted, and ran to tug at the bell-pull which would summon Annie from the kitchen.

Ella said, 'I think I shall visit Aunt Florrie, Roland. It seems ages since I've seen her and...' She shrugged.

'And you feel guilty.'

Ella laughed. 'Yes, I do. She's not getting any younger.'

Penny put her knife and fork together. 'I'm not getting younger either. I'm getting older. I'll be eight soon.'

Roland smiled, but he was aware of a frisson of alarm. He had noticed that Ella fled to Folkestone to see her aunt whenever something was worrying her, the way a woman might turn to her mother for advice. When he first met Ella she had told him that he would never meet her parents. He understood nothing of the reasons for the family rift because Ella, when questioned, said simply that it was 'a matter of the heart' that she preferred to forget. He had been so in love with her that he had refrained from pursuing the matter. In later years she had steadfastly refused to talk about it and, with both her parents now dead, Roland could see no point in opening old wounds. Although he would have liked her to confide in him, he had let the matter drop.

Watching her across the table he mentally thanked God for his good fortune. His illness had dramatically altered his quality of life and yet he still thought of himself as a lucky man. He had a beautiful wife and a wonderful daughter. Nine years ago he had been a very contented bachelor with no intention of marrying. Then they had met over dinner at a friend's house and he had taken one look at Ella and fallen in love. He had been totally smitten – his whole world turned upside down. Terrified that the difference in their ages would deter her, he was astonished and relieved when she accepted his stumbling proposal of marriage six weeks after their first meeting.

Florrie had opined that it was 'rather hurried' and had suggested a six-months' engagement. Roland's mother had also considered it a little too rushed and worried that people would suspect the worst. Even Roland, terrified of losing her, had been prepared to give her more time, but Ella had refused to listen. Three months after their first meeting, they had been married – a lavish affair with nearly two hundred guests. They had spent their two-week honeymoon in Cannes and Ella had become pregnant almost immediately. Penny had been born about a year before the polio struck.

Stifling his doubts, Roland smiled at his wife. 'I'm sure Florrie will be delighted to see you, dear.'

Annie arrived with a rack of toast and a fresh pot of tea and breakfast continued.

Penny began to plaster her toast with butter and Ella said, 'Steady on, Penny. There's enough butter there to feed an army!'

Roland asked, 'When will you go? Today?'

Ella shook her head. 'I have to wait for the doctor's report on Mr Saville. He's no better – in fact I think he's worse. I think it *may* be influenza.'

He nodded. 'Poor Nurse Baisley is fussing a great deal about the extra work.'

Penny looked up. 'Nurse Baisley said Mr Saville is a liar-bility. Does he tell lies?'

Ella's eyes flashed. 'A liability? What impertinence! When did she say that?'

'Yesterday. In the garden. She said, "He's been here three days and I'm run off my feet."'

Ella leaned forward in astonishment. 'Nurse Baisley said that to *you!*'

'No, but I heard her. She was talking to Mr Hampton.'

Abruptly Ella sat back.

Roland felt a jolt of anxiety. There it was again, that odd reaction to Hampton's name.

Ella's mouth tightened. 'Run off her feet!' She turned to Roland. 'It will do that woman good to have some extra work. You are hardly the most demanding patient, and she has a very easy life. She's growing lazy.' She reached for the marmalade, her face a mask. Before he could speak she continued, 'If it *is* influenza, Mr Saville will have to be moved to hospital. Penny, drink your milk.'

'I don't like it.'

'Don't be silly.' She turned to Roland. 'I shall go to see Florrie tomorrow.'

'Will you take a certain person?' he asked.

Penny looked up. 'That means me, doesn't it?' She looked at Ella. 'May I come?'

Ella shook her head. 'Not this time, Penny. Mrs Granger is taking you to the dentist for a check-up and–'

'I *like* the dentist.' She looked at her father. 'He's so funny and he's got lots of little fish in a glass tank which goes bubble, bubble all the time, and there's seaweed and sand. And if I don't make a fuss he gives me a comic.'

'Well, there you are then.' He smiled at her.

Ella said, 'And afterwards you can go to the park and feed the squirrels and bowl your new hoop.'

Roland stirred his tea. Had his wife made sure that Penny would be otherwise engaged so that she would be able to see her aunt alone? *Was* there something worrying her? He decided to take the bull by the horns.

'The new man, Hampton,' he remarked. 'Seems to be satisfactory – for which let us be truly thankful. Evans speaks very highly of him.'

He regretted his words as soon as they were out.

Ella's expression had changed. She said, 'I don't wish to discuss Mr Hampton, Roland. You knew what I thought about him and yet you deliberately went against my wishes.'

The swiftness of her attack startled him. 'But Evans wanted him, Ella, and...'

Ella leaned forward, her face flushed. 'You asked me to interview the man for you and I did. You then proceeded to ignore my recommendation. He's ... he's surly. I don't like him. I should have thought that sufficient reason to turn him down, but no! You have to consider Evans' wishes.'

Watching his wife closely, Roland realised that there was more to this than he had imagined.

'Ella, has this man offended you in any way? If so, you must tell me and he will go at once. With no pay and no reference. He has, hasn't he?' He leaned forward, frowning.

'No! Of course not.' She sat back suddenly in her chair. 'What makes you ask such a thing?'

He said slowly, 'I think he *has* offended you. I shall send for him and–'

'No!' She sprang to her feet, almost tipping her chair. Steadying it, she repeated, 'No! I don't want you to ... to embarrass him. Maybe he didn't mean anything. You've no need to question him, Roland. I ... oh, for heaven's sake! Just forget the whole thing.' She threw down her napkin. 'I have things to do,' she said and hurried from the room.

Roland took a deep breath.

Penny said, 'Mummy doesn't like Mr Hampton. Why doesn't she? I like him. He calls me "tiddler". I wanted to show him my handstand but Nanny wouldn't let me. Why doesn't Mummy like Mr Hampton?'

He looked into the small, glowing face and smoothed her hair. 'I don't know,' he admitted.

'Perhaps he's a liar-bility.'

'I just don't know, darling.'

Staring at the uneaten toast on his plate, he discovered that the little scene had robbed him of his appetite. He glanced at the window where the rain seemed to be lessening. Ella, he thought unhappily, you are keeping something from me. In his mind he replayed her final outburst and drew a deep breath. Ella didn't just dislike Daniel Hampton. There was something more. Was she *afraid* of him?

The following day, Ella hurried up the front steps of Sunningford. The convalescent home was mainly for elderly people who might need a little nursing after a stay in hospital. There was a library, a pleasant lounge with a piano, a wireless set and a gramophone. Outside, attractive grounds were carefully tended by a small team of gardeners.

Florence Goolden, now eighty, had had a bad fall earlier in the year, necessitating several months in hospital. During that time her housekeeper had decided to retire, so rather than engaging temporary nursing help Florrie had decided to spend the winter at Sunningford, intending to return to her home a few miles away the following spring.

As soon as Ella arrived, she had a few words with the sister and then made her way to her aunt's room where she found Florrie sitting by the window, her white head bent over the inevitable jigsaw puzzle. Like the rest of the house, the room smelled faintly of disinfectant mixed with floor polish and a faint whiff of camphor. The walls were covered with a beige and white striped paper and a large window was draped in satin curtains.

The old lady turned at the sound of Ella's knock and smiled with huge delight at the sight of her visitor.

'Ella, my dear child!'

'Not such a child, Aunt!' Ella laughed.

Florrie wagged a reproachful finger and Ella said, 'Sorry. I keep forgetting.'

'Indulge me, dear. "Aunt" makes me feel so old. Florrie will do nicely.'

Ella laid roses and a small cardboard box on the table and bent to kiss her aunt.

Florrie said, 'I thought you might bring little mischief with you?'

'Not today, I'm afraid, because we had

already made other arrangements, including the dentist. It's my fault for making a sudden decision, but I'll bring her next time. She does love to see you.'

Florrie looked at the flowers. 'They're beautiful, dear. I do so love pink roses – but you know that, of course. Ring the bell, will you? Someone will find a vase for them.' She touched the petals approvingly. 'I should have brought one of my own vases with me.'

Ella rang the bell. 'I'll bring you one next time I come.'

They waited until a young woman had carried the flowers away, then Ella sat down beside her aunt. 'St Paul's Cathedral!' she exclaimed, studying the picture on the puzzle-box lid. 'Very ambitious.' She was wondering how to introduce Daniel into the conversation without revealing the extent of her own fears. Before she could make up her mind, however, Florrie solved the problem for her.

She said, 'I've had a letter, Ella, from Daniel's father. He enclosed a letter for you and asked me to forward it.'

Ella's heart lurched as she avoided her aunt's gaze. Keeping her eyes fixed on the box lid she said, 'Five hundred pieces! Good heavens!'

'Ella. I said I've–'

'I heard you.' She looked up slowly. Daniel and his father had been estranged for years and Ella had convinced herself that she didn't care if they were never reconciled. 'You know how I feel about Edmund Hampton,' she said. 'I don't want to think about him.'

'It was a rather sad letter, Ella. He is seriously ill. He's been told he has less than a year to live.'

'We have only his word for that.'

'Ella! You can't mean that!'

Ella regretted the unkind words as soon as they were uttered, but she couldn't bring herself to retract them. It was easier to go on blaming others than to face the terrible alternative – that *she* might have been in the wrong.

Florrie said gently, 'You can imagine how he feels, can't you? The poor man doesn't want to die without seeing Daniel again and doing what he can to make amends.'

Ella stared at an oil painting on the wall – sweet peas in a glass jar. A little *too* pretty, she thought. Too 'chocolate box'.

Unable to meet her aunt's accusing eyes, she said, 'Maybe Daniel doesn't want a reconciliation. And if he does, surely it's up to him to find his father? Why do they have to involve me?'

Sick at heart, she picked up a piece of the jigsaw and turned it to and fro in her hand as the memories flooded back. In her mind's eye she saw Edmund Hampton stepping out of his motor, his face white and drawn. Having seen the car arrive, Ella prayed that Daniel was at the wheel and had run out on to the front steps behind her mother. When she saw Edmund her disappointment was acute but she lingered to listen. Edmund was pale and drawn, with lines of misery etched into his face.

'He's gone!' he told them. 'My son has gone.'

Ella's mother whispered the word. 'Gone? Oh no!' and put a hand to her mouth.

'I thought it best, Lydia.'

Ella, too, had been devastated by his words. 'Gone where?' she had asked, cold with fright.

To Edmund, her mother said, 'You'd better come inside.'

Ella followed them back into the house and, moments later, they were in the sitting room and had been joined by Ella's father. Edmund, with a glass of whisky in his hand, explained that Daniel was on his way to South Africa. His voice was hoarse and he struggled with his words. Ella, hovering in the background, received the news with mounting horror. Banished by his own father! She stood behind the chesterfield on which her father was sitting, her fingers clutching the leather with tense fingers.

'It's the only way,' Edmund told them. 'He can make a fresh start. Finish his studies out there. I can't allow him to break up your marriage.'

Her father said quietly, 'Sending Daniel away will solve nothing, Edmund. The damage is done.'

Edmund said, 'Please don't say that!'

'But ... your only child, Edmund. You'll miss him desperately.'

Edmund shrugged. 'You are my dearest friends. He has behaved abominably.'

Lydia said nothing and the three adults sat in silence, absorbing the situation. Watching them, Ella was growing increasingly desperate. She cried, *'Daniel* has behaved abominably? What about Mummy? She's just as bad. Is she going to be sent away too? Because she's older than Daniel – she ought to know better!'

Lydia muttered, 'For God's sake, Ella!' but she made no effort to look at her daughter.

Her father turned. 'Stop it, Ella. You don't understand and have no right to interfere.'

'I *have!* I loved him too! I still do.'

But they were once more engrossed with each other.

Her mother said, 'I love him, Edmund. You can't change that.'

It's as though I'm invisible, Ella thought frantically.

'I did it for you, Lydia,' he answered. 'I'm trying to undo the harm... Oh, God!' He put his head in his hands and sighed heavily.

Ignoring her mother, Ella stepped forward and faced Edmund Hampton. 'You're a wicked, hateful man! It was a spiteful thing to do, to send Daniel away.' Near to tears, she heard the tremor in her voice.

Her father turned on her. 'Please go up to your room, Ella. We'll talk about it later.'

'I won't! I shall stay if I want to! Why doesn't anybody listen to *me?* You're all so selfish. Why does nobody care how *I* feel?'

Edmund gave her a look of intense dislike. 'Because you're spoilt, young lady. A sight too full of yourself. You have the impudence to call *me* spiteful? It was *you* who found them and *you* who went running to your father.'

She found herself stammering, 'I didn't know what else to do. I was – it was so...'

Lydia said bitterly, 'It was a private moment – you must have known that much. You're an intelligent girl.'

Her father said, 'Don't try to blame Ella for what she saw.'

'I'm blaming her for what she *did*. It was malicious.'

Her father said, 'There's no call to–'

Edmund swung round. 'Don't try to defend her. We all know what she intended and why. She was jealous. Oh yes, she was. She wanted to cause trouble and she has done exactly that.' He turned back to Ella.

'If you hadn't been such a vindictive little fool none of this need have happened. The infatuation would have died a death...'

Lydia stood up, her hands clenched. 'I have told you once, Edmund, and I'll tell you again – this is not an infatuation. I am in love with your son and I always will be. I didn't choose to feel this way – it isn't easy for me – but I love him and, whether you like it or not, he loves me.'

'He *doesn't!*' screamed Ella. 'Not really.' She glared at Edmund. 'You had no right to send him away. He'll be miserable in South Africa. He'll be lonely.' She choked back a sob. 'Write to him. Bring him back. *Please,* Uncle Edmund!'

Edmund said, 'Don't be so melodramatic, Ella. We've got friends out there. He can finish his studies.'

Her father rubbed his eyes tiredly. 'Please! Stop all this, for God's sake. Ella, I've told you once to go to your room.'

Lydia set down her glass. 'There's no point in all these recriminations. I've made up my mind. If Daniel is in South Africa, I shall join him.'

The silence was complete as they all stared at her.

She stood up and looked at her husband. 'I'm sorry, but I must.' She gave Edmund a small nod. 'I know you meant it for the best but...'

'Mummy, you *can't!*' Ella was aware of a tightness in her chest. Her heart hammered painfully. Once they were together in South Africa they would never return. She would never see Daniel again! The thought was unbearable.

Lydia ignored her. 'I'm sorry we have hurt so many people, but we have to be together,' she said and walked slowly out of the room.

Ella screamed after her, 'I hate you! D'you hear me!' She looked round wildly, snatched up a heavy brass ashtray and hurled it through the French windows. Glass flew in all directions. Everyone watched as the ashtray rolled across the flagstones and on to the grass where it settled. Ella burst into tears of helpless rage and followed her mother from the room.

The following day her mother left Burleigh House; half an hour later Ella ran away to her father's sister Florrie where it was finally agreed she should stay for a week or two. In the event, she had remained there until her marriage to Roland.

Florrie's voice brought her back to the present. 'It wouldn't hurt you to read Edmund's letter, Ella. You don't have to answer it.'

Ella stared at her, waiting for the churning emotion within her to die down. At last she said shakily, 'You always did love jigsaws.'

117

Florrie's kindly face flushed. 'Forget the wretched jigsaw, Ella. I'm talking about a sad old man who–'

'He called me a vindictive little fool. I shall never forget that. He blamed *me!*'

Florrie sighed. 'Maybe you were to blame. Partly, at least.'

'Florrie!'

'Well, you were very young and we all do and say things in the heat of the moment...' She fell silent but, seeing that Ella's lips were pressed firmly together, she went on, 'Edmund's been trying unsuccessfully to trace his son and is hoping you might have an address.'

Ella tossed her head. He sends his only son to the other side of the world, she thought angrily, and now, when it suits *him*, he wants to find Daniel. He doesn't deserve to see him again.

'*Can* you help him, Ella?'

Ella considered the question. Of course she *could* help him. She knew exactly where his son was. But why should she help Edmund after what he had done to her all those years ago? When she had been in the depths of despair, almost suicidal, he had had no compassion. He had called her vindictive, so maybe she should live up to her reputation. 'I don't think so,' she said.

'Oh, Ella!'

She was aware that her aunt was watching

her unhappily and that perhaps her reaction was extreme, but she was unwilling to be generous. The memories had stirred up so much grief and anger that her head was throbbing and she had to take deep breaths to calm herself.

'He sent Daniel away,' she said. 'I loved him and he sent him away.'

Florrie shook her head gently. 'Edmund was trying to save your parents' marriage. He felt tremendous guilt, poor man, that his son should behave so badly. He and your father had been friends all their lives. Surely you knew how close they were, especially after Edmund's wife died.'

'Well, it *didn't* save the marriage, did it?'

'No, but at least he tried. No one could have guessed that your mother would follow Daniel.'

Ella felt a moment of triumph. Yes. The plan had backfired. She almost said *Serve Edmund right!* Instead she said, 'And Lydia died because of it.'

Startled, Florrie said, 'What on earth do you mean?'

Glancing at her aunt, Ella saw that her expression had changed, but stubbornly she pressed on. 'If she hadn't gone out to join Daniel she wouldn't have been stung by that insect, and she would never have got blood poisoning and she would still be alive today.' She gave Florrie a challenging look.

For a moment Florrie closed her eyes but the colour in her cheeks was rising – always an ominous sign.

She opened her eyes and drew a deep breath. 'Ella, it's time you faced facts, my dear. Daniel loved your mother – rightly or wrongly. He loved her and cherished her. They were happy together for the little time they had. He did *not* love you. Trying to believe that he did has caused you a lot of unhappiness.' Her voice softened. 'Why don't you let it rest, Ella? You can't change anything. He's gone from your life...'

But he's back, thought Ella.

'...and you have a wonderful husband and a darling daughter...'

Ella avoided Florrie's eyes, unwilling to see the pity there. She threw down the piece of jigsaw and walked towards the window. Everything her aunt had said was true and that hurt. She said nothing, too upset to find words, too mortified to finally accept that she had nothing to be proud of.

Florrie waited, but the silence lengthened and after a while she gave up. She said, 'I'm sorry, Ella. It had to be said. I thought we might talk about it in a sensible way, but I see you're not ready for that. So please, dear, let's forget it.'

Ella heard the conciliatory note in her aunt's voice and felt worse.

'Puzzles,' Florrie said, with nervous haste.

'Yes, I've always enjoyed them. I spent hours over them as a child. The bigger the better...' Her words tumbled out, faster and faster, to fill the uncomfortable void. 'And now I've got all the time in the world. Mind you, we do get magazines and newspapers, but I whizz through them in no time. It's quite hard to fill the days when someone else does all the cooking and cleaning and even changes the bed linen... So, any news? How's the Autumn Fair coming along?'

Ella crossed the room and sat down on the edge of the bed. The Autumn Fair? Yes, think about that, she told herself. How *was* it coming along? 'Nothing very different from last year really, but we did have some excitement we could have done without.' She described Mr Saville's collapse. 'I've notified his godson and he's hoping to get back to England shortly. I hope you'll feel up to attending the fair, Florrie. It wouldn't be the same without you.'

'I won't have anything for the bric-à-brac stall this year, but I'll think of something even if it's only a large box of chocolates for the raffle.'

She looked a little happier, thought Ella. Dare she bring up the subject of Daniel's return in view of what had been said? She had no wish to hear further recriminations about her former behaviour, but she was desperate for advice.

'We'll send a car for you,' she said.

'An outing! It will be a wonderful treat, Ella!'

Ella frowned, momentarily distracted by the delight on her aunt's face. Was it such a treat just to get out of Sunningford, she wondered. Florrie must be missing her own home. She asked, 'Are you sure you like it here, Florrie? You promised you'd tell me if you were not happy. I wish you had agreed to come and stay with us until you're able to go home.'

'Oh, I'm happy enough, dear. The staff are wonderful and I've plenty of company.' She gave Ella a long look. 'Are *you* happy? When you spring a visit on such short notice... I thought, "Ah, Ella has a problem and she's brought it to me." I'm so pleased to be of use to someone.'

Still uncertain, Ella began to frame a denial but instead heard herself say, 'Daniel's back in England. In Kent, actually.' She picked up a piece of jigsaw and studied it, searching for a way to begin.

'Back in Kent? Good heavens! So you *do* know where he is.' Shocked, Florrie searched Ella's face anxiously. 'Why didn't you *say?*'

Ella ignored the question. 'He's working for us as an assistant gardener and ... and I can't bear it.' Her lips trembled.

'A *gardener?* I thought he was studying to

be a lawyer.'

Ella shrugged. 'It obviously didn't happen.'

'And working at Burleigh House? How – how *difficult* for you!' She frowned. 'He had no right to–'

'He didn't know. He didn't recognise the name Gough. It was just as much a shock for him...' She stared down at her hands which were clasped in her lap. 'I shouldn't burden you with this but...'

'Ella! I may be nearly eighty but I still have my wits about me and I can survive a little bad news. Or even a *lot* of bad news. How on earth did this happen?'

Haltingly Ella outlined what had happened while her aunt listened in thoughtful silence.

At last she said, 'And have you spoken to him? About the past?'

'Not exactly, but we did speak. It was rather dreadful. I was trying to explain that he couldn't stay on but he... Florrie, he *begged* me to let him stay. Said he had debts.' She closed her eyes. When she opened them again she said, 'I was so sorry for him. He looked so scared. I feel as though I shouldn't bring more trouble upon him and yet I can't have him near me.'

Her aunt looked grim. 'He should have stayed in South Africa. Did he say why he came back?'

Ella shook her head. 'I think he would

have told me more, but I didn't want to hear it. I expect he hates me.'

'Does it matter what he thinks of you?'

'Of *course* it does!' The words were out before she could stop them. 'No!' she corrected herself hastily. 'Of course it doesn't but – oh God! I hate to see him hurting like that. So terribly *down*. He had such a wonderful future before ... until he and Lydia... Oh, damn everything! I don't know what to do.' She stared wildly at her aunt. 'It seems as though the past is coming back to haunt me... I don't want to make the same mistakes again but I have Roland and Penny to think of. I *have* to do what's right for them.'

There was another silence and then Florrie sighed. 'He has to leave Burleigh House,' she said.

'But how?'

Her aunt went on, 'Did you ever tell Roland what happened? About you and Daniel?'

Ella shook her head.

'Then if he doesn't know, you can't expect him to understand why you feel the way you do. He needs to realise that Daniel *has* to go. Tell him it was a silly infatuation. A schoolgirl crush on an older boy.'

Ella laughed mirthlessly. A schoolgirl crush? If only that were true. How easy everything would be. She said, 'Roland would know at once if I lied. He would realise that I didn't love him when we married. He's very perceptive and he would see it in my face.'

'Ah! Now that *is* a problem. Poor Roland.' Her aunt hesitated. 'I think he could bear it if he knows you love him *now*. Do you think you do?'

Ella swallowed but her throat was dry with tension. 'I've never loved him the way I loved Daniel, but I've tried to be a good wife. I gave him Penny and... I suppose it's easier since his illness.' She didn't elaborate. Her aunt had never married and Ella didn't think she would understand. Making love to one man while thinking of another was a terrible betrayal and Ella wasn't proud of herself. She went on, 'For what it's worth, Daniel is married.'

'Happily married?'

'I don't know. He didn't tell me himself, but he mentioned a wife to Penny.' She smiled. 'That child chats to anyone and everyone. Heaven knows what she's been telling him.' She stood up, clasping her hands nervously. 'I wondered if I could bribe Daniel to go. Offer him money.'

Florrie's eyes widened. 'Ella! You must be mad! Bribe him to go? But suppose Roland finds out?' Her eyes widened. 'Have you got any money of your own?'

'Some jewellery. I could sell some.' She

drew a long breath. 'It does sound rather extreme but... Daniel must know how difficult it is for me, though if he has debts and I cause him to lose his job... But if I allow him to stay and – and something happens...'

Her aunt looked startled. 'Between the two of you? Is that likely?'

Ella sat down again. She fitted the piece of puzzle into the half finished picture. 'I thought so,' she said. 'It's a piece of that window.'

'*Thank* you, dear.'

Oblivious to her aunt's tone, Ella picked up another piece and stared at it unseeingly. She could feel her composure crumbling and was afraid that at any moment she would break down.

Fortunately, at that moment the young woman returned with the roses. 'And would you like a tray of tea?' She put the vase on the windowsill.

Florrie said, 'What a good idea. Thank you, we would.'

Ella remembered the box she had brought with her. 'And would you bring two plates, please?' Turning to her aunt, she said, 'I brought some cakes.'

Florrie said, 'Let me guess – chocolate éclairs!'

They both laughed and Ella, grateful for the interruption, took control of herself once more.

Her aunt said, 'So tell me about Penny, bless her.'

Ella searched for something to say. 'She's blooming. Dancing classes are the latest craze. Tap, not ballet. Oh yes! She's going to a birthday party and ... she's beginning to enjoy her version of tennis. Roland spoils her, of course. He adores her.'

Florrie placed a piece of puzzle and then another. 'He adores you, too, Ella. He's given you everything you want. You mustn't let anything happen that would hurt him.'

Ella sighed. 'I should never have married him, Florrie. It was utterly selfish of me. I thought, "If I can't have love I'll have money!"' Her mouth quivered. 'But it's no substitute. Oh God, Florrie! I've done everything wrong and there's no way to put it right.'

The tears began to trickle down her face and she snatched a handkerchief from her pocket and dabbed furiously at her eyes. She heard the woman come in with the tray and turned her face away, but her heaving shoulders betrayed her.

The woman said, 'Oh dear! Can I...?'

Florrie said, 'No, no! She's just a little upset. Please don't worry about it.'

The door closed and Ella continued to sob while Florrie busied herself with the teapot. Seeing that Ella was still crying, she said, 'Come here, dear. Let me hold you.'

Ella slid from her chair to the floor and rested her head in Florrie's lap. She felt the small, frail hands on her head and for some time neither spoke. When finally Ella had no tears left, her aunt patted her shoulder.

'There are more handkerchiefs in the top left-hand drawer,' she said. 'Help yourself and then we'll tackle these éclairs.'

For Ella the hot sweet tea was very welcome and she bit hungrily into the choux pastry.

For a while they talked of this and that and Ella wondered why she had thought that Florrie could help her solve anything. Perhaps she had expected too much, but simply being able to talk about her troubles had been a relief and she was grateful for that.

Suddenly Florrie said, 'So what will you do, Ella? About Daniel, I mean. What are your choices?'

Ella wiped a smudge of cream from her chin. 'I suppose I can say nothing and risk a – a disaster of some kind. Or I can confide in Roland and let him help me make a decision.' She couldn't think of any other options open to her.

Her aunt said carefully, 'Do you think you are still in love with Daniel? Is that the truth of it, Ella?' When there was no answer she went on, 'I do hope not for your sake, Ella. After the way he treated you and your mother...'

Ella gave her a sharp look. 'I don't want to talk about Lydia. She had no right to love him. She was *married*.' Avoiding her aunt's eyes, she snatched up a piece of the puzzle and jammed it into the wrong place. 'Get *in*, damn you!'

'It doesn't fit there. It's the wrong blue.'

'Who cares!'

Without a word Florrie removed the offending piece. The awkward silence lengthened accusingly.

Crushed, Ella said, 'I'm sorry. I'm being perfectly beastly and you don't deserve it. I don't know what's the matter with me.'

Her aunt rested a hand on her arm. 'It's so strange to hear you of all people asking for advice. I wish I could help you, dear, but the truth is I don't know what to say for the best.'

Ella nodded. 'There's no easy answer. What would you do if you were me?'

Florrie hesitated. 'I'd confide in my husband.'

Ella thought about Roland and tried to imagine how she would break the news to him.

The prospect filled her with dread.

Chapter Four

When Ella returned to Burleigh House she was met in the hall by Nurse Baisley.

'It's Mr Saville,' she said, with barely. concealed triumph. 'He took a turn for the worse and I had to call in Doctor Clarke.'

Ella said, 'Oh dear! That is worrying news.'

'He didn't want any breakfast and complained of a bad headache. Around one o'clock I found him struggling for breath. He was very flushed. I thought the fever was returning and I didn't think I should take responsibility for him. You weren't here so I asked Mr Gough's advice.' Her expression was smug. 'The doctor agreed with me that hospital was the best place.'

Ella screwed up her face in dismay, imagining herself in the same situation. 'Poor Mr Saville. He'll be terrified.'

Nurse Baisley frowned. 'He wasn't in a fit state to be terrified. He was in a bad way. Flu can be very dangerous. My sister died of it in the 1918 outbreak.' She made no attempt to hide her hostility. 'I never did think keeping him here was a sensible thing to do, if you don't mind me saying so, but no one asked for my opinion. If he'd gone straight to the hospital when he first collapsed–'

'But I thought the fright would kill him!' Ella protested. 'I thought I was *helping* him.' She handed her coat to Annie, who had heard her arrive. 'I thought he might recover in a day or two – that maybe it wasn't flu.'

'Well, if you'll pardon me, Mrs Gough, you were wrong. The doctor's sure now that it *is* flu. And it is highly contagious. Mr Gough is worried that Penny might catch it. I tried to reassure him, but who knows?'

'Penny?' Ella felt a flicker of unease. 'But she had no contact with Mr Saville. How could she catch it?'

The nurse folded her arms. Never a good sign, thought Ella.

'But *I* was, Mrs Gough, and I've been in contact with the child. I've been in contact with most of you including your husband.'

Ella thought, she is positively gloating, damn her! She gave the woman a hard look. 'Then we'll have to look on the bright side, won't we?' she told her. 'Personally, I've never been one to panic.'

Nurse Baisley stiffened visibly. 'I am *not* panicking,' she said. 'I am merely pointing out that your kind but somewhat rash action might have repercussions.'

Ella longed to slap her. 'Let's not cross our bridges–'

'If Mr Gough were to catch flu in his weakened state–'

It was Ella's turn to interrupt. 'I'll talk to him about it,' she told her.

'I have a responsibility for him. Mr Gough is *my* patient.'

'He is *my* husband.'

Nurse Baisley gave a dismissive sniff. 'Your husband's health is my main concern. That is what I am paid for. If he goes down with flu everyone will blame me and I–'

'Yes, well, thank you for keeping me informed.' Ella glanced pointedly at the hall clock, challenging her to continue, but it appeared that Nurse Baisley had gone as far as she dared.

'I told the doctor you would probably telephone him when you returned,' she said coldly. 'Now if you'll excuse me, I have my duties to attend to.'

The nurse turned on her heel and stalked back across the hall and up the stairs. Wretched woman! thought Ella, She was genuinely sorry about Mr Saville and she *would* telephone the doctor or speak to someone at the hospital, but right now she had other matters on her mind and certainly more to worry about than a nurse with a grievance. Ella's visit to Florrie had convinced her that she ought to take Roland into her confidence. Now was probably not the most propitious time, but there never would be a *right* time to tell him about Daniel Hampton.

Outside the library, she paused, gathering her courage and muttering a prayer for help. She had to tell him enough so that he would understand her problem with the new gardener, but not so much that he would blame *her* for what had happened. It meant treading a fine line, but she thought she could do it. At last she drew a deep breath and went in. Roland's wheelchair was pulled up beside the fire and he was reading a newspaper. He folded it at once when he saw her and put it to one side.

'My dear,' he said. 'You mustn't blame yourself.'

Startled, she stared at him. 'Blame myself?'

'Hasn't Nurse Baisley told you?'

'Told me? Oh! About Mr Saville, you mean. Yes, she did.'

'Take no notice of her, Ella. She does love a drama. He's been making progress – or so we thought. Even Doctor Clarke was not prepared for his sudden deterioration. Take no notice of Nurse Baisley. You acted for the best, Ella.'

Ella leaned down to kiss him. 'Thank you,' she said, truly grateful for his kindness. 'She has done her best to make me feel guilty.'

'I thought she would. She means well,' he said, 'but nurses do get very possessive about their patients and I'm afraid she worries about me for no good reason. She seems to think that being confined in a wheelchair makes me vulnerable to every passing germ!'

Roland held out his hands to her and she took them in her own. Was it her imagination or did he feel hot? She pushed the thought away. Nurse Baisley's doom-laden words were affecting her judgement.

Her husband went on, 'She's forever closing the windows in case I sit in a draught. I sometimes wonder whether we really need her.'

He patted the chair beside him and Ella sat down. She was tempted to consider losing the nurse but it might create more problems than it solved, she thought, and pushed the idea from her mind. At the moment she had more important matters to talk about.

She took a deep breath and rushed headlong into her speech. 'Roland, I have something to tell you. I hoped I...' She was aware of his slight intake of breath. 'I can't make it easy for you – or for me – but I do promise you...'

His expression changed. He took hold of her hand so tightly that it hurt. 'Don't! *Don't!* If it's another man I don't want to hear it, Ella. I *won't* hear it and I *won't* release you.'

Ella stared at him in astonishment. 'Another man? Oh Roland, no! At least...' In fact it was another man, but not in the way he imagined. 'Darling, there's no one. Not now.'

The pressure on her hand relaxed. 'You mean that? I thought...'

'There's no one but you.' She stifled the small doubt.

His face sagged with relief. 'Oh God, Ella. You frightened me. I thought for a moment. I know I can't be all that I should...'

'Roland, *don't!*' she begged. 'That's never been an issue between us. Never. It's simply that there *was* someone else many years ago.' He was listening intently and she stared down at her hands, praying that he would hear her out without further interruptions.

'I loved him but he didn't return my love.' She took a quick look at his face and was reassured by his expression. He was curious but he was not angry. At least she didn't think so.

He said, 'You'd better tell it all, Ella. Put me out of my misery.'

'Please promise you'll understand, Roland?'

'I promise I'll try.' His nervous attempt at a smile went straight to her heart. 'I'm sure I will.'

Ella closed her eyes, unable to watch his

face. 'I was seventeen,' she began. 'Because I was still at school no one thought of me as a woman.' She glanced at him quickly. If he laughed she would never forgive him. He didn't. 'My father had a very good friend named Edmund. He had a son, four years older than me. The family had made its money in South Africa generations ago. Land mostly. We went on holidays together to Paris and Rome...'

She had a sudden vision of the catacombs – gloomy and claustrophobic. They had walked through in single file and she had contrived to follow immediately behind Daniel, loving the lithe young body that moved ahead of her, wondering what held him back from those three simple words...

Roland said, 'One big happy family.'

He spoke lightly but Ella guessed at the tension behind the words. She started again. This was the difficult part. 'The son fell in love – with my mother.'

'Your *mother?*'

She nodded. 'No one had any idea but ... but I had fallen in love with him too. I thought he loved *me*. I thought how perfect it was. Then it came out – about him and my mother.'

'Lydia, in other words.'

She nodded. 'After – after everything went wrong I refused to call her anything else. I was almost suicidal...' She swallowed. 'The son and Lydia settled in South Africa.'

'Good Lord!' He shook his head in astonishment.

'That's when I went to live with Florrie. Edmund moved away to Yorkshire.'

Roland said, 'So you had lost the young man. My poor darling.' He kissed her hand. 'My poor little Ella.'

'Not long after that I met you and ... and you were so good to me. And good *for* me.'

He said, 'And I never had the slightest inkling that you had gone through so much. You were so bright and gay. It must have been ghastly for you.'

'The thing is, Roland, that the young man obviously fell on hard times. He's come back to England. Oh, don't worry. He's married now but – but he's working for us as a gardener.'

It took a moment to register and then she felt him recoil with shock.

'Working for us... You mean *Hampton?* You were in love with *Hampton?*'

She nodded. 'At the time he was studying law.'

'My God, Ella! How on earth ... ? Good grief, this is incredible. Impossible! Did he know when he applied for the job?' He looked at her with narrowed eyes. 'Did *you* know?'

'No. He knew our family had once lived here, but now I'm Ella Gough. We recognised each other when I went out to interview him and he was as shocked as I was.'

'Rather humiliating for him, I imagine.' Roland tried not to sound too pleased.

'I didn't know what to do. So I tried to persuade you–'

'–not to take him on! So *that's* what was worrying you! Oh, Ella!'

He tried to pull her close but she held back. 'I told him I wanted him to leave, but he begged me to say nothing. He was desperate for a job. He has a great many debts. I do feel sorry for him, Roland, but...'

Roland released her abruptly. 'Don't be! He's got to go,' he said. 'Anything else is unthinkable. I'll give him a reference – a reasonable reference – that mentions only his work. I'm not going to mislead anyone about his integrity. It will be a case of what I *don't* say, not what I *do* say.' He shook his head. 'Evans won't like losing him, but he'll have to make the best of a bad job.' Ella tried to interrupt but he held up his hand. 'No, Ella, it is now my decision, not yours. I won't have that type of man in my house a moment longer. He must leave today.'

'Today? Oh, Roland...' Ella was suddenly nervous. 'Couldn't he work out his notice? I mean – should we make an enemy of him?'

'An enemy? What could a man like that possibly do to *us?*' He drummed his fingers on the table edge. 'Today. Yes... I'll tell Evans I have private reasons. The real reason need go no further.'

Ella felt helpless. He was punishing Daniel because Ella had loved him. She knew what he was doing better than *he* did.

He said, 'Don't fret, darling. He'll be out of this house before he can say Jack Robinson! You need never set eyes on him again. I shall send for him and you will remain in the sitting room until he is gone. And make sure Penny stays upstairs with Mrs Granger. He is not to be allowed to speak to anyone. No goodbyes.'

'Oh, but–'

He held up his hand. 'Nothing. The two of you have nothing to say to each other ever again.'

Now, she thought, he is punishing me.

He went on, 'A man like that deserves no consideration. I only wish you'd told me this earlier.'

Ella stood up and realised she was trembling. It had all happened so fast. As she left the room she tried to reassure herself that she had made the sensible – the *only* – decision in the circumstances. And Florrie had thought it the wisest course. If Daniel had stayed she could not imagine what might have happened. Or rather, she *could*. As it was, she was far from confident that sacking him would end the matter and was horribly afraid she had made matters worse. Knowing Daniel, it seemed unlikely that he would accept this blow without retaliation.

Ten minutes later, Evans stood before his employer, trying to understand what he was being told about his new assistant gardener. On the other side of the desk, Mr Gough looked unusually flushed and dabbed his face from time to time with a folded handkerchief. His expression, however, was thunderous and he was not mincing words.

When at last Mr Gough stopped for breath, Evans said, 'Sacked? You mean – we're getting rid of him? But why, Mr Gough? Hampton's a good, solid worker. I don't understand and that's a fact. I've no complaints at all. None. In fact I'd go so far as to say that Hampton...' He faltered.

'You're not listening, Evans!' His employer was almost shouting now. 'I've just told you that this is a private matter. Nothing at all to do with his gardening skills. Forget gardening. There is more to it. More at stake.' He looked exhausted and leaned back suddenly, breathing heavily. 'It has been brought to my notice that Daniel Hampton's morals are not all they should be.'

He stopped and pressed the handkerchief once more to his face and neck. 'So damned hot in here,' he muttered. 'Open that window, will you? Let in a bit of air.'

With an ill grace, Evans did as he was asked. Brought to his notice? Who was that then? Not Mrs Gough again, poking her nose in where it wasn't wanted?

Mr Gough went on, 'I have my wife and daughter to think about and Hampton has to go.'

Evans felt as though all the stuffing had been knocked out of him. He was so pleased with the young chap and they got along so well. He decided he would have one last try. It was worth a rollicking if it meant he could keep Hampton.

'I don't want to talk out of turn, sir, but isn't there nothing I can say?' His employer's mouth tightened but Evans went on. In for a penny... 'One more chance, sir? I mean, was it very dreadful, this morals business?'

Before he had finished he was regretting the attempt. Mr Gough had reddened angrily.

'You can take my word, Evans, that it was and that I do know what I'm doing!' he snapped. 'Nobody who might corrupt my family or one of my servants is going to remain in my employ. Send Hampton to me at once.'

Evans was aware of a deep sense of failure. He was also very curious. What on earth had the poor chap done to deserve such harsh treatment? He said, 'Should I say anything about...'

'If he asks why, tell him he'll know soon enough. And don't waste your pity on him, Mr Evans. He isn't worth it.'

Five minutes later Roland faced Hampton across the table. He had left the man standing because he wanted to get things over as quickly as possible, but that meant he now stared up into the gardener's handsome face – a face he now hated with a totally unexpected passion. Unexpected because he was not aggressive by nature, preferring to win his battles with words. He had once been called pompous and that had hurt, but he had recognised the jibe for what it was – the last thrust from a weak opponent. Now he was surprised to discover a deep anger within him. If he hadn't been immobile he might have struck the man across the face. Words would have to suffice, he thought, but he would leave the swine in no doubt of his opinion.

He said, 'I have just learned from my wife about your unpardonable behaviour in the past and the trouble and distress you caused both to her and to your families.'

The thought that Ella had once loved this man hurt more than he had expected. He felt as though the wretch had stolen something from him – as indeed he had, for it was to this man that Ella had first given her heart. In a way she had come to *him*, Roland, with an absence of innocence. There was, too, the unbearable thought that first love was always the most passionate, the one that was remembered into old age, the one with which all the others were compared ... and sometimes found wanting.

Suddenly Roland's heart was pounding with anxiety and he found himself wondering what kind of relationship had existed between this man and Ella. Had they kissed? Had he fondled her? The thought made him ill. Ella had loved Daniel Hampton but he had trifled with her affections and had then broken her heart.

The man said, 'She told you then?' He seemed surprised.

'Obviously.' He must not lose his temper, Roland told himself desperately. His only advantage was his superiority. 'I am quite disgusted by what my wife has told me, and I now regret having taken you into my employ. You must realise that in the circumstances you cannot stay here. I shall pay you until the end of the month and will give you–'

'Just a minute!'

The wretch had lost some of his poise and his eyes were blazing. Roland wondered how he had ever been taken in by him.

Hampton said, 'What is this? Don't *I* get a hearing? Don't I get a chance to tell *my* side of the–'

'No, you damned well don't!' Roland's voice had risen and he struggled to retain his composure. 'If I say you're sacked that's the end of it. Your side indeed! I've heard all I want to hear from my wife, and a very shabby story...'

The gardener leaned his hands on the desk and thrust his face forward. Anger made him ugly, Roland thought with pleasure.

Hampton said, 'But you haven't heard it all, have you? And you don't *want* to hear it all – because you're too bloody scared you'll hear something you don't like!'

The man was breathing heavily, his face contorted with rage, which suited Roland very well. Now that it had developed into a row he need feel no pity for the man. He began to speak but Hampton gave him no chance.

'I don't suppose your wife told you how much of the trouble was *her* fault. Oh, I don't deny she caught us in the act and that couldn't have been pleasant, but she was quick to punish us. She couldn't get to her father fast enough to tell it all! To send him down to the summer-house ... a charming thing to do, don't you think?'

Roland stared at him. 'She – she *saw* you and her mother...' He sat back, shocked by the image the words had conjured. Seventeen-year-old Ella had stumbled upon a man and woman ... God Almighty! 'You're disgusting!' he whispered. 'Utterly depraved!'

Hampton drew back slightly and Roland saw that the thrust had wounded him. His expression changed. 'Disgusting? That's where you're wrong. I was in love with Lydia, but Ella couldn't–'

'In love with another man's wife!'

'Yes. These things do happen. Lydia was going to ask for a divorce. She was only waiting until Ella was older. She wanted to spare the girl–'

'Spare her? An impressionable girl finds her mother and a young man together in a – a compromising...'

Hampton straightened up. 'For God's sake, man! We didn't *intend* her to find us like that. She'd been following me everywhere, so that Lydia and I rarely got the chance even to talk together.'

'Oh God! That poor child!' Roland felt sickened by the whole sordid story. He picked up an envelope and tossed it across the desk. 'There's the money in lieu of notice. Take it and get out of my sight before I change my mind.'

Hampton stared at the envelope with

obvious reluctance.

Roland said, 'And after the way you've spoken about my wife you should be thankful you're still getting any kind of reference at all.'

There was a fraught silence.

Hampton's shoulders sagged. 'I've earned a reference. What happened in the past has no bearing on how well I work.'

'All you've earned is my disgust.'

'I'll ask Mr Evans for a proper reference!'

'Ask Mr Evans?' Roland clutched at the table, fighting off a sudden wave of dizziness, and drew in his breath. 'You've got a bloody nerve, Hampton! You'll ask Mr Evans nothing because if Mr Evans were foolish enough to go against my wishes, *he'd* be the next one to be dismissed. Now get out of my sight. Stay away from my family! If I see you anywhere near this house I'll have you arrested!' There was a slight pain in his chest but he tried to ignore it.

He repeated, 'Now get out!' He was frightened by an ugly rasping in his throat as the pain intensified. He clutched at his chest, doubled over in the chair.

For what seemed an age, Roland was aware of the other man staring at him. He wanted to say, 'Get the nurse!' but he couldn't speak. His throat was tight and there was a roaring in his head. He thought, I'm dying, and this bastard is going to stand there and let it happen...

As a blackness enveloped him he slumped forward in his chair. After a moment of terror he knew nothing else.

Downstairs in the sitting room, Ella sat beside the fire, waiting for Daniel to leave the house. Suddenly she heard footsteps on the stairs and bit her lip. She mustn't see him; mustn't speak to him. To be fair to Roland, she must let him go out of her life forever.

'Ella!'

The hurrying footsteps stopped abruptly and the door swung open. Daniel stood there, his face flushed, his eyes full of bitterness.

He said, 'You husband's had some sort of fit. Now are you satisfied?'

She leaped to her feet. 'Oh God!' she whispered. 'Is he – where's the nurse?'

He stood in the doorway, blocking her way, his eyes blazing. 'I'm leaving, Ella. I've lost my job. I hope you're bloody well pleased with yourself!'

Ella could hardly bear it. He was leaving. Not only was the past still unresolved between them, but now he had the present disaster with which to blame her. She had lost the chance to ask for his forgiveness and they would part once more as enemies. Nothing had changed.

'Daniel, you don't understand—' she began, then remembered her husband. 'I must find the nurse!' she cried. 'Let me pass!'

Pushing aside his restraining hand she forced her way past him and ran up the stairs, shouting for Nurse Baisley.

Daniel's voice followed her. 'If he's dead, *you* killed him!'

As the nurse hurried towards her along the landing, Ella heard the front door open and slam shut. Later, it would seem to Ella that Daniel's departure had brought a storm of misfortune down upon her head.

When Doctor Clarke arrived twenty-five minutes later, Ella almost dragged him up the stairs towards the library.

'He's conscious, doctor,' she told him, 'but very weak.' She hurried into the room where Nurse Baisley was sitting by Roland, holding his hand. Frightened, Ella hung back as the doctor moved towards the patient. The nurse gave her a scornful look and stood up.

She said, 'He's very cold, doctor, so I've put a blanket around him. He thinks he fainted, but he *did* have some chest pain.'

The doctor leaned over Roland. 'Mr Gough? I'm Doctor Clarke. I hear you've had a nasty turn and I'll just take a look at you, if I may.'

Roland said, 'I'm quite all right now. It

149

was just – just the – I lost my temper ... stupid of me.' He raised his head, found Ella and smiled weakly. 'Nothing to be alarmed about.'

Ella gripped the back of the nearest chair.

Nurse Baisley glanced at her. 'We can manage now, Mrs Gough, if you have things to do elsewhere.' She gave her bright, professional smile which said, 'We don't need you.'

Ella hesitated. She didn't want to stay, but nor did she want to be summarily dismissed by May Baisley. If she *did* go, the doctor might think she was avoiding her responsibilities. She forced herself to look more closely at her husband. He was very pale, his hair was dishevelled and saliva trickled from his colourless lips. She shuddered, a hand to her mouth. 'Don't die, Roland,' she begged soundlessly.

Doctor Clarke looked at Ella. 'Has your husband suffered from heart trouble in the past?'

'No, he hasn't.' She moved a little nearer.

The nurse said, 'If he has, it will be in his records.'

The doctor straightened up. Turning to Ella, he lowered his voice, 'Any history of heart disease in his family that you know of?'

'Not that I'm aware. His mother died of tuberculosis many years ago and his father was killed in a riding accident.'

Nurse Baisley folded her arms. 'Since I've been Mr Gough's nurse he has never shown any symptoms of heart trouble. I would recognise them, I assure you.'

'Well, that's reassuring.'

Ignoring her, Ella said, 'Can he stay here, doctor – at Burleigh House, I mean – or will he need to go to hospital?'

The doctor turned to her. 'I don't think we should move him yet, but he may have to go in for some tests as soon as he's well enough.' He smiled. 'Mrs Gough, if I may have a word downstairs?' He gave her a meaningful glance with a slight tilt of his head and Ella understood that he didn't want to say too much in front of his patient. He went on, 'The nurse and I can manage for the moment.'

Now that the doctor had given her leave, Ella was willing to go. 'I'll be in the sitting room,' she told him.

As she hurried from the room she heard the doctor say, 'Now we're going to take you into your bedroom, Mr Gough.'

Downstairs, Ella rang for Annie and told her to bring a small brandy. Then she sat down on the edge of the sofa and clasped her trembling hands, staring into the fire as Daniel's accusing words rang in her ears: 'If he dies, *you* killed him!'

She tried to force from her mind the

image of her husband, hunched in his chair and drooling. Suppose the doctor was wrong. He was very young. Suppose it *was* a heart attack? If so, would he ever recover? She recalled the man she had married, fit and in control of his life. First the polio and now this had happened and she felt horribly responsible because it was her revelation about Daniel which had led to this latest disaster.

She wanted to feel nothing but relief that Daniel was once again out of her life, but if she were totally honest she knew she would miss him. There had been a certain frisson each morning, knowing that at some time during the day she might catch a glimpse of him.

'Well, he's gone!' she reminded herself and pressed her fingers against her eyes to keep back the tears. 'He's gone and good riddance!' She thought of him as he pushed past her, his eyes blazing. 'I don't need you in my life, Daniel Hampton!' she muttered. 'Please God, I *don't!*'

Annie came in with the brandy and said, 'Are you all right, Mrs Gough? It's been a trying week, hasn't it? First poor Mr Saville and now the master. And Dan going–' She clamped a hand to her mouth guiltily. 'Oh, I didn't mean – I'm sorry.'

Ella said, 'Yes, it was a shame he had to go but – we had our reasons.'

'Yes, Mrs Gough.'

Ella lifted the glass to her lips and was relieved to see that her hands no longer trembled. 'That will be all, Annie, thank you.'

Annie reached the door and then hesitated. 'He was a decent sort, though, wasn't he? Whatever he did. At heart, I mean.'

Ella said, 'At heart? Yes, I'm sure he was.'

She waited until she was alone again and then downed the brandy in one gulp.

Later that same night, Lizzie stared at the sheet of paper in her hand. She was sitting up in bed, putting in her curling rags. Her flannel nightdress fitted closely round the neck to keep out draughts and her face was shiny with Ponds cream. Dan lay beside her, staring up at the ceiling which was patterned with the glow of the street light shining through the casement window. She was trying, albeit unsuccessfully, to hold a conversation with him, but so far she was doing all the talking while her husband replied with monosyllables.

She read aloud: *'To whom it may concern, Daniel Hampton has carried out his duties satisfactorily while in my employ. He was punctual and willing.'*

Her mouth was a thin, hard line. 'Punctual and willing.' Gough had damned him with faint praise. So much for the wonderful new job! The idiot had got himself sacked before the first month was out.

'This is *it?*' she asked, waving the paper. 'This is your reference. Jesus, Dan! It's worse than no reference.' And all because he'd met the wife before and she'd fancied him and he'd snubbed her. She passed it back to him and they eyed each other warily. It was well past midnight, but sleep was out of the question. Dan had come home just before nine, drunk and quarrelsome, and it had taken a deal of patience to shake the truth from him. It all boiled down to the fact that he'd mucked things up. The new start was already over. She felt sick with anxiety and anger.

She said, 'It's all *her* fault. Spiteful cow!' She watched him from the corner of her eye, daring him to spring to the woman's defence, but he simply nodded. She separated another lock of hair, licked her forefinger and thumb and dampened the hair ends.

Dan found his voice at last. 'You can't blame *him*. He was in a nasty situation. It was Ella's decision; it must have been. She didn't have to tell him. I wasn't going to make any trouble.'

At least she'd got an answer out of him. Lizzie picked up one of the rag strips and folded the hair into it with practised fingers. She said, 'Don't keep calling her Ella. It was

"Mrs Gough" until this happened.'

'It's her name, that's all.'

'You said she was nothing to you, so she's just your employer's wife.'

'My *ex*-employer!'

She rolled up the hair and tied the ends of the rag. 'I hope he dies. Serves them right! D'you think it *was* a heart attack?' She began on the next curl.

'I expect it was. A very minor one. He was clutching his chest so he must have been in pain. If he dies I don't know where it will leave her. I don't know where their money comes from.'

He sounded worried and she glared at him. 'No need to sound *sorry* for him. If he dies, I hope it leaves her in queer street. See how she likes it. You're not still attracted to her?'

'I never was. That was the problem. She was just a child ... well, not *quite* a child, but certainly not a woman.'

She stared at him, defeated. He looked so ugly when he'd been drinking – slack face and piggy eyes. What had happened to the Daniel she had first met, she wondered despairingly. They had been such a handsome couple and so happy together. He had been such a catch. Lizzie had never expected him to marry her – she would willingly have lived in sin with him, but oh no! He had insisted on doing the gentlemanly thing. It wasn't *much* of a wedding in that awful Register Office, but they were married and she had the certificate to prove it. Now they were stuck with each other and it seemed nothing could go right for them.

'You don't deserve this, Dan.'

He shrugged but said nothing. Lizzie sighed. Although he'd never said so in so many words, she was sure he blamed her for the disaster over Frank's pub. How could she have known he was going to cheat them? The memory of that terrible week still haunted her. But *this* disaster was Dan's fault and that made her feel marginally better. It evened things up a bit. She tied the last curl, patted her hair and slid down into the bed, then glanced sideways at her husband. 'Dan, what are we going to do?'

He lifted his head slowly. 'How the hell do I know? If we don't pay the rent soon, Rudge will have us out on the street.'

'We could sell something.'

'Such as?'

Lizzie shook her head. There was nothing left except the furniture and that was hardly worth selling – except the grandfather clock.

'Your clock,' she said, her chin jutting. She knew it was the only remaining link which Dan had with his former life, left to him by his grandmother and very valuable, according to him. She had never understood why it meant so much to him. To her it was just a clock and a rather ugly one at that. It told the time. It chimed the hours, the half-hours and the quarters. There were sleepless nights when the sound almost drove her mad.

He said, 'Maybe.'

She looked at him, in shock. 'Sell it? You mean it?'

'I said "maybe".'

'You've never said that before.'

'We've never been so bloody poor before!'

Despite her own misery, Lizzie found herself touched by the echo in his voice and, suddenly moved, she bent over and kissed him. Usually, a sign of affection from her brought an immediate end to whatever hostilities existed between them. She considered it her secret weapon but tonight, to her surprise, he ignored the gesture and she drew back, suddenly fearful.

'I'm sorry, Dan,' she said. 'About everything.'

He turned his head and gave her a long look. 'You're not as sorry as I am,' he said, and the despair in his voice terrified her.

Next morning, just before seven, May Baisley rose, washed and dressed with a happy heart. Roland Gough was unwell. He needed her now more than ever and that thought thrilled her. She would waken him with a tray of tea as usual, but today she would be unable to help him into the bathroom for his shower and shave. Today she would give him a wash, and maybe later she would be asked to give him a blanket bath. She would render these intimate services with true delight.

When she first came to Burleigh House it had puzzled her that his wife seemed so uncaring; but now she enjoyed the knowledge that she, May Baisley, was the only woman who loved him. The fact that this love had to be kept hidden made it even more exciting. It amused her to appear coolly professional while harbouring such intimate thoughts in her heart. To May, Roland Gough was a wonderful, decent, God-fearing man and it annoyed her to hear other members of staff disparaging him as they occasionally did. Mrs Granger had once called him 'a dry old stick', but what did *she* know about the man? They rarely met. Annie had wondered why Mrs Gough married someone so much older, but it was glaringly obvious to May. Ella Gough had been after his money. She was a gold-digger.

May pulled on her blue dress, added the white apron and went to the mirror to adjust her white cap. The uniform suited her, she knew, and she imagined that to poor Roland she must appear as a vision of competence and kindliness by comparison with his hard-hearted wife. It was true that Mrs Gough had offered a bed to Mr Saville, but that was a gesture – a way of impressing the new doctor. Mrs Gough had never so much as lifted a finger to look after the old man. Oh, no. That had been left to *her*. It was, 'You can manage, Nurse, can't you?' No request. Just an order. But that was Mrs Gough all over. Impulsive and headstrong. Too used to getting her own way, like all beautiful people. Not that May minded the extra money but she was glad when they had taken him to hospital and she was once more free to give all her attention to Roland.

'Mr Gough should never have been taken in by her charms,' she told her reflection. 'He made a bad mistake there.' She smiled at herself, watching the way her eyes crinkled.

Certainly he couldn't love his wife. May wanted to believe that. Sometimes in the seclusion of her bed she allowed herself to daydream about him. Her favourite fantasy was the one in which Ella Gough died suddenly and Roland came to realise that a more suitable woman was already waiting to step into her shoes.

'Very nice!' she told herself. She dabbed a finger in the Vaseline, rubbed it into her hands and then smoothed her hair. She had to wear a cap, but she liked to think that the hair that *did* show had a gloss to it. She moved the mirror to check Mr Gough's diary. Some days one of his friends would call in; the old doctor had sometimes come for a game of chess. She opened the book and ran a finger down the page.

'Uh-oh!' The bank manager was due at 4 pm. Well, that would have to be cancelled. There was no way Roland was fit to discuss financial matters.

She pinned on her cap, hurried along the passage and down the stairs and knocked on the door of the dining room where Mrs Gough would be already at breakfast with Penny.

'Come in.'

As May went into the room, Mrs Gough said, 'Good morning, Nurse.'

She looked harassed, thought May, immediately arranging her own features into an expression of quiet calm.

Penny looked cross. 'Mummy said I have to eat my fried tomato! Ugh! I hate fried tomato!'

Mrs Gough said, 'Then you shouldn't have asked for it, should you? I told you you wouldn't like it, but you insisted. Now you must eat it.'

'But it's *horrible!* It's all *slimy!*'

'Don't be silly. You've already eaten most of it. There's only one mouthful left.'

May smiled kindly at the child. Typical of Mrs Gough to bully her. She had no understanding of young children and no patience. Poor Penny. She gave the child a little wink and whispered, 'I don't like tomatoes either.'

Mrs Gough said, 'Please don't encourage her.' Reaching for the tea-pot, she refilled her cup. 'What is it you want, Nurse?'

May looked at her with dislike. How like the woman! Her husband has suffered a heart attack and she doesn't even enquire after his welfare. Doesn't want to know what sort of night he's spent. How typical.

She said, 'The bank manager has an appointment with your husband at four o'clock, I thought you'd probably want to cancel it. Mr Gough's in no fit state to...'

'How is he this morning? Did he sleep well?'

Better late than never, thought May. 'A rather restless night, thank you, Mrs Gough. He's still asleep, but I'll wake him presently and after I've washed him I'll send down to Cook for a lightly boiled egg and brown bread and butter, cut very thin. Shall I send word when he's fit to receive visitors?'

She saw from her employer's expression that the last sentence was a mistake.

'Please don't bother. *I* shall decide when to visit my husband.'

'Very good, Mrs Gough. And you will remember to cancel the bank manager's appointment?'

Penny said, 'Ugh!' and glared at her forkful of tomato.

Mrs Gough's smile was thin and cold. 'I may decide to see him myself. You can safely leave the matter in my hands.'

Penny said, 'I can't eat it. I *won't*! I'll be sick,' and glared at her mother.

Mrs Gough said, 'I'm afraid you won't leave this table until you do!'

May Baisley decided she had heard and seen quite enough. She withdrew without waiting to be dismissed. Closing the door behind her, she wondered if Mr Gough had any idea how strict his wife was with his little daughter. If she ever saw her chance, May decided, she would mention it – in her usual joking way, of course. She made it her business, whenever possible, to let Mr Gough know just what sort of woman he'd married.

Chapter Five

Ella approached the bed with a smile that hid her real feelings. She was in fact very disturbed by her husband's appearance. Propped against the pillow, he was very pale and there was a gleam of perspiration on his forehead. The doctor had told her it *might* have been a mild heart attack, but might just as easily have been caused by over-excitement brought on by what he called 'the unfortunate argument'. Immobility played havoc with the circulation and undue exertion was best avoided. More than anything, she thought, Roland looked depressed. This was not the time to tell him that Enid Granger had given three months' notice.

Nurse Baisley was sitting at the window, writing a letter, but she stood up as Ella entered the room.

Ella said, 'I'd like to speak privately with my husband, please, Nurse.'

'Certainly – but do remember that he is not to be tired. He seems to be running a slight temperature. I do hope it's not the flu.' She gave Ella a meaningful look which she ignored.

'It's not,' Ella told her. 'I've spoken with the doctor. If he thought it was flu he'd have told me. Of course I won't tire Mr Gough. He will tell me himself when he has had enough.'

She remained standing until the nurse had removed herself and her writing to her own room next door.

Roland gave her a wry smile. 'She means well.' He patted the bed. 'Come and sit down, Ella.'

Instead, Ella drew up a chair. 'Aren't you hot with that roaring fire?' she asked. 'You're perspiring and that can't be good for you.'

'I think I'm providing my own heat!' he said with a slightly apologetic laugh. 'I feel a bit feverish, but I'll live. She tells me you visited the hospital. How is the old boy?'

'Making progress. Now that he's over the shock of being there he's beginning to enjoy all the attention. He tells me his godson's on the way back from America. He's arranged a transfer to London so that he can travel up each day.'

'Very considerate when you think he's not even a relative; just a godson. But how's that little scamp of mine, bless her?'

'Penny?' Ella laughed. 'She's as difficult as ever. A free spirit – that's what Mrs Granger calls her.' Ella thought of the struggle over breakfast, but she didn't think it worth retelling. 'I was glad to hand her over to Mrs Granger.' Which makes me a bad mother, she thought. 'Mrs Granger has a way with her that I lack.' She hoped that her husband would deny this, but instead he laughed.

'Well, dear, she doesn't take after me, that's for sure. No one could call me a free spirit – not even when I'm well!'

Ella rolled her eyes. 'I know! She takes after her mother! I'm sorry about that!'

They both laughed and Ella thought how wonderful it was of Roland not to refer to yesterday's revelations and the scene with Daniel. He hadn't reproached her, although she knew that it was sacking Daniel which had made him ill.

She smiled. 'I really came to say that Mr Carter from the bank is coming at four and–' She held up a hand as he began to interrupt. 'I will see him, dear. I just want you to advise me before the meeting.'

'You, Ella?' He looked startled. 'I'd really rather you didn't. He can wait until I'm recovered.'

Ella took hold of his hand. 'No, he can't, Roland. The doctor says that what you need is complete rest. At least a week in bed. If the symptoms persist you may need a short stay in hospital.'

'He didn't tell me anything of the kind,' he protested.

'Of course not. He doesn't want to worry

you. I can deal with Mr Carter if you prepare me. Tell me what to say and–'

Roland put a hand to his forehead. 'I've told you, Ella, I don't want...' He broke off, shaking his head, then reached under his pillows and produced a handkerchief with which he wiped his face.

Ella watched him anxiously. 'Are you all right, dear? Shall I pour you a cold drink?'

'No, no. It's nothing.'

'So tell me about Mr Carter's visit.'

'Carter is coming to discuss some shares which are sliding badly. And we have rather a lot of them. I won't pretend I'm not alarmed and I thought I should ask his advice. If we sell now we shall lose a lot of money. If we wait and they don't recover...'

'We'll lose even more.'

'The old dilemma. I would rather you didn't get involved, dear, to be quite honest.'

Ella leaned forward. 'But you aren't up to it, darling. You're supposed to be resting and–'

'How can I rest,' he cried, 'when we stand to lose so much? I need to make a decision and Carter must help me. He's the one who recommended them in the first place.'

'What are these shares, Roland?' Ella felt woefully ignorant.

'They're Spanish shares. Mainly copper. Had them for donkeys' years and they've done well, but now they're mining copper in other countries. Bringing the price down.'

Ella nodded but her eyes had narrowed. 'Shouldn't he have told you about it before now?'

Roland hesitated. 'The fact is, Ella, that he shouldn't have told me about them in the first place. It's not a bank manager's job...' He was slipping sideways on the pillows and Ella leaned over to help him. 'They shouldn't involve themselves. They're supposed to suggest you consult a broker, but we were playing golf ... nineteenth hole and we'd had a few drinks over lunch. He was feeling expansive, I suppose, and ... well, it was a tip.' He tapped the side of his nose.

Ella looked at him, concerned. He really did look very weary. She stood up, remembering the nurse's warning. Nurse Baisley would love something with which to reproach her.

'I must leave you, then, Roland,' she said. 'I'll telephone Mr Carter and tell him you're not well enough to see him. I'll find out what I can, shall I?'

He hesitated. 'I'd rather you didn't worry yourself, darling,' he told her. 'Tell Carter I'll be in touch in a day or so and he's to let me know if there's anything that needs urgent attention. Don't get involved in the technicalities, Ella.'

She leaned forward and pressed a kiss into

his hair which was damp with perspiration. 'I'll send the dragon back to you as I go down.'

She left the room with her mind already made up. When Mr Carter arrived she would deal with the matter herself. Mr Carter might not like dealing with a woman, but he would have to get used to the idea.

Promptly at four o'clock the bank manager was shown into the sitting room and Ella rose to meet him, hand outstretched. Mr Carter was short and rotund and wore small, round-lensed spectacles.

She said, 'We did meet once before – when my husband's father died. That was some years ago.'

'I do remember,' he said, with enough hesitation to suggest otherwise. 'I'm so sorry to hear about your husband. How is he this morning?'

He settled himself comfortably into the proffered chair as Annie came in with a tray of tea and biscuits. While Ella poured for them, she gave Mr Carter a brief report on Roland's condition.

Mr Carter tutted sympathetically. 'What a worry for you, Mrs Gough.'

She nodded. 'And hardly the best time for him to be worrying about these shares,' she told him.

He glanced towards the door.

Ella smiled. 'My husband won't be joining us,' she told him. 'I'll be acting for him, so to speak.' He looked startled, but she didn't give him time to protest. 'My husband feels these Spanish shares are falling a little too fast for comfort.' She gave him a hard look. 'If I have to make decisions for my husband I need to know all the facts, Mr Carter.'

Was it her imagination or did he look uneasy?

He said, 'I really don't think that a woman – that is, ... I mean no offence, Mrs Gough, but – you do understand, I'm sure...' Nervously he nibbled a garibaldi biscuit.

'No. I don't think I do.'

'As soon as your husband is well enough...'

The biscuit crumbs had apparently gone down the wrong way and he began to cough, scrabbling in his pocket for a handkerchief.

She said, 'Try a mouthful of tea.' When he had recovered she prompted him. 'The shares, Mr Carter?'

'Ah ... yes. They certainly aren't performing well at the moment, Mrs Gough. Disappointing, that's the word.'

'Whichever word you choose, Mr Carter, the value of the shares is going down instead of up and I – that is *we* – are not prepared to sit back and wait for them to go even lower. I understand from my husband that you

169

also own some?'

He looked flustered by the directness of her approach – as well he might, she reflected.

'So, Mr Carter, may I ask if you have sold any of yours?'

'Have I...?' He stared at her indignantly. 'Really, I don't think you should ask such a question, Mrs Gough... That is, I really don't think I should be discussing this with you at all–'

'You have, then.'

'I *may* have sold a few...' He took another mouthful of tea.

Ella said, 'Then why didn't you recommend that my husband did the same? A quick telephone call? As one friend to another.'

He wiped his mouth. 'Because I shouldn't be giving advice on shares, Mrs Gough. You should take professional advice, but...' He lowered his voice. 'As one friend to another, perhaps it might be wise to sell maybe half of the holding.'

'As many as that?'

He nodded.

'And what sort of loss would that entail? Are we talking hundreds or thousands of pounds?'

His round face crumpled. 'Oh, that is hardly – I mean, one shouldn't look at it quite that way, Mrs Gough. You have to balance gains and losses over the years. There were dividends... Hopefully they will go up again ... before too long. Oh, dear. You really should talk to your husband, Mrs Gough, before making any rash judgements. And do please take further advice.'

He glanced at his watch and finished his tea.

Ella stood up abruptly, forcing him to do the same. She was not impressed. Let's hope he's better at golf, she thought. 'Thank you for coming, Mr Carter. I shall pass on your advice to my husband and will most certainly be in touch with our broker.'

To soften her words, she smiled her charming smile and shook his hand before calling Annie to see him out. Then she looked through the telephone book and found the broker's business card. A Mr Dennis Varley. Her conversation with him was short and very one-sided.

'Metals are always volatile,' he told her. 'Those particular shares are slipping badly.'

'So sell them all, please. At once.'

'Certainly. You're doing the wisest thing, Mrs Gough. They fluctuate, but those shares have done well until now. Reinvest whatever we get for them. Aim to protect your capital and to bring in some income. Safest bet is fifty-fifty. Equities plus government stock. Treasury bonds. And a few blue chips – Rolls-Royce are good. If not, I'll drop you a line with all the details.'

'Thank you, Mr Varley. I'm–'

'Not at all. Glad to be of help, Mrs Gough. Goodbye.'

The following afternoon, her mood dampened by a light rain, Lizzie knocked at the door of No. 19, a bundle of £1 notes clenched in her hand inside her coat pocket. Her head was thumping and her face was white. It had been a bad day *all* day and paying over rent money to Mr Rudge made it worse. Two boys passed her, kicking a tin can between them, and in Lizzie's fragile state the noise sounded thunderous.

'Must you!' she snapped, but one of them lifted two fingers in a rude salute.

'Why, you cheeky little devil!' She lunged after him, but he dodged and they ran on laughing.

The door of No. 19 opened and Lizzie saw a large, unhealthy-looking woman with a scarf tied turban-style around her head.

'Well?' Mrs Rudge demanded.

'I'm Mrs Hampton. It's about the rent.'

'You'd best come in off the step.'

The passage smelled of stale cabbage and the walls were a depressing brown. The kitchen was large but the furniture was unimpressive. Lizzie wondered what they spent all their money on.

'What name?' Mrs Rudge took down a

pile of rent books. 'Hampton?'

'Yes. I've brought you four weeks' rent. It's all I've got.' This was a lie, but Lizzie was prepared to try. In fact they owed seven weeks and she had enough to settle the arrears, but if she could hold back even a small proportion of it she would.

Selling the grandfather clock had proved a disaster. Their visit to the 'clock specialist' had been a humiliating business. 'Wood worm' the dealer had told them, shaking his head. He also insisted that the back had been replaced with an inferior wood, and that the clock face was seriously dis-coloured, and he had tutted sadly over the mechanism which had been 'criminally neglected' for many years. He had offered half the sum Daniel expected and refused point blank to improve on the offer. Dan was upset that he should have to part with it at all, but to do so for such a small sum...

Lizzie had stood by helplessly as the two men haggled, but the dealer recognised desperation when he saw it and was quick to take advantage of their plight. After settling the rent arrears there would be very little left.

Now Mrs Rudge selected one of the notebooks and flicked open the pages. 'Oh, yes. Hampton. Pay up in full or get out. My husband's sick of you. He can let that flat tomorrow to better tenants.'

173

'Five weeks then.'

Mrs Rudge's mouth tightened. 'You'd best go,' she said, 'before my hubby gets back. He'll give you "five weeks"!'

Lizzie wanted to slap the grey, podgy face, but still she couldn't give in. 'Six, you miserable old–'

The push the woman gave her knocked the breath from Lizzie's body. Gasping, she clutched at a chair to save herself from falling.

Mrs Rudge glared at her. 'You a bit slow or what? It's seven weeks' money or we call in the bailiffs. And I don't think your la-di-da hubby would like to see your home dumped in the street! Be a bit of a come-down, wouldn't it?'

Lizzie felt bile rise in her throat. She longed to punch the stupid face. She'd come off worse in a scrap because Mrs Rudge was a lot heavier, but it would be worth it if it wasn't for Dan. He'd never forgive her.

With reluctance, she held out the money.

'About time too!' Mrs Rudge licked finger and thumb and began to count the notes. She looked up. 'It's ten bob short. Think I'm daft or something?' She held out a plump hand.

Lizzie found four half-crowns and handed them over with a bad grace. 'I hope you rot in hell!' she muttered savagely.

174

The small eyes gleamed with malice. 'If I do, you'll be there with me! Now get out – and remember, we're watching the pair of you. Any more trouble and you're out!'

She led the way back to the front door and opened it. Lizzie searched in vain for a cutting remark on which to retire but, white-faced, stepped out on to the pavement without saying a word. As she walked back towards the flat her thoughts were bitter, her throat was tight and her eyes ached with unshed tears.

That evening Penny was wandering through the shrubbery at the far end of the lawn. She had a skipping-rope in one hand but she had lost interest in it. Staring up into the trees, she waited in vain for a glimpse of a squirrel but saw nothing but birds. Glancing back, she saw Mrs Granger talking with Mr Evans. He was shaking his head and shrugging his shoulders, but she couldn't hear what was being said.

'Half a pound of tuppenny rice, half a pound of treacle...'

Penny sang and thought about Daddy who was very poorly, and Mummy who was very busy, and the party to which she had been invited. A *party!* She smiled to herself, imagining how she would look in the pink dress with the ribbons; and Great-Aunt Florrie was knitting her a little pink bolero to wear with it if it was chilly. Mrs Granger would make ringlets in her hair with the curling tongs. She wondered what she would take as a present...

'Hey! Tiddler! Over here!'

She turned towards the voice and was astonished to see nice Mr Hampton peeping out at her from behind one of the trees.

As she ran towards him he said, 'Hullo, Penny!'

She cried, 'Have you come back to work for us again?' and realised suddenly that she had missed their little talks. 'I don't think Mummy meant to be unkind,' she added. Penny had heard Annie talking to Mrs Granger, and she had said that Mummy was unkind and that had been worrying her.

He crouched down beside her and put a finger to his lips. 'Can you keep a secret?' he asked. 'It's very important, but I think you could do it. You're seven and that's quite grown-up.'

'I'll be eight soon,' she told him eagerly. A grown-up secret!

'Very *important*,' he repeated. 'It's a letter for your Mummy. I want you to give it to her, but that's the secret. I don't want anyone else to know. Not Mrs Granger. Not your Daddy. No one.'

'Not even Lucy Barnes? I'm going to her party. I'm–'

He shook his head.

176

Penny sighed. How would anyone know that she had an important secret if she didn't tell them? 'Can I tell them I know a secret if I don't tell them what it is?'

He shook his head again and looked very serious.

'Could I just *whisper* it to Daddy?' She gave him a hopeful smile.

To her surprise he looked upset. 'No! *No*, Penny! If you tell Daddy or anyone else it will spoil the surprise.'

'Daddy's very poorly. The doctor had to come.'

'I know... Is he going to get better?'

She blinked. 'Of *course* he is!' For the first time she wondered.

He glanced around him. 'So will you help me with the secret? Will you give a letter to your Mummy?'

She nodded.

'Good girl.' He pulled an envelope from his pocket. 'You'll have to hide it, won't you, because no one must see it except your Mummy. Now where can we hide it?'

'Up my jumper, under my coat?'

He beamed at her. 'Of course! How clever you are!'

Obediently she tucked the letter inside her jumper. 'I wish you *were* still working for us,' she told him. 'Mr Evans was very cross when you went away. Cross with Mummy and Daddy, I mean, and Annie said it was a damned shame and Nanny said they must have had their reasons and–'

'They *told* you all this?' He was frowning.

'No-o ... but I heard them in the kitchen.'

He tweaked her nose gently. 'Don't you worry about it, Tiddler.' He stood up. 'Now I have to go, otherwise someone might see me and then it won't be a secret.'

'Will you come again?' She smiled up at him. 'We could have another secret.'

He gave her a strange look. 'I don't know, Tiddler. We'll have to wait and see.'

And then he was gone and Penny turned to see if Mrs Granger was watching. Seeing that she was still talking to the gardener, Penny ran across the grass, giving them a wide berth, and went into the house by the kitchen door. Stopping only to eat a handful of currants which Annie gave her, she went in search of her mother and handed over the secret.

The meeting started five minutes late but, after a little chivvying from Ella, Miss Spinney quickly launched into a reading of the last meeting's minutes. Mrs Grey was knitting, but from time to time she nodded her acceptance of the points in question.

'...The list of tombola prizes was read and it was agreed that Mr Saville had done very well. However, we still expect further prizes, many of which have been promised and will come in on the morning of the fair...' Miss Spinney paused. 'I suppose I should have put something in about Mr Saville's collapse but...' She looked at Ella.

Mrs Grey said, 'But it didn't happen during the meeting, so how can you include it?'

They both looked at Ella, who suddenly realised she was the focus of their attention, and said, 'Sorry. What was the question?'

Miss Spinney explained and Ella said, 'Mention it in today's minutes. Fortunately we can say that he is making good progress.'

As Miss Spinney read the rest of the minutes, Ella allowed her thoughts to revert to a letter which she had brought with her in her handbag. A letter from Daniel in which he asked for a loan. He had confessed to a deep revulsion for even daring to ask and for having to beg, but told her they found themselves in dire straits and he knew of no one else who might help him. He had said he would come to the end of the garden the next day in the hope that she would be there. The letter had contained words which she knew by heart:

In spite of my angry words when I left Burleigh House I cannot think harshly of you for long. You are so like Lydia...

Ella drew a deep breath. *You are so like*

179

Lydia. Was that meant to be a compliment, she wondered, because if so it was somewhat double-edged. The abiding memory she had of her mother was of her naked arms and legs wrapped around Daniel Hampton on the window seat of the summer-house. Try as she would, Ella had never been able to forget that scene. Even her mother's death had not softened Ella's heart towards what she saw as a double betrayal.

'...*so like Lydia.*' There was a physical resemblance, she knew from the photographs. Ella sighed. The repercussions of her own spite had echoed down the years, bringing none of the sweetness that was supposedly the fruit of revenge. Instead she had inherited a legacy of bitterness and loss.

Miss Spinney said, 'Here we are then,' and handed Ella the book which she signed with her usual indecipherable flourish, wondering why they bothered with these formalities. Unfortunately she had insisted years ago that the meetings be conducted in a businesslike way. Now she would find it difficult to suggest that it was not necessary.

Mrs Grey said, 'I popped in to see him and he was so pleased to have a visitor. He still looked very pale, poor thing, but all he could talk about was being allowed to go home.' She held up her knitting. 'I'm knitting him some gloves. Grey ones. Well, grey goes with anything, doesn't it. He's going to feel the cold when he *does* come home. It's so hot in that ward. I said to him, "How can you bear it!"'

Miss Spinney smiled. 'So you finished the socks?'

'Oh yes. Finished and posted off.'

Ella made a big effort to forget Daniel's letter. Referring to her notes she said, 'Annie has produced a menu for the teas – almost the same as last year but sausage rolls instead of ham sandwiches – and since my husband is ill we need another volunteer to run a "Pick-A-Straw" stand.' Seeing Mrs Grey's blank look she said, 'Raffle ticket numbers are rolled up small and pushed into some of the straws. If you draw one of these straws you win sixpence.'

Miss Spinney added, 'It costs a penny or tuppence to pick a straw and only some of them win. They did it at the school fête. It's a nice little money spinner. I could do that.'

Ella said, 'Thank you. And I've spoken to the bank about change for the floats and Janet Bell is going to bring her gramophone along and some records.'

Mrs Grey started a new row. 'Some music! How perfectly lovely.'

'Something light and cheerful,' said Miss Spinney.

Ella smiled. 'Of course. And ... what else? Oh yes! The vicar's sister suggested a competition for the most beautiful baby, but I thought probably not. What do you think? It's so hurtful for the losers.'

Miss Spinney wondered whether a best-behaved dog competition would be a better idea, and while they discussed this Ella considered Daniel's letter. She had to decide what to do. If she *did* lend him money and Roland ever found out, he would be appalled by her subterfuge; yet she knew that Daniel would *never* have asked for help unless he was truly desperate. She wanted to help him, but that meant helping his wife also which complicated the issue for her. In a convoluted way, Ella felt that being poor was the woman's punishment for marrying the man Ella herself had loved... *Had* loved? Startled, Ella considered. She had loved Daniel for so long that she had taken it for granted. Was it still love that she felt for him or something else?

Mrs Grey was saying, 'All those dogs chasing around. I don't think so.'

'I agree,' said Ella. 'No dogs. No beautiful babies and no children's fancy dress. We had tantrums last time we tried that. Accusations were flying thick and fast!' She laughed. 'We nearly had a riot on our hands.'

'Did we?' Miss Spinney looked baffled.

'You weren't here that year,' Mrs Grey told her. 'You were away in Watford nursing your sister.' She rolled her eyes. 'Dreadful, that was. People claimed that the mothers had helped some of the children to make the costumes – it was supposed to be all their own work – and little Angie Betts started to cry – she was an elf if I remember rightly, and there was some argument about her wings – and Mr Betts was really *very* rude to the vicar and–'

Annie knocked and came in. 'Sorry to interrupt, Mrs Gough, but there's a Mr Marriott to see you.' She looked rather flustered.

Ella frowned. 'Do I *know* a Mr Marriott?'

'He says you do.'

Miss Spinney said, 'Marriott? Isn't that Mr Saville's godson? The one in New York?'

Annie said, 'He did say something about Mr Saville. I didn't catch it all because I'm in the middle of an argument with the butcher.' She rolled her eyes. *'Another* one!'

Ella excused herself from the meeting and hurried from the room. So the prodigal godson had come home at last! Mr Saville would be in seventh heaven.

Charles Marriott was standing in the hallway, his hat in his hand. He was slim, with sandy hair and an engaging smile. He seemed to be staring at her.

She said, 'Mr Marriott. How nice to meet you.'

He held out his hand. 'Thank you – for seeing me.'

They shook hands but Ella was disconcerted by the way he was looking at her. Not simply admiration – she was used to that and recognised it easily. 'What is it?' After a moment she withdrew her hand.

'Was I staring?' His expression changed slightly. 'Please forgive me... It's you. It's incredible. You're just how I imagined you. My godfather mentioned you frequently in his letters. I began to feel that I knew you.' He smiled again. 'I've just come from the hospital.'

'He's much better than he was.'

'I was pleasantly surprised. We talked for ten minutes or so. And I learned of your kindness, of course. I don't know how to thank you.'

'It was the least I could do. No one expected you to get back to England so quickly.' She hesitated, wanting to invite him to stay for a cup of tea but aware of the committee waiting for her in the dining room. 'I'm engaged at the moment, but–'

'Oh, please! I didn't want to interrupt anything. I just had to thank you in person.'

Suddenly Ella remembered Roland. 'I wonder if you could spare ten minutes to meet my husband? He's normally confined to a wheelchair, but–'

'The polio. Of course. I'm so sorry.'

Ella frowned. 'You *knew*?'

'Godfather is a great letter writer. He

184

wrote to me about it at the time. I was in Montreal then.' He smiled. 'I'm afraid you have few secrets, The Goughs featured regularly in the correspondence.'

'I'm flattered,' she told him.

'I'd love to meet your husband.'

'Splendid. Roland's somewhat under the weather at the moment, and has to be in bed. He may have had a mild heart attack, though we hope not. He gets so bored, and would love some company. You two have quite a lot in common, actually. You've both travelled.' She smiled. 'You don't play chess, do you?'

'I do. One of life's pleasures, as far as I'm concerned. Maybe when he's feeling better...'

Ella looked into the humorous grey eyes. She liked his easy-going manners and the soft voice with its noticeably transatlantic drawl.

She said, 'He usually spends most of his time in the library when he's up and about. He *can* walk, but with great difficulty and considerable pain. Also his right arm was slightly affected. Such a blow, because he loves to write. He manages with a typewriter, but it's slow work and so frustrating for him.'

'What's he writing?' he asked as they went up the stairs.

'He'll tell you all about it.'

She led the way into the bedroom and made the introductions. Moments later she slipped away, leaving the two men talking animatedly together.

Ella decided that Miss Spinney and Mrs Grey could wait a little longer for her return and went in search of Penny. Ever since her daughter had delivered Daniel's letter, she had been worrying in case Penny mentioned it to anyone else. She found her daughter with Mrs Granger in the garden. Penny was wheeling a doll's pram containing Jessica, her best doll, a teddy bear and a rabbit which Florrie had knitted for her.

Penny regarded her mother crossly. 'They're being naughty,' she told her. 'I've told them I shall smack them if they won't be good.' She leaned over the pram, wagging a small finger. 'Do what I tell you *when* I tell you.'

Mrs Granger laughed. 'Now where have I heard that before!'

Ella hid a grin. 'What have they done?'

Penny gave the pram a little shake. 'They're squabbling ... and Jessica's been crying.'

Before Ella could ask the reason Mrs Granger lowered her voice. 'According to Penny, Jessica's been crying because she wants a little brother.' She raised her eyebrows. 'Because Meg's got a little brother.'

'Oh dear.' Ella raised her eyebrows. 'A tricky one, that. I think Jessica is going to be disappointed.' She went on, 'Leave her with me for ten minutes. I feel like a breath of fresh air. Pop inside and have a cup of tea.'

'Thank you!' If the nanny was surprised she hid it very well.

Ella waited until they were alone and then smiled at Penny. 'Thank you for giving me the surprise, Penny,' she said. 'I do hope you haven't told anybody.'

'Only Jessica – and she won't tell.'

Ella let out a sigh of relief and hugged her daughter.

Penny asked, 'Was it a nice surprise, Mummy? Mr Hampton's letter?'

A nice surprise? Hardly – but she couldn't disappoint her daughter. 'A lovely surprise,' she agreed. 'Thank you. You are very good at secrets, Penny.'

To Ella's surprise the child suddenly turned and clung to her. Ella stared down at the little girl. The unaccustomed display of affection touched her and all thought of Daniel deserted her as she bent to kiss the top of Penny's head. 'Only a week to go to the party,' she reminded her. 'We shall have to go into town and buy those pink satin ballet slippers Daddy promised you. And a present for Lucy.'

There was a short silence, then Penny said, 'Is Mr Hampton *ever* coming back?'

In that moment Ella saw quite clearly that it was never going to happen. Daniel had a wife now, and if he felt anything for Ella it was simply because she reminded him of Lydia.

'Lydia!' she whispered and at that moment the first small doubt appeared in her mind. Ella had carefully nursed her hatred, convincing herself that her mother must have encouraged Daniel. Must have initiated the relationship. Suddenly she wondered about the truth of that. Just before her departure, her mother had tried to explain, but Ella had rushed from the room in tears of rage. Lydia had gone after her and slapped her. An hour later her mother had gone. Ella had never seen her again.

Ella swallowed hard. If she *lent* Daniel the money, the debt and its repayment would tie them together. She would never be free of him. Yet she dared not *give* him the money. Much as she would like to help Daniel, she would have to refuse. She would see him once more and explain.

She kissed her daughter. 'No, Penny,' she said. 'I'm afraid Mr Hampton has gone for good.'

The barman stopped coughing and raised his eyebrows. 'Another one? Are you sure that's wise, sir?' he asked.

Daniel regarded him with bleary eyes. 'Mind your own business!' he told him. Who the hell did he think he was? He stared into the mirror behind the bar and was not encouraged by what he saw. Through the haze of pipe and cigarette smoke his face looked drawn, his eyes haggard. He looked disgusting, he thought, but who cared? Nobody in the whole damned world. Certainly not Lizzie. Certainly not Ella Gough. She was going to refuse; he knew it. He shifted his gaze, taking in the red-flecked wallpaper, the frosted window and the comfortable but well-worn seats. He could smell the rope of browning hops that decorated the fireplace, the damp serge of the customers' overcoats and the sour breath of a nearby mongrel which lay panting at his master's feet. The sort of pub he hated, he reflected wearily, so what in heaven's name was he doing here?

'There you are – but it's your last.'

The barman waited and Daniel fumbled in his pocket for some coins. Unable to see too clearly, he simply held out his hand and let the man take the required amount. He might cheat him, but so what! Nothing mattered any more. But he was damned if he would let the barman treat him like dirt.

'Who says it's my last?' Daniel asked thickly.

'I do, chum.' By way of confirmation, he

stabbed a finger into his own chest and began to cough. When he stopped he said, 'You've had more than enough. Any trouble from you and I'll call a copper. Don't think I won't.'

Daniel tried to think of a smart answer but failed. He stared at the weaselly face and watery eyes and wondered why barmen the world over were so cantankerous.

Sliding from the bar stool, he picked up his beer and made his way unsteadily towards a corner table where there were no mirrors to reproach him. He slumped into the seat and closed his eyes. Tomorrow he would go back, cap in hand, to Lydia's daughter. She would despise him for what he had become. She might even feel a sense of triumph that he had been brought so low; might think he deserved nothing better. He took a mouthful of beer and closed his eyes.

A moment later he opened them and muttered, 'Retri-retribution...' He could still say it so he wasn't drunk. Or maybe he was. He and Lydia had been drunk that day in the summer-house. Drunk enough to be ecstatically happy, and reckless enough to throw caution to the winds and make love. Foolishly lighthearted, he had talked Lydia into it – not that she had hesitated long. It had felt so right – the very first time and in an idyllic setting. If it hadn't been for Ella...

If *only* they had waited. Lydia had agreed to ask for a divorce; they were going to be man and wife. Instead they had risked everything and lost.

'Oh, Ella!' he muttered, staring in dull surprise at the empty glass on the table in front of him. Ella ... the image of the mother she hated so much. Married to the kind of man her mother had married – an older man, kind, decent but unimaginative. Had Ella thrown herself at the first man who offered a chance to forget?

'Jesus!'

Daniel ran a hand over his face. His stomach was rumbling dangerously. Thank God Lydia couldn't see what had become of him.

A woman's voice said, 'Is this seat any-body's?'

He looked up, frowning through the alcohol, and saw a brassy woman giving him that special look. A cheap pick-up. This was all he needed.

'I'm waiting for someone,' he lied.

She gave a little laugh. 'Perhaps it's me.'

She was holding what looked like a gin and tonic. Her smiling face was bright with rouge and lipstick and the belt of her coat was pulled in tightly at the waist.

'What?' Daniel stared at her. *Perhaps it's me.* Oldest line in the book. He waved his hand. He said, 'Leave me alone, can't you!'

He didn't want to be rude, but if she persisted...

Luckily she took the hint. 'Please yourself!' she told him, the smile suddenly absent.

Daniel watched her try the same approach on a man sitting at the bar. He proved more amenable, leering and patting the seat beside him. Illogically, Daniel felt a surge of loneliness. He made his way back to the counter and pushed his glass forward.

The barman shook his head. 'I said "No more" and I meant it. You get off home.'

Daniel was aware that the brassy woman was enjoying his humiliation. Her new friend said, 'He's had a skinful!'

Pointedly the barman removed Daniel's glass. 'Go home, chum, while you still can.'

Daniel tried to summon some aggression, but he knew he was going to be sick. He stumbled towards the door and the woman called, 'Thought you was waiting for someone!' and laughed.

Somehow Daniel pushed through the door and out into the rain. The cold air hit his lungs and made him cough, which shook his stomach. Feeling a cold sweat break out on his body, he leaned against the wall. A moment later he doubled up with a cry of misery and retched over the pavement.

Chapter Six

May Baisley was standing by the window the next afternoon, watching the rain. Any sign of the magnificence of nature pleased her, and extremes of weather were particularly welcome. A severe frost, a snow blizzard, a storm – all impressed her with their excesses, and today the heavy raindrops splashing into the grass gave her great satisfaction.

'There's nothing like a good downpour,' she remarked, turning to her patient with a smile. 'I always think it freshens up the earth and clears the dust from the air.'

'I'm sure you're right.'

May regarded him closely. He wasn't eating as well as she would have liked and he was finding his confinement to bed very irksome.

'Would you like a game of draughts?' she asked, regretting her inability to play chess. It would have been nice to impress him with her skill, but she had long since admitted failure in that direction. Too many defeats at the hands of her conceited younger brother, she reflected. Her last client, a very dear man, had also tried to teach her but soon gave up. As she thought of him the familiar resentment surfaced. Although in his early sixties, he had been on the point of marrying her when his family intervened. She would have been well set up financially by now but the family, waiting for his money, had worked together to make him change his mind.

Roland Gough shook his head. 'I don't think so,' he said. 'My head aches. Do you think we might have some air in here? Open the window, perhaps?'

'Oh no, Mr Gough!' She hurried towards him. 'You could easily catch a chill in your weakened state. Let me pull back the top blanket a little. That will cool you down.'

'I don't want to be cooled down,' he snapped. 'I'm not hot.'

He clutched the blankets to him as though to prevent her taking them by force. He's not himself at all, she told herself. Illness does that to a man. They don't have the resilience of women, poor creatures. Her smile was understanding.

He said, 'That damned fire smokes so in this weather. Just open the window!'

May wagged a finger at him with mock severity. 'I'll open the door for a few minutes if you like. That will freshen the room without putting you in a draught.'

'I want the window open!'

'And I can't allow it. Doctor Clarke will

194

have my guts for garters if you catch a chill.' She wanted to sneak a look at him, to see how he had taken this rather risqué comment about garters, but didn't dare. It was rather exciting to have more power over him than usual. Perhaps now he would see her as a strong woman.

'There you are!' She opened the door a little. To distract him, she said, 'Miss Spinney called round earlier and brought you some calves'-foot jelly. Would you like–'

'No, thank you! I can't bear the stuff!' He frowned. 'My mother was always forcing it down us when we were children. I've never liked it since.'

'Oh, what a shame. So light and full of nourishment.' She tried to imagine him as a small boy and envied his mother. Roland could be stubborn and no doubt his mother had had many battles with him. Smiling at the thought, she crossed once more to the window and let out a cry of astonishment. Mrs Gough, in a mackintosh and wellington boots, was hurrying down the drive, half hidden by her umbrella. May's eyes narrowed. There was something almost furtive about the way her employer scurried along.

'Good heavens! What on earth is Mrs Gough doing out on a day like this?' She turned. 'She must be going somewhere important to risk a soaking.'

Mr Gough stared at her. 'I've no idea – but knowing Ella, I'm sure she has a very good reason.'

'Oh, she *must*. Poor soul. She'll get drenched!' No need to mention the protective clothing and umbrella.

'A little rain won't hurt her.'

It seemed too good an opportunity to miss. May said innocently, 'Nobody would even pop to the postbox in this rain.'

Mr Gough made no comment and at last she turned towards him. She knew him well enough to be aware that her words had had the desired effect.

She said, 'Shall I read to you? My teacher always said I had a good reading voice. Or the wireless, perhaps.'

'For the third time – *I've got a headache!*' He closed his eyes.

'Then you just lie there and rest and I'll get on with my embroidery. I'll sit by the window – daylight is kinder to the eyes.'

And I shall see when Mrs Gough returns, she thought. That might be interesting. There was gossip in the kitchen about Mrs Gough and Dan Hampton which had filtered through from a friend of a friend of Mr Evans. Some kind of old scandal, it was said, in which the two of them – Mrs Gough and Hampton – were involved. Sadly, it was all rather vague, but it was enough to tell May that Roland deserved better. Unless, of course, he had known the details when he married her. In May's eyes, if that *were* the case it would make Roland little short of a saint.

Seeing that Roland's eyes were still closed, she tiptoed to the door and closed it silently. She fetched her sewing bag and settled herself on a chair. 'I'm putting my initials on all my handkerchiefs. I do think it's important to keep up one's standards.'

He made no answer but breathed in a way which was supposed to indicate that he was asleep. May smiled. It was his way of preventing further conversation. She knew all his little ways. And loved them.

At the end of the drive, Ella turned right into the shrubbery where Daniel had said he would be waiting. The umbrella was soon causing her problems, catching in the rhododendrons and bringing down even more rain. Finally it caught and tore on the low branch of an oak tree. She struggled with it for a moment or two and then, losing patience, closed it. Ignoring the rain on her head, she glanced around. Hopefully she had been unobserved so far, but if challenged she would say she had been to post a letter. It was therefore important that her meeting with Daniel was as brief as possible. So where on earth was he? She had left it to the very last minute and now it seemed that he was going to be late.

'Ella! Over here!'

He emerged from the shadows, beckoning, and she moved to join him, her boots squelching through the deep layer of wet leaves. Daniel's thin coat was very wet, the meagre collar turned up ineffectively around his neck. His hat was sodden and water dripped from the brim. His hands were thrust into his pockets.

He looked ill, she thought, and years older.

'Oh, Daniel,' she said softly, knowing that to hug him would be a mistake.

He said, 'I didn't think you were coming.'

'I shouldn't be here. Listen, Daniel, I'm sorry about everything but I can't give you much. It isn't right – for me, I mean. Roland's been so good about it. I feel badly about deceiving him.'

'You mean you can give me something? God, Ella, you can't imagine how hard it was for me to write that letter. To ask for money. I never thought you would be my last hope... I needed this money. I'm desperate. I sold my clock yesterday.'

Ella gasped. 'The one that stood in your rooms at Oxford? *That* clock?'

They had all visited Daniel in his first year at the university and he had been so proud of the clock. He had been given permission to take it only when he had arranged special insurance. Ella remembered the reverent way he had opened the front so that they could watch the movement more clearly and smell the ancient aroma of polish, dust and what he called 'gracefully ageing wood'. It had been at that moment that Ella decided that she was in love with Daniel Hampton.

He nodded. 'I swore I'd never part with it, but I had to in the end. The devil of it is that it went for less than its true value.' He shook his head. 'I can't believe I'm where I am today. It's all been such a bloody mess, all these years.'

Ella was glad she had overcome her scruples and brought him *something*. The thought of him waiting here for her, miserable and wet, and going away disappointed was more than she could bear. This would be her last glimpse of him and she would have preferred to remember him happy and well.

She said, 'We don't have much time and I just want to say that ... that I didn't realise until now how much you loved my mother. I wanted to believe otherwise. I wanted to believe it was *me* you really wanted... Will you ever forgive me?'

'I forgave you years ago, if that's any comfort. You couldn't have known how badly it would all turn out. I'll always love her. I wish it weren't so, but it is.'

'I loved you and then I hated you and

now...' She shuddered as a trickle of rain ran down her neck, then made an effort to be practical. 'This is ridiculous. Here.' She thrust a small package into his hand. 'I can't get any money, but it's something you can sell. Roland won't know it's gone. It was my great aunt's and it's quite valuable.'

Wiping rain from his eyes, Daniel opened the handkerchief and stared at the gold band with its large sapphire and small diamonds. 'Your great-aunt's ring? Ella, I can't take this.'

'Yes, you can. You should get about thirty pounds for it. Less, and they're trying to cheat you. And Daniel...' She took a deep breath. 'I've promised myself this is the last contact there must be between us. *Ever.* I mean it. You must promise never to write to me again or try to see me or Penny.'

He shivered as a gust of wind shook the leaves above them, sending down more droplets. 'How is she?'

'Very well. You must promise.'

'If I must, then I do.'

'Don't look so stricken. It's because of what I owe to Roland.'

'He's not the man for you, Ella.'

She swallowed. 'Maybe not,' she told him, 'but that's my fault, not his. I threw myself at him to try and forget *you*. Poor Roland didn't know what was happening. But I won't hear a word against him. He's been so good to me, in his own way.'

Regret choked her and for a moment she couldn't speak. Rain spattered on to her hair and she hunched deeper into her mackintosh. Knowing that it was all over – no, it was worse than that. Knowing that there had never been anything between them saddened her immeasurably. Her youthful histrionics had caused so much unhappiness and she could never put it right; could never hope to make amends. Blinking back tears, she said, 'You must promise me that, Daniel. I need to be sure that there won't be anything else to fear.'

'I promise – and thank you. You'll never know how important this is for me ... for what I have to do.'

She didn't understand the last remark and he was obviously not going to explain, so she watched in silence as he rewrapped the ring and slipped it into the inside pocket of his coat. The rain continued unabated and Ella thought the dreary sound would haunt her for years to come. Unwillingly, she found herself thinking about his wife. What was she like – and how happy were they? He had never mentioned children. Did they have any? It hurt to imagine another woman giving him the family Ella had wanted to give him.

With an effort she said, 'You're married, I hear.'

His expression changed. 'For my sins. It was a mistake. I thought she could make me forget, but I was wrong. And wrong to drag her back to England with me. She liked South Africa and her parents are still there.' He shook his head. 'I sometimes think that all this is divine judgement.'

Ella felt helpless under the weight of his misery. 'Is He that sort of God?' she asked. 'Isn't He supposed to forgive sinners?'

'Not this sinner!' He gave her a long look that was heavy with regret. 'May I kiss you goodbye?' he whispered.

Ella stiffened. 'I'm not Lydia.'

'You're her daughter.'

'The daughter she hated.'

'She didn't hate you.' He wiped his wet face with a wet hand. 'She always loved you. Just before she died...'

Ella felt her fragile composure slipping. 'Don't tell me!' she begged. 'I don't care whether she did or not. What mattered to me was *you* – and you didn't love me, did you, Daniel? I can face the truth now.'

'No, I didn't – but I was fond of you.'

'For *her* sake?'

'I suppose so.'

She leaned forward and put one hand to his face. 'I adored you, Daniel.'

'Or thought you did.'

'No, it was real. First love is painfully real. Misguided, maybe, and hopeless from the start but – but *real,* Daniel.'

With a long sigh, she drew him close. Their kiss was a brief, sad affair, full of confusion – anguish for the present and regrets for the past.

She laughed shakily. 'Look at us! Two drowned rats! Oh God, Daniel!' Tears pressed against her eyelids. 'You must go. Please! Just go!'

The tears were warm against her cheeks as she fumbled for a handkerchief and for a moment she couldn't stem the flow. When she opened her eyes again she was alone.

When May saw Mrs Gough returning she glanced quickly at her patient and, seeing that he was genuinely sleeping, put down her sewing and hurried silently from the room. Watching from the landing, she saw that Annie had been summoned and watched as Mrs Gough took off her mackintosh and sat on a chair while Annie pulled off her boots.

Annie said, 'You're wet through, ma'am!'

'Please don't fuss, Annie.'

'And look at your poor old brolly! It's got a nasty tear in it.'

'It must have been when the wind caught it. It probably snagged against the railings. I'll have to fish out one of the others.'

'Shall I bring you a hot drink? It might save you from getting a chill.' Annie peered into her mistress's face. 'Mrs Gough! You've been–'

'Yes, yes! Bring a pot of tea to my room, please, Annie.'

She was struggling to sound normal, thought May, but not succeeding. There was a tell-tale tremor in her voice.

'Very well, Mrs Gough.'

So what had Annie seen, May wondered with growing excitement. *'You've been–'* what? Crying? Was that what Annie was going to say? May's lips tightened. Mrs Gough was definitely up to something and she was determined to know more. She wasn't in the habit of gossiping with the rest of the staff, but she would try to speak to Annie over supper. Somehow, too, she must alert Roland to his wife's odd behaviour. Nothing too obvious, but he must be left in no doubt about her true nature. May went quietly back into his bedroom, her mind already busy with ideas. Ella Gough might well have feet of clay, but she could prove a formidable enemy. If there was going to be a battle, May needed to be ready for it.

That evening Ella took Penny to see Roland. She had warned her daughter that her father was very tired. As they went in, Nurse Baisley came forward with her usual false smile.

'Penny, dear! How nice of you to visit your

daddy. I know he's missed you.' She took hold of the little girl's hand and went on, 'We've got a nasty headache and a bit of a temperature, I'm afraid. Better if you both keep your distance, I think.'

Penny said, 'What's a tempacher, Daddy?'

He smiled. 'Nothing to worry about, darling. But it's good to see you. Soon be the party day, won't it?'

She nodded. 'A few more days. Can I sit on the bed, Daddy?'

Nurse Baisley said, 'I think not, Penny. Just in case Daddy has caught the flu from poor Mr Saville.'

Startled, Ella said, 'Flu? Do you really think–'

'I'm just being cautious, Mrs Gough.' Nurse Baisley folded her arms. 'I never did think it was a wise move to bring him into the house. I was going from one to the other, you see.'

Ella looked at her husband. 'How do you actually *feel?*'

'It's my head. I need some fresh air, but apparently opening the window is against the rules.' His tone was irritable, Ella noticed with surprise. He was in a strange mood.

Penny asked, 'Why is it against the rules, Daddy?'

Nurse Baisley had flushed angrily. 'I simply suggested that the cold air might...'

Ella bridled. 'It certainly *is* rather stuffy in here.' She walked across to the window, unfastened it and pushed up the lower half. 'Five minutes won't hurt you,' she told Roland, ignoring the nurse. 'They're very keen on fresh air at Sunningford, so it can't be exactly dangerous.' She turned to Penny. 'Show Daddy the picture you coloured for him and then you had better go back to Mrs Granger.'

Nurse Baisley gave Ella a challenging look. 'I think perhaps you should curtail your own visit, Mrs Gough,' she said. 'Your husband is rather tired.'

Ella's smile was frosty. 'I think I'll decide how long I stay, but I'll bear what you say in mind.'

Roland turned to Nurse Baisley. 'Why don't you go downstairs and have a cup of tea and a chat? I'm sure you could do with half an hour away from the sick-room.'

The nurse hesitated, then said, 'You're always so considerate, Mr Gough. That would be most welcome.' She walked to the door and went out.

Roland duly studied the picture Penny had drawn for him. 'A horse and cart. How clever of you, darling!'

When Penny had left the room Ella drew up a chair beside the bed. 'So are you going down with the flu, Roland?'

'Of course not. She fusses... Thanks for

the fresh air! We had a battle and I lost. She's so domineering, that woman.' He took her hand. 'So ... what have you been up to today?'

'Very little really. I've designed a poster for the Autumn Fair and the printer's coming to fetch it first thing tomorrow. I spoke to the broker and confirmed the changes to the investments. It was less trouble than I expected.'

'You should have left that to me, Ella. I feel so damned useless.'

'I have to warn you that we lost quite a lot on the copper, but you were expecting that.'

He nodded. He seemed distracted, she thought.

'But there's nothing we can do about it,' she told him. 'I'm not prepared to go into mourning over it and you're not to, either. It's only money.' She laughed without much conviction.

He shook his head. 'You only say that because you've never been without it.'

Ella was silent, thinking of Daniel.

Roland said, 'Is that all then? All that you've done today?'

'Yes.'

'You haven't been out, then?'

She laughed. 'In *this* weather? Roland, please!'

'You're usually busy with correspondence until lunchtime.'

'Not today. I didn't feel up to letter-writing somehow, but I must get in touch with–' She broke off, alerted by his expression. 'What is it? Why the interrogation?'

He stared at his clasped hands. 'The dragon said you'd been to the postbox.'

Ella felt suddenly cold, undeceived by the too-casual tone of her husband's voice. He had set a trap for her and she had fallen straight into it. Before she could collect her thoughts, he went on.

'She said you were soaked through and had torn your umbrella. I thought it must have been something important...'

'Since when has Nurse Baisley been some kind of spy?' Ella's voice shook.

He was watching her. 'So you must have forgotten.'

'Forgotten what?'

'That you wrote a letter and went out to post it. What was so urgent?'

Fear and anger paralysed her for what seemed like ages, but at last Ella found her voice. 'That damned woman! She's a trouble-maker. She's...'

'I asked you what was so important, Ella.'

Ella covered her face with her hands. She would have to tell him because the truth was less damning than anything he might imagine. 'I didn't want you to know she began. She looked up. 'I had to see someone...'

'Daniel Hampton, I suppose?'

'Yes. It wasn't my idea, Roland, but it seemed best at the time. I was so worried about how you would see it. He sent me a letter asking for a loan. He said he was desperate and–'

'And you believed him.'

'Yes. He had no job and a worthless reference... I was going to ignore it, but then I thought he might ... might keep badgering me and I wanted it all to be over. I wanted him out of my life forever. I met him at the end of the drive and gave him my great-aunt's ring.'

He frowned.

She said, 'I've never worn it because I don't like it. It's rather a heavy stone and it doesn't suit my hand. I made him promise never to get in touch with me again.' She swallowed hard. 'He looked terrible. A thin coat and...'

'Save your pity!'

She said nothing.

'And is that all? Nothing else happened? Nothing else was said?'

'Isn't it enough?'

'God, Ella, you're such a fool.' He put a hand to his forehead. 'I'll have to take a couple of aspirins.'

Miserably Ella looked at him. 'Aren't you going to say anything else? About him?'

'I think you've made a mistake, but it's too late now. I doubt if we've seen the last of

Daniel Hampton. You've shown yourself to be gullible. Easily manipulated. He'll ask again; they always do.'

Ella stood up and walked to the window. 'I thought it was for the best. I trust him. I'm sure he meant what he said.'

'You've been a fool, Ella. I'm sorry, but you have. You've been taken in by a con man. That's all he is...'

She swung round, her voice rising. 'Don't call him that. You don't know him as I do. He won't break his promise.'

'Of course he will. That was just the beginning. Christ Almighty, Ella. Why didn't you come to me?'

'Because I knew you'd be unwilling to give him a chance.'

Roland glared. 'He played on your pity, Ella, and he's no doubt laughing about you – what a soft touch you were. Can't you see him for what he is? Or don't you want to admit that he's not the charmer you thought he was?'

'I tell you he's genuine. Daniel Hampton has integrity. You're prejudiced because I once loved him.'

'It sounds as though you still do.'

'You must think what you damn well like!'

He stared at her balefully. 'We'll see, won't we?'

Ella fought to keep calm. 'And Nurse Baisley is getting a sight too sure of herself.

I object to her reporting on me ... and I dislike the way she tries to monopolise you as though I have no say in your welfare.'

His smile was unkind.

'What?' she demanded.

'Nothing.'

'No, tell me. I know that look!'

'I thought how like you this is. Attack is the best means of defence, isn't it? I criticise your behaviour because you lie to me about Hampton and you pick a quarrel with the nurse. She wasn't reporting on you, as *you* put it. All she said was, "Oh dear, poor Mrs Gough" – or something similar. How was she to know you had something to hide?'

'I don't like her – and neither do you. You call her the dragon.'

'For God's sake, Ella!' He sighed heavily. 'My head is thumping, I feel like death, and the last thing I want is an argument about that bloody man.'

'I'll call the bloody nurse, shall I?'

He stared at her with obvious irritation. 'Now you're being childish.'

Ella's anger, quick to rise, faded as quickly. She felt exhausted, penitent. If he had caught the flu... Slowly she turned back to him. 'It was unwise to keep Mr Saville here. Nurse Baisley was right about that. I'm sorry.'

'Forget it.' He closed his eyes, shutting her out.

'Shall I get your aspirins?'

'No, thank you. We pay someone to do that. Go and find Penny. Give her a hug and a kiss from me. I think she's lonely.'

Ella experienced another rush of guilt. Was her daughter lonely? She had never even noticed. 'I'll ask Annie to let her make some pastry,' she suggested.

Roland opened his eyes. 'It's *you* she needs, Ella, not Annie.' He turned over and drew the covers around him. 'And shut the window before you go, please? I'm feeling shivery.'

Mortified, Ella hovered uncertainly. The abrupt dismissal rankled. She wanted to defend herself, but her confidence was at a low ebb. She closed the offending window with a bang and stalked out of the room with an appearance of defiance. Once outside, however, her steps faltered as she thought of her daughter. Lonely? Why hadn't *she* seen that Penny was lonely? If only they had been able to have a second child. She closed the door and, thoroughly demoralised, leaned back against it.

'Ella Gough,' she whispered. 'You don't seem able to get *anything* right!'

She blinked back tears. Stop feeling sorry for yourself, she thought. Think about Penny. There was a new jigsaw puzzle somewhere. The teddy bear's picnic, was it? Teddy bear's something, anyway. She brightened. They could do that together and tomorrow afternoon, if it stopped raining, she would take Penny to the park.

Just before six o'clock that same evening, Lizzie groped under the doormat for the key and let herself into the flat.

'Dan! I'm back!'

There was no answer, so she lit the stove and filled the kettle before taking off her coat which was still damp from the rain. She hung it behind the back door and stood for a moment listening for sounds from the front room which served as the bedroom.

'Dan!' She went through into the passage and into the front room which was empty. 'Where are you?'

She was in no hurry to tell him her news, which was that she had been turned down for two jobs. Back in the kitchen, she spooned tea into the pot and added boiling water. Without giving it time to brew properly, she poured herself a cup and added three spoonfuls of sugar. The baker had said they'd already taken someone on, but had given her a rock cake by way of consolation and she had eaten it on the way to the second place. This was a small builders' merchant who wanted a girl in the office, but Lizzie couldn't use a typewriter so that was a waste of time. She had offered to learn, but they couldn't wait.

Wrapping her hands round the cup, she sipped the tea, blew on it and sipped again. Maybe Dan had had better luck, although he was not very hopeful that he would get another job as a gardener. That disgusting reference! She sighed. Damn the Goughs to hell! Even the kid. But mostly damn Ella. It was her fault they were in this mess. From what little Dan had told her, it was Ella who had lost him his job – Ella who had had a schoolgirl crush on him and spied on him when he was courting and then got him into trouble with his girlfriend's family.

'Spiteful bitch!' she muttered. 'You think you're so wonderful... Well, you're not. You're a spoilt little madam!' Although Dan had denied it, Lizzie strongly suspected that Dan had been in love with Ella. He had said she was beautiful and there was something in his voice when he spoke about her. Dan could lie, she knew that. There had been several occasions when she had caught him out.

'Ella bloody Gough!' She had a sudden desire to see the woman for herself. Maybe she would. Maybe she'd think of an excuse and go to the house. She could pretend to be looking for him; ask if he worked there. Pretend to be his long-lost sister... But then she'd probably only see the maid. People like Ella Gough didn't open their own front doors.

A faint mewing came from somewhere behind her and she turned. When she opened the door of the cellar the black cat sprang out, mewing loudly.

'What are you doing in there?'

She closed the cellar door firmly. The animal had been lurking around for a couple of weeks, trying to curry favour, but Dan had said 'No'. He liked dogs and had agreed that, when they could afford it, they would get a puppy. When they could afford it. *If.* She sighed. The cat wrapped itself around her legs, purring.

'Out!' said Lizzie, opening the back door. She grabbed the cat and dropped it on to the sodden back doormat. It glared at her, arching its back, but she closed the door on it – and then opened it again. She poured some milk into a saucer and put it down, watching while the animal lapped greedily. When the saucer was empty she picked it up.

'And don't you tell!' she warned, putting the cat outside again. Closing the door, she went back to her cup of tea. For a moment or two she allowed herself a fantasy in which Dan came bursting in with wonderful news. If he did, they would rush out to get fish and chips. If not it was egg on toast.

Five minutes later Lizzie drained the cup, kicked off her damp shoes and made her way along to the bedroom to find her

215

slippers. As she leaned down to pull them out from beneath the bed, she felt a wave of nausea and straightened up. Her face was pale and there was a sheen of perspiration on her forehead as she waited for the faintness to pass.

She covered her face with her hands and groaned. Sure in her own mind that she was carrying Dan's child, she was finally acknowledging the fact that she wanted it. If *he* wanted it. What terrified her was the thought of *having* it. Giving birth to it.

'Oh God!' she whispered. In her mind the birth of a child had meant the death of her older sister. The baby had lived only five hours, but her sister had outlived her by only a day. Lizzie stared sightlessly into the past, seeing herself in her nightdress, aged six, crouched on the stairs with her sister's screams still ringing in her ears. Cold and frightened, the child overheard the hurried consultations in the hall below.

They had forgotten all about her, assuming her to be fast asleep in bed. Lizzie had wanted a glimpse of the baby she had been promised, but instead of the excitement she expected she had sensed a deepening anxiety that grew into panic as her father failed to return with the doctor.

She was still on the stairs, her heart racing uncomfortably, as the midwife came out into the hall with a small, silent bundle wrapped in a piece of white sheeting. Catching sight of Lizzie, the woman's face crumpled.

'Best get back to bed, lovey. There'll be nothing to see.'

'I want to see the baby.'

'*No*, lovey.' Tears ran down her face. 'There's nothing for you.'

Lizzie was aware of an unknown threat. 'I want to see Brenda.'

'Brenda's very ... tired.' She sniffed hard and fumbled awkwardly for a handkerchief to dab her eyes. 'You go back to bed like a good girl and don't wake young Frankie. Your mother'll talk to you by and by.'

Obediently, Lizzie had retraced her steps to the bedroom she still shared with four-year-old Frank. As she slid back into bed, she was shivering...

'Oh, Dan!' She was shivering *now*.

The horror of that night and the sad weeks that followed were indelibly printed on her memory. 'Please, Dan,' she whispered fearfully, 'don't let me die.'

Ella turned the page. 'And the three little pigs lived happily ever after.' She closed the book.

Penny sighed happily. 'They always say that,' she said. 'Does everybody live happily ever after? Do we?'

'I think so.'

Ella put the book on the bedside table while Penny snuggled deeper into the bed. A blue rabbit, a pink pig and Jessica the doll were carefully tucked in beside her.

'Night-night, Penny,' said Ella. 'Sleep tight.'

'Shall we say our prayers again, Mummy?'

'No. I'm sure God heard them the first time.' She kissed her daughter.

'Can I have a drink of water?'

'No. It's time to go to sleep.'

'Will you leave the light on?'

'Yes. And tomorrow, if the weather improves, we'll go for that walk in the park, and if they're dry enough you can go on the swings and the roundabout and...'

Penny said sleepily. 'We might see Mr Hampton.'

Ella stared. 'Mr Hampton?'

'The gardener man.'

'What makes you think we might meet him?'

'He goes to the park. He told me he did.'

'With – with his *children?*' Ella was holding her breath. Suppose they met Dan with his wife and children? She didn't know how she would bear it.

'He hasn't got any, and that makes him sad.'

'Then why does he go there?'

'To be on his own and to look at the flowers. He hasn't got a proper garden. He looks at the flowers and he thinks.'

Ella was busily absorbing this information when Annie knocked on the door.

'It's Mr Marriott, called to see Mr Gough. I put him in the sitting room.'

'Who's Mr – oh! the godson. I remember. Did he say what he wants?'

'He's brought something for Mr Gough.'

'Tell him that I'll be down in a moment to talk to him.' She gave Penny another kiss and two small arms wound themselves around her neck. The child smelled of soap and fresh linen and Ella breathed it in. Poor Daniel. No 'tiddlers'. She tried to imagine him walking in the park, alone with his thoughts.

'Mummy loves you,' she said as she straightened up. 'See you in the morning.'

Downstairs Charles Marriott waited, a small brown paper parcel in his hand. In grey slacks and a tweed jacket, he looked comfortably at ease. He smiled at the sight of her and she was surprised just how pleased she was to see him again. Since their first meeting she had forgotten all about him, but now she returned the smile with a lightening of her heart.

'I'm afraid Roland isn't up to visitors today,' she began as they sat down.

'I'm sorry to hear that.'

'He did so enjoy your visit the other day

and seemed to be improving, but today he has a headache and is resting now.'

He smiled. 'I should have rung first. I picked up a lot of bad habits in the States.'

His laugh was pleasantly low and his suntanned face made his eyes look very grey. Ella said, 'Roland is running a temperature. The nurse thinks it may be flu ... oh!' She looked at him anxiously. 'I didn't mean...'

'That maybe he caught it from my godfather?' His eyes darkened. 'I do hope not. That would be too unfair after you had been so kind. Whatever can I say?'

'There's no need for you to say anything. I did what seemed best at the time and I don't regret it. If I was wrong...' The nurse's accusing words still troubled her, however, and now Roland's anger had increased her doubts. 'My aunt warned me once not to take on too much blame!' she said. 'She's a wise old lady and I know she's right but...' She attempted a light laugh though her voice shook. 'Anyway, it's probably just a feverish cold.'

He regarded her with a thoughtful look on his face. 'You mustn't be too hard on yourself. We all make mistakes.'

'Not like mine!' The words came out with unexpected bitterness.

Charles' expression changed. 'Don't be too sure, Ella. My mistake had fatal

220

results... I was holidaying in Sorrento with a close friend a good few years ago now.' He swallowed. 'Poor Don ... I talked him into a midnight swim although he wasn't keen. It was simply bravado on my part... Somehow he drowned.'

'Drowned! How *dreadful* for you!' Ella was horrified.

'We'll never know how it happened, that's the awful thing. There was no strong tide ... no rocks. One minute he was there and the next – nothing. Silence. I thought he was kidding about at first. Trying to scare me... They called it misadventure.' He shrugged. 'I still go over and over it in my mind searching for answers, but I no longer blame myself. It took a long time, but eventually I came to terms with it. I don't think he'd want me to suffer for the rest of my life. So whatever happened in *your* past is over, Ella. You have to go on with your life.'

Ella longed to be reassured, but found herself blurting out a confession. 'But it was different for me. You see, I *was* to blame. It was no accident. I *wanted* to cause them – I deliberately...' She faltered. There was no way she could tell him, no reason for him to care. 'The trouble is that it's still going on, years later...' Daniel's haunted face was crystal-clear in her mind. Ella drew a deep breath. 'I think we should talk about something else,' she suggested. 'May I ask about the intriguing-looking parcel?'

He looked as though he might say more, but decided against it and gave the parcel a little tap. 'This is a diary which was given to me a few months ago by a woman whose great-grandfather fought in the Civil War – the American Civil War. It's quite fascinating and I thought your husband – apart from enjoying reading it – might find it a suitable subject for one of his articles.'

'I'm sure he'd find it fascinating. Would you like me to give it to him, or would you prefer to call in again with it? You'd be very welcome.'

'I think I'd like the excuse to call again,' he told her with a smile. 'I enjoyed talking to him and I know a lot of the background to the diary which he would find interesting. What I'll do is leave it for him to read, and then we can discuss it when I come next time.' He stood up.

Ella hesitated, standing up also. 'Would you like to stay to dinner? I'm sure Annie will manage a little extra, but it won't be wildly exciting. I think it's a beef pie.'

His regret was obvious as he said, 'I'd love to accept, but I've been invited to dine with a friend.' He glanced at his wristwatch. 'Will you ask me again some time?'

'Certainly. I had intended to – Roland was very keen – so perhaps we could arrange it when he's better. Have we got an address or telephone number for you?'

Outside in the hall, Charles gave her the details and she wrote them in the telephone book. Then she looked up at him. 'And thank you for your kind words. I'd like to feel better about myself, but it's not easy.'

He took both her hands in his and looked steadily into her eyes. 'Listen, Ella. Try to see it this way. Looking back, would you do the same again? Knowing how it turned out and where it led? If not, then you're not the same person that you were then. You were obviously much younger when whatever it was happened?'

She nodded, longing for reassurance. 'I was seventeen, but I knew exactly what I was doing. I was in a vengeful fury.'

'I was twenty-one when Donald died.' He stared into the past. 'His parents were *so* understanding. They didn't once reproach me, although he was their only child. Can you imagine that? There isn't a day that passes when I don't think of him. It must be so much worse for them. Birthdays, Christmas...'

Ella sighed. 'It wasn't like that for me because it *wasn't* an accident. It was...' She shrugged. 'Malice aforethought!' Never, she thought, could she tell this man how badly she had behaved, how much she had longed to inflict pain.

'But why go on suffering after all these years? Punishing yourself won't undo the harm, Ella. People change. Life goes on. You have to let the past go.'

She tried to smile, but her mouth felt stiff.

'Poor Ella,' he said softly. Suddenly he stepped closer and, ignoring the startled look on her face, put his arms around her. He said, 'Don't worry. It's just a token of sympathy from a fellow-sufferer.'

Almost at once he released her. 'Well, I'll be on my way and look forward to hearing from you sometime. Please give Roland my best wishes. I hope he feels better soon.'

Ella closed the door behind him. Charles Marriott, she reflected. What a kind man! Not that she could take much comfort from his advice, but he had been well intentioned. As she turned back her brow cleared. She would see how Roland was feeling and give him the diary Charles had brought for him.

As she went up the stairs, Ella was remembering Charles's words and at the same time wondering what they could serve when he came to dinner. Outside Roland's room she stopped, her hand on the doorknob. It dawned on her that in fact she *did* feel a little happier. Could she stop punishing herself now that Daniel was out of her life forever? She had given him the ring; tried to make amends ... Perhaps the worst *was* over. Perhaps she *could* allow herself to forget. She drew a long breath. Perhaps, after all, she could make a fresh start.

Chapter Seven

The letter came in the first post two days later. Ella stood in the dining room and opened it. The words had been cut from a newspaper or magazine, giving it a crazy, almost humorous appearance. It was brief and to the point:

...Put twenty pounds in a strong envelope and leave it in the summer-house after ten tonight or tomorrow. Tell the police and you'll see your story in all the papers...

Blackmail! *Blackmail.* Ella, suddenly weak, groped for the nearest chair and sat down. She read and reread the letter and still she found it hard to believe. More than anything, she was unbearably hurt and shocked by the betrayal. After his promise. After all she'd said to Roland in Daniel's defence...

'Oh God, Daniel! Don't do this to me!' she whispered. The words were barely audible as she struggled for breath. She felt as though someone had dealt her a resounding body blow somewhere below her heart. Amidst the chaos of her thoughts was the grim realisation that her husband had been right; she had been an utter fool. Stupid and gullible.

'You – you utter swine!' The use of an oath did nothing to relieve her misery. She had felt so ... so superior, taking pity on him, generously giving him her ring. While he thanked her with sweet words, he had known that he would blackmail her. The thought of their kiss made her cringe with disgust.

'Hypocrite!' She crumpled the letter, on the point of tearing it to shreds when another thought restrained her – one that added immeasurably to her distress. The man she had loved was blackmailing her and this piece of paper was *evidence*. Which meant that a crime had been committed.

Annie came into the room with a tray. 'I've done you some kidneys this morning to go with the bacon. Mr Gough had some as well, although I don't know whether he's eaten them. Nurse Baisley says he's very poorly. Bit of a chill. Nasty draught from the window, she reckons.'

Ella said, 'From the window? Oh... Yes.' She thought she might faint and leaned forward as soon as she was alone to rest her head in her hands. Breathing slowly, she tried to ignore the queasiness in her stomach and to control the violent shivering that had attacked her entire body.

'Sweet tea!' she murmured and poured herself a cup with unsteady hands. Cooling it with extra milk, she sipped it gratefully and tried to think. There must be something she could do; some way out of the appalling situation into which she had blundered.

'Eat something,' she told herself. Her appetite had vanished, but if she left the food untouched Annie would be suspicious and start asking awkward questions. She chewed a mouthful of bacon and buttered bread and forced it down her unwilling throat. At all costs she must prevent Roland from discovering what had happened. She told herself that he wasn't fit for any more worries, but the truth was that she couldn't bear to tell him. Even Roland would be tempted to gloat – and who could blame him, she thought with bitterness. He might not actually say, 'I told you so', but it would be implicit in every word he spoke. She would have no answer to that; he had been proved right.

Ella washed the food down with a mouthful of tea. Thank goodness Penny was eating in the nursery with Mrs Granger this morning – and that Roland wasn't sharing the meal. He would have seen at once that something was wrong.

'Think, Ella, *think!*'

She studied the postmark, but it was blurred. The name and address were in block capitals – probably written with his left hand so that if he were ever to be challenged in court he could insist... She frowned. In court? Did that mean she was seriously considering going to the police for help? Surely that was the least desirable course of action. She read the note again: *'Tell the police and you'll see your story in all the papers...'*

Ella felt panic taking hold. If Roland saw the old scandal resurrected in the newspapers he would be devastated.

One option was to send Daniel the money, but that would most likely prove to be the thin end of the wedge. And how was she to get hold of such sums without Roland finding out? With a groan of frustration, Ella pushed away her plate. She had never imagined that the day would come when she would hate Daniel Hampton, but today her thoughts towards him were anything but fond.

'I could willingly kill you, Daniel!'

If only he could get run down by a bus, fall under a train or be struck by lightning ... but the chances of fate intervening on her behalf appeared remote.

Unable to bear the uncharacteristic direction of her thoughts, she pushed back her chair and moved restlessly to the window. That damned summer-house! The scene of the original crime was now to witness further unsavoury incidents. The thought of Daniel creeping through the shrubbery to retrieve the money infuriated her, but there seemed to be no way round the dilemma. She couldn't even write to him to beg him to spare her because she didn't know where he lived.

'I have to get out of here!' she thought with desperation. Hurrying into the hall, she struggled into a warm coat and let herself out into the garden. She walked across the damp grass towards the summer-house and, reaching it, opened the door and went inside. That's where they had been, she thought. Stretched uncomfortably along the bench seat, wrapped in each other's arms and oblivious to her presence. For a moment then she had watched, fascinated, until the soft animal sounds they made seemed to echo inside her head. Naïve though she was at the age of seventeen, she had realised what was happening. Her mind filled with the thought of revenge, she had raced into the house with her mother's entreaties ringing in her ears. She could still see the dread in her father's eyes as he ran past her towards the summer-house. From the safety of the old swing, Ella had listened through her own anguished sobs to the angry cries and heated exchanges as the row broke over the betrayed lovers.

'And now it's your turn for revenge, Daniel,' she whispered. 'You waited long enough, I must say, but your timing is perfect.' She sat down on the narrow bench and glanced around. The windows were mildewed and there was a small drift of dead leaves in one corner. 'And so is your sense of place.'

She sat there for what seemed like forever, held by memories, fuelled by anger and weighed down by despair. For a second time her life and the lives of those she loved would be shattered. There was a terrible and inescapable irony in that.

The police station was unusually busy at three o'clock that afternoon. The desk sergeant was admitting two drunks who had been fighting, another constable waited nearby with a sulky woman with bleached hair and a young cadet was being given a tour of the premises. Ella hovered inside the entrance, trying to gather her courage. There was a strong smell of carbolic overlaid with something worse, and stark grey walls did nothing to lighten the unsympathetic atmosphere. Swing doors at the far end of the corridor allowed cold air to gust in and Ella shivered. One of the overhead lights was minus a bulb, the other dimmed by dust. Behind the counter, two policemen studied a wall map, talking in lowered voices, while another wrote at a small desk, his pen labouring across the page. No one took any notice of her and, for something to do, Ella examined a notice board. It bore a variety of lists and a poster of a man wanted for armed robbery. A child's blue glove had been pinned to one corner of the board.

The sulky woman caught sight of her.

'Who you staring at?' she demanded.

Ella, her throat tight and dry, could only shake her head and look away. A large clock on the wall ticked loudly, as though signalling her forthcoming humiliation. Two policemen banged in through the far door, rushed past laughing excitedly and disappeared through into one of the offices. She wondered what they had found to amuse them and whether her own story would cause further sniggers. Not that she intended to disclose everything. As far as possible the past would remain hidden if she had her way.

'Can I help you?'

The sergeant was free now and was looking at her enquiringly.

'I'd like to speak to someone about this letter.' She handed it to him and waited.

From somewhere nearby a door clanged and a man's voice shouted incoherently. This was followed by a fierce banging on what she imagined was a cell door.

'Shut your noise!'

Further banging and a stream of obscenities followed.

'I said pack it in!'

She wondered if blackmail was punished by a jail sentence...

'You'd better see Detective Inspector Hall,' said the desk sergeant, picking up a telephone and dialling to another room. 'Woman with a blackmail note,' he said. Replacing the phone, he gave her an impersonal smile. 'He's coming down, if you'd like to wait there.'

He indicated the chair and she sat down again. The clock showed that she had only been there seven minutes. It felt longer.

The detective took his time. He came down ten minutes later and the sergeant handed him the note. Impressed by her undeniable good looks, he immediately shook her hand and led her courteously up to his office. Here the cramped quarters were intensified by the one small window and the litter of papers and folders that covered every flat surface. The two of them were alone, Ella noted with relief.

When they were seated he said, 'Tell me about this, Mrs Gough.' His voice was unemotional, but his grey eyes were shrewd and his lean face not unattractive.

Ella had practised her 'speech'. 'Many years ago I did something that upset the writer of this note and now...'

He raised his eyebrows. 'You know who sent it?'

She nodded. 'Yes, but I'd rather not say. All I want...'

'But there's no handwriting. Nothing to tell you. The postmark's blurred.'

'It could only be this man. No one else knows anything.'

He raised his eyebrows. 'So it's a male.'

'Yes.' She would have to be careful.

'You have an address?'

'No, although I may be able to get hold of it.' Roland might still have Daniel's letter of application, which presumably would bear an address. 'If I can, I'll phone it through. All I really want to know is how to deal with ... with this matter as quietly as possible. I need advice. I don't...' She blinked furiously, already close to tears. 'I don't want my husband to know about it.'

'He may have to know.'

'He's very ill, Sergeant.' That was almost true.

'Detective Inspector.'

'I'm sorry.' Her carefully prepared words were slipping away. 'I wouldn't want him to know – but particularly now, because of his health. He's had a heart attack and ... and there's something else. His younger brother is an M.P. Elected in a by-election quite recently, actually, but...'

'Hmm!' He pursed his lips. 'A bit tricky. I can see that.'

'Roland would hate to do anything which

could reflect badly on his brother. And so would I, of course.'

'Mrs Gough, is what this man knows *very* unsavoury? And are the newspapers going to be that interested?'

Ella thought about it. 'It was a dreadful scandal at the time.'

'But now?'

She wavered, torn between hope and despair. Was he suggesting that she was taking the note too seriously? *Was* that what she was doing? 'I shouldn't like to risk it,' she said at last. 'It could be damaging. It certainly would be embarrassing.'

He looked at her, then smiled. 'Well, we wouldn't like you to be embarrassed, Mrs Gough. Let's take a closer look at the note.' He drew a pad of paper towards him, wrote something and underlined it. He smiled at her again and suggested a cup of tea, but Ella declined.

After a pause he said, 'Believe me, I do sympathise, Mrs Gough, but how can you expect me to deal with this if you won't tell me his name? Don't you think that's a bit unreasonable? Unless you *want* to give him the money – and all the rest he will ask for over the coming months... Believe me, treating them with kid gloves never works. If you want us to help you put a stop to this...'

'It's just that I know he's feeling desperate right now.'

'And you *aren't* feeling desperate, I suppose?'

Ella was silent, her resolve slipping away. During the day her anger had faded as she tried to put herself in Daniel's place. She wasn't going to be vindictive, but it had to stop. 'I've tried to imagine what he might do if I simply ignore the note. And I don't know. Do you think he'd give up?'

'Is he bluffing, you mean?' He shook his head. 'He'll send another demand. It happens all the time, Mrs Gough. I do have some experience of these people. And they're not "desperate", they're *evil.*'

Ella drew a deep breath. 'I don't want him sent to prison; I just want him to stop. I thought maybe you could give him a warning. A caution or whatever you call it?'

He leaned back, tilting the chair precariously, his hands clasped behind his head. 'Is this man a member of your family?' he asked.

'No. He's – he *was* – a friend of the family. There was a … bit of an upset and he blames me.'

'A former lover, then?' His tone remained neutral, but Ella couldn't meet his eyes.

'*No!*'

He was regarding her with obvious disbelief.

She said, 'Well, something of the sort.'

The silence deepened and Ella could see

how she must appear to this coldly professional man. A silly, lovesick woman who didn't want the blackmailer punished. She felt her face burn with embarrassment.

Abruptly he sat forward and made several notes on his pad. When he stopped he asked, 'How can we caution the blackmailer if we don't know his name? I hate to say this, Mrs Gough, but you're wasting my time.'

Ella met his gaze and conceded defeat. 'I'm sorry. You're quite right. I'm being unreasonable.' In a halting voice she told him as concisely as she could about the way Daniel had come back into her life, the sacking, the ring.

He finished writing and looked up. 'If you can find out where he lives, we'll send someone round later today to warn him off. If it doesn't work – and I doubt it will – we'll think again. But don't – repeat *don't* – leave any money for him. That would undermine our warning to him. If you phone tomorrow and ask for me, I'll bring you up to date.'

She recognised the note of dismissal and stood up. 'Thank you. I appreciate your help.'

As he accompanied her back to the reception area, he said, 'Try not to worry. It might blow over, though I'm not very hopeful. Anyway, we'll do all we can.'

Outside, Ella gulped in fresh air. She felt

like someone rescued from drowning. The detective had impressed her. A caution from the police would teach Daniel a lesson, and she was sure he wouldn't risk further attention from them. It was going to be all right.

Later that day Constable Smith turned the corner with an aggrieved look on his face. Quarter to seven. He should have been home by now with his feet under the kitchen table and a plate of food in front of him – probably a bit of minced beef with onion and gravy, the way Dot did it best. Instead, the dinner would be drying up in the oven.

'...Ah! Here we are.' He walked up the short path to the door, eyeing with distaste the pebbles which had replaced a front garden. Lazy, that's what some people were. How long did it take to cut a square yard of grass and stick in a few pansies?

He banged the knocker three times and waited, his mouth a tight line. Then he banged again, lifted the letter-box flap and called, 'Police!'

A woman answered the door. Probably been a looker, but a bit scrawny now.

'What?' she demanded. 'And why d'you have to yell like that? Frightened the life out of me.' She looked at him belligerently.

'You didn't answer the first time, that's why.'

'I was out the back. I can't fly, you know.'

He stood as straight as he could and looked down on her. Then he fished his notebook out of his pocket. 'Mr Hampton live here, does he?'

'What if he does? What's he done?'

She didn't look quite so cocky now, he thought with satisfaction. 'Your old man, is he?'

'Maybe.' She looked up and down the street. The curtains moved at the window of the house opposite. 'You'd better come inside,' she told him.

With an exasperated sigh, he followed her into a small front room that smelled of mildew. Refusing her invitation to sit down, he continued his questions.

'And your name is?' He took out a pencil. He'd teach her to cheek a policeman.

'Elizabeth Hampton. Lizzie. Why?'

'Is that DEN?'

She looked at him blankly.

'Your name. Hamp-DEN or -TON?'

'Oh! TON. Why d'you want Dan?'

'I just need to speak to him rather urgently. Could you tell me when he'll be back?'

'No, I can't – and I might not even if I did know. Not unless you tell me what it's about.'

He wrote slowly, with much licking of the pencil stub. 'Now that would be telling.' He gave her a mocking smile. Then he said, 'If you can't be a bit more helpful I could have you up for obstructing the police. Like to see the inside of a police cell, would you?'

The woman took a step backward. She seemed to be thinking. 'I can't tell you,' she said at last, 'because I don't know. I wish I did. If you must know, the blighter's scarpered. Done a bunk. Understand?' She swallowed hard.

Constable Smith hid his surprise. 'What – left you?'

'Yes. Yesterday. Left a note on the bedside table – and this!' She waved her right hand and he saw a ring on her fourth finger. 'Sell it, he says. How far's this going to go, eh?'

The constable shrugged, then he frowned. 'Where'd he get it, I wonder, a nice ring like that?'

'How should I know? Maybe his girlfriend gave it to him.' She folded her arms, effectively hiding the ring.

'Oh, he had a girlfriend, did he?'

'Wouldn't know. I'm not his keeper. If I was, I'd have kept my eyes on him.'

He peered suspiciously at her eyes. She'd been crying – probably over this Hampton bloke. He hardened his heart. Rule number one: never let yourself get involved.

'Might be stolen,' he said. 'The ring.' He was torn between the thought of his supper and the chance that he had stumbled on to something interesting.

'We'll never know, will we, because tomorrow I'm going to sell it.'

He hesitated. What should he do about a suspect ring? All they'd said was ask Daniel Hampton to come into the station and tell him to ask for Detective Inspector Hall. Nothing about dodgy jewellery. 'When in doubt, do nowt.' That's what his Dad had always said. He made a note of the existence of the ring, for future reference.

'What is it? Is it valuable?'

'No idea. So what's he done?'

'A little bit of blackmail.' As soon as the words were out he regretted them. Probably shouldn't have told her, but it was too late now. Not that it mattered if her old man had left her. He'd never know.

Apparently shocked, she stared at him. Then she said, 'Typical!' and then, 'Who's he blackmailing?'

'None of your business, Mrs Hampton. Unless you think you might know.'

'Well, I don't. And I don't want to know. He's gone and good riddance.'

She looked as though she'd be in tears soon, he thought nervously. He put the pencil and notebook away; it had been a wasted journey. 'I'm off then,' he said.

She followed him back to the front door and opened it. 'What'll happen to him?' she asked. 'If you find him, I mean?'

'Not up to me. It'll be up to the detectives. I'm just the messenger.' He tapped his tunic. 'I'm uniform.'

Mrs Hampton put out her tongue at the house opposite and they both watched as the curtains twitched.

'Nice neighbourhood,' she said and shut the door in his face.

Roland was sitting up in bed the following morning when Penny slipped into the room, followed by her mother. The child's face was flushed with excitement and she carried a cardboard shoe-box in her arms, bearing it carefully as though it held the crown jewels.

'Daddy! I've got my new party slippers. I've brought them to show you.'

He felt his heart lift at the sight of her animated face framed with soft curls and his eyes met Ella's. He returned her smile. Whatever she had done wrong, he could forgive her because she had given him this precious child.

He said, 'You've had fun, Ella!' He had promised himself that he would never refer to the Hampton business again. She had been honest with him, which couldn't have been easy.

She stood beside Penny. 'We tried five shops before we found what we wanted!'

Penny opened the box and spread the tissue paper. Then slowly and with huge delight she drew out one of the ballet slippers and offered it to him.

'Pink satin!' he whispered. 'Fit for a princess!'

'Do you like them, Daddy? Really truly?' She waited breathlessly.

'Like them? Of course I do. I like them so much I think *I'd* like a pair.'

Startled, she put both hands over her mouth. 'Oh, Daddy ... I don't think...' She looked at Ella, her eyes wide with doubt.

Ella laughed. 'Daddy's teasing you, sweetie. I don't think they'd look quite right on him, do you?'

Relieved, Penny began to giggle – a high, sweet sound that Roland loved. He said, 'Why don't you put them on and show me how they look?' and watched as Ella knelt to help her daughter. The sight of them together gave him enormous happiness, and he knew he'd been right to forgive his wife her youthful indiscretion. All he wanted was their happiness, because that ensured his own. There had also been some truth in what Ella said about Nurse Baisley. She was very possessive and he would have to speak to her on the subject as soon as he felt stronger. Being so dependent on her just now rendered him vulnerable, and he wanted to speak from a position of strength.

'There we are!' cried Ella and there was his fairy child, dancing around the room, her delicate arms waving this way and that while Ella clapped her hands in delight.

At that moment Nurse Baisley came into the room with a pile of newly ironed laundry and she, too, was full of admiration for the new party slippers.

'And who bought you those?' she asked.

'Daddy – but Mummy took me shopping and we went into hundreds of shops.'

'What a lucky girl you are,' she told Penny, 'to have such a kind Daddy.'

Penny stopped, arms outstretched. 'And Mummy,' she said. 'A kind Daddy *and* a kind Mummy!'

The nurse looked flustered. 'Of course, Penny,' she said. 'I didn't mean...'

Ella smiled. 'Of course you didn't.'

Roland was watching the nurse. *Had* she intended a slight by that innocent-sounding remark? And had Ella been aware of it? Certainly even Penny had noticed the tactless words.

Penny said, 'They match my party dress – and I'm giving Lucy a big, big, *big* box of paints and three paint-brushes. All different sizes.'

The nurse said, 'What a lovely present. Won't she be pleased.' Averting her face, she hurried towards the chest of drawers and began to put away the laundry.

Penny abandoned her dancing and approached the bed. Admiring her new slippers, she said, 'I don't want to learn tap any more. I want to go to ballet class. Can I, Daddy?'

Before he could answer, Ella said, 'Oh, but you have only just started a term, sweetie – and there's the concert. The dancing display. When that's over, we'll see.'

Penny turned lustrous eyes on her father. 'Dadde-e-e?'

He laughed. 'Mummy's right, darling. We'll talk about it later.' He looked appealingly at Ella. 'A term's such a long time, isn't it, when you're young?'

Please grant your little girl's wish, he said wordlessly. Tap or ballet – what did it matter? They could afford to lose the money. He wanted to spoil the child, but there was so little he could do. Trips to the park or the zoo were out of the question, and he couldn't even watch his daughter as an angel in the school play. When she had told him about Sports Day, he had felt such deep disappointment. He felt he had failed her, but the thought of arriving in a wheelchair was unbearable.

Ella said, 'Daddy's right, of course.' She smiled at him. 'Ballet lessons it is, as soon as the display is over. I'll write to Miss Bell and then we'll find a good ballet class.'

Roland opened his arms and Penny scrambled into them. Ella bent down to share the embrace. Unseen, Roland's eyes filled with tears of joy. From now on, he vowed, there would be no more problems; no more recriminations. The past was over and done with. *This* was how it was going to be.

Just before seven o'clock that evening, Ella rang the police station and asked to speak to Detective Inspector Hall. She had chosen the time carefully. Roland was upstairs, Penny was in bed and Annie was busy with the dinner. She knew she had nothing to fear from Nurse Baisley, because it was her evening off and she had gone to the cinema.

The detective's news was not encouraging.

'I'm afraid he's not at the address you gave us, Mrs Gough. It seems he's left his wife, and we don't know where he is.'

Ella closed her eyes. 'Does that mean you won't be able to caution him?'

'It does, yes. Unless we can find out where he's gone, but his wife was most uncooperative. It seems he just walked out, leaving a note and what sounds like the ring you gave him to sell.'

Her head came up sharply. 'He gave her my ring?'

'Told her to sell it.'

Ella was ashamed to realise that she was almost pleased Daniel had left his wife, even though it made things worse for her. Before she could stop herself she asked, 'What's she like?'

'There's no description. Our constable merely commented that she had been crying.' He went on. 'I assume you aren't going to put out the money?'

'No. So he might go to the newspapers.'

'Maybe he thought you just *might* come to us, and he decided to disappear.'

Ella shook her head. 'So he knows where I am, but we don't know where he is.'

'We couldn't actually prove anything, Mrs Gough, if we did have him. Unless there were fingerprints – which there weren't. Our chaps dusted them. Nothing; he must have worn gloves. If the note's typed or written we stand a better chance, but these cut-out words...' He let the sentence die.

Ella stared desperately round her as though in search of escape.

He said, 'We'll need a description of him if we're to look out for him. He won't have left the vicinity – not if he's still hoping to collect the money. He might think your nerve will break.'

'I think it will break!'

He laughed. 'Well, if we can't find him to caution him, our best hope is that he'll show up tonight. Remember he doesn't know what you're going to do. He must know you *might* come to us. We'll watch your house and grounds tonight, discreetly of course.

We could fill a bag with fake money, leave it in the summer-house and lie in wait for him. If he appears we'll nab him.'

'Oh dear...' It was getting worse. 'Would that mean charging him? I mean, would it go to court?'

'Hopefully. Blackmail is a criminal offence, Mrs Gough. You must accept that. You can't expect to take up valuable police time and then, when we catch him, let the fellow get off scot-free. You would have to be very naïve to think that reasonable.'

Ella sighed. 'You're right, I know. So what do we do now?'

'We wait, Mrs Gough.'

It was one of the longest nights Ella could remember. The clocks seemed to mock her, striking the hours and the quarters, measuring the extent of her disquiet as she tossed restlessly in the moonlit room. It was longer than the night following Roland's heart attack ... longer even than the night which followed her quarrel with Lydia and her flight to Florrie. Time and again, Ella left her bed and crossed to the window to stare out into the shadowy garden. If Daniel came in search of the money, she might glimpse his indistinct figure as he moved towards the summer-house. But she saw nothing and finally slipped into an uneasy doze just before six when it was almost time to get up.

Deeply apprehensive, her mind had ranged freely, imagining the worst that could happen. Suppose, in a fit of irrational anger, Daniel had already notified the newspapers? There was nothing to stop him, even if he thought the money would be his by morning. Panic-stricken, Ella decided to get hold of the papers the moment they arrived and search them for anything incriminating before allowing them to be seen by anyone else. Going to sleep so late, however, meant that when she opened her eyes and looked at the clock it was nearly eight o'clock.

'Oh no!' she muttered and scrambled out of bed. She must get hold of the newspapers. She grabbed her dressing-gown and pulled it on as she ran along the landing and down the stairs.

Too late. Nurse Baisley was standing in the hallway with the papers in her hands.

'Oh!' Instinctively Ella clapped a hand to her mouth. Of all people, it had to be Nurse Baisley. But why was *she* down so early? Surely she couldn't *know?* Ella felt cold and then hot. Had the wretched woman looked at any of them?

'I'll take those,' she said and almost snatched them from the nurse's hands.

Nurse Baisley, already in uniform, gave her a startled look which was heavy with disapproval. 'Good morning, Mrs Gough!' she said pointedly.

'Good morning! Yes.' Ella searched for any sign in the woman's eyes that she had already examined the newspapers and found some embarrassing revelations. The nurse seemed unperturbed.

'I just need to look at these for a moment,' Ella stammered and, unwilling to prolong the encounter, she turned away towards the stairs. She was half-way up when the nurse spoke.

'May I have my magazine, please, Mrs Gough?'

Ella stopped in mid-flight and turned. 'Your magazine?'

'*Nursing Monthly*. I am billed separately for it. I doubt it would be of interest to anyone but a qualified nurse.'

Ella regarded the smug face with loathing, then flipped through the papers and found the required journal. 'Here you are,' she said. Without another word she hurried upstairs and back into her bedroom. If Dan *had* gone to the newspapers, he would hardly have chosen *Nursing Monthly*, she told herself, feeling slightly hysterical. Jumping back into bed, she combed the papers for anything about her or Daniel or her parents.

'Nothing!' She closed her eyes. 'Thank you!' she whispered, though whether to God or Daniel she wasn't sure.

She tried to take courage from the absence of any scandal, but commonsense told her that it was too early to hope that Daniel had had a change of heart. It was more likely that he would try again to get the money. Once he had told all, there would be no reason for Ella to pay for his silence. He needed her to pay and to keep on paying.

As she began to relax the phone rang and she heard Annie answering it.

'...Who? Mr Hall? She's expecting you to call? I'll fetch her right away.'

Ella rushed downstairs again, glancing first at the other doors on the landing to reassure herself that no one would be listening. She must be careful how she answered; try to keep it as non-committal as possible.

Annie handed her the phone. 'A Mr Hall,' she whispered, 'I didn't recognise the voice.'

'Thank you, Annie.' She waited as the housekeeper returned to the kitchen.

'It's Mrs Gough. There's nothing in the—'

'That's why I'm ringing. We didn't expect this. It's not in his interest to end it all so quickly and without earning a penny. I shall need that description some time this morning, and the sooner the better. Can you be overheard, Mrs Gough?'

'It's possible but I don't think so – not at the moment.'

'Well, our blackmailer didn't turn up, but he may have been scared off. We had a bit of a problem with a woman, drunk as a lord, weaving around in the road. It meant that our man had to move her.'

'Arrest her, you mean?'

'Watch what you're saying, Mrs Gough!' he reminded her. 'Remember you may be overheard. But no, she wasn't arrested. My constable simply moved her on – marched her down the road and left her in the hedge. So Hampton either got cold feet or was put off.'

'Or came when your man was absent?'

'Possibly. Pity, but these things happen. We'll make a start on the guest houses and small hotels, although from what I hear he couldn't afford those. Then we'll try anyone who has advertised rooms to let over the past week or so. He's got to stay somewhere. I don't suppose you know who his friends are, do you? Anyone who might let him sleep on the sofa for a day or two?'

'I don't. Sorry. I really don't know much at all about his present life.'

'Never mind. We'll alert the beat bobbies – give them something to do. You haven't got a photograph, I suppose?'

'A pho–' She stopped abruptly and cast anxious eyes around her. 'Nothing recent, I'm afraid. His wife might have one – oh!' Damn! If anyone *was* listening, she was giving too much away. Looking upward, she scanned the landing for shadows but saw nothing. Then a fresh thought struck her. There was an extension to the phone in her husband's room. Oh, God!

'So you'll call in with a full description – as soon as you can?'

'Yes!' She was longing to get him off the line.

'And if you happen to discover his whereabouts you'll let us know? I don't want to frighten you but if he's in a volatile state, broke, left his wife – that sort of thing – he may be hovering on the edge of obsession. On the other hand, they might be in it together. A conspiracy. Could turn nasty.'

Obsession? Conspiracy? I'm already frightened, she thought. 'Of course I'll tell you if I – I'll do what you ask.'

'I'm just saying that we have to think of everything. We should never underestimate the opposition.'

Ella's nerves were raw and any sympathy she might have felt for Daniel was rapidly disappearing. Her thoughts swam and she put a hand to her head. *Obsession!* The word had an ominous ring to it. Suppose he hadn't disappeared; hadn't left his wife? She might have been lying. Daniel might be hiding out at their flat.

The detective was still speaking, but the

words meant nothing to her.

Unable to bear any more, Ella said, 'Yes,' and replaced the receiver.

Suppose Daniel *had* turned against her, as the detective had suggested? Or was becoming obsessed? Perhaps this was just the beginning and he meant her real harm. She shivered. Suppose he was embarking on a terrible revenge...

Chapter Eight

Florrie sat in her chintz-covered chair and tried to concentrate on the music. The pianist, a middle-aged man, was playing his usual selection of old favourites. His visits broke the monotony and she always came down to swell the audience. To her right, in the circle of chairs, an elderly woman dozed with head well down, snoring lightly. To Florrie's left was what she thought of as 'a poor old thing' – a very large woman, ninety any day now, who muttered incessantly to herself. Further along a stick-like man stared at the pianist and nodded in time to the music.

Mrs Barrett, another member of the select circle, leaned forward and caught Florrie's eye. 'I'm expecting my nephew today,' she confided. She was generously proportioned, with a schoolgirl complexion which Florrie envied. 'Have you met him?'

'I don't think so.' Ernest had been expected ever since Florrie had come to stay at Sunningford, but he rarely appeared.

'Ernest. Oh, but you *must* have. Very fair. He's coming today. I'll introduce you.'

'I'd like that.' She smiled.

Mrs Barrett nodded. 'Last time I gave him my husband's gold cufflinks. The *good* ones. He didn't *ask*, mind you. Oh no! Not Ernest. But he always admires them and I thought "Why not?" We have no children of our own and my husband always wanted him to have them. Why does he have to wait until I die, I asked myself. So I gave them to him. He was *so* delighted.'

I'm sure he was, thought Florrie. Lonely old aunts must be fair game for avaricious nephews.

The pianist turned as the melody ended. 'Anyone know the title of that one?' he asked with forced joviality.

No one volunteered.

Florrie felt sorry for him. '"After The Ball",' she offered. 'It was my mother's favourite.'

'Was it *really?* Well, that's splendid. Well done, Miss Goolden!'

Mrs Barrett said, 'It was on the tip of my tongue!'

He rewarded them both with a beaming smile, probably grateful that there were some people in his small audience who appreciated his expertise. He played well and gave his time voluntarily. He asked, 'Do you have any favourites?'

'I do love the old music-hall songs,' Florrie told him. 'What about "Daisy, Daisy?"'

'*Excellent* choice. "Daisy, Daisy" it shall be

for the lady on my left!' and, with another beaming smile for her cleverness, he settled down to rattle through it.

Florrie began to hum the tune softly to herself, but just then the door opened and all heads turned as Ella entered the room carrying a parcel.

'Ella!' Florrie waved her hand. Now what has happened, she wondered with a frisson of expectation. It was quite wrong of her, she felt, to hope for a little excitement, but Sunningford was hardly an exciting place to be and she did enjoy these glimpses into the world outside. Coming here for the winter had seemed a good idea, but she was already longing to return to her own home.

'Florrie!'

'My dear! How lovely! A surprise visit.' Uncomfortably aware of Mrs Barrett's envious expression, Florrie held out her hands in greeting. The thought that Ella occasionally sought her advice meant that an elderly aunt couldn't be as useless as she sometimes feared. Now, looking at the girl's face, she saw the dark circles under her eyes and a tenseness in her expression.

Ella hesitated. Dazzled by the attractive young visitor, the pianist abandoned his music and hurried forward. 'There's a spare seat if you'd care to join us?'

Ella smiled. 'Thank you, but I have some

– some family business to discuss,' she told him.

Disappointed, he suggested that between them they could help Florrie back to her room.

'There we are!' he said triumphantly as they lowered Florrie to a chair. He gave Ella a radiant smile. 'Glad I could be of help, ladies.'

'Ladies?' Ella said, as soon as they were alone. 'If he knew my sorry history...'

Florrie said, 'Don't talk such nonsense, dear. Of course you're a lady.'

Unwrapping the parcel, Ella handed her aunt a glass vase. 'For your flowers,' she said with a smile.

'You remembered! Oh, you are a dear!'

Ella sat down beside her. 'Those people all look so dreadfully dull. I know it's not for long, but who do you talk to, for heaven's sake?'

'One or two of them are not too bad, Ella, and I talk to the staff when they aren't rushed off their feet. They're mostly very pleasant.'

'You don't regret coming to stay here then?'

'Of course not!' Florrie hoped she was convincing. As Ella still looked dubious Florrie indicated the jigsaw. 'I've nearly finished it.'

Ella busied herself, studying the picture. 'This must be the original St Paul's – before it was burnt down?'

'It is. It's called "Old St Paul's".'

Ella picked up a piece of the jigsaw, studied it carefully and placed it with a small satisfied sound. 'A bit of window,' she explained. 'Part of the transom, actually.'

'Transom?' Florrie laughed. 'Getting rather technical, aren't we, dear?'

'It's Charles, Mr Saville's godson. He's very interested in architecture. It's something of a passion with him.' She picked up another piece and put it down again. 'They get on rather well, he and Roland. They seem to share the same interests, but Charles has done all the travelling Roland can no longer do. He's coming to dinner, but I forget when it is.'

She's delaying the moment, thought Florrie, hearing the forced brightness in her niece's voice. Oh dear! Not very promising. She said, 'Never mind Old St Paul's. Come and sit down and tell me what's happening. I'm all ears, as they say.'

Ella sat down reluctantly, but said nothing.

Florrie said, 'It's going wrong, isn't it? I can see by your face.'

'Horribly wrong,' Ella admitted. Without further ado she described the attempted blackmail.

Florrie cried, 'The wretch! I'd like to wring his neck!'

261

'It gets worse,' Ella told her.

Florrie listened with growing anxiety as her niece spoke of Roland's collapse. 'That was my fault,' she said. 'I urged you to confide in him.'

'It was nobody's fault,' Ella argued. 'We couldn't have known how it would affect him. But you do see, Florrie, why I can't tell Roland anything about the blackmail?'

'No, I don't. You are taking too much on those slim shoulders of yours!' Florrie took Ella's hand in hers. 'You say Roland's recovering, that it might *not* have been a heart attack. He's not a child, Ella, and you should allow him to help you. He's your husband, and he loves you. Think about it.'

'But I've upset him so much already. I've fallen off my pedestal – and that's hard for him. He always thought me so perfect, and now he can see that I'm no better than anyone else.'

'But no worse, dear, surely.' Florrie smiled. 'I think your pride is clouding your judgement here.'

'I'll think about it.' Ella swallowed. 'But if it gets out of hand – if the police can't find him...'

Florrie frowned. 'It sounds so unlike the Daniel Hampton I remember. He was such a charmer... Oh, sorry, Ella, but you know what I mean. He had such lovely manners – and that wonderful smile...'

'Well, he's not smiling now!... Sorry, I didn't mean to snap. I keep thinking that if only we had met under different circumstances... Oh, God! I'm such an *idiot!*' She pressed her fingertips against her eyes.

Florrie was touched by a deep sorrow. 'You don't still love him, Ella? You *can't.*'

Ella turned to her with an agonised expression. In a tight voice she said, 'No. No, I don't. How could I after – after all that's happened?' She spread her hands in a helpless gesture.

'Well, that's a relief. Blackmail is so ... so *cowardly.*'

'And it's a *crime!*' Ella covered her face with her hands. 'The police were at pains to point that out to me. Roland was right; Daniel has made a fool out of me. How *could* he, Florrie? He knew that I trusted him.'

'It looks bad, I must admit. I'm afraid it shows him for what he is – a thoroughly undesirable character... Or rather, what he's become.'

She gave Ella a sideways glance, but her niece was now staring at the jigsaw, apparently absorbed in the architecture of the famous cathedral. After a moment Ella reached out and picked up one of the pieces. 'Part of the dome,' she said and tried to press it into place. It didn't fit, but she left it there and Florrie knew that, despite her brave words, Ella still loved the man.

While Ella talked with Florrie, Lizzie sat alone in her kitchen sipping port from a cup. She had discovered the half-empty bottle at the back of the cupboard – a reminder of happier times. Christmas probably... But had they been happy at Christmas, she wondered? Maybe. Maybe not. Maybe they'd never been happy. And bloody Ella was the reason ... or was it bloody Lydia? She screwed up her face in an attempt to concentrate, but her thoughts skittered uneasily from past to present and she couldn't quite grasp anything.

When Win poked her head round the door, Lizzie was too depressed to scream at her.

'Can I come in?'

'I suppose so. Who bloody cares!'

Win hovered just inside the door, waiting for encouragement. She said, 'Drowning your sorrows?'

'Something like that.' Lizzie shrugged. 'Well, don't just stand there. Get yourself a cup.' Neither mentioned the row that had kept them apart.

Win poured herself a drop of port and sat down. 'Has he gone for good?'

'Yes. And good riddance!'

'Len thought he had. I said, "Never" but he said, "Well, where is he then?" and I thought, "No, he's right. I *haven't* seen him." You're well rid of him, Liz.' She took out a packet of cigarettes and lit one.

Lizzie said, 'I wouldn't mind a fag. Can you spare one?' If Win refused, she'd be out on her ear.

'Taken it up again, have you?'

'Why not! Who cares? Dan's not here to nag. I'd like to know where he is, though. Just so I can kill him!'

'You wouldn't.'

'Or kill myself. Who'd miss me?'

'You don't mean that.'

'What d'you know about anything?' She tipped the last half-inch of port into Win's cup.

Win looked at her through narrowed eyes. 'Now what?' Lizzie demanded.

'You could be up the spout, Liz. I'm telling you. I can tell by your eyes. They always give it away. You should go to the doctor, really you should.'

'My *eyes?*' Lizzie jumped up and stared at her reflection in the mirror over the sink. Did she really look any different? Her eyes stared back, slightly reddened maybe – but then she'd been howling her eyes out.

Taking a long draw on the cigarette, she blew the smoke at her reflection and watched it fade and reappear. 'That's tiredness.' She meant misery; hopelessness; anger. With everything and everybody. But the initial fear was followed by a sudden flicker of hope. If she *was* expecting, then Dan might come back. It might be the only way. She said, 'Get away! Course I'm not.'

He'd always wanted a family. She tried to imagine herself with a baby and a couple of toddlers and resisted the urge to shudder. But it might not be so bad. Win seemed to manage OK. If it would make Dan happy... She sat down again without comment.

Win said, 'Nice ring. Where d'you get that?'

Lizzie held out her hand and they both made admiring noises.

'He left it for me to sell. Wrapped it in the letter. Wish I needn't, though. I might pawn it and then when I win the pools I'll get it back.'

'Didn't know you did them.'

'I don't, but if.'

'Where'd Dan get a ring like that?'

'Off her, I expect.' The familiar jealousy surfaced again. 'Smug cow! I'd like to wipe the smile off her face. If I saw her in the gutter, I'd step over her.'

Win said, 'Look, I'll come with you to the doctor if you want.'

'No thanks. No offence, but I can go by myself. I'm not a kid.'

'So you will go?'

'I suppose so.' She held up crossed fingers and they both laughed.

Five minutes to go and he could shut up shop. The pawnbroker made it a rule never to close before half-past five. If he lost one transaction each day, it could make the difference between profit and loss. Sure enough, the bell jangled and he looked through the grid to see a youngish woman enter. He pushed his spectacles up on to his nose. It was usually the women. The blokes couldn't do it; too much pride. This one could have been pretty once. Same colour hair as his wife. He liked redheads. He had a feeling he'd seen this one before, but not recently. He fingered his beard and smiled.

She said, 'How much for this?' and held up a slim hand to show off a ring.

'That depends.'

When she pulled it from her finger and handed it through to him, he could see at once that it was better than average. He looked from the ring to its owner. Dodgy, was it? He studied it, frowning, then shook his head. 'Christmas cracker, was it, ducks?'

'No, it was *not*. You can see that for yourself.'

'So what are these stones?'

She shrugged and he regarded her with growing suspicion. 'You don't know, do you? Pinched, is it? Do I look like a ruddy fence?'

'It was given. A present.'

'Come off it!'

'My husband gave it to me. He *did!*'

'Put it this way – how much d'you need?' Sometimes he was lucky when they didn't know the value and asked for much less. This was a very nice ring, he thought, examining it. Faceted sapphire, dark, with some banding. Probably close to two carat. Claw setting. Three diamonds on each shoulder. Better not to know how she came by it.

'I want twenty-five pounds.'

'Pull the other one!' Nice freckles over her nose and under her eyes. Freckles always made a woman look younger. He'd like to give her more money, but business was business.

'I mean it.' She gave him a hard look.

'Sorry, missus.' He offered it to her with a short laugh, willing her not to take it.

She hesitated, then took the ring. 'I think these are diamonds–' she pointed '–and this might be a sapphire.'

Quickly he took it back. He didn't want to lose it. 'Diamonds?' She was right, but she was guessing. He shook his head again. 'If they're diamonds they're very poor diamonds. Look, ducks, since you're in a bit of a spot I'll give you five pounds. Take it or leave it.'

Her expression wavered and she swallowed. 'Look. The truth is my husband's done a bunk and I've just come from the doctor. He says I'm expecting. I need this money more than you'll ever know, and I need twenty-five pounds...'

'He walked out on you because you're up the spout? Nice man!'

'He went before I knew. And yes, for your information he *is* a nice man.'

They waited. He took out a handkerchief and blew his nose. Fancy leaving a nice bit of skirt like this one! There were some funny blokes around. Dress her up with a nice fur collar and a decent coat, put a smile on her face and a dab of lipstick; she'd look a million dollars.

She said, 'Twenty, then. It's a good ring. They could be diamonds. How d'you know they're not? You haven't looked through the eyepiece thing.'

She was smart too. 'Because I don't need to. Because it's my job to know, that's why. I didn't fall off a Christmas tree, ducks. This beard says I've been around a long time.' He tugged at it, beginning to enjoy himself. Should have gone on the stage.

'D'you think I'd last in this business if I couldn't recognise a diamond when I see it?' He gave a snort of amazement. 'I'll give you ten, but I'm a fool to myself. Never could resist a hard-luck story.' He'd get it for £10 and she'd never redeem it. He'd sell it for the best part of £40.

But now there were tears on the way and the fight was going out of her. Poor kid. He watched her brush a hand across her eyes. Oh no! Don't cry!

Her mouth trembled. 'Fifteen – or you can bloody give it back.'

'Fifteen? It'd be daylight robbery!'

To his surprise she thrust out her hand. A strand of reddish-gold hair clung to her cheek. Expecting, was she? So her old man hit the jackpot... He was tempted to hand back the ring and call her bluff, but as he hesitated two tears slid down her freckled cheeks and he knew that he was beaten. Never could resist tears.

With a loud, exasperated sigh he reached into the till, drew out three fivers and laid them on his side of the counter.

Prolonging the agony, he fiddled about, putting the ring into an envelope and reaching for a pen.

'When you going to come in for it?'

She blinked hard. 'I don't know. A week or two. Three, maybe.'

'There'll be a weekly charge and–'

'I know how it works, thank you. Always in your favour!'

Hoity-toity! He said, 'You're the one wants the money.'

He scribbled down the details on his pad, tore off the top copy and pushed it through with the notes. She snatched them up without a word of thanks.

As she turned to go he came round from behind the counter and followed her to the shop door. He turned the notice round so that it read 'Closed' and stood between her and the door.

'So you're all on your lonesome. Want a bit of company, do you?'

'I've got plenty of friends.'

'I bet. Gentlemen friends, are they?'

She gave him a look that told him he was wasting his time and he opened the door and stepped aside. Worth a try, anyway.

'Don't spend it all at once, ducks,' he said with a grin.

She gave him a spiteful look and said, 'Go to hell!'

He shrugged as he slid the bolt. There was no pleasing some people...

Lizzie went straight round to Win's, where the kitchen was in chaos. The fire was smoking, the baby was crawling around in the crumbs, wet washing hung on a string overhead and Meg was sulking in a corner with her thumb in her mouth. Lizzie told Win about her less than perfect day.

Win whistled. 'Fifteen smackers? Good God! That must have been some ring.'

'He diddled me, but I'm going to need it. You were right about the kid.'

Win whooped with triumph. 'What did I

say? I can always tell. When's it due?'

'April twelfth according to the doctor. A spring baby, he said, and all the summer to look forward to.' She shook her head despairingly. 'Just as well, with all those nappies to dry. Sometimes I hate this country. At least in South Africa we had decent weather.'

Meg said, 'Where is South Africa, Auntie Liz?'

Win gave her a dour look and said, 'Mind your business, Miss Nosy Parker.' She turned back to Lizzie. 'And is everything OK with the baby?'

'As far as they can tell. Who's to say? No, it's *me* that's in trouble. "Take things easy," the doctor told me. He gave me some sleeping pills to make sure I get plenty of rest. Doctors! He shook my hand as I left and said, "Congratulate your husband for me, Mrs Gough." What do they know – or care? They make me sick.'

'He's right though, Liz. You must take care of yourself.'

Lizzie gave a short laugh. 'That's where you're wrong, Win. It's Dan who should take care of me. He got me into this. He should *be* here!'

Win patted her shoulder and searched for a way to change the subject. 'What a palaver we had last night with this one,' she said, drawing Meg to her. 'Crying her eyes out over that ruddy party. Lucy-blasted-Barnes. It's this afternoon. Probably started by now. I've told her, "You weren't invited so you can't go." But would she have it? Grizzle, grizzle! I thought Len was going to thump her.'

Lizzie sat up suddenly. 'I'll get her in.'

Win stared at her. 'In? In where?'

Lizzie grinned. 'Into the party! If she wants to go, she'll go.'

Meg said, 'Go where? What?'

Lizzie said, 'Has she got anything nice to wear?'

'She's got her blue spotted frock but–' Win frowned. 'What are you on about?' Lizzie looked at Meg, her gloom apparently forgotten. 'I'll take you to the party, love. I'll *make* the snooty woman take you in. I'll *shame* her into it. Win – you got a decent ribbon for her hair?'

'Yes, but–'

'You get her dolled up while I get her a present to take.' She looked at Meg. 'Don't stare at me like that. I'm not mad – not yet!' She laughed. 'I've got a box of hankies. Lace ones. Never been opened. I'll wrap them up and I'll be back in ten minutes.' To Win she said, 'No time for curlers. Just brush her hair and stick in a nice big bow.'

Win still hesitated. 'But suppose she says "No"...'

'She won't. I know her type; she'll give in

to avoid a scene.' She stood up, her face flushed with excitement. 'Ten minutes!' she said and winked at Meg.

The child looked at her mother. 'Can I?' she asked breathlessly.

Lizzie pointed over her shoulder. 'Don't you recognise me?' she asked. 'Can't you see my wings?'

'Wings?' Meg moved round to examine Lizzie's back. 'No,' she said.

'That's because they're invisible. They do that sometimes. But they're there. That's because I'm your fairy godmother!'

Penny was hurrying round a row of chairs and waiting breathlessly for the music to stop. Mrs Barnes was playing 'Here We Go Round The Mulberry Bush' and as soon as she lifted her hands from the keys the children hurled themselves on to the chairs. At the end of each round Lucy's granny took away one of the chairs. Lucy, resplendent in her black ankle-strap shoes, had been the first to be 'out' and Penny had tried hard not to feel pleased. Now there were only four children left. Penny felt quite desperate. She was so near to winning the prize which stood on the mantelpiece, resplendent in yellow tissue paper and pretty gold ribbon.

The doorbell rang and Mrs Barnes stopped playing. Penny hesitated. Was this because someone was at the door? As the other three children threw themselves on to the seats, Penny was transfixed with horror. She had lost her chance – but *was it fair?*

Mrs Barnes said, 'Now who on earth can that be? Everyone is already here.'

Penny said, 'Mrs Barnes, did you–'

But Lucy's mother had left the room and Penny drifted out after her. She was trying to gather her courage to ask the dreadful question – had Mrs Barnes *meant* to stop playing the piano? Or was it because of the bell? She threw an agonised glance in the direction of the mantelpiece. Penny was sure that as long as she was polite, asking Mrs Barnes wouldn't be a bad thing to do – and Mummy and Mrs Granger would never know.

A woman stood on the doorstep with Meg Cutts beside her. Penny recognised her; she sometimes brought Meg to the dancing class.

'Sorry we're a bit late.' The woman pushed Meg forward. 'This is Meg Cutts. I'm her Auntie Lizzie. In you go, dear, and give Lucy her present.' She smiled at Mrs Barnes. 'She wasn't sure she was invited, but I said to her mother, "No one would leave one child out of a party. Not even Mrs Barnes".' She smiled. 'Not if all the rest were invited. It would be too cruel.'

Meg tried to squeeze past Mrs Barnes, but

she put a hand on Meg's shoulder.

She said, 'Did Meg have an invitation? A *printed* card?'

'We're sure she did.'

'With her name on it?'

'She must have lost it. She's been so looking forward to it. You know how children are.'

Penny smiled at Meg, who was squashed between Mrs Barnes and the doorframe and wondered what sort of present she had brought. Lucy's main present had been a scooter with red wheels, and Penny was going to ask for one exactly like it when her own birthday came around.

Mrs Barnes said, 'If she didn't have an invitation, then I'm afraid she wasn't–'

'I told you. She must have lost it.'

Penny stared at Meg's auntie; she had stopped smiling and looked rather cross.

'It's – it's a matter of numbers,' Mrs Barnes told her. 'We only have eight crackers and–'

'I've never seen a box of eight crackers. It's nearly always six or a dozen!'

'And I made eight jellies–'

'That's good, because she doesn't like jelly!'

Penny was astonished, she thought *everyone* liked jelly. She gave Meg a little wave and another smile.

Mrs Barnes went on, 'And only seven

presents to take away. It just isn't...'

Meg's auntie leaned forward so that her face was very close to Mrs Barnes' face. 'If you think I'm going to break this kid's heart by taking her home again, you've got another think coming!'

'Well, really!' Mrs Barnes took a step backwards and Meg seized her chance and slipped inside. 'You've got a nerve, coming here like this. What sort of woman are you, for heaven's sake!'

Meg gave Penny a shy smile.

'We're playing Musical Chairs,' Penny told her, 'but I think I'm out. Anyway, it's nearly over. Come on. I'll show you.' She took the girl's hand and led her into the room, where Meg handed Lucy the present and the children gathered round to see it opened.

'It's grown-up hankies,' Meg told her, 'With a-nishalls.'

'Thank you.'

Susan Wells said, 'But it's an "E". Your name starts with "L".'

'No, no!' Meg explained. 'It stands for "Ever-so-grown-up". Auntie Lizzie told me.'

Lucy beamed. '*Thank* you, Meg.'

Penny said, 'I gave her a box of paints.'

When Mrs Barnes came back into the room, her face was very red and Penny wondered if she was going to get the flu.

Promptly at six-thirty, Ella arrived at the house to collect Penny. As she waited on the doorstep, another woman appeared.

Ella smiled at her. 'Poor Mrs Barnes. I expect she'll be glad to see the back of them!' She laughed. 'Children's parties are always so exhausting.' She held out a hand. 'I'm Ella Gough, Penny's mother.'

To her surprise the woman's expression changed. Or had she imagined the narrowing of the eyes? Seconds later, she was smiling again as she shook Ella's hand.

'I'm Meg Cutts' aunt,' she said. 'Her Mum's a bit off-colour, so I said I'd fetch her home.'

At that moment the door opened. Mrs Barnes smiled at Ella, but her face froze when she saw Meg's aunt. To Ella she said, 'Do come in, Mrs Gough.' To the aunt she said, 'I'll send her out.'

Puzzled, Ella followed Mrs Barnes into the hall where all the girls milled around, tired but happy. Penny ran up to Ella, bright with excitement. She was already dressed to go home and carried a small present wrapped in gold paper.

Mrs Barnes said, 'Come along, Meg.' She took the child's hand, hurried her to the door and pushed her out none too gently. Then she closed the door and leaned against it. Catching Ella's surprised look, she said, 'She's got the cheek of the devil, that woman! Actually gatecrashed the party with that wretched niece of hers. Told me she'd lost the invitation, but I knew she was lying.' She gulped in air. 'Brought her along with a present, would you believe, and practically *pushed* her into the hall. Wouldn't take no for an answer – and so rude!'

Ella said, 'Oh dear. How difficult for you.'

'What could I do? It wasn't the child's fault.' She ran a hand over her face, struggling with her anger. 'I daren't tell my husband. He'd be furious!'

Penny danced up to them, eyes shining. 'Mummy, can they all come to my party?' she demanded. 'I said they could.'

Ella said, 'We'll see, sweetie. It's not for a long time yet.'

'I've been good. Mrs Barnes said I have!'

Ella tweaked her nose gently. 'I should certainly hope so, Penny!'

Mrs Barnes said, 'Oh, she has. A very sweet child.'

Penny took a deep breath. 'We played Postman's Knock and Pass The Parcel and Musical Chairs, but I didn't win anything, and we had dear little cakes with pink icing and I gave Meg some of my jelly – and Sarah was sick but not much and the birthday cake had seven little dwarves because Lucy is seven...' She paused for breath.

Mrs Barnes bent over one of the children.

'You've put your shoes on the wrong feet, dear.' To Ella she said, 'That's why I didn't ask the woman in just now. I know it was impolite of me, but I just couldn't do it. I don't want that kind of person inside my home. I don't know what my husband's going to say.' She put a hand to her chest, breathing heavily. 'She was *extremely* rude! It was all I could do not to strike her. Quite frankly, I think she's a bit ... well, you know.' She tapped her forehead.

'It's possible, I suppose,' said Ella. 'Come to think of it, she gave *me* a funny look, too, when we met at the front door. Goodness knows what *I've* done! I don't even know the woman.'

'Believe me, you don't *want* to know her...' She broke off. 'Sarah, don't jump about like that, dear. You'll be sick again.' She rolled her eyes. 'I couldn't believe how much this child tucked away. My mother thinks she must have hollow legs!' She took out a handkerchief and dabbed carefully at her face. 'Well, that's another birthday over. What an afternoon! I'm worn out but the children have enjoyed themselves and that's the main thing.'

More mothers were arriving and Ella and Penny said their 'goodbyes' and left. To their surprise, Meg and her aunt were still outside and the woman gave Ella a warm smile while the two children began an earnest conversation.

'So this is Penny. Meg's often spoken about her. I thought they were probably in the same class at school but Meg says "No".'

'Penny goes to Havenbridge.'

'Havenbridge? Where's that?'

Before Ella could respond Penny chipped in, 'My teacher's called Miss Meacher and she's ever so pretty. She's always laughing, and she has a box of special toffees and if we're especially good–'

'Oh! A box of special toffees!' She gave Ella a challenging look. 'Private then, is it?'

Ella nodded.

'*Very* nice! Expensive, I bet.'

'We think it reasonable.' Ella decided she didn't like the woman's tone. In fact she didn't like the woman, full stop, and she had no wish to be drawn further into conversation. 'We must go,' she said firmly.

Penny tugged at her hand. 'Can Meg come to tea one day, Mummy?'

Ella groaned inwardly. 'I expect so. It rather depends...' On what? She thought frantically. 'Where does Meg live?' Please let it be a long way away...

To her surprise, the woman's smile vanished. 'What's it got to do with you?'

Ella said, 'Well, if Meg's going to come to tea...'

'She isn't. She ... her mother doesn't allow

it.' She turned and grabbed Meg's hand. 'We're going to be late,' she told her. 'Say "Goodbye".' Before the child could speak, she began to drag her away along the pavement.

Ella heard Meg say, 'Late for what?' but the answer was inaudible.

She watched them go. Mrs Barnes was right; there was something very odd about Meg's aunt.

Ella took Penny up to the study to tell Roland all about the party. When Penny finally ran out of superlatives, she was sent off to find Mrs Granger and get ready for bed.

Roland looked at Ella. 'Isn't she wonderful – our daughter? It's nice to see her happy.'

Ella nodded. 'Any news from the police while I was out?' Against her better judgement, she had told Roland about the note and he had taken it better than she could have hoped.

'A little. The ring turned up – in a pawn-shop. Routine check.'

Ella's heart beat faster. 'Was it Daniel? Did they get a description?'

'It was a woman, Ella. They think he might have given the ring to his wife. They went straight round to the flat but there was no one there. They got a key from the neighbour and had a good look round.

Nothing incriminating. Neighbour claims that the wife did pawn a ring yesterday. She boasted that she'd got fifteen pounds for it.'

'Fifteen? That ring's worth–'

'Ella, the wife's expecting a child.'

Ella felt as though all the breath had been knocked from her body. A child. Daniel and Lizzie...

When she spoke she was struggling to sound as normal as possible. 'So they might be in it together, Lizzie and Daniel.'

He looked at her with compassion for a long moment. 'It rather looks that way.'

Ella could only nod her head. If she spoke she knew her voice would break, and she couldn't bear Roland to know how shaken she was by the news.

Mercifully, a knock on the door interrupted them.

'Come in!' cried Roland.

Evans came into the room, his cap tucked under his arm, a broad smile on his face. 'Evening, Mrs Gough. Evening, sir.'

Ella could only incline her head wordlessly. She felt as though she was drowning in air.

'How was he – the latest chap?' Roland asked. 'What was his name?'

'That's what I've come about, sir. Berry's his name. Tom Berry. Very nice chap, he is. Very suitable.' He gave Ella a quick glance and she lowered her eyes. He was no doubt

283

hoping that this time she would refrain from interfering.

Evans went on, 'Got a wife and two kiddies, and very keen for regular hours. Not so knowledgeable as Hampton, I must admit that, but he's willing to learn. Been working in a plant nursery for two years, so he reckons he's picked up the basics. He's waiting downstairs 'case you want to size him up, sir.'

'If you want him, Evans, that's good enough for me. Has he accepted the wages and the hours and so on?'

Ella was recovering. She breathed deeply and regularly, telling herself again and again that the news meant nothing to her. Only partly convinced, she was nevertheless bringing her emotions under control.

'Oh yes, sir,' Evans replied. 'He's sturdy, too, sir. Very strong. Used to be an amateur boxer years ago, but he's given it up. Wife didn't like it. Women are like that – begging your pardon, Mrs Gough. He'll start to-morrow if I give him the go-ahead.'

'By all means.'

Again Evans glanced at Ella.

She said, 'He sounds an excellent choice, Mr Evans. Your judgement is usually very sound.' To her relief her voice sounded reasonably steady.

Evans tutted. 'Except that youngster – the one before Hampton. I certainly slipped up

284

there – lazy little devil, he was.'

Roland said, 'No one gets it all right. Go down and put this chap's mind at rest. He can start in the morning.'

'Right, sir. Thank you, sir.' He gave his hair a deferential tug and left the room beaming.

Roland said, 'All's right with the world, then – at least, Evans's world.'

So he was going to let the subject drop. For that Ella was truly grateful. She promised herself she would never mention the child; would never think about it; would never allow it to cause her the slightest anguish.

'All's right with *my* world,' Roland told her gently. 'Come here and kiss me, Ella. I'm so lucky to have you as my wife.'

She was startled by the intensity in his voice. 'Even though I bring you all these terrible problems?'

'You've brought me years of happiness, Ella.' He made a balancing motion with his hands. 'And you've given me my darling Penny. All this weighs heavily in your favour, you see.'

'But right now?'

'The blackmail, you mean? There's been no further development. I think we've called their bluff. If they've any sense, they'll disappear before the police catch up with them.'

'Oh God, Roland, I wish they would.' She

leaned over and kissed him.

Roland put his arms around her. 'Sleep with me again, Ella, as soon as I'm over this. I can't make love to you, but I'd like to go to sleep with you in my arms. It's been such a long time.'

Ella knelt beside him. 'I'd love that, Roland,' she told him, then rolled her eyes. 'But ... come back to *our* bedroom? What's Nurse Baisley going to say about it?'

He laughed. 'To hell with the dragon!' he told her. 'I've missed you.'

'I've missed you, too.' She realised with a sense of shock that this was true. They *had* been drifting apart and she had done nothing to prevent it. She had allowed Daniel's ghost and Roland's disability to create a gulf between them, and now she must put matters right.

His arms closed round her in a fierce embrace and Ella felt her eyes fill with tears. There was more than one kind of love, she reminded herself, and from now on, whatever happened, her one thought would be to make this dear man as happy as he deserved.

Chapter Nine

They first realised that Penny was missing at five minutes past four the next day, when Enid Granger went to the school to meet her. When the school playground was at last empty, Mrs Granger went in search of her.

'One of the tinies?' The caretaker scratched his head. 'As far as I know they've all gone home,' he told her. 'You'd best see the headmistress or her class teacher.'

'Miss Meacher,' Mrs Granger told him. 'Class three. Where is that?'

She followed his pointing finger and hurried along the corridor. Half-way along she saw the headmistress, Miss Stobart – a tall, cheerful woman she had met several times before.

'Penny Gough?' she said, in answer to Mrs Granger's anxious enquiry. 'I thought they'd all gone home, but maybe she's helping her teacher. You know how they are about being "monitors". Milk monitor, blackboard monitor...' She set off in the direction of the classroom with Mrs Granger hurrying to keep up with her. 'It makes them feel so important, and it's probably their first taste of responsibility. I can still remember giving out the straws when I was about seven.' She laughed. 'Ah, here we are.'

She led the way into the room, which was bright and modern with small chairs and desks. Pictures adorned the walls and a mouse in a cage had pride of place on a table by the window. A young woman with dark hair was pinning up an alphabet frieze, but she turned with a smile to greet them.

'Miss Meacher, this is Mrs Granger, Penny Gough's nanny.' She looked round the room. 'Oh dear. She's not here. Did you actually see her leave the school?'

'Penny?' She looked surprised. 'Not really. She was in the cloakroom with the rest of the children. I remember rebuttoning her coat for her.'

Mrs Granger said, 'I didn't see her come out. I was here a moment or two before four, as usual. She always waits just inside the gate. Oh, dear! I can't think what to do next. I can't go home without her.'

Miss Meacher said, 'Maybe she started walking to meet you?'

'But I'd have seen her!' Enid's voice rose as panic set in. 'We'd have passed each other. Oh heavens! We must telephone the police. If anything's happened to her, I'll–'

The headmistress held up her hand. 'Please, Mrs Granger. We should stay calm. I'm sure there's nothing wrong. I'll telephone to her parents. It's possible

Penny's walked all the way home on her own.'

Enid clutched at the idea. 'Oh, yes! That'll be it, I expect. Oh dear! My poor heart's racing.'

'Come into my study and sit down while I phone, Mrs Granger.' She patted the nanny's arm in a comforting manner and led the way to her study.

Unfortunately, the phone call did nothing to reassure them.

'She hasn't ... oh, dear. That is worrying... No, I can't explain it, I'm afraid Mrs Granger was here just before four as usual, but Penny had gone... Well, of course we'll search the school but I really don't think... You'll get in touch with the police? Do you think that's necessary at this point?... Very well, then. Good. Yes, of course...'

The word 'police' did nothing to reassure Enid. 'She's not there, is she?'

Slowly the headmistress put down the receiver. 'I'm sorry, Mrs Granger. Penny hasn't gone home.'

Miss Meacher's face crumpled. 'That poor mother!' She was silenced immediately by a sharp look from the headmistress.

'I've promised we'll search the school – we must enlist the caretaker's help.' She put a hand to her head. 'This *has* to end well, Mrs Granger. I have great faith.'

'But suppose something's happened to

her,' cried Enid. 'Suppose someone's *taken* her!'

'Abducted her, you mean? *Kidnapped* her? But why should they?' The headmistress looked surprised. 'It's usually the children of millionaires who get kidnapped.'

She's trying to appear calm, thought Enid, but she noted the headmistress's fingers tapping restlessly on the desktop.

Miss Stobart smiled at her. 'We mustn't alarm ourselves just yet. She's probably gone home with one of the other children. They do that sometimes.'

Enid suddenly saw that this *was* a possibility and some of the terror left her. Yes, that could be the answer. 'Oh, I do hope so!'

The headmistress's smile was determinedly positive. 'We'll find her, never fear. Mrs Gough is contacting the police and they'll no doubt come here. While we're waiting we'll search the building.'

Ella put down the telephone and stared blankly ahead. They'd taken Penny. She *knew* it. Daniel and Lizzie had stolen her child.

'Oh, please God!' she whispered and put out a hand to steady herself. She hadn't paid over the money; she had gone to the police – and this was her punishment. There was a terrifying blackness in front of her eyes and she felt icy cold. They had taken her bright, wonderful daughter; she might never see Penny again. The thoughts seemed to echo round the hallway, grotesque and terrible.

'They've taken Penny!' The words were almost inaudible. Looking at herself she staggered to the downstairs cloakroom. Looking at herself in the mirror, she saw the face of a stranger – pale and wide-eyed.

'Penny!' she whispered.

If they laid a finger on her daughter she would kill them both...

Ella ran the tap, filled her cupped hands and rinsed her mouth. Then she splashed cold water over her face which was beaded with perspiration. Already her mind was wrestling with the problem. Where would they take Penny? What would they do to her? Surely Daniel wouldn't harm her? She breathed deeply, struggling against faintness. She must be strong for Penny's sake.

Outside the cloakroom she stood for a moment, leaning back against the door. Annie, coming out from the kitchen with her arms full of ironed linen, stared at her in concern.

'Mrs Gough! You look terrible! Are you ill?'

'The phone call ... it's Penny. They can't find her!'

Annie looked at her blankly. 'Can't find

her? Who can't?'

'Penny's missing! Mrs Granger went to the school as usual, but she's gone.'

'Oh, no! She can't – I mean, surely – I mean how do you know? For sure?' She clutched the linen to her as though for protection.

'I just know,' said Ella. 'I have to go down to the school to talk to the police. If Penny turns up–'

'Oh, she will, Mrs Gough!'

'If she comes home you must ring the school immediately...' she pointed out the number in the telephone book, 'to let us know. And if she does come home, don't let her out of your sight. Do you understand?'

Annie nodded, white-faced. 'Where's Mrs Granger?'

'Still at the school.'

'Little monkey! She's probably wandered off. I did that once. Followed one of the boys home because he said he was going to marry me. I was six at the time. My mother gave me a smack on the legs for the fright I gave her.'

Ella stared at her. If only she could believe that. 'I don't think she's gone willingly.' But she couldn't expect Annie to understand; the housekeeper knew nothing about the demand for money. 'Oh God, Annie! If anything's happened to her...' She snatched a handkerchief from her pocket and wiped away the tears. 'I mustn't give way; I know I mustn't. And Annie, not a word to Mr Gough. He need not know there's anything wrong – at least, not yet. I'll tell him when I absolutely have to. He's not in a fit state for a shock like this.' This was his beloved daughter.

Annie nodded. 'I won't say a word. I swear it. He dotes on the child. It would break his heart if–'

'Don't say it!' She held up a hand. 'Don't even *think* it!'

Ella rang for a taxi and pulled on a coat while she waited for it to arrive. Her arms felt like lead and there were cramps in her stomach. She was still waiting when the bell rang. Rushing to open it, she found Charles Marriott on the doorstep. His smile faded as he read her expression.

Before he could speak she said, 'Charles? What are you doing here?'

'You invited me to dinner, remember?'

Ella stared at him, utterly confused. 'Today? Was it today?' She wanted to scream. All she could think about was her missing daughter.

'It was,' he said gently. 'You said, "Come early if it's a nice day and we'll take Penny to feed the ducks in the park."' As she still stared wordlessly, he said, 'If it's not convenient...'

Ella tried to speak but could only manage

a choking sound. 'It's Penny–' she began, then the tears burst forth and his arms were round her as she clung to him in a paroxysm of terror. Dimly aware that Annie had joined them, she heard Charles say, 'Don't worry. I'll look after her, Annie.'

If only he could, Ella thought, gasping for air, desperate to control her fear. If only he could wave a magic wand and turn back the clock. If she had Penny in her arms now, she would never let her go.

'Come and sit in the car,' he said, guiding her down the steps.

They sat together in the back seat. Gradually her tears came to an end and she began, haltingly, to explain what was happening. Fortunately he grasped the situation straight away and took charge.

'So you were on your way to the school?' he said.

She nodded, wiping her eyes and breathing deeply. 'I thought you were the taxi.'

He pointed down the drive. 'Here it comes now,' he said, 'but you don't need him. I'll take you wherever you need to go. Wait here and I'll pay him off.'

Emotionally exhausted, Ella could only watch and wait.

'Excuse me, but are you Mrs Gough?'

Surprised, she turned to see a young man at the car window. He held a letter in his hand and she was immediately defensive.

'Who are you?' she demanded sharply, although common sense told her this could hardly be a kidnapper delivering a ransom note.

'Tom Berry, ma'am. The new gardener. A chap just asked me to hand you this. Wouldn't give his name. Said you'd know.'

So it *could* have been. In seconds the insecurities rushed back to fill her with dread. 'Thank you,' she stammered. 'What did he look like?'

He described Daniel and she nodded. With an effort she managed a friendly smile. 'I hope you're settling in, Mr Berry.'

'I am, thank you.'

She waited a moment, watching him go, afraid of what the letter might contain. It would be a demand for a lot of money, she knew that much, but as long as they got Penny back unharmed she would gladly hand over every penny they owned, and Roland would feel the same. She was tearing open the envelope when Charles climbed back into the car.

'This came,' she told him.

'You think it's a ransom note?'

Ella nodded and began to read it out: *'Dear Ella, This is to let you know that I have left Lizzie. There is nothing to keep us together now and she will be better off without me.'*

She said, 'It isn't,' and read on silently:

...I left her the ring you gave me, with instructions to sell it. The money will keep her going for a while.

I have found another job – handyman, with a cottage to go with it. Hardly well paid, but I have a roof over my head and meals provided. I doubt you will ever want to contact me, but if you should need me the address is above.

Please forgive me for all the grief I have caused you. I hope you may one day think kindly of me. I wish you and your family all the best.

Sincerely, Daniel

Ella reread the note with growing bewilderment, then handed it to Charles. It was not the letter of a man who had recently been blackmailing her. He was giving her his address – and he was hardly likely to do that if he feared a visit from the police. She felt unreasonably pleased that he had left Lizzie and delighted that he had a job and a roof over his head. But if he wasn't the blackmailer, who was?

'It was Lizzie!' she cried. 'It has to be Lizzie.'

So if Lizzie had sent the blackmail letter, had she also taken Penny? Ella thought frantically.

'I've changed my mind,' she told Charles. 'I must talk to Daniel. Take me to this address. Do you know it?'

'Yes.'

Moments later he had cranked the engine and they were on their way.

Daniel's greeting was far from warm. 'What the hell are you doing here?'

She ignored his obvious irritation. 'I spoke to your employer. He said I could have ten minutes of your time and no more. Daniel, someone has taken Penny.'

'Taken her? How do you mean?'

'She's disappeared. We think someone's kidnapped her; we believe it's Lizzie.'

'Lizzie? How could she – I mean, why should she?' His look of bewilderment was genuine, thought Ella. He had not been involved in the blackmail, and for that she was deeply thankful.

'Someone sent me a blackmail demand,' she told him, 'immediately after I gave you the ring – which she pawned. I'm ashamed to say that I thought it was you, but that's not important right now. Finding Penny before she comes to any harm is what matters. Would Lizzie do something like that? Is she capable of kidnapping a child?'

He looked dazed. 'I wouldn't think so, but ... she was always rather wild. Rather unpredictable. If my leaving her...' His eyes widened. 'Oh God, Ella, I hope this isn't my fault.'

297

Ella struggled to stay calm. 'I don't care whose fault it is. Could Lizzie do it, Daniel? Could she take Penny? I don't want to send the police off on a wild-goose chase. You know her...'

'The police?'

He hesitated and her fragile calm almost deserted her. 'Daniel! Tell me. I don't have much time.'

'I daresay she *could*.'

'And – and would she hurt Penny?'

He regarded her unhappily. 'Not normally,' he said.

Ella wanted to scream. He was protecting his wife. She said, 'But...?'

'She gets a bit uncontrollable when she drinks. That's really the only time – the only way she might do something stupid.'

'Stupid? Or do you mean violent?'

'I don't know. I suppose it's possible.'

Ella tried to ignore the image this created in her mind. 'If she has taken Penny, where would she hide? Does she have any friends who would hide them both? Think, Daniel, *please*. I have to find her. Every minute counts.'

'If she's not at the flat, try the people next door. Or Mrs Levine, the old lady upstairs. Ella, shouldn't you leave it to the police?'

'No. I must do something. Anyway, the police will be at the school by now and I can't waste time telephoning.'

'Shall I come with you? I'll ask for time off. I'll–'

'No need. I've got a friend with me... Thanks, Daniel.'

Ella was already running back the way she had come. He called after her, but she didn't stop until she was back in the car. Then she gave Charles the new address and leaned back against the seat. She felt better for having something positive to do. As they drove, her desperation was giving way to a fierce determination. She was going to find her daughter – and God help anyone who tried to stop her.

May Baisley sat at the kitchen table, fuming. The child had disappeared and they were keeping Mr Gough in the dark. They were treating him like a child. It was quite disgraceful.

Annie faced her across the large scrubbed table, her hands wrapped around a cup of tea. Behind her, the stove threw out a comforting heat, and the smell of steak-and-kidney pie filled the air.

Annie shook her head. 'At least the poor soul's got someone to help her. That Mr Marriott's a very decent sort.'

Evans was propped against the door jamb, unwilling to enter with his muddy boots and too lazy to remove them. Tom Berry sat on the back step, enjoying the sunshine, saying little.

May put down her tea. 'Decent? *Decent* men don't embrace other men's wives,' she told Annie. 'Anyway, Mr Marriott's almost a stranger. They've only known him a few weeks.'

'Hardly a stranger if he's invited to dinner. And Mr Gough likes him.'

'Liking's one thing.' May threw her a dark look. *'Trusting's* another. How can they trust a man they hardly know? And as for liking – I daresay some people liked Crippen, but that didn't make him a decent man.' She felt rather proud of this and was pleased to see that Annie was momentarily silenced. 'I'd say that Mr Marriott was taking advantage of her – unless, of course, she encouraged him.'

Annie's eyes narrowed. 'You implying something, Nurse? Because if you are, I shall make it my business to–'

'I'm implying nothing. Simply making a comment.' May regarded her with dislike. If only the silly woman wasn't so loyal. Talk about blind devotion! If Mrs Gough stole the Crown Jewels, Annie would think up some exonerating circumstances. 'But if Mr Marriott had his arms round her...'

Annie rose to the bait. 'You *are* implying something! You just be careful!'

Mr Evans peered nervously over the rim of his mug and said, 'Now, now, ladies!'

300

May glared at him. 'You stay out of this. I don't know why you have to stand there, anyway. You're letting in the cold air.'

Annie said, 'Pay her no heed, Mr Evans. You don't take orders from this one. And I like a bit of fresh air.'

The two men exchanged glances and Evans muttered something which made Tom Berry laugh.

May snapped, 'What did you say?' but they grinned at each other like two schoolboys. Really. Men!

Annie said, 'He was just comforting her that's all. There's no harm in a man finding a woman attractive.'

'But she's *married!*'

'So what? She's still attractive. He's not making eyes at her and...'

'Not yet, perhaps.'

'...and she's not leading him on.'

'How do you know?'

Annie wagged a finger. 'You know your trouble, Nurse? You've got a very nasty mind.' She left the table and began drying the cutlery, tossing the knives and forks into the drawer with as much clatter as possible.

May stiffened. 'And *your* trouble, Annie, is that you've been here so long you can't see the wood for the trees. Mrs Gough's no angel. She's got faults like everybody else.'

'Meaning?' Annie turned to glare at her.

May sipped her tea. 'Meaning that pretty

women attract men like bees to a honey pot, and it's up to the woman to see that they keep their distance. I wouldn't let a strange man hug me if I had a husband like Mr Gough.'

If only! Perhaps Mrs Gough would run off with Mr Marriott, leaving the way open for *her*. If this fantasy ever became reality, she would give Annie her marching orders without a second thought.

Annie said, 'Nobody'd want to hug *you!*'

Mr Evans gasped and a mouthful of tea went down the wrong way, making him splutter and spill what was left of it. Tom Berry brought in both the mugs and retired to wait nervously on the doorstep while Evans readied himself to leave.

That does it, thought May furiously. Annie would go without a reference. She put down her tea with great deliberation. 'I *beg* your pardon?'

'Granted,' said Annie. 'I'm glad I'm not like you – always thinking the worst of people. If Mrs Gough wants the news kept from her husband, then she has a very good reason and it's none of your business. *I* understand her if you don't. She wants to save him from the agony of knowing unless he really has to. What's the point in upsetting the poor man if the girl's going to turn up? Mrs Gough is doing what she thinks best and while you're in my kitchen

I'll thank you to–'

'Your kitchen? Don't fool yourself – you just work here like the rest of us.' She glanced towards the men for support but they had disappeared, closing the door behind them. May snorted, '*Your* kitchen, indeed!'

She thought she had Annie beaten, but the wretched woman recovered quickly and pointed an accusing finger at her.

'Well, I may *just work here,* but at least I'm not making a fool of myself over my employer. Oh, don't bother to deny it. We all know you're soppy about him.'

May felt the colour rush into her face as she stared at the housekeeper.

'Well! I ... I don't – I...'

The shock was tremendous and she struggled for words, feeling her cheeks burn with embarrassment. Had they known all along? But no, that was impossible. She had been so discreet.

Annie went on, 'Mr Gough this and Mr Gough that! You really thought we didn't know? Huh! You're a bigger fool than you look.'

Stricken, May rose from her chair on legs that felt stiff and unresponsive. She must get out of the kitchen.

Annie had the audacity to laugh. 'Don't like the truth, do you!' she taunted.

May kept her face averted as she made her

way to the door. How on *earth* had they guessed?

Annie called after her, 'Pot calling the kettle black!'

May's wits had deserted her and she could think of nothing suitably cutting to say in reply. Stumbling along the passage, she reached the stairs and clutched the handrail, willing herself to master each step as she made her way slowly upstairs. She was trembling with humiliation. How dare Annie speak to her like that?

'Stupid, ignorant woman,' she muttered. Her throat felt tight. What hurt most was the loss of her secret. Annie had tarnished that by her coarse jibes and May knew she would never forgive her. Mrs Gough should know better than to employ such a woman.

She was trying to feel hate instead of grief. Hate would be easier to deal with than the terrible sense of loss which enveloped her. May doubted if any man had ever looked at Annie twice, let alone entrusted himself to her care. She reached the landing and paused for breath and to gather her resources; she felt strangely weak, but she fought against the desire to hide away in her own room. Once there she would throw herself on to the bed and weep, and they would see her reddened eyes and know...

May drew herself up and set her chin.

'Stupid, ignorant woman!' she repeated

and focused on Annie. What gave her or anyone else the right to think they knew better than Mr Gough's own nurse what was best for him? He was a grown man; he deserved to know what was going on. He had a *right* to know – and she had a good mind to tell him herself...

'I could do it!' she whispered, coming to a sudden halt outside the bedroom. She had a wonderful vision of herself bending over her patient, explaining gently what had happened. She could see the gratitude in his eyes. 'Thank you, Nurse. Oh, thank you,' he would say. He would then decide on the best course of action. He'd probably call the police. Maybe he'd ask *her* to do that for him. By the time Mrs Gough returned from her harebrained chase, the matter would be under control.

'I could *do* it!'

She closed her eyes, hearing again Annie's spiteful jibe: 'Nobody'd want to hug *you*.' Wouldn't they? Wouldn't Mr Gough give her just a small sign of gratitude? Maybe a little peck on the side of the face? A tiny sign was all she asked; a hint that in other circumstances he might want to do more.

She longed to tell him, but did she have the courage to go against them all? This might be her best chance of moving a little closer to her patient; starting a new phase in the relationship.

'Tell him!' she urged herself.

She took three deep breaths, fluffed up her hair around her cap and opened the bedroom door. Mr Gough was listening to the wireless, but he turned eagerly as she came in. His smile faded as he saw that she was alone.

'Any sign of Charles Marriott?' he began. 'He's coming to dinner. He's supposed to be here by...' He stopped, obviously alerted by her manner. 'What is it, Nurse?'

If only he would call her 'May', she thought. Just once. She crossed the room and bent over him. He smelled of Knight's Castile and hair pomade and the top two buttons of his pyjama jacket were undone. A few more inches and she could have kissed his bare chest, she thought. Her breath caught in her throat as reluctantly she drew back a little.

'Mr Gough, I have something to tell you,' she said huskily. For a moment her courage failed and she fussed with his pillows. Then, greatly daring, she laid a hand on his shoulder. 'Something has happened, and rather foolishly your wife is determined to keep this from you.'

'Happened? What's happened?'

'It's probably nothing...' Again May felt a ripple of unease. 'At least... The point is that I feel you have a right to know.' This was proving harder than she expected. She began again. 'When Mrs Granger reached Havenbridge, Penny wasn't there...'

He listened in silence, open-mouthed with shock. Ashen-faced, he clutched at May's wrists, pulling her closer.

'My daughter?' he whispered hoarsely. 'My daughter is *missing?* Good God, what are you saying?'

He was hurting her wrists, but she made no attempt to disentangle herself. At least he was holding her.

'I thought you would want to know,' she told him. 'Mrs Gough wanted it kept from you, but I disagreed. "He's not a child," I told her. "He's entitled to know the truth." I felt it my duty–'

'Missing since when? Tell me!' His hands fell away from her wrists as he started to shake.

'–my duty to you, Mr Gough. Just because you're an invalid doesn't mean you have no right to know. She should–'

'Missing since four o'clock? Is she lost? Is that it? *Tell me,* for Christ's sake, woman. Has someone taken her?'

Alarmed by his reaction, she watched in horror as he threw back the bedclothes. 'Oh, no, Mr Gough! You stay right where you are! I insist.'

She put her hands on his shoulders, but he threw her off with surprising force. 'We have to do something. I must get downstairs.'

May made a grab for the bedclothes and tried to cover him, but he had swung his legs sideways and was trying to stand up.

'But you're not well enough!' she cried. 'Get back into bed! For heaven's *sake*, Mr Gough!' She watched with growing panic as he levered himself upright. 'You mustn't... There's nothing you can do. The police are dealing with it.'

'The police?' He stared wildly round the room. 'Fetch my clothes, woman.'

'Mr Gough, *please.*' He had never spoken to her like that before. 'They're doing all they can. They'll find her.' This was not at all how she'd imagined it.

'Get me some clothes, damn you!'

He swayed suddenly and she rushed to help him. 'I'll get your clothes,' she promised. Anything to keep him there. 'You just sit on the bed. You're really not well, Mr Gough, but I'll try to find some clothes.' She clasped her hands in despair, seeing only too clearly what Ella had so wisely anticipated.

'Oh God!' He groaned, one hand to his chest. His eyes closed, then opened in alarm. She waited breathlessly until his expression relaxed.

Then she said, 'Just slip you feet under the bedclothes while I – really, there's nothing else you can do, Mr Gough. Your wife's gone to the school. She went in the car with Mr

Marriott to talk...'

His face brightened. 'Marriott? Well, that's something. He'll help her. He's a good chap, Charles Marriott.'

She hesitated. 'Yes, he is.' Thank goodness Annie couldn't hear her.

He screwed up his face and closed his eyes. When he opened them, he said, 'Marriott will sort things out.'

'Of course he will.' She ground out the words, wondering what Mr Gough would say if he knew 'the good chap' had been seen with his arms around Mrs Gough while she sobbed on his shoulder. Briefly May was tempted, but decided in the circumstances to save that for later. She watched him anxiously. Mrs Gough would have something to say to her if he insisted on dressing himself and trying to help.

She said, 'Why not leave it to your wife and Mr Marriott? For all we know they might have found her already. Probably have. They could be on their way home right now. Is there any point in upsetting yourself?'

By way of an answer, he pressed his hand against his heart and said, 'Christ Almighty!'

'Are you all right?' Her own heart fluttered in sympathy.

'I don't know.' He doubled up. Now he was clutching his left arm, his clenched fingers white. His breathing was laboured.

May decided to take advantage of his momentary weakness. She said briskly, 'Get right back into bed, Mr Gough. You're over-exerting yourself.'

Instead he lurched sideways and almost fell from the bed. She tried to manoeuvre him, but he slipped further and fell on to the floor. His face was contorted in agony and May was forced to acknowledge the attack for what it was.

'Oh, my godfathers!' she whispered. She knelt beside him. 'Mr Gough. *Darling!* Don't die!'

He made a sound that was little more than a moan. When he tried to speak the words came out in an incomprehensible jumble. His eyes rolled in his head and his curled-up body tightened. She was desperate to help him, but experience told her there was nothing she could do for him. She must get the doctor. No, better still an ambulance. He would have to go to hospital for emergency treatment. Struggling to her feet, blinking back tears, she rushed into the next room to the telephone and called the operator.

'Get an ambulance here as quickly as possible,' she gasped and added the address. 'My employer is having a heart attack.'

Penny lay on an old blanket on top of a heap of coke in a corner of the cellar, feeling

310

rather aggrieved. Her hands were tied together in front of her by a piece of cord and there was another piece round her ankles. She thought her mother ought to come and take her home. She stared at Meg's Auntie Liz and wondered where Meg was.

Auntie Liz said, 'What are you staring at?'

'Nothing.'

'Well, don't.'

Hastily Penny looked away. There was a spider on a web in the corner of the wall and she watched it for a few moments. When it did nothing interesting, she took another look round the cellar. The walls had once been white but were now very dirty. There was a small window. Someone had hung a sack over it, but a dim light showed round the edges. Penny wondered whether she could get out through the window and run away, but it was high up and Auntie Liz would see her trying to climb up the wall.

In one corner there were three cardboard boxes full of what looked like old clothes and an enormous pile of newspapers. She knew without looking that Auntie Liz was sitting on the only chair and that she was drinking from a bottle which stood on an upturned tea-chest beside her. Also on the tea-chest was an alarm clock, a folded scarf and a thermos flask. Leaning against the chest was a broom.

'I'm thirsty,' Penny grumbled.

'Too bad!' Auntie Liz glared at her. 'You can have some hot milk later, but not yet. Do you good to go without for a change. Spoilt little brat!'

'I'm not!'

'Course you are. Private school. Fancy uniform. All that.'

Penny said, 'Can I play with Meg?'

'No, you can't. And stop asking questions.'

'Where is she?'

'That's another question. Just shut up, will you? My head's thumping.'

'But why can't I?'

'None of your business.' Auntie Liz took another drink from the bottle and lit a cigarette.

'Your hands are shaking!' Penny told her.

'I won't tell you again! Shut *up!*'

Her fourth mouthful, thought Penny, who had been counting them because she had nothing else to do. She had decided that she hated Auntie Liz because she told lies. When she came to the school, she was all smiley and told Penny that Mummy had said she was to go with her because they were going to meet at the shoe-shop, where Mummy would buy her some black patents like Lucy Barnes's shoes. *Exactly* like them, with ankle-straps and a button. But they didn't go to the shop; they went for a long ride on a bus and then got off and got on

312

another bus, and then they went to a baker's and bought two currant buns and ate them walking along the street – which Nanny said was vulgar – but they never did get to the shoe-shop.

When it got dark they got on another bus and came here, and Auntie Liz stopped being nice and smiley and everything was horrible.

Penny wriggled until she could sit up. 'I want to go home.'

'Well, you can't. Get that into your head. And don't turn on the waterworks. It won't wash with me.'

She blew out smoke and to Penny's surprise it turned into a lovely little ring and floated up to the ceiling.

Penny was trying hard not to cry, because if she did Auntie Liz had said she would stuff an old sock into her mouth and she didn't like the thought of that.

She said, 'Are you going to sweep up? It's very dirty in here.'

'Sweep up? *Sweep up?* No, I'm *not.*'

'What's the broom for, then?'

Auntie Liz glanced at it. 'To chase away the mice.'

Penny smiled. 'I had a mouse once. It had a dear little cage with lots of sawdust and a dear little wheel and it–'

'I don't want to hear about your mouse. Nasty things!'

'It had dear little whiskers and a lo-o-ng tail...'

'I said–'

'I called it Mickey, but when it had some babies we had to call it Minnie and...'

Auntie Liz grabbed the broom. 'One more word from you and I'll wallop you with this!'

Penny gave up trying to be nice. 'I'm telling Daddy about you!' she said.

Auntie Liz said, 'Listen a minute... I can hear someone!'

Suddenly Penny heard it too. It sounded like footsteps somewhere outside. She opened her mouth to shout, but Auntie Liz leaped from the chair and clapped a hand over her face. The hand smelled of cigarettes.

'Not a squeak, d'you hear me?'

Penny could only nod.

The footsteps stopped and there was the sound of someone knocking on a door.

Penny thought it was probably Mummy or Mrs Granger come to take her home. She tried to open her mouth to call out, but the hand tightened. Penny bit it, and Auntie Liz slapped her leg so hard it made tears come into Penny's eyes.

The voice outside called again 'Liz? It's only me – Win. You in there? You all right?'

There were different, heavier footsteps. 'Take a look through the front window, Len.

I couldn't see nothing through the letter box. I don't think she's come back.'

A man's voice said, 'I could force the door.'

'Force the door? Are you mad?'

So it wasn't Mummy after all. Tears of disappointment trickled down Penny's face, but Auntie Liz shook her violently. 'Stop grizzling or you'll get another slap!' she whispered.

The man said, 'She's not here, Win. Give it up. Who cares, anyway? I'd like something to eat if you've finished chasing around after her ladyship.'

'I only thought – you know – she was in a funny mood this morning. Very low. Talking a bit wild.'

'What? Liz do herself in? Never!'

'It happens. 'Specially in her condition.'

'That selfish cow? Give over!'

Grumbling, the voices faded, and the footsteps moved away.

Auntie Liz took away her hand and said, 'Stupid tart!'

The mention of food reminded Penny that she was hungry. 'Is it tea-time yet?'

'You had a bun. What more do you want?'

Penny sighed noisily. At home with Mrs Granger they always had sandwiches and *then* a cake or some biscuits. Penny was getting cold. She looked towards the window; there was no light coming round the sack over the glass now. She said, 'I don't like the dark.'

Auntie Liz pulled a torch from the bag and switched it on, standing it on end so that the faint beam shone up on to the ceiling. She said, 'Time for your milk and then you can go to sleep.'

'I'm not sleepy.' Penny tried to look at the clock. She was trying to remember what Miss Meacher had told them about the big hand and the little hand.

'You will be!'

'But it's not my bed-time!'

'It is because I say it is.' She picked up the thermos flask. It reminded Penny of the picnics they had had in the summer, and remembering them made her want to cry.

Auntie Liz unscrewed the top of the flask and it turned into a little cup. She poured hot milk into it. 'Drink that!' she said. 'All of it.'

'Has it got sugar in it?'

'Oh, for heaven's sake! Just drink the stuff.'

Slowly Penny began to sip the hot milk.

'Hurry up. There's another cupful in there. Don't want to waste it, do we?'

Smiling a funny smile, Auntie Liz lit another cigarette.

Chapter Ten

The light was failing as Ella and Charles reached the school. Once inside, the police informed them that Penny was no longer on the premises. They had looked everywhere inside the building – every classroom, the hall, the cloakrooms. Then they had searched outside – the playground, the toilets, the shed where some of the teachers kept their bicycles. They had even investigated the boiler room.

The constable gave a little shrug. 'I'm so sorry,' he said.

'She's not here,' said Ella, her panic mounting with every minute that passed. 'Oh, God! She's not here!' Her shrill words hinted at the growing hysteria within.

Charles put his arm around her. 'Be strong, Ella,' he said softly. 'You can deal with this.'

Ella stared at him. 'I really don't think so,' she admitted, but hearing herself utter the treacherous words was a shock. She had been so strong since Roland's illness, congratulating herself on her ability to organise without fuss; revelling in her ability to make instant decisions; proud of the way she managed her own life and the lives of those around her. Now, within the space of a few days, her self-confidence had been stripped away, leaving her totally vulnerable. The disappearance of her beloved child had been the final blow.

'Yes, you can.' Charles's arm tightened. 'I'm here, and we'll deal with it together.'

She flashed him a grateful glance and then turned to the constable. He looked much too young, she thought unhappily. His smooth face was unlined, his expression a little too earnest, his uniform tunic too large round the neck.

She said, 'Shouldn't you be sending out a description of her? We're wasting so much time. Penny could be–' She stopped, appalled. She had almost said 'dead', but that wasn't possible. 'She could be in serious trouble. What about the hospitals? She may have had an accident.' An accident, she thought fearfully, might be the best they could hope for. An accident was not the result of malevolent forces at work. If Penny had been knocked down by a motor car there could be no malicious woman responsible for her disappearance. An accident – any accident was something from which she could recover. But being snatched by a crazy woman filled with hate...

They had gone through to the headmistress's study. The young constable was saying something and Ella tried to concentrate.

'...a few details, Mrs Gough?' He waited, his notebook and pencil poised.

'Details?' What was he talking about? She felt as though she were in a fog of incomprehension – like the worst type of nightmare where suddenly you are no longer in control.

'Your daughter's description – unless you have a photograph of her with you?'

'Not a recent one, I'm afraid.'

'Then a few details – age, appearance and so on.'

'Oh yes! I'm sorry.' She swallowed but her throat was dry. 'Seven years old, shoulder-length hair, blue eyes, wearing a school uniform...'

'Which is?' he prompted.

Her mind was a blank. What *was* the school uniform?

Miss Stobart said, 'A navy-blue gym slip and white blouse.'

He said, 'Shoes?'

Everyone was looking at Ella. She stared back. Shoes. The word meant nothing; her mind refused to function. She heard Mrs Granger say, 'Brown lace-ups. Her coat's a sort of fine tweed with velvet collar. A fawny brown...'

She thought, 'Poor Mrs Granger'. Touching the nanny's arm, she said, 'Don't blame yourself.'

Unfortunately the kindly meant words were more than the nanny could bear and her eyes filled with tears.

Charles said, 'We'll find her. You'll see.'

The constable turned to the headmistress. 'If I may use your telephone...'

'Of course.'

Ella made an effort to collect her thoughts. 'Ask for Detective Sergeant – sorry, Detective Inspector Hall.'

They all waited as the constable passed on Penny's description. When he finally put the phone down he turned to Ella. 'They'll be looking for her on the streets. They've already checked the hospitals, and there's been no accident involving a child.' He smiled. 'I really think she's probably wandered off, Mrs Gough.'

'No,' Ella insisted. 'She's been taken by a woman called Mrs Hampton. I just know it! Why didn't you speak to Detective Inspector Hall? He understands the background to all this.'

'D.I. Hall was out on another case, I'm afraid. Expected back in about an hour. Can I give him a message?'

'Just tell him what's happened. He'll know what to do.'

The constable started to put away his notebook, then changed his mind. 'If you're right about this woman Hampton – where might she take the child? Any idea?'

Ella shook her head. 'I suppose she's got friends but I don't know who they are. Her neighbours might know.'

'I'll report back to the station and pass this on to my sergeant.'

They all walked out to the playground where his bicycle leaned against the railings. No one spoke as he rode away.

Ella said, 'He's much too young. Too inexperienced.'

Charles squeezed her arm. 'They have their procedures. At least we know she hasn't been involved in an accident.'

Miss Stobart glanced at Ella. 'I shall wait here for a while in case Penny comes back to the school.'

Mrs Granger said, 'I'll stay with you, if that's all right with Mrs Gough. Then if she turns up I can take her straight home.'

If. *If?* Ella turned to Charles. 'I'd like to talk to the Hamptons' neighbours. They might know something.' They *have* to know something, she told herself. A seven-year-old child couldn't simply vanish.

They found the Hamptons' house and tried that first. No one answered their knock. They rang the bell. Silence. By the light of the street lamp they made their way round to the back through a wooden gate, passing the coal hole, a small, low window covered with rusty iron mesh and a brimming dustbin without a lid. From the top of a fence, a black cat jumped down and ran to greet them. At the back of the house Ella pressed her face to the scullery window. The place certainly appeared to be empty but, peering through a gap in the net curtains, she saw that someone had left a milk bottle on the draining board. About an inch of milk remained. She also made out a badly chipped sink with one tap, a few unwashed plates and some cutlery. Beyond, on the table were the remains of a loaf of bread, a butter dish and a crumpled cigarette packet. She thought that if this was Daniel's home she could understand him leaving it.

'Someone's been here,' she said, 'but when?'

Charles had examined the garden shed. 'No one there.'

Together they surveyed the garden where, at the far end, they saw signs of Daniel's handiwork: a row of cabbages, another of onions, a small wheelbarrow full of weeds. The thought of him living and working in this depressing place brought tears to eyes, but she blinked fiercely.

'We'd better try the neighbours,' she said.

An elderly woman on the left side of the Hamptons could tell them nothing. Or preferred not to. She didn't even open the door, but pushed up a window and spoke from there. Obviously callers after dark were not welcome in this part of the town. Ella couldn't blame them. There was a dismal aspect to the street which the lamps failed to dispel.

'I keep myself to myself,' the woman told them. 'Never been one to stick my nose in. They'll all tell you that. What she does next door is her own business.' She closed the window before Ella could ask any more questions.

They had better luck on the other side where a blonde woman answered the door. Seeing two strangers silhouetted against the street light, she left the chain on the door and squinted at them through the crack.

'The Hamptons?' she repeated, regarding them with obvious suspicion. 'And who might you be?'

'My name's Mrs Gough. I need to—'

'Mrs Gough?' Her surprise was evident. 'The one what got Dan the sack? I hardly think you'd be very welcome even if she *was* in, which she's not. She never had a good word to say about you, that I can say.' She slid the chain and opened the door a little wider, staring at Ella with undisguised curiosity.

Ella said, 'My little girl's missing. She wasn't at the school. We think she may have left with someone else. I have to—'

A small girl pushed her way forward and Ella, startled, recognised her at once. 'Meg?' she said. 'Meg Cutts?'

The woman said, 'So? I'm Win Cutts, her mother.' To the child she said, 'You know this lady?' She made it sound like an accusation.

Meg smiled shyly at Ella, who narrowed her eyes. '*You* live next door to the Hamptons?' She glanced at Charles, who raised his eyebrows.

Ella said, 'I met Meg and her aunt at Lucy Barnes' birthday party.' Her mind was racing.

The woman nodded. 'That was Liz Hampton. Meg calls her "Auntie" but she's not really.'

Ella was stunned. 'So *that* was Dan – Mr Hampton's wife!'

Lizzie Hampton had been able to identify both Ella and Penny, but had concealed her own identity. It *had* to be significant. She turned to Charles. 'So Lizzie knew me and she knew Penny. Meeting us out of the blue like that – is that what gave her the idea?'

'It's certainly possible.' He turned to the woman. 'So you've no idea where she could be?'

'None at all. Saw her this morning early but not since.'

A thin, dour man appeared behind the woman and said, 'What's up now?'

Ella said, 'I'm looking for my daughter, Penny.'

The woman told him, 'She's asking about Liz, but I told her we don't know no more'n what she does.'

He said, 'And don't want to, neither. If she's done a moonlight flit she won't be missed. She was trouble, that one.'

Win said, 'She had her good points, though. Credit where credit's due, Len.' She turned to Ella. 'And she was crazy over her old man. It properly knocked her for six when he left.'

Ella felt a flash of unwilling solidarity with the absent Lizzie. She said quickly, 'The house seems to be empty.'

Win said, 'It is. We went round earlier. Not a dicky-bird. There's an old girl upstairs. She never goes out. A bit past it, but she might know something.'

Charles held out a ten-shilling note. 'If this Lizzie does turn up, would you call the police? They need to talk to her.'

As Win raised her hand, Len reached for the note and stuffed it into his pocket. 'What's the silly cow done then? Robbed a bank?'

Ella wanted to bang their heads together. They were not the sort of people she understood; they seemed callously indifferent and it was galling to have to ask them for help. Suddenly she turned to Charles. 'I wonder if

Daniel spoke to his wife about Penny? She told me they chatted one day while he was with us.' Her suspicion deepened into certainty: Daniel's wife had taken her daughter. If these people knew *anything,* she must frighten it out of them.

She said, 'Mrs Cutts, I have reason to believe that Lizzie Hampton has kidnapped my daughter. It's a police matter. If you know anything at all...'

The woman's eyes widened. 'Kidnapped your daughter? Liz? I don't believe it!'

Charles said, 'The police are looking for her at this very moment.'

'Please!' Ella said desperately. 'Do you have *any* idea where she might be? She obviously wouldn't bring her here, but she must have other friends or family?'

The woman shook her head. 'A brother Frank, but he's in the nick. Mind you, she was in a very funny mood last night. Smoking like a chimney and knocking back port. Fine mother you'll be, I told her. She kept—'

Ella broke in, 'Fine *mother?*' She had forgotten. 'Of course, Lizzie Hampton's expecting a baby.'

'Well, it won't be an elephant, will it! April, the doctor said. Spring baby.'

'Does her husband know?' Now her heart was beating erratically. Surely Daniel knew his wife was pregnant? But he hadn't mentioned it.

'No. Poor cow was scared to tell him, them being in debt and everything. Then he scarpers. She wasn't too pleased. Left all on her own with a kid coming. *Very* nice!' She shrugged. 'She kept saying there was only one way out. "I'll have to do it!" she says, over and over. "Have to do what?" I said, but I couldn't get any sense out of her. I said to Len, "She's going to do herself in!" He didn't believe me, but I wouldn't put it past her. Jump off a bridge or something. Chuck herself under a train.'

Ella was glad of the reassuring pressure of Charles's hand on her arm.

'Could Liz have meant something else? Could she have meant she'd have to kidnap my daughter? Ask for a ransom? To get some money.'

Win and Len exchanged shocked glances.

'God knows!' Win said at last.

Ella was trying not to think about the pregnancy. Daniel's baby would be born into poverty and crime – and he didn't even know he had a child on the way. Perhaps Lizzie intended to keep it a secret. Or to try and get rid of it. She felt an overwhelming despair. It was all too sordid for words.

Suddenly she had to get away from them. She would go home – or to the police station. Maybe Detective Inspector Hall would be there by now. But first she thought they should try the old lady who lived above the Hamptons.

She said, 'Well, thanks for your help. We'll try next door.'

They walked back into the street and up the steps of Daniel's house. Charles put his finger on the top bell and left it there. After a long wait they saw a light come on at the top of the house and a shadowy figure descended the stairs.

An elderly lady opened the door. She was tall and painfully thin and smelled of lavender. Peering in their direction she asked, 'Who's there? Who is it?'

Raising her voice, Ella apologised for calling after dark.

The woman shook her head. 'I don't see too well these days.'

Ella explained who she was and asked her if she had any knowledge of Lizzie Hampton's whereabouts.

'Lizzie downstairs?' She cupped a hand to her right ear.

Ella shouted, 'Yes!'

'She's been out all day, that's all I know.'

'You're quite sure?'

'What's that?'

Ella raised her voice again and repeated the question.

'Am I sure?' The old lady nodded. 'Quite sure. I thought I heard her come back, but then it was all quiet. No wireless. No doors banging. And I've not seen hide nor hair of him either. I sometimes hear him in the garden, calling to her to put the kettle on because he's nearly done.' She leaned forward confidentially. 'I've got a nasty feeling he's left her. I heard her crying last night – and the light in the passage was on all night. *He* always turns it off last thing. She's good-hearted – do anything for you – but a bit noisy. Not that it bothers me.'

'Have you heard any children?'

'Any what?'

'Children.'

'Children? She hasn't got any children. Little Meg comes round from next door.' She smiled. 'Brings her doll. Sometimes she does her dance steps for me. Nice little thing.'

Ella looked at Charles. In a low voice she said, 'It's hopeless. She doesn't know anything. We might as well go.'

They thanked her, then retraced their steps to the car. Collapsing into the passenger seat, Ella watched Charles walk round to the starting handle. When the engine sprang to life he climbed in and put the car into gear.

'Where to?'

'We'd better go home,' she said. 'I'll have to tell Roland. I was hoping against hope he needn't know but... Or maybe we should go to the police station first. Oh God! I don't know what to do any more.'

The car moved forward as Ella stared through the windscreen in a baffled silence.

Charles glanced at her. 'I'm taking you back to Burleigh House. You've had a tremendous shock, Ella, and you need to rest a while. You can talk it over quietly with Roland and wait for news there.'

Ella could only nod.

The small group of hospital staff stared down at the figure in the bed. The patient was very pale and still and appeared to be sleeping.

The consultant scanned his notes and turned to the young registrar. 'You did well.'

The man flushed at the rare praise. 'Thank you, Mr Grey.' It had indeed been difficult and twice he thought they'd lost him. He had been very close to panic, although he would never admit it. It would have been his first death. Sweat still beaded his forehead, but the nurses had been wonderfully supportive. Bringing the patient back from the brink had seemed nothing less than a miracle.

The consultant said, 'So he's stabilised?'

'Just about. We had to sedate him. I think he could have another attack at any time.' He hesitated. 'To be honest, I'm not very hopeful.'

'Hm. Do they know what brought it on?'

As the registrar hesitated, the nurse said,

'Apparently their daughter's disappeared. Just a youngster. Missing from her school. It was the shock.'

'Thank you, nurse.' His smile was dismissive and she took the hint and hurried away.

The staff nurse said, 'The wife's in a terrible state. She's obviously devoted to him.'

The consultant pursed his lips. 'Were you on duty when he was brought in?'

'No, Mr Grey. That was Staff Nurse Tibbs. She was going off duty, but she told me what had happened. Apparently the patient can't walk without pain, so he's usually in a wheelchair – with a private nurse.'

'There's money, then?'

'Apparently.'

'Hm. What was it – an accident?'

'I'm sorry, Mr Grey. I'm afraid I don't know.'

The consultant referred once more to his notes. 'Ah! Polio, I see. Probably weakened the heart.' He glanced at the staff nurse. 'And the wife – where is she now?'

'In the waiting room. She's very tearful.'

'I'll go and speak with her.'

'Thank you, Mr Grey.'

The registrar led him out of the ward and into the small waiting room. As they entered a woman in a navy-blue coat jumped to her feet. She was crying and her face was blotched. She clutched her chest and cried, 'Don't say he's gone! Please! Don't say–'

The consultant held up his hand. 'No, no! So far so good, but you must understand that your husband's condition is far from satisfactory–'

She looked startled; opened her mouth to speak, then closed it.

He continued, '–but he is still alive, and we're doing all we can for him.'

'Thank you...' She seemed to be thinking hard. 'May I see him? May I sit with him?'

'I don't see why not, but he's been sedated and is sleeping deeply. Please don't try to talk to him.'

'I have to talk to him. I need to tell him... Oh!' She pressed a balled-up handkerchief against one eye and then the other, but the tears continued. 'If anything happens to him I – oh Lord! I'll never forgive myself...'

'Please, Mrs Gough. Do try to pull yourself together!' The consultant's voice was kind but firm. 'You mustn't blame yourself. Anyone can have a heart attack. In the circumstances and with the patient's history, it was always a possibility.' He glanced outside and caught the eye of the waiting registrar who, taking his cue, stepped in.

Before he left the room the consultant whispered, 'Don't mention the missing child. She's already almost hysterical.'

'Another cup of tea, Mrs Gough?' The registrar smiled. 'And a biscuit? We don't want *you* collapsing on us, do we? You've had a bad shock.' His soothing words softened the consultant's brisk departure. 'If you care to come with me...'

'No!' She shook off his hand. 'I'm going to sit with him. He might regain consciousness and I need to talk to him. I want to be on hand, you see.' More tears flooded her eyes and she covered her face with her hands.

'Oh God!' she whispered. 'What have I done?'

Lizzie shook the torch with a muttered oath. 'Don't you ... dare!'

For a moment it flickered, then the thin beam continued. She should have thought of getting some new batteries but she hadn't. Carefully she shone the light round the cellar, peering carefully into each corner, alert for anything that moved.

'Nothing there.' Momentarily reassured, Lizzie stared across at the sleeping child who lay sprawled across the ironing blanket. The whisky had blurred her vision slightly, but it had also lulled her into a false security. She no longer felt afraid; no longer wondered whether she had done the right thing. Everything was going to be all right.

Earlier Lizzie had removed the cord from around Penny's wrists so that she could drink the milk, and now one small arm was outstretched, as though asking for help. Lizzie stifled a pang of guilt. At least the kid had stopped asking those endless questions. With a struggle, she got to her feet and took a few reluctant steps closer to her prisoner.

'Ruddy kid!' Her voice lacked conviction.

A long sigh escaped her. *If* Dan knew about *their* child, he might come back. If he did and if he *promised* to stay with her, she could probably bear it. Some kids were OK. Even the Goughs' kid looked OK asleep, but when she was awake she was such a clever-clogs. She didn't miss much – except the hot milk. Lizzie grinned faintly. She'd swallowed that one!

She dropped to her knees beside the still form. The child was *so* still.

'Oi! You!'

There was no reply, not even the flutter of an eyelid. Lizzie was aware of a slight unease but she shook it off. The sleeping pills had worked a treat. Penny had drunk the milk, good as gold, even thanked her for it. Now that *was* good manners and she liked that. Not like Meg from next door. Not a bad kid at heart, but a proper little tomboy with her blinking handstands and cartwheels and suchlike. Noisy with it, too. When she wasn't shrieking she was bawling her head off. Mind you, it was all about upbringing and Win Cutts was hardly the best mother in the world. As for Len... She shook her head despairingly and thought about Dan. Now Dan would be a good father. He'd set a good example.

She raised her voice as much as she dared. 'Penny! D'you hear me?'

Her slight unease deepened. In the torch's dim light the fair curls clung damply to the small, perfectly shaped face. The mouth was softly curved. A pretty little kid actually. Gently Lizzie pushed back one of her curls. Her little girl would be pretty – no doubt about that – with her and Dan as its parents. Or a sturdy little boy the image of Dan.

If only Penny didn't look so *pale*. Maybe it was the torchlight. Lizzie grabbed the girl's arm and shook it.

Nothing...

Lizzie swallowed hard. How many of those pills had she given her? Four? Six? More than that? She couldn't remember.

She said, 'No idea!' because she needed to hear a human voice. Then, with a sound that was half-way to a sob, she laid down the torch, leaned over the girl and grabbed her by the shoulders. 'Wake up, damn you!'

The head with its fair curls flopped like that of a rag doll and Lizzie felt a rising panic. She shook Penny violently and was rewarded by a faint moan. Closing her eyes, she clutched the child to her, weak with gratitude.

'Penny! *Penny!*'

Hugging her, she thought again of her own son. A little boy for Dan to play with. She imagined them chasing around the garden with shrieks of laughter. Or a daughter... Dan would make her a swing and push her to and fro, and her curls would fly out and her little legs would kick with excitement... She smiled. It might not be so bad.

She closed her eyes suddenly. Suppose someone stole *her* kid! Christ, she'd go mad.

Releasing Penny, she scrambled to her feet. It came to her forcefully that she had done a terrible thing. If Daniel found out he would never forgive her. He would never come back to her. But...

'You're not coming back, are you, Dan?' she murmured.

She must finish what she'd started. Still, it could have been worse. At least the kid was OK. She was alive; just sleeping.

The torch was flickering again and, turning, Lizzie snatched it up in a rage. 'You *dare* go out!' She shook it, walking back to her chair. The whisky had all gone. She was sobering up and didn't want to.

Sitting down, she switched off the torch to save what there was of the battery. She'd look for another one when she went upstairs. There were still things to be done. The letter about the ransom for a start; it had to be sent to the Goughs. She had sat up half the night snipping and pasting. If she caught the late collection it would reach them tomorrow morning... Yes, that was it. She must go to the postbox at the end of Church Lane and on the way back she would buy some more fags.

She put a hand to her head which was throbbing. She needed another drink, but she dared not spend any more money until she was sure the Goughs were going to cough up. She tried to think if she had overlooked anything. Ah yes! She gave a little nod. Someone might come snooping around and Penny might start to yell.

'The scarf,' she muttered. But now the idea of a gag had lost its appeal. Damn and blast! She should have done it earlier when she was in the mood.

At least the kid wasn't going to object. Carefully Lizzie wound the scarf round Penny's mouth and tied it in a knot at the back of her head. It wasn't easy with the child flopping around like that and when it was done Lizzie wiped sweat from her face with the back of her hand.

'Breathe through your nose,' she told Penny. 'OK?'

There was no reply. No indication that the girl had heard; no sign that she even knew about the gag. The fear surfaced again as Lizzie leaned close but could detect no sign

337

of life. Had she overdone those blasted pills?

'No!' Of course she hadn't. It wasn't as though they were poison or anything. She would wake up soon.

'Don't be such a fool, Lizzie!'

Lizzie forced herself back to the chair and sat down heavily. She felt so terribly tired. Better not to look at the girl. She turned off the torch and closed her eyes; she'd go upstairs later, but not just yet.

Before Ella had a chance to get out of the car, Annie was running down the steps.

Ella called, 'Something's happened!'

Charles said,' Perhaps they've found her.'

'No. It's something bad!' Ella was already hurrying towards the housekeeper. 'What is it, Annie?'

She could see by the woman's expression that the news was not good and her hopes plummeted. The worst had happened; they had found Penny dead. Why else would Annie look so distraught? She tried to concentrate, vaguely aware that Charles was now beside her.

'Is she all right? Tell me quickly!'

'There's no news of Penny.' Annie's expression was anguished. 'It's Mr Gough, ma'am. They've taken him–'

Ella gasped. For a second or two darkness closed in. 'They've taken *Roland?* Oh, my God!'

'No, no, Mrs Gough. Not *taken* him. I meant, to the *hospital.* He had a heart attack. I'm sorry but he's ... he's really ever so poorly.'

Ella could only stare at her. 'A *heart attack?* But what brought it on? He doesn't *know* about Penny.'

Annie shook her head, glancing at Charles as though for support. 'Mrs Gough, he *does* know, I'm afraid. Nurse Baisley told him.'

'*What!*'

'We tried to stop her, but she said he was entitled to know. Wasn't right to keep him in the dark, things like that. Next thing we know she's screaming from the top of the stairs that the ambulance is on its way. When it came she insisted on going with him. I expected her to ring us with news, but not a word. I rang the hospital but they said he was ... that he's in a critical condition. Oh, Mrs Gough! You don't think he'll die, do you? He looked so white and his eyes were closed...'

'Of course he won't die.' Ella felt dazed. The extent of the new crisis numbed her mind. Her thoughts, once so chaotic, now slowed down. It seemed impossible to think clearly, let alone make a decision. After a moment she looked at Charles.

He said, 'I'll take you to the hospital, Ella.'

She stammered, 'To the hospital. Yes, of course. But Penny...'

Annie said, 'And your Aunt Florrie phoned and I told her what had happened. I'm sorry if I did wrong, but I was still in a state of shock myself and I simply blurted it out. Anyway, she said she's coming over...'

Ella clutched at the thought of further support. 'Is she here?'

'Not yet. She's coming over by taxi with a few things in a suitcase. She says you're going to need her. I've made up one of the spare rooms and lit a fire.'

'Thank you, Annie.'

'And Miss Spinney turned up and–'

'Oh, good heavens! I forgot about her.'

'I sent her away. I said you'd be in touch. I just said that Mr Gough was taken to hospital. Nothing about Penny.'

'Oh, Annie! What would I do without you?'

It seemed incredible that elsewhere life was going on normally, while her daughter was missing and her husband was at death's door. Without protest Ella allowed herself to be guided back into the car. She closed her eyes and leaned back against the seat. It would be wonderful to have her aunt with her through whatever the next few days might bring.

As Charles put the car in gear Ella said, 'Florrie is elderly, but she's very sensible. You'll like her.'

'I'm sure I shall.' The car rolled forward.

'You'll have to give me directions. I don't know my way around yet.'

Although confused and in a state of shock, Ella directed him and eventually they reached the hospital.

Charles said, 'Why don't you go ahead, Ella, while I park the car? Then I'll come and find you if I may.' He put out a restraining hand. 'And Ella, don't give up hope. Roland has so much to live for. He's going to pull through, I know he is.'

'Thank you.'

Ella jumped out and hurried up the steps.

'Don't die, Roland!' she whispered again and again.

Once inside she made her way to the reception desk, where a small woman was filling in a form.

'Roland Gough,' Ella explained. 'He came in an hour or so ago with a heart attack. I came as soon as I heard.'

'I remember.' She referred to a sheaf of papers. 'Here it is. Gough, Roland Edward. An emergency call. Ambulance, wasn't it?'

'Yes. How bad is it? Can you tell me?'

'You'll have to ask the doctor. I just deal with the paperwork.'

Ella leaned against the desk, still trying to catch her breath. 'May I see him?'

The receptionist frowned. 'I doubt it. Are you another relative?'

Ella stared at her. 'I'm his *wife*. I'm Mrs

Gough. Surely I can see him?' Seeing the woman's expression change, she said, 'Who did you think I was?'

The woman stared at Ella. 'Well, the fact is – I think his wife's already here.'

Ella fought back a scream of frustration. 'His *nurse* is here. *I'm* his wife! Now can I please see my husband?' Her voice alarmed her. It was strident with suppressed anxiety and a growing anger. She told herself to keep calm; that it was pointless to antagonise the staff.

The receptionist shrugged. 'Well, you'll have to speak to Sister. Straight down the corridor to the stairs on the left. At the top, turn right and right again. Ward 3A. Or you can use the lift.' She pointed.

'Thank you!' Ella pushed herself away from the desk and walked unsteadily towards the stairs. When she found them, they seemed interminable, but she reached the top at last and hesitated. Left or right? She went to the left, realised her mistake and turned back.

Ward 3A was a fair-sized room with about sixteen beds in it. Overhead lights threw the room into gloom and the smell was a mixture of antiseptic and floor polish. Some of the beds were hidden by curtains and from one of these a flustered nurse emerged and hurried to the telephone on a desk in the middle of the area. Here a sister in her dark blue uniform pored over some paperwork. Ella looked at each bed until she saw May Baisley sitting beside one of them, clasping the patient's hand. Ella felt a jolt of anger.

She walked to the sister and said, 'I'm Mrs Gough. I would like to see my husband.'

The sister glanced up. 'Mrs Gough?' She frowned.

Before she could go on, Ella said, 'The lady sitting with him is his nurse. She came in with him because I was out at the time. She can go home now that I'm here.'

The sister stood up and held out her hand. 'Mrs Gough, I'm so sorry. She was so upset – we all rather assumed... It was all rather hurried at the time, as you'll appreciate. I'm Sister Peterson.'

She led the way towards Roland's bed, her shoes squeaking on the polished floor. At that moment May Baisley turned. Seeing Ella, she snatched her hand away from Roland's and stood up guiltily. So ... thought Ella. The nurse has a soft spot for her patient. So how did the wretched woman feel, knowing that she had provoked this attack; knowing that she was responsible for his predicament? Ella was surprised to find that she felt almost sorry for her.

May Baisley said, 'He hasn't opened his eyes. He doesn't seem to hear me.' She

343

addressed her remarks to the sister, avoiding Ella's eyes. 'I was – I was trying to warm his hands. He's so cold.'

The sister said, 'I'm afraid I'll have to ask you to leave now, Miss Baisley. There's been some confusion but his wife is here now. Perhaps you would like to wait at Reception? I expect you'll want to ring for a taxi.'

'No. I–'

Ella forced a brief smile. 'I have Mr Marriott with me. He'll take you home and then come back for...'

May Baisley gave her a look of evident dislike. 'Be beholden to that man? Never!'

Startled, they watched her turn away. With her head high, she made her way unsteadily towards the doors.

The sister said, 'Poor soul. She's taken it badly, I'm afraid. They often do. Professional pride, I suppose.'

Ella had turned her attention to her husband. Taking hold of his hand, she was startled. 'He is cold!' she exclaimed.

The sister laid a hand across his forehead. Her eyes narrowed. 'His temperature certainly is dropping,' she agreed. 'I'd better call the registrar.' She hurried back to the telephone and Ella sat down in the chair May Baisley had vacated. She leaned across and kissed her husband's face. 'Don't die, Roland,' she begged. 'Don't leave me.'

In his white hospital gown, Roland seemed unfamiliar and somehow remote. Beneath the grey hospital blankets he looked like a stranger.

Gently she began to rub his hands in an effort to warm him. Finding this a useless exercise, she kissed them instead.

'I'm here now, darling,' she told him. 'It's Ella. I'm sorry about everything. About Penny. They'll find her, I know they will.'

Suddenly his eyelids fluttered and his lips moved.

'Roland!' Hope flared within her as she leaned closer. 'What is it? I'm sorry, I can't understand you.'

He mumbled something that was mainly incoherent but Ella caught the word 'Penny'.

'Roland, they're looking for her. They're doing all they can. You mustn't worry, darling. You must concentrate on getting well. What would our little Penny do without her daddy?'

Abruptly his eyes opened and he stared straight out at her. 'Promise ... find her...' he muttered.

'I promise, Roland. We'll find her safe and well. You'll see.'

If only *she* could believe that! She hated deceiving him, but there was nothing he could do to help and she wanted to minimise his anxiety. 'The police have a description of her. They think she probably just wandered off. Apparently it's not uncommon. Poor Mrs Granger is beside herself, but it was nobody's fault. They're all on the lookout for her.' She prayed he wouldn't recognise the false tone of optimism.

Her words seemed to have calmed him. As he relaxed back into the pillow and closed his eyes, Ella allowed herself a quick look round the ward. Two of the men were sitting up, one holding a magazine, the other a book. Another, younger man sat dozing in a chair beside his bed.

At that moment Sister Peterson re-appeared with a young man whom Ella correctly assumed to be the registrar. He took a long look at the patient, then took the clipboard from the end of the bed and studied the notes.

He gave a slight nod to the sister who said, 'We'll leave the doctor alone for a moment, Mrs Gough – he needs to examine your husband.'

Something about the way she took hold of Ella's arm sent a frisson of fear through her. 'No... Wait!' she cried. She looked again at Roland and from him to the doctor who was leaning over him, shining a torch into his eyes.

The sister said, 'Perhaps a cup of tea...' and tightened her hold on Ella's arm.

'No!' Ella jerked her arm free. She looked at the doctor. 'He's worse, isn't he? You can tell me.'

The doctor was taking Roland's pulse.

'He's getting worse!' Ella cried. 'He's so cold. Is it a coma?'

The nurse said, 'Please, Mrs Gough. I think it would be better...'

Studiously the doctor avoided her eyes. He untied Roland's gown and applied a stethoscope to his chest.

Ella swayed and almost fell as the truth dawned. 'He's not...' The word was too terrible. Instead she whispered, 'He's not going to recover, is he? Oh God!'

Clutching the sister for support, she allowed herself to be lowered on to the chair.

The doctor said, 'I'm afraid he won't recover, Mrs Gough. I'm afraid ... it's already too late. We've lost him... I'm so dreadfully sorry.'

Looking at him, Ella could see that he *was* sorry. He said, 'It was very peaceful. He just slipped away.'

Probably a very new doctor, she thought dully. Not used to death.

'*Death*,' she whispered. Now it was said. She gazed at Roland. He looked so peaceful that she envied him. 'Oh, darling!' She swallowed. It seemed incredible. Impossible.

She patted his hand, blinking hard. Her tears would have to wait. First she must find Penny. Roland had made her promise. She kissed him on the forehead.

'Goodbye, darling. Please forgive me. I'm so sorry I wasn't...'

Sorry I wasn't a better wife – that's what she wanted to say, but with the doctor and nurse so near she felt unable to finish the sentence.

The registrar held out his hand and she took it. 'You have my condolences, Mrs Gough, but it was a massive attack. We did everything we could. I thought – but it wasn't to be.'

She nodded, not trusting herself to say more. After a last look at her husband she turned away. The sister followed, her shoes squeaking. The sound made Ella want to weep. She knew that in the years to come, when she remembered Roland's death she would hear that sound.

The next ten minutes passed in a dream. She signed papers without reading them and answered questions she barely understood. Tomorrow they would release 'the body'. Resentment rose within her. Already her husband had become 'the body'. Why was he no longer 'your husband' or 'Mr Gough'? It was all so thoughtless; so unintentionally cruel. She shuddered as she walked out of the building into the darkness where motor cars passed, two people chatted beneath a lamp post and a policeman walked his beat. Nobody knew or cared that Roland had gone from her life forever. It felt like an insult. She pushed the thought away.

Promise... It had been Roland's last request.

'I'll find her,' she said aloud.

In a daze, she stood on the steps, fighting off the grief that waited to overwhelm her. She had lost her husband, but she had also lost her daughter and giving way to grief would make it impossible to carry on. She promised herself that she would remain strong until Penny was safe. Only then would she give way to her feelings. She became aware that someone was calling her name and, turning, saw Charles Marriott hurrying towards her.

He said, 'How is he–' and then stopped as he saw her expression. 'Oh, no!' he whispered.

She looked at him dry-eyed. 'They did all they could.'

'Ella! What can I say? I'm so sorry.'

Ella nodded. 'Did you see Nurse Baisley?'

'Yes. She came running down the steps. Nearly bumped into me. I started to speak to her, but she muttered something I didn't catch and hurried past.'

'She must have known he was dying,' said

Ella. 'She must have waited long enough to hear...'

'I was going to offer her a lift back to Burleigh House, but I didn't go after her. I wanted to be here for you.'

'I think she cared for him. All those years and I didn't guess...' She drew a deep breath. 'I promised Roland I'd find Penny. Charles, if you can bear it I want to go back to that house. I'm going to break in and search the place.' She watched him trying to hide his dismay.

'Er – shouldn't we let the police do that?' He took hold of her hands. 'You're in no fit state to–'

'What sort of state d'you think Penny's in? I *feel* that she's there – in here! Intuition, perhaps. Call it what you will. I'm going back there.' It occurred to her that there was no reason for her conviction – unless Roland was guiding her. Was that possible? At that moment it felt perfectly feasible and she desperately wanted to believe it. 'Penny's *there!*' she repeated.

'Shouldn't we ring the police first? They might have found her already.'

Ella hesitated. He thought she was being unrealistic and she couldn't blame him, but the feeling was growing within her. 'She's there, Charles.' It was the one positive idea to which she could cling. 'We'll telephone the police *afterwards.*'

He squeezed her hand. 'Look, Ella, I promise you–'

'They haven't found her, Charles. But I know where she is.'

'And if Lizzie's there?'

'I don't *care*. I want to go to the flat *now* – even if I have to walk all the way.'

To prove her point, she turned and began to walk along the street. She heard him call to her but walked on. At last she heard the engine fire up and soon he was pulling in beside her. He pushed open the door and she climbed in without a word.

Ella wondered what she would do without him. Then she wondered what she was going to do without Roland and tears sprang into her eyes. Before she could rally, her fragile self-control crumbled and she was sobbing helplessly.

Ten minutes later they arrived back at the Hamptons' flat. Before Charles could try to reason with her, Ella was out of the car and running round to the back of the house. She tried the door handle, banged on it with her fists and gave it a hefty kick.

'Lizzie Hampton! You open this door! Now! Do you hear me?'

Charles caught up with her. 'Steady on, Ella. You'll hurt yourself.'

'Penny's in there, Charles. I *know* it!'

'You can't be sure. Please calm down, Ella.'

351

'I need an axe.'

'An axe? For God's sake! Ella, this isn't like you.' He took hold of her hands. 'Look, we've just passed a telephone box. I'm going to ring the police. I'll find out what's happening and tell them where we are. Just wait here, Ella. Don't do anything rash.'

Ella nodded. She waited impatiently until he had gone and then rushed to the shed. An axe! Unable to find one, she returned to the back door with a billhook. Staring at the door, she thought, 'Wedge the end in by the lock and then twist it.'

Her stomach churned and bile rose in her throat. There was a roaring in her ears and she knew that panic was not far away. They *must* find Penny here.

Beneath her the wood of the doorframe was splintering. She watched in a kind of daze as it ate further into the wood.

She shouted, 'Penny? Are you there? It's Mummy!'

She dropped the hook and threw herself against the door. It swung inwards with a crash and a fluttering of paint flakes and Ella stepped into the room. She found a switch and turned on the light. Sink and drainer, table and chairs, a dresser and a larder. Not very promising. She shouted, 'Penny! Are you here?'

The profound silence continued. Suddenly she jumped as something wound itself around her legs and she saw that the black cat had followed her in.

Ella raised her voice. 'Penny? Can you hear me? It's Mummy!'

Nothing. Her confidence wavered in the uncompromising silence. This was breaking and entering – and there was also the damaged door.

'Search the house,' she told herself.

She rushed into the hallway and on into another room: a bathroom with an ancient geyser. Next the lavatory, then the bedroom. She stared at the rumpled bed which Daniel shared with Lizzie. *Had* shared, she amended and felt nothing. No sign of her daughter. For a moment Ella thought she was going to be sick as her stomach heaved with fear.

Charles reappeared. 'The back door doesn't look too healthy!' he remarked. 'Any sign of Penny?'

'No, Oh, Charles...'

He took hold of her hand. 'We haven't finished yet. We should wait. The police are coming...'

Ella ignored him. 'There might be an attic; she might be there. Could you explore upstairs? Ask the old woman?' A thought occurred to her. 'Do we *trust* her? She could be hiding her. Suppose Penny's upstairs – with that old woman?'

'I'll go up. You wait down here.'

He ran up the stairs two at a time. Unable to bear the inactivity, Ella went back into the kitchen where the cat was sitting in front of the larder, swishing its tail.

Ella said, 'Oh you're hungry, are you? Well, I'm sorry, but it's not my house.'

The cat mewed and she bent to stroke it. She said, 'What happened to your poor ear?' and for a moment imagined she heard a faint sound from beyond the latched door. Had Lizzie locked her prisoner *in the larder?* No, that was impossible. It only had a latch.

Voices filtered down from upstairs and she heard Charles say, 'Is there a ladder?'

So there *was* an attic.

The black cat crouched beside the larder door, pressing its nose against the gap beneath it.

Ella's mind seemed to move in slow motion. She remembered the small window they had passed as they came round the side of the house. A very low window. So maybe this wasn't the larder but a *cellar!*

She grabbed at the latch and the door swung open. She screamed, 'Charles! There's a cellar!' For a moment, torn between hope and fear of disappointment, she thought she was going to faint.

Charles shouted, 'Wait for me, Ella!' and she heard him come down the stairs two at a time.

He stared at the opened cellar door.

Ella whispered, 'So dark and cold!'

'I'll take a look. Please, Ella. Just in case...'

Now, so close to finding her, Ella was terrified of what they might discover. She closed her eyes. Would they find Penny? And if so, what state would she be in?

Charles went down the steps into the gloom. 'I can see a woman and a child...'

Please, God! *Please,* God. 'Is she – is Penny...?'

She began to follow him but he had stopped part-way down.

'She's asleep,' he said.

Ella forced herself to take a look. There was a torch and by its faint beam she saw Penny sprawled on the coke-heap. She also saw Lizzie, slouched in the chair. Neither moved. At once the neighbour's words came back into her mind. 'She was in a funny mood ... might have done herself in...'

'Charles, are they ... they're all right, aren't they?'

He was holding her back, which meant that he suspected the worst.

'Ella, let's wait for the police.'

Something in his voice sent a spasm of terror through her. He thought they were dead.

'Penny!' she shouted hoarsely. 'Penny, wake up! It's Mummy come to take you home.'

The child didn't move, but the woman

did; her eyes opened and she stared directly into Ella's face.

Ella called, 'It's me, Penny's mother. It's all over.'

Lizzie blinked. 'What?... What's over?'

Charles said, 'I can smell whisky. She's probably drunk!'

Lizzie stood up, swaying, steadying herself against the back of the chair. 'I didn't mean... I want some money. I've got to... I've got to have...'

As Ella stepped forward, Charles caught her by the arm. 'Don't touch her. Let the police deal with her, Ella.'

'Let me go, Charles.'

'Please, Ella! Wait.'

For a moment Ella held back. Charles was right. Ella knew that if she found herself within striking distance of Lizzie Hampton she would do something she might regret.

Charles knelt beside the child and spoke softly to her as he untied the cord round her ankles and removed the scarf from her face. He lifted her head, trying to rouse her. Then he said, 'I'll telephone for an ambulance.'

'An *ambulance?* Oh God, Charles! You don't think...' A wild, blinding fear raced through her. Penny was too still. She hurled herself across the cellar and crouched beside her daughter. *'Penny!* For God's sake, Penny, open your eyes. Speak to me!'

Lizzie swayed. 'She ... she's asleep...'

Ella sprang to her feet and whirled round. 'You did this to my daughter!' Before Charles could stop her she had launched herself at Lizzie and grabbed her by the shoulders.

Charles cried, 'Don't Ella! She's not worth it!'

Ella didn't even hear him. She shook the woman violently and then, with all the strength she could summon, threw her into the corner. With a cry of pain and fright, Lizzie collided with the wall and then collapsed. She slid down on to the floor, clasping her right ankle and moaning.

Ella struggled for breath. 'You heartless, wicked...' She could find no words to express her rage. She wanted to smash Lizzie's head against the wall; to beat and kick her; to reduce *her* to a silent shadow of her former self. Adrenalin coursed through her as she staggered back, gulping for air, shaking uncontrollably.

'Stop this, Ella,' she murmured unsteadily. 'That's enough.'

She daren't look at Charles. He wouldn't need words; his expression would be enough. Shame burned through her. She had descended to Lizzie's level, and she imagined Florrie's disapproval. Thank God Roland would never know. Slowly she raised her head and took a quick look at the crumpled figure in the corner. She expected to feel remorse but instead felt a surge of triumph. Serve her damned well right!

Charles said, 'Ella...'

'Don't!'

For what seemed an eternity the ensuing silence was broken only by Lizzie's whimpers. Then Ella turned back to Penny. She pulled her up on to her lap and saw at once how pale the child was. So cold and so silent. Her eyes were closed and she lay limply in Ella's arms, a travesty of the sparkling child she had once been. The small heart-shaped face was dirty and streaked with tears long since dried. Her pale curls were tangled.

Shocked, Charles knelt beside them, his face agonised. 'Ella...' he began. He put an arm round her.

Ella, hugging the child, looked at him wordlessly. At that moment they heard a car draw up outside and moments later two policemen were clattering down the cellar steps.

She looked up at them with anguished eyes. 'You're too late,' she told them. 'We're all too late. I think she's dead.'

Chapter Eleven

Daniel stabbed the fork into the ground, leaned on it and forced the spines upward. It was good soil and had been well nourished. He broke up the forkful and repeated the operation. There was something soothing about digging; something to do with the repetition and the satisfaction of seeing the hard, cracked earth transformed into a crumbling brown row.

It was a well-tended garden and his employers seemed fair-minded people. He was lucky to have been given another chance and he knew it. So far his 'handy man' skills had not been much in demand; he had changed a light bulb, chopped wood and oiled a squeaking hinge.

'Thank God for small mercies!' he muttered and smiled.

There was a large greenhouse and a well-stocked potting shed. The fruit bushes were protected with strong netting and he had been told they cropped superbly. The paths were deeply gravelled and the mower was brand new. He sighed. It wasn't what he wanted from his life, but he was prepared to make the most of it. The small cottage that went with it was hardly spacious, but he had a roof over his head and that was what mattered. Lizzie would have...

'Stop that!' he told himself sharply. He didn't want to think about Lizzie – because, unexpectedly, he missed her and because his conscience pricked him relentlessly. She had driven him to distraction and he had abandoned her, but although in some ways it was a relief to be free, he was filled with guilt and regret. Lying sleepless in the early hours, he worried about her. For better, for worse...

'Damn it!' He stabbed the fork into the ground and straightened his back.

Suppose Lizzie *had* taken Ella's daughter? He found it difficult to imagine that she would go that far or could be that stupid, but just suppose she *had?* She wouldn't harm the girl, he was sure of that. Well, almost sure. But if she had and if she were caught – it was a criminal offence and she would be sent to prison. It would be worse for her if she had demanded a ransom. Or harmed the child in any way!

'Oh, Lizzie! Lizzie!'

He also understood Ella's distress and could imagine her terror. To lose a child must be every mother's nightmare.

'Hell and damnation!' He closed his eyes. There was no way he could continue to turn his back on the problem. Lizzie's irrational behaviour was partly his fault. Indirectly it was his affair with Lydia which had lost him the job with the Goughs. Today he must accept responsibility. Without a second's thought he began to walk towards the shed where his bicycle was kept. There was no time to ask permission. If he was missed, he would have to explain.

Annie carried a tray of tea into the sitting room where Florrie, cosily ensconced by the fire, turned and smiled.

'Tea? Oh Annie, you're spoiling me.'

Annie beamed. 'Nice to have you here with us,' she said, setting down the tray which she had laid with the gold-rimmed crockery and the pewter teapot. 'I know Mrs Gough will be pleased. It's been such a shocking time – first poor little Penny disappearing and then Mr Gough taken ill like that. I don't know how she's going to manage. She always looks so calm and confident but–' She shrugged.

Florrie sighed. 'I've never been fooled by that air of self-confidence. I know her too well and so do you. All these meetings and committees and what-not. What is she trying to prove, I ask myself. Busy all the time. No time to think.'

'Exactly.' The housekeeper caught Florrie's eyes and looked quickly away, fussing over the pouring of the tea. 'Not that it's my place, but you can't help noticing these things. Always on the go, she is. Organising this and that.' She shook her head. 'I've said it many times – she'll wear herself out.'

'Poor Ella. I can't imagine what she's going through.'

Annie handed Florrie a cup of tea and asked, 'Sugar?'

'Two, please.'

Annie offered the sugar bowl. 'Had the Dramatic Society on the phone ten minutes ago asking for Mrs Gough. Wanting to know if she was going to be at the audition tonight. I've forgotten which play they're doing, but it was comedy. Mrs Gough usually has a leading part and she loves all that dressing-up. She's very good, too, as you know. We all get free tickets and it's a really enjoyable evening.'

Florrie stirred her tea. 'Happier times!' she murmured.

Annie nodded. 'Then it all goes wrong. Why is life all ups and downs? Full of nasty surprises.'

Florrie recognised the depth of the house-keeper's depression. 'Ella's lucky to have you,' she said. 'I know how much she relies on you.'

Annie blinked. 'Does she? Oh I do hope so.' She sighed. 'I told these dramatic people she wasn't feeling very well. I didn't know if I was supposed to tell everyone our

362

troubles.' She watched Florrie sip her tea. 'Do you want anything in it? A splash of whisky? My mother used to swear by that in time of trouble.'

'I don't think so, thank you.'

'Dulls the edges, she used to say.' Annie pointed to the tray. 'I've made you a sandwich because I know you must have missed your lunch. That's nice fresh bread and a lovely bit of boiled ham. Very lean and not too salty.'

'I'm not very hungry, but it was a kind thought. Thank you, Annie.'

Annie seized the tongs and added a few lumps of coal to the fire. Staring into the flames, she said, 'They will find her, won't they? Penny, I mean. I said to Cook, if God lets anything happen to that child he's lost me forever. I shall never set foot in a church again if she's ... if God lets anything...'

'Of course they will find her. Oh yes!' Florrie's conviction was slightly overdone. 'We mustn't think anything else.' She took the sandwich. 'Poor Ella...' Her eyes darkened. 'If only she would forgive herself for – for past mistakes. She's quite vulnerable really. Brittle is probably the best word.'

Annie replaced the tongs and straightened up. 'We'll have to keep our eyes on her, poor soul,' she said. 'Well, now. I must get back to the kitchen.'

'I thought I spotted Nurse Baisley dashing up the stairs.'

Annie tossed her head. 'I suppose she'll be next, poking her head round the kitchen door expecting to be waited on hand and foot. I never did like her and now ... well, it's her fault the poor man is – is the way he is. Telling him like that after the mistress said we were to keep it quiet! I never did understand why Mrs Gough put up with her.'

'Because she's a good nurse,' Florrie protested. 'Ella thinks her very capable.'

'Capable she may be, but she thinks so much of herself. We're never allowed to call her May. Oh dear no! She thinks she's a cut above the rest of the staff. She said once that she was "very close to the head of the house". What cheek! Well, I'll have to leave you and get on. Eat that sandwich if you can. It'll do you good. We're all going to need plenty of energy to get us through the next few days.'

Watching the housekeeper go, Florrie relaxed and her expression changed. In spite of her brave words about Penny, she felt desperately apprehensive.

She whispered, 'Please, Ella, come back with some good news.'

She stared at the sandwich, then reluctantly took a bite. It tasted like sawdust.

May Baisley had thrown herself face down on the bed when she returned from the hospital. She had lain there, drained of emotion, praying for a merciful oblivion which didn't come. He was gone. She had lost him ... she had also lost her reason for being. She smiled suddenly into the pillow. They had called her 'Mrs Gough' and she hadn't corrected the mistake.

'Mrs Gough!' She whispered the words into the pillow. The first and only time she had been mistaken for his wife. She would always remember the thrill it had given her. And those stolen moments beside his bed with his dear hands in hers...

She turned over and sat up. Soon the real Mrs Gough would be arriving home and there would be a scene. Mrs Gough would question her. She would question the rest of the staff, and they would tell her that the revelation about the daughter had brought on the attack. They might call it accidental death instead of natural causes. They might accuse her of incompetence or of behaving in an unprofessional way. They would never understand that her first duty was to Roland Gough.

'The police!' she muttered.

Yes, they might even involve the police. Almost certainly they would, because Mrs Gough would want to blame her. That woman would delight in incriminating her.

May thought about the look on Mrs Gough's face when she saw her holding Roland's hands.

'Jealous bitch!'

Her mouth tightened. Well, now he was hers no longer. Serve her right... But what should she do now?

'I'm going,' she said, although she had nowhere to go unless it was back to her stepmother. 'I'm going,' she repeated and slid from the bed.

From the top of the wardrobe May took down her large, somewhat battered suitcase. She took off her cap and apron and tossed them on to the bed. Mrs Gough had provided the uniform; she was welcome to it. Carrying the suitcase, she crossed to the chest of drawers and began methodically to fold and pack her clothes.

'Vests, knickers, petticoats, stockings...' The next drawer down. 'Blouses, cardigans, jumpers...'

Packing was terrifying. It meant a large step into the unknown. But the sound of her own voice was strangely comforting. In the bottom drawer she had stored her personal belongings: photographs, letters, diaries. They followed her clothes into the suitcase.

'Taxi!' she muttered and moved to the telephone to call one. That done, she moved on in a kind of daze. Her best shoes went into the suitcase which was already almost full. She glanced at the row of books on the shelf beside her bed. No, they could stay. She went into the bathroom and collected flannel, toothbrush, dental powder, cold cream and lavender water. These she tossed into the suitcase on top of everything else.

Suddenly she paused.

'My wages!'

She was owed for two and a half weeks but would they pay her – in the circumstances? She had some savings, but not a lot. A quick look in her purse was reassuring. Enough for her train fare back to her stepmother.

'You can keep your damned money!' The swearword made her feel stronger.

Ten minutes later she was ready. The suitcase bulged and she had crammed last-minute odds and ends into her knitting bag. From the window she saw the taxi arrive. She struggled down the stairs and there, of course, was Annie, her mouth open in surprise.

'Nurse Baisley. Where – I mean – what are you doing? Where are you going?'

May straightened her back and gave the woman a glacial stare. 'None of your business.'

'But what ... you can't just...' Flustered, she moved between May and the front door. 'Does Mrs Gough know? Has she *sacked* you?'

May wanted to slap the stupid creature.

'Sack me? *Sack me?* Certainly not. I'll have you know that I've never been sacked in my whole life!'

'Then it's because you caused it!' Annie nodded. 'That's it, isn't it? Guilty conscience. And so you should have. If it wasn't for you, poor Mr Gough wouldn't be ill. He wouldn't be lying at death's door. If you'd kept quiet as you were told–'

'He isn't at death's door.'

'What d'you mean? Is he better?'

May's grief had given way to a satisfying anger. 'No, he's not better. If you must know, he's dead!' she shouted. 'Understand now? Now get out of my way, Annie.' Her voice rose and May was mortified to hear that it trembled. 'I'm going and you can't stop me.'

Annie's eyes widened. She was very pale. 'Dead? I don't believe it.'

'He's dead – and I'm not needed any more, and I have better things to do with my time than hang around waiting for Mrs Gough to come home and blame me!'

They stared at each other, one furious, the other silent with shock.

Outside the taxi driver hooted.

Florrie appeared at the door of the sitting room, clutching the door jamb for support. 'What's happening? What's all the noise about?'

Annie turned to her. 'Nurse Baisley's

leaving,' she stammered. 'She says Mr Gough's...'

May discovered new strength from their unhappy faces. She gave Annie a withering glance. 'Open the door for me. My taxi's here.'

Annie, stricken, obeyed.

'But surely you should speak to Mrs Gough before you go,' Florrie said.

May said, 'You stay out of this.'

Florrie raised her eyebrows. 'Well, really! What a disagreeable woman you are!'

The taxi hooted again, and May shouted, 'I'm coming!' She was torn between staying to prolong the row and going before Ella Gough returned. There were things she longed to say, but there was no time.

She took a few steps towards the door, then paused to rest the suitcase and gave the aunt a spiteful look. 'I'm happy to say that Mr Gough didn't find me disagreeable as you do.'

The woman rose to the bait. 'What's that supposed to mean?'

'Work it out for yourself.'

Annie said, 'Don't flatter yourself, you silly woman. Mr Gough had more sense than to—'

'That's all you know!' May lifted the suitcase and staggered out on to the steps. 'Mr Gough admired me. I understood him.' She stopped again and waited for the taxi driver to help her. He came up the steps, picked up the suitcase and carried it to the waiting cab. May said, 'I was the only one who cared. The only one who loved him.'

Tears blurred her eyes and she turned and stumbled down the steps. 'I loved him,' she whispered, 'and he loved me. That's all that matters.'

She climbed into the taxi.

'Where to, missus?'

She began to sob.

'Where do you want to go?'

She couldn't answer. She couldn't think. He put the car into gear and she heard the car wheels scrunch slowly over the gravel.

'Bus depot? Railway station? Beachy Head?' He waited. 'Come on, missus. Be reasonable. I've got to know where we're going.'

Brushing the tears from her eyes, May turned to watch Burleigh House as it receded into the distance. As they turned out into the road she made a huge effort to control her grief. 'The station, please,' she told him. Then it came to her that if she went straight back to her stepmother she would be unable to attend Roland's funeral. That would be the last service she could render him, and she ought to be there. It wouldn't please the family, but she didn't care.

'No,' she amended, rapping on the window. 'Take me to a cheap hotel.'

While Detective Inspector Hall was taking control of the situation in the cellar, Daniel arrived. He caught sight of Lizzie and his face paled.

'Lizzie?'

D.I. Hall said, 'You're the husband?'

'Yes.' He turned back to his wife. 'What the hell's happened?'

Ella said, 'Isn't it obvious? She kidnapped my daughter. *She kidnapped my daughter!* I thought she was dead. Oh, Daniel!' She was on the verge of hysteria and Charles knelt beside her.

'Penny's going to be all right,' he insisted. 'You must stay calm for her sake.'

Torn between the two women, Daniel turned back to his wife. 'Have you hurt her, Lizzie? If you have...'

Lizzie swayed and, without the policeman's support, would have fallen. 'I didn't ... didn't do anything,' she told him unsteadily. 'Just a sleeping pill to keep her ... a pill to keep her quiet. She...'

D.I. Hall turned to his constable. 'Here. You take her. Keep her on her feet.'

Daniel said, 'Is she ill?'

'Drunk, sir.'

'Oh God!'

Lizzie regarded him blearily. 'I need some money, that's why. That's why, Daniel...'

'I left you the ring.'

'It's not enough.'

The inspector crouched over the un-conscious child, taking her pulse. He nodded with relief. 'She'll come round, Mrs Gough. The hospital will pull her through.'

Ella looked across at Lizzie. 'How long has she been asleep? How many pills did you give her?'

Lizzie shook her head.

Ella screamed at her. 'How many, for heaven's sake!' She pressed the unconscious child to her chest, struggling against the panic. The policeman was right, she had to stay calm for Penny's sake. Her thoughts reverted momentarily to her dead husband and she gave a little cry of anguish. If only she had been able to reassure him – he could have died content. Fresh tears pressed at her eyelids and she sought wildly for a distraction. She told herself that this was partly Daniel's fault for bringing the hateful woman to England. He had almost cost Penny her life and Ella wanted to punish him.

She caught his eye as he stared helplessly around the cellar. 'She's expecting a baby,' she told him as bluntly as she could. 'Your baby, Daniel.'

His eyes widened. 'A baby? Lizzie? But that's not possible. She's always said–'

'Ask her yourself.'

Daniel turned to Lizzie, but the detective

was in the middle of cautioning her.

'...and anything you say may be used in evidence against you.'

Lizzie cried, 'Daniel?' The words had had a sobering effect.

Daniel held up his hand, appealing to the detective. 'Wait! Please let me talk to her. Give us a moment or two.'

As Ella watched their whispered exchange she experienced a growing sense of pity for them, trapped in a web they had spun for themselves. It came to her suddenly that she no longer envied Lizzie her husband. Daniel was not the man she had always believed him to be; he was as vulnerable as the next man, with the same mix of strengths and weaknesses. She closed her eyes as her mind took a further unwelcome leap. He was as vulnerable as she was herself.

Daniel turned to the policemen. 'Do you have to arrest her? She's not dangerous. She hasn't harmed anyone.'

D.I. Hall raised his eyebrows. 'Hasn't harmed anyone? She's kidnapped a child. Terrified her, no doubt. Drugged her to keep her a prisoner.'

'I meant–'

Ella broke in, *'Hasn't harmed her?* You don't know that. How do we know what she's done to her? Penny's still uncon- scious!'

Lizzie said, 'She's not unconscious. She's

asleep, that's all. I didn't do anything to her.'

'Of course she's unconscious, you stupid woman! If she was asleep we could wake her up!'

Daniel said, 'I don't think it's as bad as it looks, Ella.'

'Well, thanks for your opinion! Don't you think you might be somewhat prejudiced?' She heard her voice rising and took a deep breath. 'Look, we don't know how much harm has been done, Daniel. Penny will probably have nightmares for months. How would you like to be a small girl taken away by someone you hardly know and kept in this disgusting cellar for hours and hours?' She swallowed hard.

The inspector said, 'Right, that's enough from you two!'

Ella ignored him. 'Not to mention giving her God knows how many pills that might have killed her. Don't you dare make excuses for her, Daniel Hampton. She's behaved abominably and it's no thanks–'

'Stop it!' D.I. Hall glared from one to the other. 'There's no need to carry on like this. Lizzie Hampton has committed a very serious crime and it is my duty to arrest her, and that's what I intend to do. There's nothing to discuss. She has to be taken to the police station to be formally charged and–'

Ella's pent-up fear broke free, surfacing as

anger. 'You can lock her up,' she shouted, 'and throw away the key as far as I care. She's a deceitful, lying little hussy!'

Daniel said, 'Please, Ella! Don't!'

She rounded on him, white-faced. *'Don't? Why not? Why shouldn't she face up to what she's done?'*

Lizzie began to cry, a thin wailing sound.

The detective swore under his breath. 'Mrs Gough! This isn't getting us anywhere.'

Ella didn't even acknowledge that he had spoken. 'And why shouldn't you face up to it too, Daniel? You dare to take her side against mine? Just because you're married to her ... just because she's expecting your child. That alters nothing–'

'Mummy...'

The word, faint though it was, caught the attention of all of them. Heads turned and six pairs of eyes stared down at Penny.

Hardly daring to hope, Ella looked at her daughter. 'Penny? Darling?' Had she imagined that small word?

Daniel said, 'Was that Penny?'

'I think so!' Her anger vanished as thought it had never been, to be replaced by a trembling hope.

All eyes were on the little girl and they watched incredulously as she stirred and rubbed her eyes.

'Penny! *Penny!* Wake up. It's Mummy

come to take you home.'

Lizzie muttered, 'I just need some money...' but no one was listening to her.

D.I. Hall said, 'She's waking up. That's wonderful!' He was beaming.

The constable said, 'Thank the Lord!'

Penny frowned. 'I don't like it here...' The blue eyes were fixed sleepily upon her mother.

'We're going home, darling. I promise.' Ella kissed her fiercely.

The detective coughed. 'Maybe a visit to the hospital first – to make sure she's quite all right.'

Reluctantly Ella agreed.

Penny said, 'Lizzie was...' Her eyes closed and then opened again. 'She tells lies... she said...' Her eyes closed again and her head lolled.

Ella shook her gently. 'Wake up, sweetie. It's time to go home.' Her voice rose fractionally. 'Penny ... look at me!'

Charles said, 'Shall I hold her for a while?'

'No!' She smiled to soften the rejection. 'I'm so thankful to have her in my arms again...'

'I know.'

'God knows what she's been through, Charles.' She drew a long breath and wished that she could hate Lizzie for the torment of the past hours. Seeing her now made that difficult.

D.I. Hall said, 'Take her to the car, constable, and wait for me there.'

Lizzie's eyes were wild with fear. 'Daniel! Don't let them take me!'

Daniel asked. 'May I accompany her? Is that allowed?'

'I'm afraid not, sir, but you can meet us at the station. She'll be formally charged there.'

'I'll do that then.' He turned to Lizzie, but she had panicked. Jerking herself free, she made a stumbling run for the steps and almost tripped. The constable dashed after her.

Daniel cried, 'Don't do this, Lizzie. You'll make things worse!'

Lizzie turned and kicked out at the constable.

'Dammit! Come here!' he cried and tried to take hold of her arm.

She was half-way up the steps by this time and, turning, she lashed out with her foot and caught the constable on the knee.

'Jesus!' he cried and grabbed his knee. But Lizzie had lost her balance and, struggling to regain it, staggered backwards. Before anyone could help her, she had plunged over the side on to the cellar floor.

As Daniel ran forward Ella experienced a growing despair. With an effort, she closed her eyes and ears to the scene and gave her attention to her daughter who was hovering between sleep and wakefulness. At that moment they heard another vehicle draw up outside.

The constable said, 'That'll be the ambulance.' He made his way painfully down the steps and grabbed Lizzie's arm.

Ella turned to Charles. 'I'll go with Penny. Will you follow us with the car? If they say she's all right I'd like to take her home.'

He nodded. 'While you're with the doctor, I'll ring Burleigh House and let them know Penny's safe.'

The ambulance man appeared at the top of the steps. Lizzie was on her feet and was sobbing uncontrollably, holding one hand to her head. A trickle of blood oozed from her temple and down her left cheek, and Ella thought at once of Daniel's baby. The same thought had obviously occurred to Daniel, who was speaking in an undertone to the ambulance man.

D.I. Hall looked none too pleased. He said, 'The police doctor can see to her, it's the child who needs to go to the hospital.'

The ambulance man looked dubious. 'It's not just the blow to the head,' he warned. 'There's just a chance – well, in her state, sir...' he lowered his voice, '...the fall might cause a miscarriage.'

The inspector made no attempt to hide his annoyance. 'Oh all right, then, but my constable will have to accompany her.'

Charles turned to Daniel. 'I'm going. I'll take you.'

'Thanks.'

What is Daniel thinking, Ella wondered. Hoping that she will lose the child?

The ambulance man was leaning over her. 'I'll take the little girl, madam.'

Ella nodded and watched him carry Penny up the steps. Charles helped her to her feet where she stood for a moment, stiff and uncomfortable. Her clothes were covered with coal-dust and there was a ladder in her stocking. She brushed at her clothes ineffectually, then gave up and allowed Charles to help her up the cellar steps.

The ride to the hospital was one Ella would never forget, and she thought the thin wail of the siren would haunt her dreams as the ambulance made its way through the streets, taking the corners too fast and weaving in and out of the traffic with what seemed like reckless abandon. Penny lay on a stretcher along one side and Lizzie lay on the other. The constable sat in silence, avoiding Ella's eye.

They reached their destination eventually and Ella and the constable climbed out. Charles drew up alongside, quickly followed by the police car with Detective Inspector Hall. Within minutes they were all being shepherded inside the hospital and Ella found herself waiting in a small cubicle, surrounded by a curtain of striped grey and white cotton. Penny was awake again and more alert – staring round and blinking at the unfamiliar surroundings. She still looked grimy and unkempt; although Ella longed to get her into a bath to remove all traces of her ordeal, she told herself to be patient. For the moment it was enough that her daughter was safe and the terrible ordeal was at an end. Making a conscious effort, Ella allowed herself to relax, easing her stiff shoulders and taking deep breaths. Miraculously, the brightly lit bustle of the hospital was driving out the nightmare of the past hours, the memory of the sordid cellar and the atmosphere of fear and violence which had combined to overwhelm her. Hopefully, the same miracle was working for her daughter, too.

Ella smiled at her. 'We're going to let the doctor take a look at you, and then we'll probably go home.'

Penny said, 'Where's Daddy?'

Ella hesitated. She hated to lie, but surely Penny had had enough to deal with without hearing that her father was dead? 'He couldn't come but...' The compromise faltered.

Penny nodded. 'And where's Auntie Liz? Did she hurt her head?'

'Yes – but don't think about her, darling.'

'Her head was bleeding.' She frowned. 'She tells lies. I hate her.'

'Never mind. She's gone now and Mummy's here.'

'Where's Mrs Granger?'

Before Ella could answer, the curtain was pushed back and a young doctor arrived to examine Penny. He was thin, with an untidy mass of curly hair.

He smiled at them both. 'Ah! The sleeping beauty's awake! Good.' He tapped Penny's nose with a friendly finger. 'Pricked your finger on a spindle, did you?' He held two fingers against the pulse in her wrist.

'No I didn't!' she told him indignantly. 'I just fell asleep.'

'Been asleep for a hundred years?'

'No!' She giggled and glanced at Ella, who felt a rush of tenderness. This was more like the Penny she knew and she felt weak with relief.

'What, no bad fairy?' He lifted her jumper and applied his stethoscope to her chest.

Penny shook her head. 'That's cold!' she told him.

The doctor grinned at Ella. 'I don't think we've got too much to worry about here. Now, Penny, open wide ... that's good. And how do you feel? Any nasty pains in your head?'

'No.'

'In your tummy?'

'No – but the coke *was* lumpy.'

'The coke?' The doctor glanced at Ella and then to somewhere beyond the curtains. Ella nodded and stood up. The doctor tucked the blanket around Penny and led the way outside. In a low voice he asked, 'What exactly happened to her? I'm afraid my information's a bit sketchy. Locked herself in a cellar, did she?'

Ella told him all she knew.

'Hmm. Quite an ordeal! Do you think she was ill-treated physically? Violently, I mean? Slapped? Punched? Man-handled in any way at all?'

Ella thought for a moment. She tried to imagine it, then shook her head. 'I don't think so. I think Penny would have said, Doctor. I would like to take her home with me. She's been through so much that I think home and a familiar bed would be best for her.'

To her relief he nodded. 'But do keep your eyes open. Any suspicious marks ... anything she might say. Don't hesitate to call your own doctor or bring her back to us. I don't want any nasty surprises but – yes, Mrs Gough, you can take your little girl home.'

Outside in the corridor, Daniel's ordeal was far from over. He knew in his heart that it was just beginning. He glanced up in time to see Ella and Penny walk out of the swing doors. As they came slowly towards him he froze. What could he say? 'Sorry' was such an insubstantial word. Unable to face Ella, he smiled at Penny.

'It's Mr Hampton!' she cried.

Daniel said, 'I'm so glad...' He felt choked. He forced himself to look at Ella, but she was staring resolutely in front of her. Not trusting herself to speak, he thought.

Penny said, 'We've got a new gardener, but he doesn't call me Tiddler. His dog's called Snip and he can beg and–'

Ella said, 'Come along, Penny.'

As they walked away, Penny turned round to wave. 'Mummy, that was Mr Hampton. Don't you remember him?'

Ella murmured something he couldn't hear and then they had gone through the doors and out into the night. Threatened with a growing despair, Daniel forced his attention back to D.I. Hall and the constable.

'I shall leave my constable here, Mr Hampton,' the former was saying in irritatingly measured tones. 'If, after her examination, your wife is considered well enough to leave the hospital she will accompany the constable to the station where she will be formally charged with kidnapping, obstructing the police and attempting to avoid arrest–'

'Attempting to...? She only kicked his

383

shins, for God's sake!'

'And assaulting a police officer in the execution of his duty.' D.I. Hall flipped his notebook shut and gave Daniel a challenging look.

Daniel fumed. 'Can she come home after she's been charged?'

'That depends, sir. Might be a question of bail.'

'Bail?' Daniel groaned with frustration as he turned away and thumped the wall with his fist. 'Dammit!' Bail. Of course. They had no money for bail. His wife and his unborn child were going to spend the night in prison.

'But you know she's ... pregnant.'

'So I believe, sir.' His tone was deliberately indifferent.

Daniel wanted to shake him. 'Ever heard of humanity, Inspector?'

'No need for sarcasm, Mr Hampton. I'm doing my job and it's not my fault if your wife decides to kidnap a little girl. Has *she* ever heard of humanity, *sir?*'

With an effort Daniel swallowed his pride. 'If there's anything you can do for her...'

'I'm afraid not, sir.'

He was saved by the reappearance of the elderly doctor who had been examining Lizzie.

'Mr Hampton?'

'Yes.'

'I'm pleased to say that there seems to be no harm done, Mr Hampton ... internally. The baby appears untouched by the fall, and we've patched up the head wound. Quite superficial, fortunately. A few stitches. Nothing to worry about.'

He was trying to reassure him, but Daniel didn't want his wife released from the hospital. More than anything he wanted her kept in overnight – that would give him a breathing space to consider their plight and decide what to do.

He said, 'But you'll keep her in, won't you, Doctor? For observation.' He gave the doctor a meaningful look.

'Well, I hadn't ... I naturally thought...' He looked surprised.

Daniel said, 'She's been through a bit of an upset. Rather out of character. I'm worried about her state of mind. In the circumstances...'

D.I. Hall said, 'The doctor's said she's free to leave! She can come with us.'

'No!' Daniel looked appealingly at the doctor. 'He didn't say that – not exactly...'

The doctor caught his meaning and wavered. 'Perhaps it would be best if she could see the gynaecologist in the morning.'

From within the room Lizzie called out, 'Dan! *Dan!*'

'Excuse me.' Daniel went into the room and found Lizzie sitting up on the examining table. Her hair was tousled and her eyes were wide with fright. She looked like a trapped animal, he thought, with a rush of tenderness which surprised him.

'Dan, I want to go home.'

He put his finger to his lips. 'Hush! You *don't* want to leave here. If you do, they'll arrest you.' He took her hand in his; it was cold and she was shivering. 'I want you to stay in overnight. I need to get help for you – money to put up for the bail. You just rest,' he told her. 'Let me do the worrying. You've got our baby to think about.'

Her eyes filled with tears. 'Oh, Daniel, do you want it? Really want it?'

'Of course I do. We're going to get over all this and then we'll find somewhere to be together and make a fresh start.' He put his arm round the thin, shaking shoulders and cursed himself for his selfishness. He should never have walked out on her. *Her and the baby.* He still couldn't quite believe it.

She clutched at him, beginning to cry. One part of his mind said 'Comfort her'. The other said 'Let her cry'. Her obvious distress would influence the doctor and might gain them a few hours' respite from the law.

'They'll lock me up. They'll take the baby away!'

'They can't do that, Lizzie. We're married and I'm the baby's father.'

'But how could you manage without me?'

'I don't know yet, but I'll think of something.'

Leaving her abruptly, he went back into the corridor. To the doctor he said, 'She's a bit hysterical. Would you...?'

The doctor went at once to his patient, leaving Daniel with the two policemen.

The inspector said, 'Well, I'll be getting back to the station to fill in a report on the incident.' He turned to his constable. 'When Mrs Hampton has sobered up...'

Daniel snapped, 'I object to that kind of talk! She's not a drunk.'

D.I. Hall raised his eyebrows. 'Is that the way she normally behaves, then? I was giving her the benefit of the doubt.'

'Look, I left her a few days ago and she then discovered she's expecting a child. That's enough to throw any woman off balance. She's hysterical.'

His words had little effect. The detective's smile was cold, the sneer thinly disguised. 'Having your child kidnapped would throw some women off balance, but Mrs Gough's not hysterical. That may be because she hasn't swallowed a bottle of whisky while standing guard over a child she had half killed with pills!' He thrust his face closer to Daniel's. 'Save your breath, Mr Hampton. All my sympathies are with Mrs Gough and that unfortunate child.'

They were interrupted again by the reappearance of the doctor, who said, 'Mrs Hampton shouldn't be moved tonight. Well take another look at her in the morning.'

D.I. Hall turned. 'In that case, my constable will stay here, outside the ward.'

The doctor gave him a sharp look. 'I will allow it on this occasion. Please remember that it is in my power to refuse.'

Meanwhile the constable moved a hard-backed chair from further along the corridor, sat down about two yards from the ward door and stared straight ahead.

The doctor gave the constable a cold look. 'The patient has been sedated and is in no condition to run away! You people...!' He shook his head.

'He's just carrying out his instructions,' said the inspector.

A plump nurse hurried up to them looking harassed. 'Excuse me, Doctor, but Mr Foote is not responding. He's vomiting again. Sister would like you to take a look at him before you go off duty.'

'I'll be there in two ticks.' He turned to Daniel. 'Come in first thing tomorrow and explain to Sister that I've given permission. Say eight o'clock?'

'Thank you – for everything, Doctor.'

Unseen by the policemen, the doctor winked and Daniel felt oddly comforted by this small expression of support. Before D.I.

Hall could stop him, he turned and made his way quickly towards the main doors and out into the darkness. He hadn't the faintest idea what he could do to help his wife, but his next and immediate hurdle was the coming interview with his new employer and some way to explain his absence.

Chapter Twelve

Charles sat in the third row and tried to keep his eyes on the speaker. Roland's brother, Claude, was talking about the deceased and deserved his attention but Charles's gaze repeatedly returned to the widow. Ella Gough sat alone in the front pew, a slim, slightly huddled figure who from time to time turned to stare at the mahogany coffin. A large display of white lilies lay on top of it and other wreaths were tastefully arranged around it.

'...Roland always looked up to me the way younger brothers do and now, looking back, I can see how close we were despite the age gap. Later we were at Cambridge together, although our paths crossed less often than one might expect...'

Charles glanced past him to the vicar and on to the eight choirboys resplendent in red and white cassocks, then back to Ella. He had fallen in love with her the moment they first met – maybe even before that. His godfather's letters had never failed to include news of 'Mrs Gough', sometimes *dear* Mrs Gough'. She had been 'kindness itself' on many occasions, as well as 'understanding and wonderfully generous'. His godfather had been so excited when the child was born and desolate when Roland had been taken ill.

Charles drew a long breath. This was hardly the time, with Roland's body not yards away and a full congregation gathered to mourn his passing, but it was impossible not to be aware that suddenly there was a chance of spending the rest of his life with Ella. Whether she would ever love *him* was in the lap of the gods, but he knew there would never be anyone else but Ella for him. He remembered the shock he had felt when they shook hands for the first time; he had been unwilling to release her. Now he longed to sit beside her, to put an arm round her hunched shoulders and whisper words of consolation. But you *can't*, he told himself. You must keep a respectful distance, now and for some weeks. Months, even. You daren't rush her; you'll only frighten or offend her. She has just lost the man she loves; she needs time to grieve, to adapt, to want to love again. Patience, for God's sake!

Claude Gough had resumed his seat and they all rose to sing the next hymn. Charles found it in the hymn book; one of his favourites. He watched Ella wipe her eyes. Then she was turning the page in search of the place. Was it one of Roland's favourites, he wondered? Was Roland's spirit with them? He wasn't a firm believer in life after death, but he was willing to be persuaded. And if Roland's spirit *was* with them, could he see into Charles's mind? He hoped not. He had genuinely liked Roland Gough and knew he had lost a potential friend. How ironic, then, that Roland had been Ella's husband. He sighed as the organ pealed and gave himself up to the music. He had a good baritone voice and loved to sing.

'Praise my soul the King of Heaven...'

Charles watched Ella lift her head to sing and wished he could pick out her voice from the rest. If only he could see her face! For a moment he allowed himself a glimpse into the future they might have together. He pictured a family, grouped round the font. Himself holding Penny's hand, Ella holding the new baby. Briefly he closed his eyes. I have waited all these years for the right woman. Please let her love me. Let *me* be the one who makes her happy.

While they buried her father, Penny was standing beside the coffee table with a piece of jigsaw in her hand, her face screwed up in concentration. She wore a dark green velvet skirt and a white knitted jumper. Less than a week had passed since she had been rescued from the cellar and the household had marvelled at her resilience.

'Blue with a greeny bit,' she announced, peering at the half-completed picture.

'It's much too hard for you, Penny,' Florrie insisted. 'You should have your own puzzle. A children's puzzle.'

The little girl scowled. 'I like *your* puzzles.' She tossed the offending piece on to the tray and picked up another. 'This one's got an edge! Browny grey with an edge.' She glanced down at her new shoes and smiled happily.

Florrie watched her with a deep sense of thankfulness. The child appeared to have suffered no serious effects. She seemed totally unaware of the danger she had been in and her main complaint, frequently repeated, was that 'Auntie Liz told lies'. Even this had mainly disappeared since Ella had stifled her doubts and bought her a pair of the much-maligned ankle-strap shoes.

Florrie glanced out at the rain. The trees, almost bare now, stood out starkly against the cloudy sky. The traumas of the past few days had tired her and she was pleased to be comfortably ensconced with Penny instead of attending Roland's funeral. She intended no disrespect for Ella's husband, but burials were a constant reminder of the frailty of life and her own dwindling years. They were emotional affairs at the best of times, but today the unremitting rain made it worse. She could imagine the sombre scene at the graveside, the mourners huddled into their overcoats and mackintoshes, struggling to hold on to black umbrellas.

Sitting by the fire with a rug across her knees, Florrie was conscious of a contentment she hadn't known for a long time. It sprang from a sense of belonging again; being part of a family; feeling *needed*.

Penny said, 'I didn't want Daddy to be dead. Why is he?' She paused, staring up into Florrie's face.

Florrie was startled. It was the first time Penny had mentioned Roland's death in her presence and she wasn't sure how to reply.

Without waiting for an answer, Penny asked, 'Are there really angels in heaven? With white wings and little gold harps?' She stole a look at her great-aunt and twisted one of her curls around a small finger.

'I don't know, dear. I've never been to heaven so I'm not sure.'

'Auntie Liz said *she* will be going to the other place. It's called Hell, and it's because she told me lies.'

Florrie was beginning to feel flustered. Why were the young so *direct*, she wondered. She said. 'I shouldn't pay much attention to that nasty woman. She's a bit – a bit mixed up.'

Penny smiled. 'I didn't pay her much attention because she was drunk.'

Florrie blinked. 'Drunk? How do you

know she was drunk?'

'She told me. She went hiccup, hiccup, and then she said "Pardon me, I'm drunk".' She laughed. 'When I hiccup, am *I* drunk?'

'No, dear, of course not.' Florrie gave her a reproving look and placed a piece of the jigsaw. 'I expect she was joking.'

'She wasn't.' Penny gave her a straight look. 'Have you ever been drunk?'

Florrie raised her eyebrows. 'Drunk? Certainly not!' she replied and, glancing at the mantelpiece clock, hoped it wouldn't be too long before the funeral ended and Penny's mother returned to claim her.

A quarter of an hour later Ella returned from the church. Charles helped her from the car and she hurried inside.

Annie, holding the door open, asked, 'How did it go, Mrs Gough?'

'Very well, thank you, Annie. A big congregation, but that was to be expected. Mr Gough was well respected.'

'Was Nurse Baisley there?'

Ella nodded. 'And she sent some beautiful flowers.'

'Red roses, I suppose!'

'They were, actually. Poor woman. I was going to invite her back here, but she slipped away.'

Ella omitted to say that she had caught sight of Daniel at the rear of the church.

Their eyes had met fleetingly and she had acknowledged him with a small nod. She wondered why he had attended the funeral of a man he hardly knew, but now she shrugged the question aside. As she took off her wet coat, she glanced into the sitting room where the funeral feast had been arranged on additional tables. A whole ham, a game pie, a salmon poached with dill. China and cutlery shone, glasses sparkled under the two small chandeliers. There was a white floral display in each corner of the room.

'You've done wonders, Annie,' she said. 'It looks very elegant.'

Miss Spinney and Mrs Grey arrived together. A few members of the Dramatic Society had come along, also the bank manager, the accountant and Doctor Clarke.

Everyone was soon inside, enjoying the warmth and hospitality after the depressing service and rainswept burial. Ella moved among the mourners with a welcoming smile, receiving their commiserations and feeling intensely bereft. From time to time she caught sight of Charles and was grateful for his help. Roland had once referred to him as a 'thoroughly decent man' and she was bound to agree. A true friend in times of trouble. Watching him now, she was sorry that he and Roland had had so little time to spend together. Odd that he had come into their lives so casually. In a way it was Mr Saville who had brought about the introduction.

She took a sip of her wine, but the thought of food held no appeal. The bank manager moved to stand beside her and shake her hand.

He said, 'So terribly sorry, Mrs Gough. Dreadful. Quite dreadful. So much to live for.'

Ella nodded. 'We're going to miss him terribly.'

'I heard about the abduction, of course. What a frightful experience for you all.'

'It was,' Ella agreed, 'but Penny seems to be getting over it all very quickly. I'm hoping things will soon be back to normal.'

He made the usual offers of help and gave way to Miss Spinney who was hovering at his elbow.

She clutched Ella's free hand. 'I remember you both in my prayers,' she said, 'and I do believe God will provide. It was a lovely service. Very moving.'

Ella smiled. After a few moments of inconsequential talk she made her excuses and moved away to speak to Charles.

'I'm going to slip away upstairs,' she told him. 'Penny is with Florrie and I want to speak to them. If anyone asks, will you tell them I'll be down again shortly?'

'Of course. Are you bearing up? I know how hard it must be.'

'I've felt better but...' She gave a wry smile. 'Will you stay on after they all leave? I have to hear the will read, but then we could relax and maybe have some dinner later. Florrie might join us.'

'I'd like that, but I don't want to impose.'

She smiled. 'I'd hate it if you said "No".'

As the low murmurs around her changed to a more relaxed hum of conversation, she took a tray of food and made her way to Florrie's room. She barely had time to put the tray down before Penny rushed towards her. Ella scooped her up and the child flung her arms round Ella's neck.

'Cuddle me!' she pleaded. She lowered her voice. 'The special way, like Daddy used to do.'

'How did Daddy cuddle you, sweetie?'

Penny looked up with wide eyes and a shaky smile which failed to hide her yearning. 'He hugged me and then, while he was kissing me, he pretended to steal one of my curls!'

Ella did her best and was rewarded by a little sigh of satisfaction. She said, 'Daddy loved you so much.'

'I was his best girl in the whole world.'

'I know you were.'

Ella exchanged a look with Florrie and kissed the top of Penny's head. I will make it

399

up to her, she told herself. I'll be mother and father to her and she will never feel unloved. She said, 'I thought perhaps to-morrow we could take some flowers from you to Daddy's grave. Would you like that?'

Penny's face lit up. 'And I could make a card for him? A sort of birthday card. I could draw Daddy and me and put kisses all round the edge!'

Ella, moved, fumbled for an answer.

'That's a lovely idea,' Florrie said quickly.

Penny looked at her. 'Will he be able to see it if he's in heaven?'

'Oh yes! He can look down. He'll be very pleased.'

Ella smiled at her aunt. Florrie's re-assuring presence was exactly what she needed, and it crossed her mind that the temporary visit might be extended in-definitely; she might even persuade Florrie to move in permanently.

There was a knock at the door and Annie came in looking flustered.

'What is it, Annie?'

'It's him! The gardener chap.'

'Tom Berry?'

'The other one – that you sent away. Mr Hampton. He wants to see you. Says he must talk to you. I told him it was a funeral. I tried to say it wasn't convenient but...'

Ella's heart was racing as she stood up. 'It's all right. I'll see him.'

Florrie said, 'Don't let the wretch upset you, Ella.'

Penny jumped up. 'I like Mr Hampton. Does he want to see me, too?'

Florrie took hold of her hand. 'You stay here with me, Penny. We've nearly finished the puzzle and I can't possibly find all the pieces by myself.'

As Florrie put a restraining hand on the little girl's arm, Ella followed the house-keeper from the room and down the stairs. Daniel was waiting in the hallway. He looked wet and miserable.

'We'll talk in the dining room,' she said. 'Annie, will you bring Mr Hampton a glass of brandy to warm him up?' She gave Daniel a brief smile and led the way. Inside the dining room, she closed the door. 'I can spare ten minutes,' she told him.

He seemed disconcerted by her brisk manner. 'May I take off my overcoat?'

'Of course. Would you like something to eat?'

He shook his head. 'I'm sorry about your husband's death.'

She nodded. 'One thing after another.' She indicated a chair. 'Do sit down.'

They both sat and Daniel said, 'Not a good year for any of us.'

'I'm afraid not. I've lost Roland, but at least I have my daughter back. I thank God for that.'

For a moment he was silent.

Ella said, 'How's your wife – and the baby?' It was hard to know what to say to him. At one moment she wanted to hug him, the next she wanted to scream abuse because of what Lizzie had done. She didn't want to have to look at him, but she dreaded the moment when he must leave.

'She's out of hospital.'

'Good.'

'She's in prison. They're asking bail.'

Ella digested the information and immediately saw the reason for Daniel's visit. He wanted her to provide the money which would release the woman who had put her through so much agony of mind and treated her daughter so badly. He would know that she was a wealthy widow who need ask no one for permission to spend the money.

He said, 'It's set at two hundred pounds. Will you give me the money?'

Her first reaction was to say 'No' but then she longed to say 'Yes'. She wondered what would happen if she *did* provide the bail money. Then again, what would happen if she *didn't?*

At that moment Annie came in with a glass of brandy and the distraction gave Ella a few moments to collect herself. Daniel drank half the brandy in one gulp.

When Annie had gone, Ella asked, 'Do you have to stay with her, Daniel?' She wanted to hear him say that he didn't love Lizzie, yet perversely she wanted him to be happy. She knew that there was no future for *her* with Daniel, after all that had happened.

Daniel downed the rest of the brandy and put down the glass. 'I have to stand by her, Ella. She'll never manage alone and – she's carrying my baby. I don't want my son or daughter born in prison or given up for adoption. I want my child to have a happy home. You won't believe me, but Lizzie's not all bad. I've got to make it work for all three of us.'

Ella drew a long breath. Did she love this man enough to help him make a new life with a woman she hated? To delay answering the question, she cast about in her mind for arguments.

She said, 'But bail only lasts until the trial. Suppose the verdict is guilty, which it must be. Lizzie will go to prison anyway.' She saw his expression change. 'Look, Daniel, I've said I will press charges.'

There was another silence, then he said, 'I'm begging you not to. They might still go ahead, but it would weaken their case if you didn't. I'm pretty desperate right now.'

Restlessly he stood up, crossed to the window and stared down into the garden. Watching him, Ella wished she had had a brandy herself. This was harder than she had expected.

He turned, staring slowly round the room, then smiled faintly. 'Remember that Hallowe'en party?' he asked. 'You were about ten and I came as the Devil and you were terrified! Your father was furious with me. Said I intended to scare you.'

'You *did!*' she protested.

'I remember that mirror.' He pointed. Lydia had draped it in black net... 'You were a bad fairy and Lydia was a witch with long green fingernails.'

'I didn't recognise you.' She remembered his devil's mask looming towards her out of the bushes. She'd had nightmares for weeks afterwards.

After a moment he said, 'Your clock's stopped.'

'I forget to wind them. It was always Roland's job before that damned polio. He used to go round the whole house – a daily ritual. He loved clocks.'

Reluctantly they returned to the matter in question.

Daniel sighed heavily. 'Look, this is what I want. I'll spell it out ... throw myself on your mercy. If you turn me down you'll ruin us – and I won't blame you.'

'I think you will!' And I'll blame myself, she thought, with sudden insight. If I don't help them it will start all over again. The guilt and the bitterness. Perhaps this was a second chance.

He said, 'All right then – I will blame you, but I'll understand. I want you to give me three hundred pounds. I'll get Lizzie out on bail–'

'*Three hundred!* For heaven's sake, Daniel!'

'I'll need a few savings. We'll have expenses. If they find her guilty they'll lock her up for years, but I'm going to keep that baby – which means I'll need someone to look after her ... or him.' He stopped and rubbed his eyes. 'Sometimes I think I'll go mad. I can't think... I just want...' His shoulders sagged and she saw the desperation in his face. 'How did I ever get into this mess?'

Ella stared back, her thoughts racing. Her feelings for this man would never go away. So *he* must go. The occasional letter or exchange of Christmas cards – she could probably bear that. But if he remained in the area with the shame of a wife in prison, struggling to pay his way, bringing up their child, she would never be free of him. Nor would he ever be free of her. They would be drawn together again and again, haunted by the mistakes of the past. Frantically she searched for a solution, but when it came she was shocked. Before she could change her mind she said, 'Listen, Daniel. This is what I am prepared to do. Provided you agree. If not, I can't help you.'

He was looking at her with a glimmer of

hope in his eyes as she steeled herself to put the plan into words.

'I will put the bail money *and* I will give you five hundred pounds.'

He gasped. *'Five hundred?* Oh God, that's–'

'Hear me out, Daniel. You may not be so pleased. With the money, you will buy tickets for South Africa.'

His face fell. 'South Africa? Oh, but–'

'Will you please stop interrupting me!' She took a deep breath. 'You'll forget about the bail and get out of the country–'

He stared at her aghast. 'What are you saying?'

She ignored the interruption. 'When they tell me Lizzie hasn't appeared for trial, I'll be astonished and furious–'

'Ella, you *can't!* I won't let you do this. It's madness!'

'I'll be furious because I'll have lost my money. It will look as though you've done a moonlight flit. They won't be able to blame me, and there'll be no one for me to press charges against. You'll get a job over there and make a fresh start.'

He regarded her wide-eyed, but she could see he was at least considering the idea.

'It's a terrible risk for all of us,' he said. 'Suppose they catch us?'

'Then I'll say I know nothing about it.' His words had shaken her, however. The possibility of recapture hadn't occurred to her. 'You'll have to make sure they *don't* catch you.'

He swallowed nervously, but she could see he was weakening. Ella prayed that he would agree before she lost her courage.

He said, 'It's a crazy idea, but it just might work.'

'I'll chance it if you will.' She closed her eyes. The longer he hesitated the more sure she became that this was yet another mistake and that she was drawing him further into the mire.

He said, 'Won't they be watching the ports?'

'They won't know you're thinking of leaving. They think you're broke, remember? Anyway, Lizzie is hardly an international criminal!' For heaven's sake, she thought desperately, make up your mind! She hardened her heart. 'That's your decision, Daniel, not mine. If you decide to go, cross to France and go on from there. I know a small hotel in Paris. Florrie and I spent a few nights there. And don't tell me you don't have a passport.'

'Of course I do...'

'It's the only way, Daniel. They'd never bother to chase you across half the world – even if they knew where you'd gone, which they won't.'

'You want to get rid of me, Ella!' He tried

to make a joke of it.

Ella nodded. 'I have to make a new life too, remember – for me and for Penny. I can't do that with you here. So don't thank me; I'm being selfish. I have to forget you, Daniel. It's best for you, too. We seem to have an adverse effect on one another's lives. Two stars that keep colliding.' She forced a smile. 'Better to be in different galaxies.'

Daniel covered her hand with his. 'I wish things could have been different.'

If she hadn't fallen in love with him ... or if he had returned her affection ... or if her mother... But now fate had them cornered.

'So?' She made her tone determinedly brisk. 'What do you say?'

'I have no choice,' he said hoarsely. 'We'll do it.'

Six days later Ella was summoned to the police station by a brief phone call. Guessing the purpose behind it, she waited in the reception area, struggling to hide the extent of her anxiety. The blue glove remained on the notice board beside a new directive about rabies. It was all depressingly familiar. Around her people came and went, escorted in the main by a policeman: a weeping woman, a drunken man, an obstreperous boy whose foul language appalled her. Minutes ticked by as

408

Ella watched, fascinated. Pockets were emptied, forms filled in and men and women were signed in or out as the occasion demanded. A young woman entered with an overweight policeman who pushed her none too gently on to the bench beside Ella. He was carrying something which he tossed on to the desk. The woman looked about twenty; she was flashily dressed and smelled of cheap scent.

'Bloody coppers!' she grumbled. 'I never pinched nothing. I paid for them stockings, but I lost the receipt. They've got a down on me. Got a fag, love?'

'No. Sorry.'

'What they done you for?'

'Me? Nothing.' She felt a frisson of fear as she said this. She *had* committed a crime; she had connived Lizzie's escape. Not only connived but instigated it. 'Conspiring to pervert the course of justice.' She wondered what the penalty was for that particular crime.

The woman nudged her with an elbow. 'Nothing? Come off it! You must have done something. It's written all over your face!'

Shocked, Ella hastily rearranged her features. 'No. It's – it's on another matter.'

And none of your business, she thought. The last thing she wanted was to be drawn into an argument. She needed time to herself to compose herself and *think innocent.* There must be nothing in her eyes to give the police the idea that she was implicated; she must appear genuinely surprised and angry. You can do it, she told herself. You can act for pleasure; now it's real. She sat up a little straighter.

The large policeman said, 'Oi! You with the dodgy stockings.' He pointed to the woman. 'Over here!'

She muttered, 'Bloody bullies!' and moved reluctantly to the desk.

'Empty your pockets. You know the drill by now. What is it – third time?'

She ignored the question and threw several packets on to the desk.

The desk sergeant said, 'More silk stockings? My, my! You will look smart. Off to Ascot, are we?' He wrote something on his pad. 'Four pairs silk stockings to the value of...?' He cocked his head enquiringly.

She said, 'Don't look at me.'

'You don't know?'

Ella saw the trap. The woman didn't.

'Oh yes?' he crowed, 'I thought you'd just *bought* them.'

Now she saw it. 'Oh, sod off!'

An older man approached Ella and she recognised Detective Inspector Hall. He had an odd expression on his face which she found difficult to read.

'Let's go somewhere quieter,' he suggested and led the way into a small office.

Ella sat in one of the two hardbacked chairs and prepared herself for the worst. The detective sat down and looked at her. 'I'm sorry, but I have some rather bad news,' he told her.

He doesn't sound at all sorry, she thought, and suddenly recognised his expression. It was triumph.

'Mrs Gough, we have reason to believe that Elizabeth Hampton has disappeared. She didn't report in this morning or yesterday, and it seems they've...' He paused, searching Ella's face for signs that she had grasped the implications of the situation. He went on, 'In other words, we think she's left the country, Mrs Gough. Well, both of them have gone actually.'

'I see.' He was *glad*, she thought. He knew how much money she stood to lose and he thought it served her right. In a way it did. She sympathised with him. They had done their best to find Penny and then, when they almost had the culprit under lock and key, Ella had made her release possible. Hardly likely to impress Detective Inspector Hall!

She tried to look confused. 'So – so she might not stand trial – is that what you mean?'

'There's that, of course, but... Well, if she doesn't return, you stand to forfeit the bail money. I'm sorry, Mrs Gough but–'

'The bail money? Forfeit the – oh no!' She

looked stricken. 'Do you mean I lose *all* of it? The whole two hundred? It's a lot of money.'

He shrugged. 'That's the way it works. It was a lot, granted. But then kidnap is a very serious crime. Your daughter could have died in that cellar.' He shrugged. 'We did try to warn you, Mrs Gough, but you wouldn't listen.'

'Yes, you did!' She sighed heavily. 'Looking back, I can see it wasn't very clever of me.'

'Putting up bail rarely is.' He sat back, enjoying her discomfiture, then went on, 'Understandable in cases where there is doubt about the guilt, but you *knew* she was guilty. To be frank with you, Mrs Gough, none of us could understand why you did it. Had you husband not died he would *certainly* have advised you against it. Perhaps your sympathies were with the woman's husband.' He waited for her to deny it, but she hesitated fatally and he went on, 'You see, Mrs Gough, he may have been involved in the kidnap, despite your faith in his integrity. Now, without a trial, we may never know the full facts.'

'I'm sure he knew nothing–'

'That's what he wanted you to think.'

'With hindsight...' Ella faltered, then with an effort she rallied. D.I. Hall had almost succeeded in sowing the seed of doubt, but

412

that was his job. He was trained to interrogate people. Keep calm, she told herself.

She looked straight into his eyes. 'Are you sure – that they've gone? Are the police looking for her? For them.' She must let him think she was more concerned about the money.

'Keeping an eye out. The usual routine.' He leaned forward. 'You could help us, Mrs Gough. If we *can* find them, you won't lose your money. Do you know anywhere they might have gone? Any friends who might–' He looked round as the door opened. A young policeman said, 'Oh, sorry, sir!' and closed it again. 'Any friends who might shelter them? Any family?'

'I don't know anything about the wife. Mr Hampton has a father living somewhere in Yorkshire, but that's all I know. No address.' She regarded him earnestly. 'But he and his father quarrelled years ago. I doubt if he'd make contact in these circumstances. Too ashamed, I should think.' She frowned with feigned concentration. 'Of course they did spend a few years in South Africa. That's where they met. They probably have friends out there.'

His disappointment showed in his face. 'But ... how could they afford the fare? A passage to South Africa – *twice?*'

She shrugged. 'Sold something, maybe.'

'Not very likely. You saw their flat. I don't recall any family silver. No old masters on the wall.'

She ignored the sarcasm. 'Maybe they borrowed it?'

'Who from?'

Clasping his hands, the inspector rested his forearms on his knees and stared at his shoes, apparently deep in thought. Ella wondered whether her performance had convinced him. She felt fairly confident that she had sounded reasonably innocent, but minutes passed and he didn't speak. Was he trying to test her, Ella wondered. Hoping to draw an unguarded comment from her, perhaps? Was this a recognised procedure for undermining a suspect's confidence? She must say nothing.

At last he straightened up. 'And you're absolutely sure you have no idea of their whereabouts? I'm sure I don't need to remind you that it's an offence to withhold information.' His tone and expression were distinctly unfriendly. 'Might be construed as obstructing the police in the execution of their duties.'

She felt a jolt of fear. He suspected the truth; she had underestimated him. 'I'm sorry,' she stammered. 'If I knew anything at all...'

As he stood up, his expression was withering. 'So that's it then, Mrs Gough,' he said coldly. 'You can't help us, so we can't help you. Your money's forfeit. Every penny of it. Gone! And for what? To save a pair of undesirables. Not to mention a great waste of police time and resources.'

Ella stood up and discovered that she was trembling. 'It's my own fault.'

'It most certainly is.' He opened the door and shouted for someone. A young constable appeared.

D.I. Hall said, 'Show Mrs Gough out, Baines,' and walked out of the room. No 'Goodbye'. No handshake.

Ella followed the constable out on to the steps. Neither spoke. She saw Charles on the other side of the road, smiling, opening the car door for her. Returning his wave with feigned cheerfulness, she determined to tell him a carefully edited version of what had taken place. The interview had depressed her and, as she waited for a gap in the traffic, it didn't help to know that her fall from grace had been entirely of her own making.

That evening at dinner, Ella and her aunt sat at one end of the dining table facing each other across the tureens. Florrie ate heartily, enjoying the pheasant casserole. Ella nibbled at her portion without enthusiasm until at last Florrie put down her knife with a deliberate clatter and a resigned sigh.

'Ella! You've got to talk to someone,' she told her. 'It might as well be me. And don't pretend there's nothing on your mind. I know you better than you know yourself.'

Ella placed her knife and fork together and pushed back her plate. 'I'm not hungry.'

'I can see that!' Her aunt regarded her with exasperation. 'What happened at the police station?'

Ella took a sip of water and said, 'Nothing really. I told you when I came home.'

'You said merely that you'd lost your money because they'd fled the country. Charles was with you and I didn't want to press you. But I know you, Ella. There's more to it.'

Ella stared at the ceiling.

'Ella!'

'It was not a pleasant experience, that's all. I had to sit with the ... the dregs of society. A shoplifter asked me what I was "in for". I ended up feeling no better than she was. Feeling sorry for her, in fact. There but for the grace of God... The police were decidedly unsympathetic.'

'Poor you. I'm so sorry.'

'Coming home in the car, I kept thinking that if Roland had been with me, they'd have treated me differently. It brought home to me how very alone I am without him.'

'It's not easy, Ella, but you're strong. I've been alone for most of my life. You learn to

416

manage. I think you're doing very well. The last few weeks have been full of unpleasant surprises, but you've dealt with them all.'

'But have I dealt with them in the right way? I sometimes wonder just how smart I really am!'

Florrie laughed. 'We all feel that way sometimes. Nobody gets it *all* right, Ella.'

'And there's Penny.'

'She perfectly all right. She's a bright child and you're getting to know her better.'

'She adored Roland. I can never take his place.'

'You don't need to, dear. You have your own place in her life.'

Annie came in to clear the plates and they waited in silence. When she brought in a lemon meringue pie, Ella regarded it blankly.

Ella said, 'I've been thinking, Florrie. I don't want you to go back to Sunningford. I know I'm not the easiest person to live with, but this is such a big house. You could have your own rooms, bring some of your furniture and be as independent as you wish. Won't you think about selling your house and coming to keep me company?'

Florrie helped herself to a slice of the pie. 'Eat some, Ella. Keep your strength up.'

'You haven't answered me.'

Florrie cut another slice and placed it in front of Ella. When Ella started to eat,

Florrie said, 'I would love to live in Burleigh House, but only while you need me. What if you ever remarried?'

'I doubt I will,' Ella told her. 'And even if I did, you would still be welcome to stay. You'd be part of the furniture by then,' she joked. 'Love me, love my aunt! Shall we take that as settled? Penny would be so thrilled.'

Florrie reached out and took hold of her hand. 'We'll take it as settled – and thank you, dear.'

'The pleasure's mine,' said Ella with a broad smile, and she meant it. At least she had got *something* right.

Two weeks later the Autumn Fair was upon them. Obligingly the weather brightened and a surprisingly warm sun emerged from behind the clouds. This meant they were able to hold the event in the garden instead of inside the barn. Seeing so many happy faces around her, Ella was glad that she had allowed it to go ahead. Penny always looked forward to the event with wild excitement and Ella was sure that Roland wouldn't have wanted it cancelled on his account. She was still in black but Penny was resplendent in her pink party dress although, at her own request, she wore a black ribbon in her hair.

The telephone rang incessantly with last-minute queries, but at five past three Annie came hurrying to Ella in the dining room with news of an unexpected caller.

'It's Mr Hampton,' she told her, 'on the telephone, but–'

'Mr Hampton?'

'Not our Mr Hampton. He says he's his father. *Edmund* Hampton.' She looked anxious. 'He says he *must* speak with you and, if you won't agree, he'll travel down from Yorkshire and call in person.'

'But he's *ill!*' She frowned. 'And how did he find me? How did he know...?' she began, then rolled her eyes. 'Florrie told him!' she muttered.

Annie said, 'He sounded rather strange. Shall I say you're not available?'

It was tempting, but Ella knew it was not the way. This was one more opportunity. 'I'll take it, Annie, thank you.'

She walked slowly out to the hall and picked up the receiver. 'Ella speaking.' In her pocket she had the card she had received that morning from Paris. Daniel had written, 'Paris is superb. Hotel fine. Leaving in ten days' time.' No signature. Nothing the prying eyes of the police could register if they were watching the house.

'Ella, I have to know where he is!' The voice sounded weak and strained, but she recognised it instantly. 'I badgered Florrie unmercifully. You mustn't reproach her, Ella.'

'I won't. She did what she thought was best.'

'She told me about the kidnap. What can I say? It was a terrible thing to do.'

'I know, but it wasn't Daniel's idea.'

'Thank God for that! But your aunt told me they'd left the country. You took a risk.'

'I think I got away with it.' She took a deep breath. 'I'm sorry you're ill. I should have answered your letter. Please forgive me.'

'I have to see him. I only have a few months. Six at the most.'

'I had a card from them this morning. They're leaving for South Africa in about a week.' She gave him the name of the Paris hotel and the telephone number. 'If you're not well enough to travel to Paris, you could talk to him.'

'South Africa? I don't understand. Florrie said they had very little money.'

She hesitated. 'I gave them some.'

There was a moment's silence. 'That was very generous, Ella. But I'm leaving him everything. There's a big house here in Wetherby. I want to share it with them for the little time I have left, and then it's theirs.'

Ella was surprised to feel nothing. No sense of betrayal that her carefully laid plan was being undermined. Instead she had a strange feeling of inevitability, as though fate was taking a hand.

'That will solve most of their problems,'

she said. Yorkshire was a long way away. Far enough. 'With a little luck you might even live to see your grandchild.'

'That would be a bonus,' he told her, 'but I'm not going to be greedy. I just want to see Daniel – to hold him in my arms... And this Lizzie person? You've met her, Ella. Can she possibly make him happy?'

'Anything's possible.' Ella kept her tone neutral. 'With the baby and no financial worries – at least they'll have a better chance than before. Daniel says she loves him.'

'Please God she does!'

At that moment Miss Spinney appeared with a small cake on a plate. 'Oh, there you are–' she began.

Ella indicated the telephone and Miss Spinney whispered, 'Oh, sorry!' and put the plate on the hall table. 'One of Mrs Grey's lemon-curd tarts!'

'Thank you.' To Edmund she said, 'I have to go. There is an Autumn Fair gathering pace around me.'

'I haven't said how sorry I am about your husband. I do wish you happiness, Ella. I'm so sorry ... about that and – and everything else. I was hasty, and stubborn. He takes after me, I'm afraid.' His voice broke. 'And poor Lydia... It was a cruel way to die...'

Ella heard herself say, 'They had a few happy years together. Don't reproach yourself.'

'I hope Daniel will forgive me.'

'He will,' she said. 'He's changed. We all have.'

'I always hoped you and he...'

'He didn't love me.' The silence lengthened.

'I'll go after them,' said Edmund. 'I can be in Paris the day after tomorrow.'

'Are you sure you have the strength? The crossing might be rough.'

'I stand more chance if I can see him face to face. Thank you for your help.'

'You're welcome. And God bless.'

Ella replaced the telephone and stood thoughtfully nibbling the lemon-curd tart. Then she went back outside and at once Penny rushed up, her face glowing with excitement. With Florrie's help, she had made some tiny lavender bags decorated with lace, and she was selling these from a small trug which Florrie had lined with green velvet.

'They've all gone, Mummy! Every one. I gave the money to Aunt Florrie.'

'That's wonderful.' She bent down to kiss Penny and then straightened to survey the scene. Poor Roland! He had always insisted on attending, wheeling himself around and finding a kind word for everyone. He would have approved, she thought.

Tom Berry had mown the lawns first thing that morning and the grass looked in peak condition. Eight trestle tables had been set up in a wide horseshoe arrangement and chattering groups were gathered round them. The cake stall, the bottle stall, the tombola – all were drawing eager customers. Ella began to stroll towards the tombola stall where Mr Evans was determined to win the bottle of whisky.

He had just won a box of ladies' handkerchiefs and was eyeing them with disfavour. 'I'll have two more goes,' he said.

The stall-holder looked at him. 'You sure now?'

''Course I'm sure.'

'You've already had more'n a dozen. You could've *bought* a bottle for that!'

The old man frowned. 'I never have!'

'I'm telling you!'

'Well, I'll be darned!'

Shaking his head at his own folly, he considered the handkerchiefs. 'Reckon Mrs Granger might like these,' he muttered and set off in search of her.

Ella moved on. Florrie, with a warm rug over her knees, sat beside a baize-topped card table which supported a large glass jar filled with sweets. As Ella arrived, a small boy had handed over his penny and was trying to guess how many sweets were in the jar.

'A million!' he suggested.

'Not quite a million,' Florrie prompted.

He reconsidered, his face contorted with effort. 'Five?'

'More than five.'

He looked at her suspiciously, as though she might be trying to confuse him, but at that moment his mother arrived to help him out and they settled on three hundred and fifty-three.

Seeing Ella, the mother laid a sympathetic hand on her arm. 'Poor Mrs Gough, you're being so brave. And the weather is so kind.'

Ella smiled. 'Roland wouldn't have wanted us to cancel it.'

Florrie nodded. 'We're all determined to look forward and not backwards.'

The woman took her son's hand. 'Well, it's all one can do, isn't it? Life must go on.'

Ella continued to mingle with the crowd and finally glanced in at the barn where Annie reigned supreme over the refreshments. Cucumber sandwiches, sausage rolls and fairy cakes formed the basis of the tea, and a selection of these was carefully arranged on doilies and selling for sixpence a plate. Crockery and a tea urn had been hired from the Village Hall, and as usual Mrs Granger had volunteered to fill the cups. The last time they would see her here, Ella reflected. Penny would miss her. Nurse Baisley – who had always sold tickets at the gate – had been replaced by the young verger who had a smile for everybody and appeared to be enjoying himself immensely.

The vicar's sister, carrying a newly purchased coffee sponge, stopped to speak to Ella. 'I'm taking this cake home and then I'm coming back,' she told her. 'I don't want the icing to melt. We're so grateful that you let us go ahead. The funds from the Fair are always so necessary.'

Ella smiled. Nod and smile. It wasn't so easy this year, but in a few hours it would all be over. She thought about Edmund and wondered how his meeting with Daniel would go. Hard to imagine him embracing Lizzie, but she was going to bear Daniel's firstborn. It was something of a trump card.

'Some of the proceeds go towards the old folks' Christmas party, you see.'

Ella nodded. They *always* went towards the Christmas party, but if the vicar's sister wanted to tell her again she was prepared to listen.

'How is young Penny taking the death of her father?'

Ella raised a hand in greeting as Janet Bell's mother passed her. 'She's tearful at times, but getting better than I had dared hope.'

'And the other dreadful business? We were all so shocked.'

'She talks about it quite naturally.'

'But to be kidnapped!'

'She slept through most of it, thank

goodness. And, of course, the woman wasn't quite a stranger.'

'But then to flee the country while on bail! I said to my brother, "It's amazing how some people's minds work!"'

Amazing, thought Ella. Hopefully the police would have stopped looking for them by the time they returned with Edmund Hampton.

She was rescued by the appearance of Charles's car, which drove slowly up to the front steps. Ella brightened. 'Excuse me, please.'

Charles had had a meeting in London and hadn't been certain when he would be back. She watched him scan the crowd before she waved to attract his attention.

'Ella!' He smiled broadly as he hurried towards her. 'Everything going well, by the look of it!' He looked at her more closely, concerned. 'You look so tired. Will you be able to rest when this is over?'

She nodded. 'Florrie read me the riot act and she's right. I've been doing too much lately and now that Roland's dead... Anyway, I've decided to retire from the Dramatic Society.'

'Will you miss it?'

Two young boys began to dodge round them, shrieking excitedly. One tripped and fell and Ella reached down to help him up.

Charles laughed. 'Whenever I got too

excited, my godfather used to say, "It will all end in tears!"'

'And it did!'

'Invariably!' He laughed.

The boys ran off and Ella addressed the question. 'Will I miss it? I don't think so. I've also given up as chairman of the Tennis Club. They can still use the court and they'll manage without me. And Mrs Granger will be leaving, did I tell you? I'm going to need much more time for Penny.' She smiled. 'How about you? Did your day in London go well?'

'Well enough. I was clearing out godfather's flat in Baker Street—'

'I was hoping he'd feel well enough to come today.'

'He sent his best wishes, but didn't feel up to it. Just lack of confidence, I think. He's doing quite well generally.' He pulled a small package from his pocket and unwrapped it. 'I found this in a little antique shop. I thought Penny might like it.'

She stared at the delicate silver frame with delight. 'Charles, it's beautiful!'

'I thought that perhaps you could find a rather special photograph of the two of them – Penny and Roland.'

For a brief moment Ella felt hurt, almost excluded, but immediately recognised the significance of the idea. Father and daughter together, as they never would be again.

She, God willing, had years of togetherness with her daughter. She said, 'That's so thoughtful, Charles. It's a wonderful idea.'

'Perhaps you could surprise her – put it by her bed while she's asleep so that she can find it in the morning?'

Ella was touched by his kindness. For a bachelor, he had a surprising understanding of children. 'A rather special photograph.' But why hadn't *she* thought of it? She felt a flash of guilt but resolutely pushed it from her. She was learning.

'You ought to have a family of your own,' she said.

He shrugged.

Ella gave in to her curiosity. 'Was there never anyone special? Or shouldn't I ask?'

'There has never been anyone, but then I've never really looked.' He grinned. 'Too lazy, perhaps – but I'm still hopeful. Not too late to start a family.'

Penny ran up to them waving the empty trug. 'Look, Mr Marriott! I sold all my lavender bags. Every single one!'

'What a clever girl!'

She flashed him a quick smile, then turned to Ella. 'And Mummy, I had a go on the tombola because I wanted the doll, but I won a picture of Sidmouth so you can have it if you like. They're looking after it for me.' She turned to Charles. 'Would you like some tea, Mr Marriott?' She lowered her voice. 'It costs sixpence, but Annie always lets us have it for nothing because this is our garden. It's very nice tea. Do you like sausage rolls?' She had taken his hand and was tugging him away in the direction of the barn. But almost at once Penny glanced back over her shoulder. She said to Charles, 'We can't go without Mummy.'

'I'm coming,' Ella told her, smiling, 'but I'm too tired to hurry. You two go ahead and find a table for three.'

Ella walked slowly after them, watching her daughter skipping with excitement beside Charles, her blonde curls dancing around her head. Penny glanced back again.

'Mummy! Come *on!*' The well-loved voice was tinged with impatience.

'I'm coming!'

With a smile Ella quickened her step, then stopped again. For a moment she watched Charles and Penny settling at a table. He leaned forward and said something which made her daughter laugh. As she joined them, Ella had the strangest feeling – that she had stepped out of the shadows of the past and glimpsed the future.

This Large Print Book for the partially sighted, who cannot read normal print, is published under the auspices of

THE ULVERSCROFT FOUNDATION